MENACE

WOLVES OF IRON VALOR MC BOOK 2

DEX HAVEN

UNDER A TEXAS SKY PRESS

For inquiries or permissions, please contact:

mailto: dex@dexhavenauthor.com

Website: DexHavenAuthor.com

DEDICATION

MEAN MAN

Thank you for making this life a reality. And for the laughs. I'm glad you kept me from being a lone wolf. They tend to go feral, you know?

EPIGRAPH

"For where thou are, there is the world itself, and where thou are not, desolation."

Shakespeare- Henry VI

TRIGGER WARNINGS

This book contains some dark themes that include a physically abusive father and brother, abduction, graphic intimacy, and violence—but as always there is a triumph-centered resolution. Guaranteed HEA. I don't believe in giving away the journey before it begins, but I do believe in honoring your peace. If you know certain topics are hard for you, I encourage you to trust your instincts and read with care. Check my website for a more complete list. I don't believe it's possible to cover everyone's triggers. This book is intended for readers 18 years old and older. Read responsibly. www.dexhavenauthor.com

CONTENTS

Chapter 1

King Declan Calloway

The courier's throat bobbed as he read King Dominic Madison's decree, his voice trembling like a cornered rabbit's. "Failure to produce Savannah for her union with Prince Dominic will be seen as a breach of the Blood Pact... and grounds for further action."

Glass shattered in my fist before he finished. Whiskey and blood dripped onto the portrait of my daughter—her painted green eyes still defiant beneath the crimson smear.

"Further action?" I hissed, stepping over the shards. The boy scrambled backward, parchment crumpling in his grip. "Your king mistakes my patience for weakness. Tell Madison his alliance burns with the next sunset if he dares—"

A choked gasp cut me off. The fool had gone pale, staring at the wolves' mounted heads above my desk—their frozen snarls a reminder of what happened to those who crossed the Eastern Shifters. I seized his collar, the stench of his fear sour as rot. "Run. And pray your king's threats outlive my daughter's rebellion."

He fled, leaving the decree amid the wreckage of her portrait. Savannah's laughter seemed to echo in the splintered frame. This was her masterpiece: a shifter king humiliated, a peace treaty crumbling. My hunters outwitted at every turn. I crushed the parchment, its wax seal cracking like bones. Let Madison rage.

Let the packs howl. I'd raze the continent before letting a traitor's blood dictate my legacy.

The report in my hand hissed as whiskey seeped into its ink. Sightings near the Iron Peaks. Three hunters dead. A shadow with my daughter's face. I traced the claw marks gouged into my desk—old wounds from the last time she'd tested me.

You should've learned, I thought, meeting her painted gaze. Ghosts didn't frighten me. But living, breathing defiance? That I'd break.

I stared down the insolent eyes of my daughter in the faded portrait on my desk, a grim specter of rebellion and ruin. My breath felt thin as I dropped the latest report from my hunters atop a useless pile. Savannah's disobedience was a living thing, gnawing at me, and I half expected to find the damn frame empty each time I looked up. A growing silence crushed the walls of my study as the rage swelled. Shadows crawled the surface of my desk, reports, and promises of punishment, all smothered in her defiance. I had warned her. I had promised her. It was not concern but certainty that hardened me. Savannah would have no peace in this world or the next until she bent her will to mine. I crushed the latest report in my fist and let it drop beside the others. Even ghosts would tire.

A dim glow from a single lamp fought against the creeping dark, spreading flickering light across the mounted heads of wolves I'd known in other days, other fights. I resented the weak flames for their similarity to the daughter who still evaded me. They burned and burned, only to fade in the end. The stale reports from my so-called hunters piled up in testament to their failures, crumpled paper haunting my study like Savannah herself. She would not get the best of me, not as long as I had breath. I stared her portrait down again, unable to look elsewhere. The air felt thin. The walls pressed close.

I wiped the blood from my hand, grabbed another glass, and poured. Let the anger fill me more than the whiskey did. Her absence wouldn't last forever. She wouldn't outlast me. Another failed report slid from my hand, the sound of it settling almost as infuriating as the report itself. I promised my daughter that she wouldn't get away with her insolence. With this mockery of her own kin. Her image was a sneer in oil and canvas, eyes a haunting green that questioned whether I could break her at all. I could. And I would. And I hoped she was alive and well to know the pain that awaited her.

More letters. More empty words from useless men who still couldn't find her. I set my jaw, reading through them again. Reports of shifters vanishing across my kingdom. They'd grown in number and frequency, especially over the last few months. My initial anger told me that Savannah was among them. But only until I calmed myself with drink, with repetition, with a cold fury that knew her better. I refused to entertain weakness, to allow even a fleeting thought that she was anything but alive and mocking me with every evaded hunter.

I should have been worried. A weaker king might have been. But I knew my daughter, and more than that, I knew myself. I fought back anything that felt like fear and instead focused on Savannah's rebellion, how she could turn on her own family. Her own blood. There were consequences for everything. And she would come to understand them all. Her portrait was a spiteful whisper on my desk, testing me. Daring me to flinch or look away. I would not.

I forced a grim smile as I piled the reports higher. My own defiance was iron. I crushed paper after paper, reading them each time with a vicious certainty. Let the girl hide. Let the coward run. She would come crawling back before I even thought to blink. I promised that much to myself and to the pale light and shifting shadows, and the promise ran through my veins with a conviction hotter than blood.

Savannah was gone. Her refusal was absolute. But my certainty was greater than hers, greater than anything she could imagine. Her delicate portrait lay before me, fragile and unguarded and everything she wasn't. The rage in me swelled again, familiar and violent, and I dared to crush one of the damn reports a little harder than before. As if I could break the paper and not my own hand. I would get the better of her. I would get the better of them all.

I allowed a moment's hesitation, a flicker of something weaker than I'd known in years. I let myself fear that she'd gone the way of the other missing shifters. My hand almost paused in its ritualistic tightening of another failed report. My breath almost slowed. Almost. But that wasn't who I was, and it wasn't who she was. I swallowed more whiskey, trying to keep control. It wouldn't happen again.

Glass felt heavy in my hand as I let anger choke away concern. I told myself she was stronger than that. More conniving. I let my thoughts drift away from whether she was lost and instead forced them to settle on her punishment. On what she would face once she was brought back here, empty frame or not.

I drank deeply, settling the fire and the rage, and made my decision. Hunters were clearly not enough. I would need to set more of them on her trail, push them harder, further, more desperately than ever before. Savannah would not win. Not this time. She'd think she had, as all cowards do. But I knew better.

It wasn't her safety that concerned me. Never that. It was her shameful, treacherous refusal to bend to my will. She would find no peace in this world or the next. And I would not rest until I saw her kneeling before me, eyes wide, understanding her place at last.

I set the whiskey down, steadying my hand, letting my mind wander to places darker than the night outside. I would ruin her. Break her. That was her destiny. Her defiance was no match for mine. She wouldn't outlast me. Neither would Dominic who deigned to threaten me.

My pacing was a furious, relentless rhythm.

How dare they hold me accountable? How dare they think to threaten my rule? How dare they accuse me of breaking this alliance? This treaty. This farce of a marriage. My footsteps echoed my rage, punctuating the silence like a heartbeat.

I felt betrayed, but not by King Madison. I would show them what true betrayal looked like. Savannah thought she could slip through my grasp, that she could leave a stain on my honor, my pride, my name. I'd ruin her first.

The cold air settled on my skin. My breath had gone ragged with each explosive burst. My hands shook. There were moments I felt like a child in the storm of my own anger. Moments when her refusal, their demands, became more than I could bear. But only moments. And then the rage was back; it filled me more than blood, more than air.

Let them have their ultimatum. Let them believe they could scare me. Let the coward Madison and his pathetic son think they'd get what was mine. Let Savannah try and defy me. Her defiance was just like the boy—thin, brittle, easily broken. I refused to bow, refused to even consider the consequences of a lost alliance, a weakened throne. She'd pay for this with her life, with her soul. I didn't care which.

My anger spiraled, and I welcomed it. It became a living thing, a twisted mockery of her cowardice and my strength. Savannah's treachery had one last chance to run, and it was up.

There was no blood, no family. Only revenge.

Her defiance was insurmountable, and I laughed bitterly at the challenge of it all. At the thrill and promise and impending certainty of seeing her brought to heel. I stopped pacing, stopped in my track of thoughts that doubled back on themselves, that began and ended with fury. She couldn't hide forever.

The thought was a comfort. She'd feel my anger across every mile, every dark shadow, every forgotten place she thought she could find refuge in. Her heart wasn't that strong, her soul not that lost. I would reel her back.

Her life was mine to dictate. Her future was already decided, and no alliance, no empty threats would keep her from it. I was a force of nature, and she was a fool.

I picked up the scattered letters.

Savannah's blood ran in my veins, and I would see it drained before I saw it cold. Before I saw it running free. She was a coward, and I would hunt her like one. Her choices were ashes, and my will was iron. She'd face me at last, and I'd have the last word.

My son Callum entered the room, too much like myself for either of us to stand it. His smile bordered on smug as he lingered in the doorway, eyes catching the remnants of my shattered resolve. My heart beat savage and quickly as we stood apart, daring the other to give in first. I wasn't sure we could have been called kin at all. Our blood felt too thin, too cold, too dangerously like my daughter's, the daughter I refused to name. Callum and I were bound by stubborn arrogance and by a shared desire to see her brought back in chains. He stayed near the door, feigning respect. But I knew him. Knew the way his eyes lingered on me, the way they caught on glass shards and whiskey stains. I would break him next, if I had to. I let the thought go. He was not Savannah, not the ghost that haunted me, and I held his gaze while the room spun. He finally looked away, claiming her name with that same smug smile.

I turned my back, steadying myself with the rage that never seemed to leave me. It burned brighter when I faced him, when I remembered how close to the edge she had pushed us.

"Father," Callum said. His voice was smooth and unflinching. "The situation with Savannah is growing worse. You're aware, of course, that the Midwestern pack will hold us accountable."

"Do you think I fear their judgment?"

"I think," he said, staying close to the door, "that they'll push until we break. Unless we act quickly."

I felt a ghost of the rage I'd thrown at the stone fireplace. A ghost of the daughter who dared defy me. I stayed near the window, daring him to think my back was a weakness.

He wouldn't. He knew me better than that.

"I plan to take care of it," I said, words harder than iron, more biting than the air between us. "There are specialized hunters ready to leave this afternoon. They'll bring her back. At any cost."

"And what cost do you expect?" he asked. He stayed near the door, distance calculated. Too much like my own.

"Any cost."

He nodded, approval mixed with that infuriating self-satisfaction. I knew that look. Knew it too well, and I hated him for being so much like me. "What if it's not enough?"

"Do you doubt my ability to control this?"

He finally stepped further into the room, acting as if he owned it, owned us, owned the damn situation I refused to acknowledge. "I'm not sure she'll come willingly," he said.

I turned to him, caught the smugness before it spread, captured it with words I knew would shatter the space between us. "No daughter of mine will defy me and live to tell about it."

He had the sense to flinch. The nerve to recover quickly. "It's just," he said, the haughtiness returning, "that this was never supposed to be difficult."

"Then increase the bounty. Get your hands bloody if you need to. It makes no difference to me."

He let the moment pass, let his own fear catch up to him. His confidence drained and was replaced by something more useful. He was smarter than I gave him credit for. I almost admired the boy.

"I'll spread the word," he said, no longer questioning me. "She can't hide forever. We'll have her."

I let his words echo, my own distrust of them weighing heavy on my heart. It wasn't that he believed them. It was that I wasn't sure I did.

"Do that," I said.

He paced slowly, the soft steps of a man too confident, too assured. Too young to know that he would not last in the shadow of my rage. The shadow Savannah threw across this family, this house, this kingdom. He looked at me with a smug approval I couldn't bring myself to crush.

Not yet.

Callum believed in this. In us. In what it meant to have a king for a father. He didn't see the curse of it, not like the coward who ran from it all. I couldn't afford his naïveté, but I needed him for now. For this. He left me alone in the study, alone with thoughts that circled back to her. That dug deep into my chest and took the breath from me.

Savannah's defiance was a betrayal too raw, too real to hide. She'd pay for it with blood and tears and a lifetime of silence. We would have her back.

The pressure in the room grew heavy, unbearable. Like the last months, like the countless nights and countless hopes gone shattered. I steadied myself with the thoughts of how to ruin her. How to ruin the weak pack that thought to threaten us.

Her rebellion was a mark on us all. It scarred me, scarred her brother, scarred what remained of our power. Callum couldn't see it. Not yet. But he would. I'd make sure of it. And then I'd break him too, if I had to.

I waited for him to return. Waited for him to be as stubborn as me, for him to share this burden like it was his own.

Callum was like a ghost, but not the one I feared. Not the one that haunted me through every night and every breath and every moment my own strength became weakness.

I thought I heard her voice. I thought I heard it, and broke it, and let it bleed into the night. I thought I had more time.

Her name wouldn't leave me, but I refused to speak it. Callum was her image, and he knew it. It kept him on the edges; it kept him in the dark. It kept him, and I hated him for it.

But I hated her more.

The night would not end. Her refusal would not end. It was another game, another false sense of hope and control. We'd bring her back. It was all I could think, all I could allow myself to think. The certainty was consuming, destroying.

I wouldn't outlast this.

It felt like waiting for the gallows, like knowing your place and denying it all the way down.

Bronwyn hovered in the doorway, her fingers worrying the lace at her sleeves. She still wore that damnable floral perfume, cloying as guilt itself.

"Declan...?" Her voice frayed at the edges. "Will you dine with us tonight? The cook prepared beef wellington—"

I didn't turn from the window where moonlight carved shadows across the eastern plains. "You think my appetite hinges on beef wellington while our legacy rots?"

A pause—the soft hitch of breath she always failed to stifle. "They said... they said there may have been a sighting?" Her hope curdled my teeth. "Does Callum think....?"

"Callum thinks nothing without my order." The glass trembled in my grip; liquid fire bled down my wrist as I turned slowly toward her crumpled face—that face I once took pride in breaking before dignitaries who might have desired it more than duty demanded of me now. Our daughter had evaded me longer than dignity allowed. "Savannah will kneel for Madison's whelp, whether she crawls back or is dragged."

Bronwyn flinched as if struck yet dared step closer—foolish woman still reaching through walls built long before vows were choked out between us... her blue eyes pooled with midnight grief she mistook for strength.

"She's your child," she whispered fiercely, so fiercely it almost resembled a spine.

My laugh cracked ice across marble floors beneath which generations of Calloway wolves snarled restlessly beneath stone tombs already forgotten by time but not blood-debt.

"She stopped being a child when defiance became her creed," I spat, watching satisfaction bloom as crimson drained from lips pressed tight. Her hands trembled now not with fear but rage.

Bronwyn retreated first, as she always did, clutching at pearls draped over collarbones bruised more often by silence than fists these days. She halted at the threshold.

"Find her alive," she murmured, voice splintering. "Or bury me beside her."

Her footsteps faded down corridors colder than our wedding bed had ever been.

I finished off the bitter dregs, tracing maps marked with failed searches. Savannah would learn the consequences of defiance against the crown.

Chapter 2

Menace

Sawyer. Her absence stained the room where we met to assess the wreckage of her captivity, and I felt it burn into me while the scent of coffee, whiskey, and day-old pie pressed into the room. She'd been here six weeks now, and the mystery of her remained. We sat in a rectangle of leather chairs, tension hanging between us like another lost mate. My fingers drummed against the table, unbidden and uncertain. Bronc loomed over the worn wood, organizing our priorities: burn, retrieve, recover, report. Details spilled over the table in messy tangles of speculation. My mind worked itself raw as I pieced it all together, overanalyzed, recalculated, failed. Bronc's eyes met mine. "What do you know about Sawyer's time in that lab?"

"Not much. It's a difficult subject to broach." I felt the chairs close in around me, the clutter of papers spread like doubts, and I couldn't stop thinking about how I'd neglected my car dealership. Everything I'd built seemed on the brink of falling, waiting on me to make sense of the madness and move. Two months of being absent. We accomplished the goal. Got our Luna back. That's a victory. I brought back a treasure, too. One I know next to nothing about. Except for the fact that she's mine. My business would be fine. I've got a great general manager. Still felt like I should be there. I gritted my teeth and waited, half ready for Bronc to chew me out and half hoping he would. I'd spent a lifetime wrestling things into order. Except for this. Except for her.

The worn leather squeaked beneath me as I shifted my weight, tried to lose the thoughts of Sawyer that slipped into every empty space. I breathed in the tang of old coffee, let the sounds of shifting chairs and shuffling papers force me back. "Prioritize," Bronc barked, drawing the room into his rhythm. "We're not done 'til every name's been accounted for and every family's been contacted."

I blinked, finally focusing on the room. Ghosts in leather cuts, scrawled lists like confessions, and Bronc standing at the head of it all like the wrath of God. Liam Baucaum didn't flinch as he flipped through Juliet's notes, scattering details like premonitions, shaking the room with his resolve. I absorbed what I could, pushed away what I couldn't.

Wrecker's low rumble took over as Bronc handed him the spotlight. He traced a thick finger over printouts and digital files, translating them from hieroglyphics into tragedy. "So far, Juliet's counted sixteen recovered and seven unaccounted for," he began. His gravel voice added weight to every number. "Anderson, R." He continued down the list with surgical precision, calling each letter and name into its own small grave. "Lindsey, C. Marks, G." I couldn't bear to listen. I couldn't look away.

Wrecker moved through the list, a countdown to the one name I knew I'd never hear but ached to. Others followed his words, but I already knew the punchline. Absence. My name this time. My sentence to watch as each piece of her shattered further from reach. I listened through the entire alphabet, pretending this time I'd been wrong, knowing damn well I never was.

"It's not here, man," Wrecker concluded, the files closing under his heavy hands like the lid of a casket.

Bronc's eyes shot toward me, keen, unforgiving. I tensed. Here it comes, I thought. He held his stare on me until I felt every bone in my body snap, then shatter. "Bridger," he said, dropping the nickname as if invoking another name might force it to appear, "you heard anything else? It's clear nobody is looking for her."

He waited, silent, until my own voice clawed its way up and out. "We've been taking things slow," I admitted. "It's been a rough re-entry."

"Rougher than not knowing?" Bronc demanded.

The shame hit like a second bullet, driving deeper than the first. I'd left her past alone, too afraid to push when she'd already come so close to shattering. Or maybe it was me I feared breaking. The edges had grown so damn sharp these past months.

"It's all I can do right now to keep her from running," I said. Her steps were distant echoes across the open plains, across an entire country I could never close between us. Not fast enough. Not sure enough.

He didn't really get it. We had no history. She didn't know if she could trust me. It had only been a few weeks. She was free of that nightmare, and I didn't want her to relive it. I wanted to give her more time.

"Look, I'm trying to give her a little more time. She doesn't know if she can really trust us. Trust *me*. After what she's been through? I don't blame her. Don't wanna push her too hard."

Wrecker kept a sharp eye on me, read me like another unsealed file. He and the other members of the Iron Valor Pack held a united front, solid as their names. He returned his attention to the task at hand. They all did. I should have, too. "Once you get more information, we can update the list. Be sure no one gets overlooked," Bronc said, already pivoting to the next priority, the next fix. "I'm trying to avoid too much heat from the council. They're gonna wanna know why we didn't bring them in. I'm gonna try to frame it like we were just trying to rescue our Luna. It didn't concern them. That's our story, and we're stickin' to it."

His relentless pace never failed to amaze me. The man was a machine. That's why he was such an effective alpha. The Iron Valor Pack/MC ran like a well-honed business. And it was. It was a living, breathing entity. A world within a world that required a leader who could focus on several tasks at once. I was so damned happy he had found Juliet. She was sure and strong. Just like him.

"Let me know what you find."

The finality of his words landed like a mark, a mate, a bloody handprint over everything I couldn't touch. It marked me as a man he counted on to simply handle his business. A promise in the form of a burden, one I'd see through at all costs.

We tangled our way through Sawyer's absence on the list and onto the next mess. Lucia Kozlov showed up at girls' night. Bronc mentioned a curious gaze that the vampire princess gave to Sawyer as she left the cabin. I can't begin to know what that could mean.

"So you had to have the, 'your college roommate is not just a vampire, but a vampire princess' talk with Juliet, huh? How'd she take it?"

Bronc's voice held some humor when he said, "Juliet took it about how I expected. Pissed, then fine."

She bounced back. Found herself. She was the anti-Sawyer. I could see the thoughts growing, shifting in Bronc's mind, and I hated him a little for it. We locked eyes. Mine narrowed. Bronc's twitched with amusement, and we returned to the conversation that I'd never left.

Juliet seemed to get stronger with every wave that crashed against her. Bronc saw that as clear as the bright pink mate mark that showed the world she was his.

"Girls' night was a bust," Bronc chuckled. "Maybe I'll tell her to have another. Without the undead crashing this time." His humor only half hid the worry.

A mirthless grin ghosted my face. "Huh. I bet Juliet still had a good time." I was hoping Sawyer would open up some. Especially with Maddie there. She could get anybody to talk. "Can't believe Maddie didn't have Sawyer spilling her guts. She's got a way of dragging stories out of people." I mentioned on a laugh. Maddie was famous for her penchant for never knowing when to quit.

The fond look on Bronc's face showed how much he loved his little sister. It twisted my gut a bit, thinking about my own baby sister I'd lost a few years ago. "Oh, I'm sure she tried. Juliet told me she felt like Sawyer had fun, but was closed off. Until Lucia got there. Then she said things really got awkward. No idea what that could have been about. Could have been nothing more than Sawyer sensing that Lucia was a vamp." Bronc rested a rough hand against the table, his frustration coming through louder than words. Lucia had that effect on people.

The space shifted around us as Bronc filled in the rest, and I pictured Juliet's defiant look as he finally admitted her best friend wasn't only a vampire but vampire royalty. Kazimir Kozlov. He used to be much more difficult when the kings were a threat. The Bratva had as much of an empire as any of the combined packs. No wonder he'd waited so long to bring Juliet into that mess. It would have bit him in the ass no matter the timing.

"Our Luna's tougher than you thought, huh?" I knew this. "You catch anything else from Sawyer before she left?" I wanted to learn something. *Anything*. Bronc didn't want to pry, but I damn sure did. I only needed a direction to go with the pieces I had.

"She looked like a ghost in those woods," he admitted. Her wild, haunted look entered my mind. "Not sure if it was the undead or my mate that spooked her more. If I were a betting man, I'd put money on Juliet."

I didn't know if he was wrong, or if I just wanted him to be. Sawyer had the look of a girl who needed protection and fought against it with every step. I held Bronc's gaze until he broke with a smirk. His confidence ate at me. I'd never been uncertain about anything in my life. Until now. But he knew what to do. He didn't even have to think about it.

Lucia's departure left me as unsettled as Sawyer, but for other reasons. He said she gave a knowing look. "How long was the bloodsucker around before Sawyer bailed?" I asked.

Bronc's reply was swift, sure, infuriating. "Long enough to shake things up. Short enough not to know how bad." The circle of cuts and names shifted. Restless. "She's headed back east."

I looked over at Wrecker. He's our guy who knew something about everybody. "You got anything that might help decipher why Lucia would give any kind of odd look at Sawyer?"

His laugh made sense. "You'd need a fucking map to follow anything that Lucia Kozlov does, man. She might have liked her shirt or her hair. Hell, she might swing that way. Fuck if I know."

I ran my hand down my face. Vampires. He's right. A look could mean a hundred different things.

The glow of Wrecker's laptop flared like an uninvited spark in the dim room. Cold light reflected from highball glasses and sweet tea filled Mason jars and washed across grim faces as we turned from vampires and girls' nights to something more tangible: spreadsheets, missing money, an inside man. We couldn't afford doubt or loose ends, not with the rest of the operation stalled and not with the pace we'd set for the rest. Skeeter's betrayal lit the room like the one verifiable fact we could focus on, and this time my mind stayed sure as we closed the net around him.

Wrecker held the room in thrall, casting numbers and letters into black and white truths. "With Juliet's information, there's no doubt. It's him," he said. The sheets had familiar data in foreign places, scrawled notes that showed how far we'd missed the mark. The light from the projector spread like a stain, details casting longer shadows than even I had expected.

Skeeter's small-time betrayal stung, but his access worried us more. It fit like another goddamn piece, sure as Bronc's bite and just as vicious. It wouldn't end with one man. It never did.

My lips set like a tomb, like the grave I'd be putting that boy into. "How long?" I asked.

"Been going on for years," Wrecker said. "Started back when Axel kept the books. Small at first. Less than a grand a month. But then last March, after Axel disappeared, it picked up." He drew his fingers over the bank records like a map, an architect of treason. "Last deposit was yesterday. Someone's gotta be using him. This is more than Skeeter. Question is, who? Bigger question is why? That son of a bitch has been a patched-in member of this club for over twenty years. Been a member of this pack his entire life."

I heard that clear enough. We'd start with the man and finish with whoever pulled his strings. The lines and columns lit our plans as fast as Wrecker called them, a more orderly run than I'd had in months. "We're not waiting to find out who," I said. "Bronc?"

His answer was as sharp and deadly as expected. "Same as we always do. Round up every last son of a bitch." The circle around us grew tighter as he spoke, flanking him, anchoring him. Supporting the push of a freight train across the Texas plains, and nothing could stop it.

Arsenal shifted the focus back to action instead of outcomes, filling the void of every ghost in the room. "This time tomorrow, he'll know better." He grinned like the vengeful devil he was, eyes cutting the room for loose threads. Finding none.

Loose threads. They choked me like a hangman's noose these last months, and I wanted nothing more than to cut them all. This was one I'd snip. It was the only one I could.

"He expecting anything?" I asked, as though I hadn't heard the reply before it came.

"Works next to me every goddamn day as though he's still family," Bronc answered, leaning into the leather of an enforcer's chair. "That they're in the clear."

I could see the strain it had put on our Alpha. With what he'd just gone through with Juliet, this was a burden he didn't need, and it made me want to drive my fist through Skeeter's face. This man would lay down and die for this pack, so to see it repaid with betrayal made the blood boil in my veins. My eyes scanned the faces of my brothers around the table. Big Papa, Arsenal, Doc, Wrecker, all of us wore the same murderous look.

We all leaned in with him, sharing his look of imminent triumph. A look I hadn't seen since we bashed in the doors of that lab weeks ago.

"Figure it'll just be me and Bronc," I said, sorting names like card tricks. "Then Wrecker, Arsenal, Papa. We need y'all for the haul in." Their feral grins returned the expectation. They'd take care of it all right. I couldn't wait. I couldn't fucking wait. "Doc, you can come if you wanna. Figured you'd like to sit this one out. It's basically just gonna be a grab him and go."

Doc didn't get his hands dirty on every run we made, being a healer and all.

"I'm good sitting it out. As long as I'm notified immediately upon completion." He answered with no sign of grief.

Papa asked the big question. "We gonna just lock him up and let him stew until we're ready to shake him down?"

Bronc was thoughtful. "Yep, we'll hold him. I want him secured while we're handling the council shifter disappearance notifications. One major crisis at a time. But I want my fucking shop theft stopped. Skeeter has stolen his last dime from me." Bronc gave a single, satisfied nod. "We know where it's headed." He stood, a monument to everything the rest of us tried to be. "We've got a plan. It executes tomorrow. Tonight, the wolves run."

Our confidence cast shadows as we rose, solid as the cuts we wore, dark as the purpose we took to the field.

The shift tore through me like wildfire, bones cracking and fur erupting from skin—painful yet familiar, a gateway to freedom. My paws hit the earth as my human thoughts blurred into instinct, into hunger for speed and moonlight. The forest blurred as we launched forward, pack leaders surging like shadows given purpose. Wind ripped through my coat; pine needles and frost sharpened the air in my lungs. This was primal truth—no laws, no walls, just movement. Just pack.

We wove between trees in a symphony of snarls and panting breaths, each stride synchronized by decades of muscle and blood memory. Bronc's massive black form cut through the dark ahead, our Alpha's presence a beacon none dared outpace. But tonight wasn't about hierarchy. It was about teeth bared in grins, claws shredding terrain as we raced toward nothing and everything. The bond between us thrummed louder than heartbeats: together, we were avalanches. Together, we were lawless gravity.

A fallen oak loomed in our path—Bronc leaped first, a black shadow against the sky. I followed without hesitation, muscles coiling mid-air as moonlight bathed my underside. For a breathless second, I floated weightless...then slammed back into rhythm with Wrecker and Doc flanking me. Their warmth brushed my fur; their resolve mirrored mine. Threats would come—they always did—but I grinned wider. Let them. We'd tear through steel for this brotherhood, crush throats for this thrill of belonging deeper than bone.

When Bronc's howl fractured the night—low, defiant—ours answered in unison. The sound shook stars loose from clouds. No hunt tonight. Just running. Just proving to the shadows that we owned them. Every snap of underbrush beneath our paws was a vow: try us.

The pack wouldn't break.

The world would bend.

And we'd savor every scar it took to make it so.

Chapter 3

Sawyer

It was a devil's choice. The kind that left my hands trembling around a cup of tea and my heart a snared rabbit's heart beat inside my chest. Even in my tiny apartment, with its warm tones and welcoming furniture, it left me breathless and broken. He'd found me. There was no other way to read Lucia Kozlov's unexpected appearance at girls' night. My father had sent her to drag me back to Martha's Vinyard like a captured prize. Kazimir and my father must have mended fences. Last I knew they hated each other.

The only other explanation was that fate was playing a cruel game of coincidence. I suppose it was possible that Lucia was truly Juliet's friend and was concerned about her. Seems ridiculous that Lucia could truly care about *anyone*. But Juliet had that effect on people. Hell, I fell in love with 'all things Juliet' within hours of meeting her. She is Goddess-blessed, and the perfect Luna for her pack.

So, this left me with a frightening dilemma. Did I run again? Did I abandon my new life and Menace in an attempt to protect him and the Iron Valor pack? Or did I risk staying, keeping my true identity a secret, as I continued to lie to the man who I believed was my fated mate? If I told him who I truly was, the circumstances of why I lied, what would that look like? What would Menace expect his Alpha to do? I was terrified to find out.

Menace was a man who valued integrity. He was ex-Delta Force, for God's sake. Loyalty and honesty are what kept his men alive. And here I was, lying straight to his face every day. It was a lie by omission, but a lie was a lie was a lie.

The couch groaned under my weight as I sagged back, the soft floral fabric suddenly a straitjacket pinning me to the harsh reality of my past. Tapping fingers against a porcelain teacup, darting eyes to the window, I sat like prey expecting a predator to pounce. It would take my father's men no time at all to reach me. A deep, raw ache threatened to split my ribs as I thought of Menace and the devastation I'd leave behind. I felt my wolf pace behind my ribs. She was having none of it. She refused the idea of leaving who she'd already considered her mate. My agitated state only increased.

There were no options that didn't tear me to pieces. There was no decision except staying that didn't leave me broken. And staying came with its own terror.

Memories of my father and his controlling grip paraded through my mind. I saw him, King Declan, with eyes that matched mine in shade but held no warmth. There he stood, always looming, a tyrant in the guise of a loving parent. Even across the country, his power extended like claws. My thoughts flitted to Bronwyn, my gentle mother, who couldn't summon the strength to help herself, let alone me. Griffin, my younger brother, was sympathetic, but he knew the danger of trying to aid my escape. My older brother Callum believed in duty above all else, and his obedience to our father was absolute. When I'd sought freedom, I was on my own.

My life in Martha's Vinyard was little more than a gilded prison, with a future planned by others. Shipped off to private schools, where I begged to earn a music degree and allowed it only because it served the family's prestige. I was a bargaining chip, promised to another pack's king as a strategic pawn. I didn't see a way that I could ever escape it.

It was almost too similar to what Juliet had just lived. Granted, her fiancé was a madman, but as far as her false identity and hiding in plain sight were concerned, the parallels were uncanny. If only my father didn't care where I was, like hers.

The minutes stretched out. I tried to busy myself by reading a book I'd found on the bookshelf. *Pride & Prejudice*. Even Mr. Darcy couldn't ease my worries. My options of whether to stay or run kept streaming through the back of my mind. Running became increasingly dangerous. A lone wolf would eventually turn feral. The cards were stacked against me.

It would be another cowardly retreat. And before being tortured in Harrison's lab, I was no coward. I'd faced down men in alleyways in New York and held my own. I didn't like this frightened version of myself. But I was afraid for more than just myself. With Menace and Iron Valor in danger, there was no time to waste. My resolve to stay weakened like the dying daylight on the walls.

The remnants of my old life lingered heavy. Those eleven months on the run before landing in Harrison's clutches had been a horror show I didn't want to repeat. First Manhattan, trying to stay alive on the streets of New York. My every footstep seemed to echo with my father's anger as I ducked down alleyways and into shadows, always looking over my shoulder for the men he sent to find me. Each day stretched into eternity, weighed down by fear and loneliness. I kept moving west until I'd wound up in the Ozarks. I thought I'd be safe among the pines. Then I'd had to shift to keep my wolf from losing her mind. Apparently Harrison's men had seen me. That's when the true nightmare began. It was only Menace breaking down the door and busting my chains that gave me my first glimpse of hope after months of anguish.

Dairyville was the last in a series of desperate grasps at freedom, and the first place I had started to believe it was more than a mirage. Until Lucia Kozlov. Until girls' night and that sickening sense of fate crashing down. How could I leave? How could I stay? I was at war with myself, and both sides were losing. The bindings on my heart grew tighter. My father's shadow loomed. It left no room for hope.

This town and these people were the love song I had given up on. A few precious weeks of pretending I could live my own life. Everyone I'd encountered here had been gentle with me. Kindness like I'd never experienced in my life. I'd only ever known people treating me with deference. Like a princess. The freedom of a false name and a new identity opened my eyes to what life could be. Each piece fit together into a puzzle of lies that only my own foolishness could believe. But I wanted to believe it. I wanted Menace. I wanted the life and love he seemed to offer without words.

For the first time, I could see it: a reckless, blinding vision of a future that I didn't want to surrender. The way he looked at me. The warmth of his presence. The steady force that held me together when I should have shattered.

Sawyer Galloway. Not quite a lie, not quite the truth. A girl who thought she could run forever but couldn't even manage another day.

Ms. Pearl had been a savior of sorts. I remembered arriving, wrapped in a blanket in Menace's arms. Her warm eyes had seen the empty horror in my eyes. She knew I needed something that felt safe. Something that felt like my own. She mothered me in a way that even my own sweet mother could not. Was never allowed to.

Leaving her would be another tearing in a heart already split wide. I wanted to believe in my strength. In Menace. That I could choose to stay and protect the dream I had barely begun to live. But I was my father's daughter, bred for flight and the preservation of his empire. The cowardice that threatened to consume me felt ingrained, a legacy of running.

The air felt thin and useless, each breath barely enough to keep me conscious. My chest rose and fell like an engine out of control. Like my mind, my pulse refused to slow, frantic with the fear of abandoning everything good and true in a hopeless effort to protect it.

But it was a broken knowing. If it turned out wrong, I couldn't run from myself. The sharp-edged pain of losing Menace would cut too deep. His absence, my failure—each option left me skinned to the bone. The tug in my gut that I'd felt for him. The more I was around him, the stronger it became. It was a constant pull. I felt certain he was my fated mate. He seemed to be a part of me somehow. Beyond feelings, beyond explanation.

The memory of his hands on me—soft and confident, nothing like I'd expected—brought heat to my face. This older, dangerous man, who I'd loved since the moment we met, held back as if I might shatter. As if a twenty-four-year-old virgin, kept pure by her father's design, was too delicate for him. His restraint was an unsolvable mystery. He couldn't know I wanted him to let go. I craved the beast he kept locked down. I'd seen him the night he'd stormed my cell. He was a wild man that night. For some reason, *that* is what I longed for. Was he disgusted by my innocence? I wasn't fragile. Goddess knows I'd weathered so many storms.

The air settled around me like a shroud. It held me tighter than any prison. The effort of holding myself together turned each second into hours. Each thought to ash.

Menace was the life I wanted. This town was the family I needed. Lucia's discovery forced my hand. I didn't know if I could trust her. Her relationship with Juliet was what I'd pinned my hopes on. She'd never cause her or her pack harm.

In the distance, I heard the song of wolves. I recognized Menace's howl. My soul and heart instantly calmed. How could I ever abandon that? Him?

I didn't know who I was anymore. Sawyer? Savannah?

A coward in two parts.

Water splashed against ceramic like the erratic flutter of my heart. Even the soothing motions of washing the teacup left me hollow and restless. If I stayed, if I dared risk everything, would Menace accept the real me? It would have been easy to believe in fate, in a destined mate, in the strength of our bond, but he was cautious where I was desperate. It wasn't just my father's threat I faced. It was my own fear that Menace wanted a woman, not a virginal princess preserved for a loveless match. I set the cup on the drying rack and watched the water drain, feeling as fragile as the porcelain.

I clutched the edge of the counter as if it could keep me tethered to this reckless plan. Staying. Letting the call of my heart, not my father's will, dictate my fate. The name Savannah felt like a bad joke, as foreign and distant as the world it belonged to. Sawyer was a bolder soul, one I could only hope to embody when I was free from the shadows of Martha's Vinyard and duty. But the specter of inexperience haunted me as much as Declan's power. It dogged my every breath.

I believed in what I felt for Menace, in the promise I saw in his eyes. If I stayed, I would have to tell him the truth. About Declan. About being promised to another. He might not even want to touch me after that. Would his restraint turn into a permanent withdrawal, leaving me more alone than ever? The thought that he could walk away at any time and never look back brought me to the edge of despair.

A subtle ache settled deep in my bones whenever he wasn't near. It grew stronger by the day, this longing that ate away at reason and left nothing but blind, reckless need. Maybe this was what being mated felt like. But if he truly *was* my fated one, wouldn't he have taken what was his?

I moved through the tiny space, restless and unsettled. Each shadowed corner of the apartment, each carefully chosen piece of furniture, spoke of a home that I could lose at any moment.

Or was it a home I'd never really had?

Menace was the constant, the true north that I had to believe in.

Just then, a shadow filled the doorway. Strong. Indelible. I met his eyes and was lost to their heat. His hunger stole my breath away, stole the words from my throat. I stood frozen and wanting. Then he stepped inside. The door clicked shut. The distance closed. A shift in the world. In me. His presence was magnetic, more real than any fear that had gripped my heart. Jeans hung low on his hips. His chest was damp, a hint of sweat. Of man. My father, my past, my every fragile doubt seemed absurdly distant.

"I had to see you," he said, and I drowned in it. His words. His scent. His need. Everything was Menace.

The moment stretched thin and breathless between us. Electric tension sparked and snapped, leaving the air heavy with unspoken promise. My body burned with a need I could barely understand, but I felt it at the core of me, pulsing and raw. Desire flooded every vein, setting my skin ablaze with the unbearable longing to close the last inches between us.

"Sawyer," he murmured, his voice a deep, rough caress. The sound of my name on his lips broke something inside me, tore down the walls I'd built, and left me exposed. It was enough to make my knees weak and my heart pound so fiercely I feared it might burst. "I couldn't stay away."

He took a step closer, and I felt the world narrow to the charged, impossible space that held only us. Only this. Only now. His scent—earth and forest, power and want—enveloped me, seeped into my bones and took root. It left me helpless and breathless, a girl with nothing left to lose.

Nothing left to fear.

The single light over the kitchen peninsula flickered above us, a strobe to mark the dizzy spin of my thoughts. My hands twitched, reaching for him, then pulling back as I hovered on the edge of reckless abandon.

Of losing myself completely.

His gaze never left mine. Hazel eyes shimmered with promise, with hunger, with the same reckless need that tore through me. That made me want to forget every terror, every plan, every doubt I'd harbored.

When he touched me, I thought I might shatter. His hands, strong and sure, cupped the back of my neck and pulled me in. My breath hitched. My pulse exploded. There was no hesitation, no holding back, only the fierce press of his lips on mine, unyielding and absolute.

It set fire to everything.

I melted against him, against his solid warmth and the unrelenting surety of his touch. The world shifted, dizzy and unfocused, a blur of light and dark as he pulled me closer.

"I tried to go home after our run. Saw your light still on." He had my head in his hands, fingers massaging my scalp as his breath brushed my lips.

"You need to lock your goddamn door," he said. Then, his lips crashed onto mine. Consuming every thought in my head except for his taste, the feel of his lips, his tongue, as it dominated my mouth.

My arms reached around his waist as I held on for dear life.

He slowed his assault on my mouth, easing into soft, simple kisses across my mouth and face. His breath came in pants until he was back in control of his emotions. My breathing slowed as well, and I looked into his beautiful hazel eyes that tonight were more gray than anything.

"I don't want you to stay away." I told him.

He kissed my forehead. Serious, suddenly.

"I'll be by in the morning about seven. We need to talk about your future around here. I need to get back to my regular schedule at my auto dealership, and I want to be sure you are squared away."

This was not the conversation I expected after those kisses. "Oh, uh, okay. That sounds great. I'd like that. I guess." I know I sounded like an idiot. Gah. I needed to try to sound more mature.

"Uh, I mean, yes, I'd like to know more about where I can fit in around here."

His grin was so beautiful. Standing in my house with his six-pack on display, sweat-soaked hair, looking like sex on a stick, after all but fucking my mouth with his tongue, he wants to have *this* conversation.

He gave me another forehead kiss. "Good. I'll see you in the morning at seven sharp, Red. Lock this door and set the alarm." He said over his shoulder as he shut the door behind him.

I followed him to the door to lock it. "See you in my dreams, Bridger." I whispered under my breath as I set the alarm. I knew at that moment I was staying.

CHAPTER 4

MENACE

I sat outside Sawyer's apartment, a goddamn masochist. There was a fresh and dangerous pull between us, the lights in her window taunting me with their late-night glow. I didn't know the first fucking thing about her except I couldn't get enough of the taste of her. She was more than what she seemed, a delicacy my wolf had already claimed in a far more honest way than I could bring myself to admit. I drummed my fingers on the steering wheel and let a low growl escape my throat, struggling to find some honorable ground between claiming her secrets or claiming her body. The truth was, I didn't know which one I'd take first. If she were smarter than she looked, she'd be miles away by morning.

She'd come from money; that much was obvious. Too much polish. Too much refinement. I'd seen girls like her before, but none had been a match for my wolf. Not one. The fire of her hair and the stubborn way she held herself told me she was more than just another pretty face. They told me she'd hold out. That she'd burn me with her spirit before she gave in. And damn if that wasn't what made me want her more.

I tapped the wheel again, watching as shadows shifted in the room above, making my heart and wolf pound in tandem. Even if I knew nothing about her past, I had to give her credit for one thing: she'd ditched whatever easy life she'd had to take a gamble on something darker. On something rougher. On something that would make or break her. I could feel the fine thread of her vulnerability stretching all the way to the truck, a lifeline I'd either pull tight or let slip.

And goddamn it, she was too young. Thirteen years was a sizeable difference. Her voice and the edge in it echoed through my head, taunting me with the knowledge that I'd already claimed her in every practical way. I wasn't sure if she was crazy or just gutsy, but my wolf had recognized her and hers. He'd settled in, curled up like he already had what he wanted.

How the hell was I supposed to make this work?

I growled low again, my breath clouding the cab in front of me. There were so many pieces to this puzzle I couldn't even begin to map it out. The only thing I knew was that she was meant to be with us. With me.

I stared at her window, the shadow of her moving through my mind like a memory I hadn't earned. The instinct to protect her flared hot and fast. What the hell did I know about her? About someone so proper? Wasn't much, but as far as what kind of future she'd have here? What kind of job could I arrange for her? I could sure as shit tell she didn't belong in a waitress uniform. No, it would take a hell of a lot longer to get her on my payroll than Bronc's.

There was nothing tying her to this place but me and her secrets.

I exhaled, the breath as sharp as my need. I needed to find a place for her within the pack before my instincts outpaced my patience. At least that way she'd be less likely to run, less likely to fade, less likely to leave me in the wreckage of another unfinished life.

But damn, I didn't just want her to stay. I wanted everything. And it was tearing me apart.

I clenched the steering wheel, watching as her lights finally went out. The ghost of her smile haunted me through the darkened glass, sweet and fleeting. The words she'd whispered as I shut her door, her certainty that she wasn't afraid, cut through me like a blade with no mercy. I smiled to myself. *"See you in my dreams tonight too, Red."*

The pieces fell into place, and I let the silence sink into my bones. I shifted gears and drove into the dark. Tomorrow was the first step in getting her settled into her new life.

There was a fresh and dangerous pull between us, even in the bright morning air. She opened the door before I knocked, breathless with surprise. Like I'd shattered every impression she'd ever formed. Like I'd given myself away in one sudden motion. Her face was alive with expectation as I crossed the threshold, knowing I'd claimed another part of her and not caring how fast the next followed. Not caring if it was her secrets or her body. Her fingers gripped the door, shock coiling through her, making her the most beautiful thing I'd ever seen. I kissed her forehead.

"Thought you'd guessed by now," I said. Let her stare at the side of me she hadn't seen before. Her in dark leggings, ankle boots, and a green sweater, every line as young and flawless as the curve of her parted lips. Me in a dark tailored business suit. The new dynamic hit us both hard. Even harder than I'd planned. I didn't want to give her a chance to second-guess things, so I quickly got her in my truck and headed us into town.

We sat across from each other; the diner in town was the perfect place for breakfast and our discussion regarding what came next. "I knew you were complicated, but this is more than I imagined." Her voice was full of wonder, the words taking form like she didn't trust them yet. She lingered over her cup of coffee.

"I'm full of surprises," I said, feeding the tension. Watched her eyes continue to study me. "One of them being I own one of the largest Ford dealerships in the country."

She let out a small breath, not quite a laugh. I liked the way it sounded. Liked the way it brought her shoulders down, easy and natural. "You *are* full of surprises," she said, teasing me with the lightness of it.

Then she gave me a sideways look, dark green eyes surrounded by thick lashes, the most seductive thing I'd ever seen. I wanted to reach across the table. Caress her flawless porcelain cheek just to break the distance between us. "And the other surprises?" She asked, voice tentative.

I smiled, slow and wide. "Confidential." Her hair spilled around her, coiled and burning with intensity. Just like my need to have her. "I might let you in on 'em." The teasing came out darker than I'd planned. Rougher. She wasn't backing down. She wouldn't give in first. I waited. Let her make the move. Let her reach out with her vulnerability and test the waters.

It was her turn to surprise me. She held my gaze without flinching. "Mysteries can be fun to unravel, I guess."

I laughed, the sound surprising us both. "Guess you'll have to find out," I said. Her frustration made her even more beautiful. I let it play across her face until I couldn't stand the distance anymore.

"Guess I will." Her coy smile only made her features more intriguing. But as much as I loved the flirtatious banter, I knew I had to steer us into more serious conversations. I reached for her hand across the table.

"Tell me what your plans are, Sawyer. For the future." My voice was more of a demand than I'd meant it to be. Her breath caught slightly as she contemplated her answer. She had changed from the damaged woman I'd rescued those weeks ago. She'd been seeing Penny, our pack therapist, a few times a week. I hated to ask how that part of her life was progressing, but I had to know. "Are you ready to move forward? I know it's not my business, really. But I can see how much you've changed since you've been seeing Penny. I thought maybe it was time for you to take the next step and integrate more into pack life. And I certainly don't want to pressure you, but everyone in the pack who is able plays a part in keeping the community running. Do you have any skills or areas you're passionate about where you think you might want to contribute?"

"I have a degree in teaching and music," she said finally. She swallowed, the moment tightening. Breaking over us like a wave. "I'd like to teach or even give private piano lessons."

The words opened the door for me, and I wasn't going to let it close. Her dream was within my reach. "You want to teach?" I repeated. Her earnestness cracked me wide open. It was unexpected and perfect. "That's amazing." Her look of confusion made me smile.

"I thought that would be an unreachable goal there for a while," she muttered as she got a faraway look on her face.

I knew she'd gone to a dark place. Fucking Harrison's lab where she'd been tortured and abused. I squeezed her hand. "Hey, look at me, Sawyer." She slowly came back to me. "You're safe now," I told her. "I swear to you. I will never let anyone hurt you again."

The quiver of her lip as she smiled told me she wanted to believe that. The look in her eyes told me she didn't quite think it was true. She immediately put on her signature Sawyer 'happy face.'

"So, what's so amazing about me wanting to teach?"

"What if I told you I had an opening?" The raw need in my voice gave away more than I'd planned. More than I cared to keep hidden.

"An opening?" Her confusion was sharp and sweet.

"For a teacher," I said. "At the Pack school."

She froze, an arrow in flight, an emotion I hadn't expected freezing us both in place. Her questions. Her fears. Her body alive with uncertainty. Her expression transformed as she realized what I was offering her. Her hope filled every corner of the room, so bright it almost blinded me. Her green eyes. Her flushed skin. Her parted lips. The image was burned into my skull. Her voice was breathless. "A music teacher?"

I held the moment. Trapped it like an animal in my ribs. "Exactly." Her desire hit me hard.

"Are you serious?" I bit back a smile.

"More serious than you know," I said. Every word precise. Tactics honed in on what mattered. She believed me. Her face told me everything. Every shift, every crack in her hesitation. Every nuance of her willingness to step off this cliff with me.

"I don't know what to say." Her voice was music. Pure and clear and full of all the things I needed to hear. Her willingness to give this a shot. Her willingness to give *me* a shot.

"Say you'll do it." The words came fast. I couldn't hold them back. "Say you'll consider it." Say you'll take me. Her eyes met mine. They were weapons. Blades. They pinned me in place.

"Yes." That was the only word that mattered, and she said it. The sunlit room became our cathedral, a holy place where we were the only true believers. Where nothing else could exist but us. Where we would write our story, long and hot and full of fire.

"Good." I said the word slow. Savored the taste of it. My wolf was roaring in satisfaction that we were providing something that our mate wanted. It seemed ridiculous. She wasn't my mate. But something deep inside said she *was*. "Let me see what I can arrange. You might be able to start in a couple of days." I leaned back, trying to regain my control. Trying to mask the burn in my gut as I texted the school principal.

"Really?" She glowed. Her energy set me on a course I couldn't reverse. A course I didn't want to reverse.

"There will be a few things to work through, but I can make it happen." The morning light seemed too bright, our own private universe expanding with each breath. "I'll take care of the paperwork."

"I don't understand how you can offer me this. I thought you owned an auto dealership."

I patted her hand. "Let's go to the school and I'll explain more about how things work with the Iron Valor Pack."

The sign for Bridger Hardin, Sr. Elementary loomed like a goddamned threat as we pulled in. Sawyer looked out the window at it, and I didn't need to have a bond to tell me her nerves were high. She tried to hide it, but I could tell by the way she wrung her hands together. I parked and put a steadying hand on her knee.

"Wait, Bridger Hardin Elementary. Is the school named after *you*?"

"My grandfather actually, thus the 'senior.' When I donated the money to build the school, I wanted it named after the greatest man I ever knew. Hunters killed my father when I was very young. My granddad stepped up and even though he was older, he was a stand-in father to me and my siblings. A damn good man." She listened so intently as I told her about him.

"I'm sorry about your father, but your grandfather sounds like a wonderful man. The kind of man anyone would love to have as a father figure." She spoke quietly. The look on her face led me to believe she didn't have the same paternal experience. Tonight I was going to insist she came clean with me about who she actually is.

As we entered the brightly lit building, I caught the hard edge of footsteps before the woman they belonged to appeared. My ex-Karen's eyes swept from Sawyer to me with careful control, but I knew what ran beneath the surface. "Bridger," she said, lips tight around my name like it was something she couldn't quite swallow. "Good to see you again." This is the woman who had dreamed of being my mate. After six months with her, I knew that would never happen.

Sawyer stood with a wariness that bordered on vulnerable, the other female bringing out some instinctive caution that would make things interesting for us all. I introduced them, and Karen's look turned appraising. She paused for a long, assessing moment before speaking. "You're here about the teaching position?"

Sawyer nodded, the blush in her cheeks giving more away than I knew she'd want. "Bridger told me you're looking for a music teacher. I'm Sawyer."

"Yes." Karen folded her arms and gave me another unreadable glance. "I'm the principal, Karen Day. And he tends to make decisions for the school at times."

"Karen," I said, letting the weight of my voice carry more meaning than my words, "I know she's the right choice."

A cold spark lit her eyes. It sent an almost visible shift through Sawyer, who absorbed it with wide curiosity and remained uncertain of her footing. "Well, you should see the music room. Follow me."

I let Karen take the lead and trailed behind with satisfaction cutting through my veins. We reached a long hallway lined with brightly colored doors. The tour moved forward with the kind of tautness I was growing to enjoy. Karen's composure frayed a bit when she spoke again. "Will you be living with the pack full-time?"

Sawyer glanced over her shoulder, eager for the chance to express what she hoped I'd hear in the response. "That's my plan."

"That's a lot of commitment for someone new to the area," Karen said, each word deliberate and charged.

"Commitment is what she's all about," I said, feeling the tension bite like a chilly wind.

"I see." She opened the door to the music room and stepped aside for Sawyer to enter. Her tone held an edge that could have cut diamonds. "It must be very serious, then."

I followed Sawyer in and ignored Karen's last barb. The walls stood adorned with instruments and a stack of blank sheet music.

Sawyer drank in every detail, an unguarded brightness shining from her in clear defiance of the jealousy I knew burned from Karen's side of the room. She walked up to the piano in the middle of the room and sat. Her fingers flew across the keys as she quickly played a haunting and familiar melody.

"This is perfect," Sawyer whispered, pure awe in her voice as she stood.

"We do things right here," I replied, directing my comment to both of them and knowing only one would get it.

Karen's mouth tightened before she could speak again. "You must be eager to start."

"I am," Sawyer said, and my wolf sang with her excitement, rough notes that went clean through me. "Will you show me the rest?"

Karen's reluctance pushed through a thin layer of profession-alism. "This way."

Sawyer turned and followed the direction, giving me a look that sent a flare of satisfaction through every nerve.

We ended the tour with more tension than we'd begun with, and it sparked like live wires the second Karen found another chance to pull me aside. "You're taking a risk with her," she said, keeping her voice low. "You don't know if she'll stay."

"It's a risk I'll take," I answered, letting her hear how little doubt I had.

Karen's eyes moved to Sawyer, who was admiring the layout of the main office like she belonged there already. "Be careful, Bridger."

"You too, Karen," I said, the threat as open as a wound, know-ing she'd remember this when the day ended.

I walked back to Sawyer, dismissing the possibility that Karen might sabotage what I'd laid out so perfectly, and felt her anxiety mix with fresh confidence as I neared her. "It's a lot to take in," she said, but I could see from the look she gave me that she meant more than the school. "When would I start?"

"I'm thinking Monday," I said.

She swallowed my suggestion with more courage than doubt. "Whew! That's fast. But good."

"That's the good thing about being independent."

Sawyer waited for me to explain more, green eyes steady with fascination.

"We own the land, the school. Everything."

Sawyer's expression held promise, the emotion of it clear and confident now. She'd found more here than she'd expected, and it showed. "I'd love to be part of this," she said. "Is it always like this?"

"What do you mean?"

"The Pack. How it works."

"You've only seen a fraction," I told her, deciding she'd have to know everything if she was going to take the leap I needed from her. "It's more self-contained than you realize. The school is not the only place the Pack exercises independence. We try to be completely self-sustaining." I explained as we left the school.

She absorbed the information, letting it reshape the world she thought she'd entered. "How do you mean?"

"We grow our own food," I said, testing her reaction to each new piece. "Raise livestock. Run businesses on pack land and in town."

"And the school?" She sounded more sure of herself now. "I'll be teaching only pack children?"

"That's right."

Her eyes were bright. "That's as it should be."

"How independent it all is." Her words were soft, full of something close to awe.

"That's the point." I waited, my breath tight in my chest. "Keeping us safe. Keeping us secret."

She didn't flinch. Didn't look away.

"So, you think you're ready?" I pushed, wanting to hear her confirm it.

Her determination flared, a wildfire in the dark forest of her eyes. "Yes."

The force of her answer rocked through me.

"It's a lot to take on," I warned, trying to give her a way out. Knowing I didn't want her to take it. "You'll have pack parents to deal with. There will be battles to fight at times."

Her expression was fierce. Full of things she couldn't put into words. "I know how to fight."

I pulled the truck up to her apartment and put it in park. My eyes held hers, and I knew I had to say it. That it was too soon to mean everything, but not soon enough to mean nothing.

"You'll get what you want, Sawyer." The name burned in my throat. "Everything you want."

The gratitude and hope in her gaze staggered me.

"Can we talk more tonight?" she asked.

My gut tightened. I had a feeling she was ready. Tonight could be the first step to unraveling her secrets.

"I'll bring dinner."

"Okay." She got out and closed the door, my name on her lips as she did. "Menace?"

I leaned across the seat, breathless and breaking. "Yeah?"

"Thank you." Two words, and they came closer to destroying me than anything in my thirty-seven years.

I watched her until the apartment door closed. Until I was sure she was safe. Until I was ready to take a deep breath.

The drive to the dealership was a blur of uncertainty. Too many thoughts tangled up in the things left unsaid. Too many things I wanted to do to her.

I pulled into the lot, adrenaline surging when I should have been running calm and steady. The mundane rhythm of business couldn't distract me. Nothing could, now that I'd committed.

Once I hit my office door, I fell into the rhythm of work. Inventories and payroll, parts orders and tariffs. There was enough business chaos to fill the room. I was thankful I had good people to keep this place running like a well-oiled machine. My general manager was at my door several times.

"Glad to see you boss man. Even happier, Alpha has his Luna back by his side. Lydia says she's the first one to help when any of the women in the pack have a problem. She's something else."

My heart swelled, knowing I was a part of bringing Juliet home. "Thanks Ed. We were sure relieved to find and bring her and Sawyer out of that situation. Juliet has been a pillar of strength that's for sure."

He cleared his throat, remembering that Juliet wasn't the only woman rescued. "Oh hell, that's right. How is Sawyer?"

I smiled. "She's gonna be fine. Matter of fact, I think she's gonna be the new elementary school music teacher."

"I'll be damned. That's fantastic news, man. Love to hear it."

The ringing of my phone chased Ed back to his office. And put me on high alert. It seems it's time we handled up on the business of Skeeter and whatever the hell is happening with the money at the motorcycle shop. Tonight, Sawyer. Tomorrow Skeeter.

CHAPTER 5

SAWYER

Sunset painted the walls in strips of rust and crimson, a reminder of the hours I had left to tell him the truth. Shadows moved with me as I paced, frantic, with the impending confession burning a hole in my throat. Menace. He would never forgive me for hiding something like this. He would hate me as soon as I revealed who I was. My restless eyes landed on the door. I wanted to run again, but there was nowhere else to go.

My stomach growled. I hadn't been able to eat anything after breakfast. The excitement of the opportunity of being able to teach. The thing I'd wanted to do all my life and thought I'd never be allowed to and the impending doom of my confession kept me from eating. Menace said he'd bring dinner. I had to try to eat, or I'd be sick before I could tell him everything. My stomach clenched. He'd storm out the minute I said my real name. He'd walk away and leave me to a life of exile. My heart slammed against my chest. Every moment I lingered here put him and his pack in more danger. The afternoon sun turned a darker red, blood pooling beneath my feet.

A knock. The sound split through my head. I froze, imagining him on the other side of the door. Tall, imposing, the hard glint of his eyes. He'd hate me. Throw me out. Abandon me to the fates. I'd rather die than see him walk away. Tears burned. Breath shallow. Maybe if I hid here, he would give up, leave before I had to explain. God, how ridiculous was I?

My hand was on the doorknob, pulling it open before my heart made the choice. He stood like an omen on my doorstep, large and shadowed. His tee clung to his chest, and his leather cut showed the mark of his authority. I wanted to fall into his arms and forget who I was supposed to be. Wanted to dissolve into the strength of him until the rest of the world faded. But I couldn't. I opened my mouth to speak, to say what? "Hi."

Menace stepped inside, and the apartment shrank around me. As much as I ached to be near him, the reminder of how temporary this was gnawed at me. This would be the last night. I swallowed hard against the burn in my throat. It was a moment before I realized I was staring and that he hadn't said a word.

He carried a bag from Ms. Pearl's. He held it up for me to see. "I brought burgers. Best in town." His smile almost relaxed me; it was so disarming. I tried to keep my hands from trembling as I took the bag and unpacked the burgers and fries onto paper plates.

He glanced at the food, then back at me. The dark shirt stretched across his shoulders in a way that left my pulse uneven. I thought of how hard it had been to resist him, knowing what we were to each other. Knowing I would have to leave.

"Sure smells good."

We moved to the couch, his presence as much an accusation as an enticement. This shouldn't feel awkward. He's had his tongue down my throat, for Pete's sake. But I was too afraid of the pain when I finally told him. I put space between us, praying he'd be as far away as possible when he looked at me like I was a traitor. We ate in silence, the rustle of wrappers unnaturally loud.

"Wine?" I asked, more to have something to do with my hands than because I thought he'd accept.

"You're shaking, Sawyer." His voice was deep, steady. I almost wanted to believe it held a hint of tenderness, but that wasn't possible.

"Just a little bit cold," I lied.

He leaned back against the couch. There was more distance between us than just space. "I can tell something's bothering you." He talked between bites.

His hazel eyes pierced me, so sharp I felt like they left marks. A knot in my chest twisted tighter. "I'm..." A coward. "I'm fine."

But I wasn't. I was the opposite of fine, and he knew it.

We finished eating, or I pretended to. My stomach felt like an acid pit, threatening to consume me. Menace looked as if he had all the time in the world, his arm resting casually on the back of the couch. His seeming indifference pushed me closer to the edge.

I rose and poured another glass of wine, clinging to the small hope that alcohol might calm my nerves. The kitchen was small, U-shaped, the island a peninsula. I didn't turn around, waiting for the wine to stop sloshing. Waiting for my heart to stop pounding so hard I could hear it echo off the walls.

When I sat down again, he hadn't moved. If he was impatient, he didn't show it. But the set of his jaw and the narrowed line of his eyes left no doubt.

"Menace..." I hesitated. His name tasted bitter. It would be the last time I spoke it.

"You know, Sawyer is not my actual name." It spilled out before I could stop it.

That caused him to move. His arm came down as he turned on the couch to face me. He gave a short nod, indicating he already knew that. Maybe he knew everything. The blood felt thin in my veins, my skin going pale and cold. I closed my eyes against the intensity of it. He was still in the same position when I opened them, waiting.

"There's so much I have to tell you."

He didn't blink, didn't break his gaze.

"That I need to tell you."

My voice cracked, my fingers wet against the wineglass.

"Start anywhere," he said.

My heart was running faster than I ever could. I'd tried. "You'll hate me," I said.

He just looked at me, that hard hazel stare that seemed to see through layers I hadn't even begun to uncover. "I could never."

"Oh, I think you could."

It was hard to say what felt heavier—my heart or my voice. They both struggled, gasping for breath.

"Have a little faith in me," he said.

I was trembling again, but it didn't matter. I had to get through this. "My entire life is a set of strings, all attached to someone else's hand. All manipulated and jerked into a dance I've never been able to stop."

His silence tore through me. I put the wineglass down, worried it would shatter. Everything felt close to breaking.

I forced myself to keep going, to move past the suffocating air and his stoic expression. "I never had any choices."

A pause stretched between us, taut as a wire. I waited for him to speak, but he didn't.

"Everything was decided for me. The clothes I wore. My hair color, length, style. Friends, schools, hobbies, everything. I never had any say. Everything was carefully curated specifically for me. To create the perfect daughter." The person I was supposed to marry. "I thought..."

I thought he would have interrupted by now. His gaze was unflinching, cutting.

"Until finally there was a decision made for me, I would not allow. No one but myself would be the person who got to decide who I loved. *I* would be the person to decide whom I gave myself to. Me and me alone. There was only one way I thought I could be free. That was running."

He still said nothing. The wine was still in my throat, acidic.

"Are you going to say anything?" I asked, voice hoarse.

"I'm allowing you to finish."

He did not know how much it hurt to continue. No idea how heavy the truth was.

"I can't," I barely spoke.

"You can. You're doing well; keep going."

I drew a breath that didn't feel like mine.

It came out in a rush, a confession against the sanctity of silence. "I'm not like Juliet." The glass in my hand was close to breaking. "I'm not an afterthought. I'm the opposite. My father always knew where I was. Every minute of my life."

I saw his jaw tighten, his fingers drum against his thigh.

"Everything was arranged. There was no escaping him. No negotiating. It was like..."

"Like what?" Menace asked.

"A political arrangement."

His face was hard, closed. But I saw it change, recognition settling in.

My chest was a cavity, dark and empty. My words had been gutted from it.

"I ran because they were going to make me marry some-one." My voice cracked again. This time I didn't bother fixing it. "Because they wouldn't allow me to say no."

He watched me, calculating. The way I'd expected. But he didn't tell me to get out. Not yet.

"Who?"

His patience was a knife, slow and brutal.

I couldn't look at him when I answered.

"Someone my father thought would strengthen his power. Someone who didn't care whether or not I loved him. Someone cruel. Someone who needs heirs."

His eyes burned. I could feel them on me, a heat worse than his silence. My breath felt as final as a tombstone. "It was a strategic match," I said.

"Why didn't you tell me?"

His voice was rougher than before. He was beginning to see. Beginning to understand.

"I was afraid."

His posture stiffened. He was beginning to put the pieces together.

"Afraid of what?"

"Afraid of everything. I'd just been pulled from the nightmare of that lab. I didn't know if my father knew that I'd been locked up in that cell. Afraid of what people would see when they looked at me. Of what *you* would see." I cried.

I waited for him to say something. For him to cast me out with the rest of my secrets.

But he didn't.

"You're thinking of how you can run now, aren't you?" he asked.

A short, bitter laugh escaped before I could stop it. "Trying to," I said. "But not getting very far."

A choked sob climbed its way into my throat.

"When you broke down that door to my cell, it was like I'd been freed from more than what Dane had done to me. Something broke inside me when I looked in your eyes. I should have just told you who I was and had you return me. But I was selfish. I dared to hope."

His face was in his hands.

"Please," I said. "Please look at me."

He lifted his face to me, a million unsaid words in his eyes.

I drew another breath, preparing for the last cut.

"I'm not Sawyer Galloway."

This was it. I had to get the words out.

"I'm Princess Savannah Calloway."

He stood, the movement abrupt, almost violent. I flinched.

I stood as well. "Daughter of Declan Calloway." I said it to his back, a plea as much as a confession.

He turned slowly, his eyes narrowing.

"King of the Eastern Wolves." The words came out broken, desperate. "I'm so sorry."

He took a step toward me, then another. I tried to shrink back, but there was nowhere left to go.

He reached me, his breath warm against my skin. I couldn't stop shaking.

"You know how dangerous it is for you to be here."

"Yes." It was barely a whisper.

"You know what will happen when they find out."

The fear rose, drowning me.

I nodded, unable to speak.

"You think you're leaving?"

A tear slipped down my cheek.

"I think I have to. I'm trying to," I said. "It's not working."

His hand brushed against my hair. The touch was enough to break me.

"Don't." He said it like a command, but his voice was gentler than I'd expected.

"Don't what?" I asked shakily.

"Don't try."

"I can't stay." My words were so soft I wondered if he'd heard them.

He answered by pulling me closer, the way I'd dreamed he would.

I buried my head against his chest, dizzy with relief. With his scent.

"Honey and roses," he said, his breath stirring the loose strands of my hair.

"What?"

"What I smelled that night at Pearl's."

I drew back enough to look at him, heart in my throat. His face was softer than I'd ever seen.

He held me for a long time. I felt his strength seep into my bones, mending the parts that had been broken. But the truth was too heavy for one person to carry. I pulled back, fearing what might happen if I kept him close. I had already risked too much by staying. He didn't let me get far, just enough to look at him. This beautiful man, his hazel eyes molten. I wanted to remember him like this when I left.

"I don't want to run anymore," I said, my voice trembling.

He smoothed my hair away from my face.

"Then don't," he said.

"You don't understand." I put a hand on his chest, a final touch. "You don't know what I'm bringing down on you. I don't know what I thought. Going with you to the school. Sitting at that piano. Trying to act like I could have a real life."

Menace's eyes narrowed, focused. "Tell me what I don't understand. What do you think you're bringing down on me?"

I took a step back, everything aching.

He sat me next to him on the couch; the world reduced to the distance between us. He watched in silence as I tried to find words, words that would only hurt him.

"It's more complicated than you think."

"Try me."

I drew a breath, every part of me tight.

His assurance would have been comforting if it hadn't also been dangerous.

"My mother... I don't know how she stands it. All of it. She begged me to be careful. Told me I needed to find my fate."

"Looks like you found it." Menace's words were sharp and determined.

"Yes." My voice cracked.

His fingers stopped drumming.

"I feel it too. But it gets worse."

His voice was serious. "Tell me."

"The man he promised me to is Dominic Madison."

His face drained of all of its color. "The King of the Midwest?"

"And that's why I said I cannot stay," I barely whispered, tears streaming down my face.

"And I'm telling you, you're staying." He was emphatic.

The finality in his voice sent a shiver through me.

"He won't let me go."

"Neither will I."

"But..."

"But what?"

I swallowed against the growing tightness in my throat. "He'll never stop hunting for me. He made a deal with Dominic. When you saved me from that lab, I guess I just forgot. I felt something stronger than my father's wrath the moment I first saw you. I think it was hope."

"You're staying."

"You could die for this." My voice was thin and desperate.

He brushed his fingers across my cheek, sending a shock through my skin.

"Then I'll die," he said.

"Menace."

The word was a prayer and a plea.

"Savannah."

Hearing my name on his lips sent a shiver through me.

"Don't run."

"You're asking too much."

He smiled, but it didn't reach his eyes.

"It would be easier for you to just let me go," I said, everything raw.

"No."

"Please."

He pulled me to him, crushing. Consuming.

The force of it left me breathless.

"You can't do this."

His grip tightened, leaving me helpless and comforted. Leaving me exactly where I wanted to be.

"Yes," he said. "I can."

He kept me there, unwilling to let me slip away.

We stayed like that as the night surrendered to dawn, as my fear gave way to hope.

I felt the warmth of him against me, felt the tremor in his breath. He wouldn't let me leave, not even for a moment.

The rising sun caught in his hair, a burnished light that made him glow.

I'd never seen anything more beautiful.

"Not gonna lose you."

I shook my head, overwhelmed by the force of it.

"You're risking too much."

His hand traced a path down my back, sending sparks down my spine.

"That's the point," he said.

He moved us to the bedroom, each step careful and measured.

"Don't know what I'd do," he said, his voice a low rumble, "if you left."

He laid me down, as gentle as I'd ever known him. As loving.

"You'll have to find out," I said, a last attempt to sound strong.

He grinned, the tension in his eyes softening.

"Or not."

I laughed, and it felt like freedom. It felt like we had all the time in the world.

The sound of it echoed against the walls, a promise as solid as his hold.

"I'm not going anywhere," I said, knowing it was true.

He lay beside me, an anchor. A salvation.

"You can't," he said. "Not anymore."

I buried my face in his shoulder, breathing in his scent.

"I was afraid."

"I know," he said, stroking my hair. "Don't be."

It felt like a command.

It felt like love.

He stayed with me as sleep finally pulled me under, as the shadows disappeared with the coming of a new day.

He stayed.

We stayed.

Chapter 6

Menace

The day's first shadows hadn't faded from the walls when I woke with a start. Savannah's cheek was pressed onto my shirt-covered chest, her arm slung over my stomach. Her confession cut through my mind, sharper than any alarm. I could still see the fear behind her eyes when she'd whispered the truth in the dark. "Calloway," I muttered, tasting the name. Gently I removed her arm, grabbed my phone, and texted Bronc to see if she could stay with Juliet, my thumbs heavy as I punched out my request. She'd need someone besides me to talk to, someone to keep her secrets. I told Savannah as much last night, a knot pulling tight in my stomach as I thought of what it would take for her to let it all out. My shirt stuck to my skin as I pulled on my boots.

Bronc, need Savannah to stay with Juliet today. We've got too much to handle with Skeeter. The message hung there, stark and desperate. I scrubbed my hand over my face, hoping he wouldn't ask too many questions yet. Not that I didn't trust my brothers, but hell, if Savannah's secret got out too soon, I wasn't sure we'd have the time to react. The fucking King of the Eastern Wolves. I couldn't get her voice out of my head, the tremor in it when she finally said her name.

I felt the pressure building behind my eyes. This would be a fucking day. I heard her stir as I set up the coffeemaker. She came around the corner just as it started to drip into the carafe. Goddamn if she wasn't a vision with her tangled auburn hair spilling out of the messy bun that sat atop her head.

Slowly, I made my way around the butcher block peninsula to her as she stood still as a statue. Those terrified green eyes held my every move. "Hey, Red. I don't like your looking at me like a frightened lamb." My hands cupped her face as I kissed my way down from her forehead to her lips.

Loved the way her breath caught at my slightest touch.

"I'm not afraid of you.," she said breathlessly when I stopped. "But I won't lie. The situation has me scared shitless." She half laughed as she followed me to the kitchen to get the coffee mugs down from the cabinet as my phone buzzed. Her eyes widened as she saw Bronc's name flash across the screen.

"I asked Bronc if you could stay with Juliet today. I want you to tell her everything. She can keep your secret, and you need to talk to someone. She's a good one, Savannah. I trust her. You can too."

Bronc's answer was short and sweet. *Yeah, she can stay. We'll talk later.*

While Savannah changed clothes and got herself together, I thought of Declan Calloway, of what he might be doing to track her down. Savannah wouldn't be the only one he'd come after. Once he knew where she was, none of us were safe.

I thought about how the guys would react when they heard the news about who Savannah was. One shitstorm after another. I expected them to go a little ape shit. That was standard-issue behavior for such an occasion. I knew one thing was certain though: they were my brothers, and they'd stand with me, just like we stood with Bronc. Just like I'd stand with them. Hell or fucking high water. Life or death. I'd have their backs. And they'd sure as hell always have mine.

We stopped for a quick breakfast, and then I basically drove like a madman. My foot pressed heavy on the gas, the wind beating at the windows like it had fists. My heart kicked harder, thinking about how I could keep Savannah safe and hold the club together at the same time. I had to tell them what we were up against. And I had to tell them now. The conversation was light as we basically rode in silence. We must have had that in common. When I have heavy stuff on my mind, I tend to get quiet.

Then, I let myself think about Skeeter, let it distract me from the heavier weight. We'd been on to him for weeks. Felt good to finally pin him down. Knew he was behind the money missing from Bronc's shop, thought we'd scare him out into the open and call it a day. Then we saw how far back it went, and everything we knew now told us it was gonna be bigger than we thought. As most things were.

The sky was too big, the horizon too wide. Everything stretched out forever out here. The farther I drove, the farther it seemed like I had to go. I lived about five miles inside pack territory. I'd dropped Savannah by Bronc's and then headed home for a shower and clean clothes. When the pack buildings finally came into view, I felt like I'd put on armor. The air was charged with a storm I couldn't see, but I could sure as hell feel.

Parking outside the clubhouse, I cut the engine and sat there longer than I should have, mind spinning circles. I thought about Savannah and how far she'd gotten with her story to Juliet. I sent her all the good thoughts I could.

Almost texted her. My hand hovered over my phone, but I stopped. Stuffed it in my pocket. If I kept checking on her, I'd never do what I needed to do here. I slammed the truck door and stalked up to the house. This was it. The bomb was about to drop.

The compound was quiet when I arrived, but it felt like the calm before a storm. I went straight to the meeting room where the others were already waiting. Bronc looked up, a shadow of suspicion in his eyes. "The look on your face tells me I'm not gonna like this." He was seated at the table, hands folded in front of him like he was expecting a bad hand to be dealt.

"Well then, I must be doing a real fuckin' piss-poor job at facial expressions," I said, voice dripping with sarcasm. "Because you're gonna fuckin' *hate* this. Seems our Sawyer, *my* Sawyer, my *mate*, and yes, I said mate, is actually Savannah *Calloway*." I let her full name hang there, waited for them to catch up. It didn't take long.

Bronc's mouth tightened as the weight of it sunk in. Then, after a heavy sigh, "I just wish that one goddamn time, somebody around here could drop some kind of good news on me. Declan fucking Calloway," he muttered. "That son of a bitch is dangerous."

Arsenal leaned back in his chair, eyes flicking from me to Bronc, processing. He crossed his arms, the tattoos on his forearms shifting with the motion. Tension ratcheted up and crackled between us like static. "She'd better have a golden pussy." Was his fucking smartass reply. I took a step towards him. Bronc's massive hand on my chest the only thing that stopped me from causing serious bodily harm.

Bronc's glare could bring a man to his knees. "Now is not the time for your disrespectful comments about your brother's *mate*, jackass." It was like Bronc had backhanded Arsenal across the face.

"Apologies, man. This is all new. Women around here being more than pussy that is. I got your back, you know that. And hers."

The room felt too small, like there wasn't enough air to go around. I stayed at the head of the table, the pressure of their attention pinning me in place. Bronc's jaw was set, the tendons in his neck standing out as he absorbed what I'd just dropped. He leaned forward, fingers interlocked. "How the hell did you get into this mess, Menace?"

"I knew she was hiding something," I said, knowing how weak that sounded. "Had no way of knowing it'd be a bombshell like this. Figured she was unhappy with her pack at home and had an opportunity not to go back so she took it. I fucking introduced her to Karen at the elementary school. She said she had a degree in music and education. Should have heard it when she sat at the piano." My mind went to that classroom. "I don't know how she thought she'd get away with it when I ran her credentials. Guess that's why she fessed up. That and she's scared to death her father's men are going to hurt us."

"King of the Eastern Packs is a well-known tyrant," Big Papa chimed in, his voice low but steady. His heir isn't any better.

"Yeah." I nodded, remembering Savannah's confession and the fear in her eyes. "She's been running from Declan for almost a year. Went off-grid, hiding out wherever she could, until by some fluke, Harrison's men found her in the Ozarks."

The room was quiet for a moment before Arsenal asked the $64,000 question. "Why is she running, Menace?"

"Yeah, it gets worse." I looked down at my scarred hands that were flat on the table. Then I looked back up at my brothers whose lives were all going to soon be in danger.

"She ran, because her father promised her to the new King Dominic Madison of the Midwestern Packs."

Bronc shook his head. "Jesus Christ. You brought a fucking Calloway into the compound. And possibly induced the wrath of the Midwest king as well?"

"She's my *mate*," I shot back, the words coming out sharper than I intended. "And I just rescued a woman. There was no way for me to know any of this. What was she supposed to do? It's only been a few weeks. But once Lucia came by your cabin, she knew her time was up. Lucia recognized her."

Bronc ran his hand down his face. "Shit, what a mess. I'll have Juliet call Lucia. Get her to keep quiet."

I finally took my seat at the table. "Savannah is telling Juliet everything right now. I told her she was going to need a friend, and there is not a better person I know than Juliet."

Bronc's eyes shifted to me, like he was surprised.

I shrugged. "I mean it. Every word."

Bronc looked as old as I'd ever seen him. I was glad he had Juliet in his life. She gave him some balance to the burdens he always carried.

The words hung there, pressing down on us all. I could see the calculations spinning in Bronc's mind, the tactical angles he was working through. Finally, he exhaled and leaned back, fingers steepled. "What's our play?"

"We need allies," I said. "Someone with enough force to stand up to Declan."

"Rafe Mayfield," Doc suggested, speaking the name we were all thinking.

Bronc considered it, his expression hard and unreadable. "Reaching out to another king is a big move. Declan gets wind of it, he'll retaliate."

"He's coming no matter what," I argued. "Once he knows Savannah is here, he'll make a play for her. He won't care if we're in the crossfire."

Bronc's gaze met mine, searching. "Can you trust her not to run again?"

"Yeah." I thought of the look on her face when she said she wouldn't leave me. I felt it like a weight in my chest. "She wanted to, just because she's scared shitless that we can't handle her father and his men. I convinced her that we can take whatever he throws at us. Sure hope I'm right. But she's not going anywhere."

The others were quiet, but I could feel the tension winding tighter around us. Bronc rubbed his hand across his mouth, considering. "We'll need to move fast. Get to Mayfield before Declan makes a play."

I nodded, relieved to have him on board. "Soon as we've got Skeeter locked down, we ride to Alabama."

"Better not wait too long." Bronc's voice was clipped, the authority in it clear. "Wrecker, find out if Declan's sniffing around. We'll have to face him once we start informing packs about their loved ones. Word will get out about us scuttling that lab. We may already be out of time."

The lights buzzed overhead as silence settled again. Wrecker shifted, pulling out his tablet and scrolling. "Got chatter on Declan," he reported. "Uptick in movement, but no specifics. He's trying to keep the search for his daughter on the down low. Keeping it real quiet."

Bronc cursed under his breath. "Doesn't sound like him. He usually goes big. He must be pretty embarrassed his little girl slipped out from under his thumb."

"Maybe he knows we've got Savannah," I said, a chill running through me at the thought.

"Can't take chances," Bronc replied, his voice steel. "We have to get to Mayfield."

The decision felt like a live wire in the room, buzzing with risk and desperation. I stayed rooted at the table, jaw tight, wondering how much time we really had. Bronc pushed to his feet, his chair scraping back. "We go to Alabama after Skeeter," he said, his voice final.

We went over our plans to nab him. That's the easy part. He's right here, every day, all day. We just had to get the job done. Harder part might be breaking him.

Bronc repeated the plan to meet with Mayfield, as if saying it would make it easier. The others nodded, but their faces said otherwise.

The sun hung low, bleeding orange across the asphalt as we rolled up to the shop. My cut felt heavy on my shoulders, the club patch itching like a brand. Behind me, Bronc and Arsenal and the others killed their engines, the silence sudden and sharp. No need for speeches. We all knew why we were here: two years of missing cash, inventory logs thicker with lies than grease, and Skeeter's shaky hands at the center of it.

Juliet's spreadsheets had painted him guilty weeks ago—entries "miscounted," shipments "lost," pennies skinned into thousands. Axle's old fingerprints were all over it too, but that bastard had already eighty-sixed us. But Skeeter? He wasn't smart enough to run a game this slick alone. Someone else was pulling his strings. And tonight? He'd sing for us or choke on his silence.

We all strolled in like it was a regular Thursday night. Skeeter stood frozen by a gutted engine, grease smeared up his arms like war paint. His eyes darted—left to right, exit to exit—but Big Papa was already blocking the door, arms crossed. Wrecker ran his finger across the front counter like he was giving it the white-glove treatment.

"Hey fellas. Place was pretty scarce today." Skeeter stammered, backing into a tool rack. Wrenches clattered to the floor. "Just Maddie and me most of the day."

"Appreciate the hard day's work," Bronc spoke as he stepped slowly towards him. "Busy day, otherwise?"

Skeeter was glancing around the shop, trying to figure out what the hell was happening. "Not too bad. Got that Gold Wing in over there. And trying to finish this Street Glide is all. Everything okay, Bronc?"

There was Bronc's opening. Skeeter continued to use hand wipes to clean his hands.

"Well, now that you mentioned it, Skeeter. There *is* something we need to discuss."

He flinched. Sweat glazed his face even in the shop's chill. Scared, I noted—not of us, though we could make it quick if we wanted—but of whatever shadow had its claws in his spine. His throat bobbed as Arsenal tossed me zip-ties from across the room; they landed in my palm with a slap that made Skeeter twitch again. Eyes wide, he seemed to realize what was happening as he hung his head.

I gave a small laugh. "Ahh, the lightbulb might not be the brightest one in the pack, but it finally turned on. Put your arms behind your back you traitorous piece of shit."

He did as I instructed.

Bronc continued, "Twenty years, Skeeter. You're going to betray your pack after twenty years?"

I led him over to Arsenal by his elbow. He wasn't slinging bullshit like usual now. Didn't fight when Arsenal shoved him into the van outside. Just slumped against the metal floorboards, staring at nothing, mouth sewn shut by fear. Not much worse than betraying the Alpha of your pack.

Chapter 7

Savannah

The cabin was almost obscene in its warmth. Juliet and I settled in the dining area, where pastries and coffee sat waiting, ever the perfect hostess. She pushed a stack of porcelain plates in my direction and gave me a sweet smile that set my pulse sprinting. My thoughts tumbled between my father and Menace, between honesty and terror, until her Luna intuition broke the silence.

"What's going on, Sawyer? It's not like Menace to drop you off like an Amazon delivery."

My hands trembled. I barely tasted the pastry as I bit into it, chewing on it and her question at the same time. The courage to answer was in short supply.

I wondered if she knew already. If Menace had said something to Bronc. If word had spread through the pack, through the town, like a wildfire set to consume us. What would they do to me once they knew?

"I don't know where to start," I finally said, a hollow laugh escaping my lips.

"Start with Menace." Her eyes were sharp, too sharp. "Something's happening. He's concerned."

Concerned was an understatement. Terrified was closer. My voice trembled as I spoke, each word dragged up from the pit of my stomach.

"I'm not who you think I am." The confession clawed its way out, ripping me apart. I watched Juliet's expression shift, her breath catching as I explained who I was. "I understand you're new to our world and the politics of it. You've probably heard of the Supernatural Council and the territory kings." She nodded her head slowly in understanding and some confusion as to where this was going. "My real name is Savannah Calloway. I am the daughter of Declan Calloway, King of the Eastern Territory. Princess Savannah Calloway, if I'm being official."

"Oh, fuck," she whispered. Her surprise morphed into comprehension, and I could almost see the gears turning as she repeated. "King of the Eastern Territory."

"I never meant to endanger anyone." The words tumbled over each other, desperate to explain. "Once Menace rescued me..."

"You fell for him," she finished. The knowing in her voice cut through my shame, laid me bare.

I nodded, the movement feeling like defeat. Her gaze held mine, waiting for more. I struggled to find a beginning that wouldn't betray my heart as much as the end would.

"I know this will sound somewhat familiar to you. It's not that I know exactly how your life was, but I understand you had similar struggles. My entire life, I never had a moment of freedom," I started again, the words stained with the taste of my past. "Everything in my life was planned, orchestrated. Every class I took, every person I met, was part of his agenda." My father's shadow stretched long over every memory. "My father groomed me as a political pawn. I was going to be his key to the Midwestern packs."

"An arranged marriage?" Her voice held a note of something like pity, but stronger, as though she understood too well.

"King Dominic." His name felt foreign on my tongue after so long, a relic of another life. "My father's big move."

Juliet absorbed it all, her presence an anchor I didn't know I needed. "And you've been running from it."

"From him." My hands were fists on the table, shaking as I held on to something she couldn't see. "I thought I was safe in the Ozarks. I thought I could be a new person. Then Harrison's men found me, and you know how that ended."

"What did Menace know?" Her question was gentle but unyielding.

"Nothing. I just gave him the name Sawyer Galloway, Juliet. I thought I could just start a new life. Be her. Then Lucia came through your door."

Her eyes lit with the remembrance of that night. "Oh stars, that's why you both were acting so strangely!"

"Yes. She recognized me. We've known each other since we were children. At first, I thought my father had sent her. But her father hates my father. And I saw how much she loves you, so I knew it was just an awful coincidence. But she told me my father had so many men looking for me. I realized it was just a matter of time. He just hasn't made it public because it will embarrass him."

I was staring down at my hand. "I still was delusional enough to think I could hide here. But Menace told me I had to be productive. He asked me what skills I had. The only honest answer I had was that I was a certified music teacher. Then, he excitedly took me to the elementary school and introduced me to the principal, and they showed me around. I got caught up in the moment. Saw the music room, played the piano. The thought that maybe I could have this life entered my mind and heart. I wanted it so much. Menace offered me the job, and I foolishly accepted. I knew I had to tell him the truth. And here we are."

My heart pounded, reckless in my chest. "I've never been so scared in my life. But I can't imagine being without him." The admission left me hollow. My secrets spilled between us like shattered glass.

Juliet watched me closely, her eyes a mix of caution and compassion. "Does he know how you feel?"

"Yes." I looked down, unable to hold her gaze any longer. "He's afraid I'll run again. But I'm out of options. He doesn't understand what my father is capable of. Now my greatest fear is for the pack."

The room seemed to close in; the warmth suffocating as I waited for her to say something, anything.

She reached across the table, her hand warm on mine. "Declan's not the only one with power," she said, her voice firm. "Menace is Bronc's right hand, his brother. If Declan comes for him or you, he'll have to answer to the entire pack."

I wanted to believe her, wanted it more than I'd ever wanted anything. "You don't know my father. He's ruthless."

"He's not the only one." Her smile was fierce, a promise more than a reassurance. "We've faced worse than him before."

Juliet's hand squeezed mine, pulling me back from the edge of despair. "You'll have to show Menace you're not too scared to stay," she said.

"Even if it puts you all at risk?" My voice was barely a whisper, my fear laid bare.

"We can handle the risk," she replied. "Can you handle losing him?"

I couldn't. I knew that now. Knew it with every frantic beat of my heart. "I've only ever belonged to one person," I said, the words slipping out before I could catch them. "And that involved physical chains. I never want to feel that way again. I'd rather be soul-bound to Menace than any physical chain."

"He'd never hold you against your will." Her eyes met mine, steady and unwavering. "Be with him because you long for him. Because you'd die without him. Not because you're running from something else."

The truth of it settled into me, deeper than I thought possible. It took root, growing past the fear, past the doubts that had chased me halfway across the country.

Our words stretched through the morning, past the coffee and pastries, into the uncertain light of a future I never imagined having.

Menace and Bronc arrived with the weight of doom hanging on their shoulders. I'd barely digested my confessions to Juliet when Bronc's icy glare made me shrink back, his disapproval a storm cloud in the room. He loomed over the table, blunt and impatient, as Menace laid out their plan. Declan's name vibrated in my chest like a dull ache. They were going to King Rafe Mayfield, looking for allies in Birmingham. The cabin felt tight with tension as we left. Instead of driving me back to my apartment, Menace veered onto an unfamiliar road, the questions loud between us.

The silence spread, swollen and ugly, until I couldn't stand it. "Where are we going?" I finally asked, the uncertainty raw in my voice.

Menace's eyes stayed on the road, his face carved in stone. "Somewhere safe."

The words did nothing to calm the storm inside me. The flat Texas landscape blurred past as my pulse thudded louder and more erratic. I watched him, searching for a clue, but he was unreadable.

We drove longer than I expected, each mile pulling me further from the certainty I thought I had. My fingers fidgeted in my lap, twisting my fear into tangles I couldn't undo.

When he finally turned onto a quiet street lined with sprawling trees, I stared out the window, my breath catching. He parked in front of a stately colonial house, its black shutters standing in stark contrast to the crisp white siding. Boxwoods trimmed to military precision marched in neat rows.

He got out of the truck, his stride purposeful as he moved to the door.

I hesitated, my unease blooming into full-blown suspicion. The interior was just as pristine, with gleaming hardwood floors and crown moldings that felt both oppressive and elegant.

Then I saw it. My things, stacked neatly by the door. I turned to him, a storm of emotion in my chest.

"What is this?" The question came out sharper than I intended, my confusion laced with the beginnings of anger.

Menace's voice was as blunt as his expression. "You're living with me now."

The shock left me momentarily breathless. It echoed inside, the way Bronc's declaration of war had—too loud and final. My mouth opened, then closed again, my thoughts tangled and uncertain.

He moved past me, setting his keys down with the same kind of authority he wielded everywhere else. I stood there, my feet planted in rebellion, as the full weight of what he said crashed over me.

"You can't just decide that for me." My voice rose with the tide of anger building in my chest. "I've had people making my decisions my whole life. I won't—"

I stopped, the fight bubbling too hot for words. The last shreds of my control slipped away, my anger sparking like wildfire.

He watched me, unmoving, as though the storm of my rage was nothing compared to the hurricane brewing between us. "You're not safe on your own."

It was all I needed to hear for my anger to consume me completely. "I'm not safe with you, either! Declan will come for me no matter where I am." I turned, pacing the room in frantic strides. "You can't protect me, Menace. No one can!"

The space between us was charged with everything I'd confessed to Juliet. The control, the powerlessness. He thought he could keep me here, thought he could claim me like he claimed the rest of his world. But I was done being someone else's possession.

My footsteps echoed as I marched past him again and again, my frustration at a fever pitch. He was so still, so goddamn certain. It only fueled my desperation. "I don't need you to keep me in a gilded cage," I shouted, my words ricocheting off the elegant walls. "I don't need another man telling me how to live!"

"Are you done?" His voice was infuriatingly calm, the eye of a storm that I couldn't see.

I spun to face him, my chest heaving with the force of my rebellion. "I don't think I ever will be."

We stared at each other; the tension snapping like electric wires in the air. And then he moved, fast and inevitable, pinning me to the wall.

His mouth claimed mine, a branding more than a kiss. It seared through the anger, through the defiance, through everything that said I didn't want this.

Because I did. More than I ever wanted anything.

His hands gripped my arms, holding me in place, but it was my need that kept me there. My hunger matched his, demanding and insistent, said with every movement that I belonged to him as much as he belonged to me.

I felt the shift in me, the loosening of the threads that tied me to a life of compliance. Menace wasn't Declan, and he wasn't Dominick. He was mine, and I was his, and it scared the hell out of me how much I wanted to be caught in his grasp.

The kiss deepened, rough and wild, his teeth grazing my lip until I moaned into him. I was lost in it, in the ferocity of his need and mine.

The taste of him filled me, more intoxicating than the terror that had driven me for so long. I pressed against him, desperate and reckless, my fingers tangling in his hair as the last of my fight crumbled to dust.

This was what I'd been running from and toward, the intensity of it too much and not enough. He knew it. Felt it. Matched it.

Menace groaned, low and primal, as though he could sense my surrender. His grip softened, pulling me closer, his hands moving to my waist, my hips, branding me in new ways. I arched into him, craving more, craving everything.

His breath was hot against my neck, his lips tracing a line down my throat.

"Savannah." My name sounded different when he said it. Less like a threat, more like a promise.

I couldn't breathe, couldn't think, couldn't hold on to anything but the press of his body and the demand of his touch. "Bridger," I gasped, the name almost a plea.

We staggered together, a messy tangle of limbs and lust, neither willing to let go. I pulled him to me with every bit of strength I had, afraid that if I let go I'd lose myself completely.

And I wanted that. Wanted the reckless abandon that only he could give me. Wanted to forget who I was and remember only who I was with him.

He pushed me harder into the wall, harder into the truth of what we were. The intensity was a live thing between us, coiling and twisting, and the heat of it burned away the last of my doubts.

We kissed like it was the only thing keeping us alive. Like every breathless moment was borrowed from the chaos that surrounded us.

My anger melted, consumed by something much more dangerous. I wrapped myself around him, pulled him impossibly closer, wanting the risk of it, the edge of it, more than I'd ever wanted safety.

Menace. His name thrummed in my veins, in my bones, in every part of me that had been empty for too long.

I didn't care that I was living with him now. Didn't care that he made the decision for me. I didn't care because he was right. I wasn't safe on my own, not with Declan's reach longer than I ever imagined.

But here, pressed between him and the wall, claimed by the fierceness of his desire, I felt untouchable. I felt wild.

And more than anything, I felt his.

CHAPTER 8

MENACE

A thread of madness licked the edges of my thoughts as I claimed her mouth again, each breath between kisses a desperate oath. "Savannah," I whispered against her lips, "tell me you're mine." Her hands dug into my back, pulling me tighter, daring me to swallow her whole. Her body said yes in a hundred frantic ways, but I needed more. I stopped. Hauled myself back to sanity and made her say it, the words like broken glass. "Tell. Me. You're. Mine."

Her voice was a flame, scorching my doubts. "Yours," she said. "Now and always."

Her confession curled around me like smoke, choking what little restraint I had left. The fire in her words seared my need to possess her. I lifted her from the floor and pressed her against the wall, felt her pulse like gunfire beneath my lips. She was mine in ways I never thought possible, her body moving with mine, every shiver and sigh a language I'd almost forgotten how to speak.

"You're so goddamn beautiful," I rasped. "Say it again. I can't hear it enough. This feels like a fucking dream."

Her wolf flared beneath her skin. I could feel it calling to mine, setting my own wild instincts loose. It was there in the ragged edges of her breathing, in that tremor that wasn't fear but longing.

My teeth grazed her neck, the temptation of a claiming bite so strong I had to tear myself away.

"You're not dreaming," she gasped, her hands everywhere, fanning the heat between us. I was so fucking close to losing control.

"You need to understand that Bronc might be the Alpha of this pack. But I'm the Alpha of this house. Of our home. I won't be gentle with you." I growled, pressing harder into her.

The fight in her bled into something else, a complete and willing surrender. She arched toward me, her head falling back, exposing the line of her throat like an offering. "Menace," she whispered, and my name was all I needed.

"Tell me it's what you want." My grip was fierce on her hips, and I had to dig deep for the strength to wait.

Her lashes fluttered, those wild green eyes boring into mine. The submission in her gaze did things to me I didn't know I could feel. "Everything," she said, and the words wrapped around my wolf like chains, binding and freeing me in the same instant. "I submit to you. Take me. Make me yours."

Everything but the two of us disappeared. The looming threat of her father, pack intrigue and problems. There was only this: the feel of my body on hers, the taste of her skin, the unbreakable claim I'd stake. My lips moved over hers again, and my voice was an oath that went deeper than words.

"Once I start, I won't stop," I said, a promise as much to myself as to her.

The way she clung to me told me she'd never want me to.

The world blurred as I carried her, nothing more than shadow and pulse and frantic need. Our bodies fit together in a rhythm too wild to be real. Her lips traced patterns across my neck as I took the stairs two at a time. "Now," I groaned, "Savannah, I can't wait." Her laughter was a sweet curse, and I knew I was doomed. The bedroom door slammed against the wall. I set her down and simply stared at her. She was the most beautiful woman I'd ever laid my eyes on. Dark auburn hair hung in loose curls almost to her waist. Lightly freckled porcelain skin faintly pebbled under my touch.

"I need those clothes off. Now." I told her. More of a command than a request, but she followed immediately by unbuttoning her top. I noticed her hands shaking, so I took them in mine as she fussed with a button.

I tipped her chin towards me. "Hey, are you frightened?"

Her hands hesitated for a moment. "No, it's not fear. I'm just nervous I guess. I know you've seen me naked. For Goddess's sake, the way I was when you pulled me out of that lab..." She looked away.

"Savannah, stop." I took both of her hands in mine. I realized I needed to handle her with a bit more care. As her Alpha, it's my job not just to dominate her but to see to all of her needs. I backed up until I could sit on the bed with her standing between my legs. She was about my same height this way. "Let me." I told her as I began unbuttoning her shirt the rest of the way baring a pretty pale blue lace bra when I pushed the shirt off her shoulders. "Stunning," I said as my fingers traced over the delicate lace of the bra. "Turn around, sweetheart." Obediently, she slowly spun, revealing her perfectly lightly freckled back. I ran my hands across her shoulders and down her arms. Then I reached for the hooks of her bra. I eased them open, then slid my hand under the straps and slid them and the bra off. It fluttered to the floor landing silently on the plush rug under her feet. I ran my fingers lightly across her back, then kneaded her shoulders, eliciting the sexiest moan from her as her head fell forward. I then stood and gave her a little nudge forward so I could turn her back towards me.

Her head still lowered she quietly said, "Thank you... Alpha," biting her lower lip, looking up at me through her lashes.

Shit. My dick could not get harder.

"You're such a good fucking girl." I told her and kissed her forehead. Then I kneeled down on one knee and took one foot at a time in my hand and removed her boots while she watched, no doubt wondering what I would do next. Then I stood and slid my hands into the waistband of her leggings and felt the firm globes of her ass. I pushed down and drug both her leggings and panties down to her ankles, then removed them, which put me back in that one-knee kneeling position again. Only this time, her bare pussy was within reach of my mouth.

"Savannah?" I asked as my fingers came up and caressed that completely hair-free intimate area. "Do you shave here? So fucking soft."

Her pale cheeks turned an adorable pink. "As part of my grooming regimen, when I turned 21, all of that was lasered. So it's all gone permanently. I'm sorry if it's not attractive to you." She told me in a small voice as she looked down at me, her hair spilling in dark red waves well past her shoulders.

"Oh, Red. There is nothing about you that is unattractive." I told her while I continued to rub my thumbs over the velvety soft skin. "Spread your legs for me, sweetheart." She did as I asked, revealing more of herself to me. My fingers rested on her hips while my thumbs explored further, caressing the interior of the walls of her beautiful, wet cunt. Her breaths were coming in shorter pants now as she stood naked before me.

"As a matter of fact, I've never seen a more beautiful, dripping pussy. It looks incredibly delicious." My thumbs pulled her walls apart, leaving her open as I leaned in with my tongue and gave a nice long lick, lingering extra long at her clit where I gave an extra suck.

Her hands went from fists at her side to grip my shoulders so she'd keep her feet. And the beautiful sounds that escaped her lips. Moans and gasps that filled the room only drove me to give her more.

As I rose, my tongue licked from her core up her soft stomach to her round, ample breasts. When I reached her neck, my teeth lightly grazed the spot I intended to place my mark. Then my mouth found hers again. My tongue traced her lips until it claimed her mouth completely. I knew she could taste a hint of herself there.

I placed her on the bed, chest heaving like a madman. My fingers trembled against her skin, love and lust tearing me apart. "Tell me," I demanded. "Will I be the first to have you like this?"

I could barely see, could barely think past the urgency of claiming her. My hands stilled on the hem of my henley as I paused before ripping it off.

"Tell me," I said again, unable to hide the desperation in my voice. "I need to know."

Her hand reached up to touch my hip, gentle in a way that burned. "You are," she said, and the admission brought me to my knees.

"Your father," I muttered, as I ripped off my shirt. The name a curse on my lips. "And King Dominic. They wanted you to be pure for that fucking marriage."

"That's what they intended," she breathed.

Her gaze was unwavering, cutting straight to my heart. I felt the heat of it, a force that made me reckless and wild.

"I was a bargaining chip," she continued, the words laced with something like relief. "But I'm yours now, and I've never felt so free."

"Fuck, Savannah," I whispered, unable to look away from her. My jaw clenched and unclenched with every beat of my heart, every pulse of my rage. "I can't believe you survived."

She was on her knees now in all of her naked beauty and grace. "You saved me," she said softly.

The weight of her past settled over me, a shadow I couldn't ignore. My mind flashed to the jungle, to the lab where Dane kept her captive. I'd found her in that hellhole, chained to the goddamned floor. A science experiment. I saw the fear in her eyes then, and it haunted me still.

She must have seen the cursed memory pass over my face.

"It's over," she said, pulling me back to her. "I'm free. I'm yours."

My jeans hit the floor as I crawled across the bed to her, easing her back down. I stared down at her, my mind a riot of emotions. I wanted to make sure she was ready, make sure I wouldn't hurt her. My jaw was so tight it ached.

"You're sure?" I asked, my voice breaking. "After what they did."

"Yes," she cut me off, her voice firm. "Nothing can keep me from you. Not what Dane did, not my father's scheming."

The certainty in her voice was fierce as the fire in her eyes. "Dane may have done things to me, but I'm so thankful that he never got the chance to take my virginity. That means that you will not just be my first, but my only. And I wouldn't want it any other way."

Her words only increased my desire for her. Spurred on by wolf to claim our mate. There were only the two of us and our increasing desire for one another.

"I want this, Menace," she said, her hands pulling me closer. "I want you. More than anything."

Her untamed hunger matched my own, urgent and insistent. She was so fucking magnificent. A smoldering ember on the verge of becoming the wildfire that would consume every part of me.

I let the wildness take me, let it consume every part of me.

This was what we both wanted. This was what we both needed. A reckless need drove us forward. And I would not hold back.

My wolf surged through me, desperate and rough, pressing her into the bed as my mouth found the line of her throat. Her pulse beat there, frantic and insistent, a rhythm that paced my own. "Mine," I growled, the word more possession than promise. My hands roamed her skin, each touch a declaration I wouldn't take back. This was it, the moment I'd never expected, never imagined. A raw intensity broke through my restraint and shattered me completely. She *was* mine. But goddamn, I was *hers*. I felt it in every kiss, every gasp, every frantic whisper that passed between us.

My hands further explored every inch of her body. As ravenous as I was to claim her, I was ever aware that this was her first time. I wanted to make her forget Dane's hands and everything they took from her. He may not have taken her innocence, but he took too fucking much. My fingers, my touch would be the only memories she'd have from this moment forward.

She lay beneath me, her body trembling, her breath coming in shallow gasps. Her skin was flushed, her lips swollen from my kisses, and her eyes—those fucking eyes—were wide with a mix of fear and desire. I could smell her arousal, thick and heady, mingling with the scent of her fear. It was intoxicating. My wolf howled inside me, demanding I take her, claim her, make her mine in every way possible. But I held back. I needed to erase every memory of that bastard Dane, every touch, every violation. I needed her to know that this—this was different. This was us.

"Menace," she whispered, her voice trembling. "Please."

I leaned down, my lips brushing against her ear. "Tell me what you want, Red."

"You," she gasped. "I want you."

I growled, low and deep, the sound vibrating through both of us. My hands roamed her body, tracing every curve, every dip, every scar. I wanted to memorize her, to know every inch of her. My fingers brushed over her nipples, already hard and pebbled, and she arched into my touch, a soft moan escaping her lips.

"Fuck, Savannah," I muttered, my voice rough with need. "You're so beautiful."

Her hands gripped my shoulders, her nails digging into my skin. "Menace, please. I need you."

I kissed her again, deep and hungry, my tongue tangling with hers. My hands moved lower, skimming over her stomach, her hips, until I reached the apex of her thighs. She was wet, so fucking wet, I could feel the heat of her. I groaned, my cock throbbing with need.

"Tell me again," I demanded, my voice a low growl. "Tell me you're mine."

"Yours," she gasped. "Always yours."

I admired her bare pussy, smooth and glistening, and I couldn't resist. I had to have another taste as I lowered my head, my tongue flicking out to lap at her center. She cried out, her hips bucking against my mouth.

"Fuck, Menace," she moaned, her hands tangling in my hair.

I licked her again, slow and deliberate, savoring the taste of her. She was sweet, so fucking sweet, and I couldn't get enough. My tongue circled her clit, teasing and taunting, before I plunged it inside her, fucking her with it. She writhed beneath me; her moans growing louder, more desperate.

"Please," she begged. "Please, Menace."

I pulled back, looking up at her. "Are you ready, Red?"

"Yes," she gasped. "So ready."

My cock was hard, throbbing with need, and I could see the hunger in her eyes as she looked at it. I grabbed it, stroking it slowly as I looked down at her.

I pressed its head against her entrance, feeling her wetness coating me. I pushed in slowly, inch by inch, giving her time to adjust. She was tight, so fucking tight, and I had to fight the urge to slam into her.

"Fuck," I groaned, my hands gripping her hips. "You feel so good."

She wrapped her legs around my waist, pulling me deeper into her. "More," she begged. "Please, Menace."

I gave her more until I felt the resistance of her virginity. "Sweetheart, this is going to hurt, but only for a moment."

Her eyes glistened with unshed tears. "I know, I know. Just please hurry. I need..."

I thrust into her, hard and deep, and she cried out, her nails digging into my back. I paused just for a moment so she could get used to my size. Her hands had a death grip on my shoulders.

Her body arched into me, giving in to the need that burned between us. I was ravenous, reckless, more untamed than I'd ever been. Her fingers tangled in my hair, urging me on as I gave her everything. Nothing else existed. Not the pack. Not the threat of her father. Only the force of this, of us, of everything I'd never thought I'd have.

"Savannah," I groaned, my mouth crashing against hers. She kissed me back with a desperation that fueled my own, each breathless second pulling me deeper under her spell.

I'd never needed anything the way I needed her. My mind spun with the magnitude of it, a dark and endless whirlwind I didn't want to escape. She was the eye of that storm, the calm in the chaos, and I was caught in her. Helpless. Wild. Lost.

Her name was a raw wound on my lips. My heart thundered in my chest, and I knew she felt it. Knew she felt the way she tore me apart and put me back together.

"Bridger," she gasped, and the sound of my name was my undoing.

I took her finally, completely, with a savage need that ripped through the last of my control. I sank my teeth into her shoulder, marking her, claiming her as the taste of her blood filled my mouth, sealing the bond in a bite that connected us in ways I never thought possible. Her release came with my bite, her pussy clenching my cock in a vise that felt impossibly tight as my knot started to swell inside her. We were locked together, a physical manifestation of our bonding. It was as though the tumblers all fell into place and her essence began to fill every part of me. The beauty of who she was entered my soul.

The magic of it crashed through me, wild and relentless, an explosion that shattered my senses. My eyes slammed shut as I drowned in it, as I let it sweep me away. Then she leaned up, her teeth elongated, as she took my head in her hand and pulled me to her. She sank her teeth into my neck at the juncture of my shoulder.

Our connection flared brighter, hotter, filling every piece of me, setting my blood on fire. I'd never been so consumed, so possessed by anything in my life. She came again as I found my release. The impact shook both of us. Her body shuddered in beautiful waves of pleasure, and my cum filled her body to overflowing. The power of our combined climax tore the air from my lungs and left me weak and shaking. I groaned her name, barely coherent, barely able to comprehend the magnitude of what we'd done.

I was shattered and whole, a man brought to his knees by a single, searing truth:

This was what I was made for.

I would die for her.

We lay tangled in each other, bodies slick with sweat and blood. Her shoulder glistened where I'd claimed her, the mark a dark and beautiful promise. I knew that mine looked much the same. I could feel her inside me.

"Savannah," I whispered, pulling her closer, feeling the tremors in my own limbs.

"Bridger," she breathed, and the sound of it filled me with something more powerful than magic. More powerful than fate.

It filled me with her.

The room faded around us, nothing more than shadows and air and the quiet pulse of our synchronized hearts.

"Don't let go," I said, and I didn't want it to sound like a command. Goddess knew I'd chain her to me if I had to.

"Never," she replied, a vow as binding as any I'd ever heard.

I held her tight, felt the warmth of her skin, the soft weight of her against my chest. Her breath tickled my neck, and the sensation was more intimate than anything I'd known.

The bite mark pulsed with its own heat, the bond a living thing between us.

The intensity of it left me breathless, left me wondering how the hell I'd survived without it before.

"Savannah," I said again, just to feel the shape of her name on my tongue.

"Bridger," she answered, and it was all I needed.

It was everything.

I knew that we'd brought hell to our doorstep. Together, we'd face it. I just hoped we were strong enough to come out of it alive.

CHAPTER 9

SAVANNAH

Menace told me about his meeting with Bronc and the other officers of the pack. They knew my identity and that my father was searching for me. I knew they'd be heading to Alabama to visit the king of this territory to head my father and Dominic off before he could take a stand against Iron Valor. I felt terrible that I was the cause of this stress for the pack. They'd already had enough with that Skeeter person sitting in jail, apparently.

Bridger told me it was not my place to worry about pack matters. He wanted me to concentrate on taking care of myself. I love him so much. Never in my life had I had anyone put me first. It was a new sensation. They'd also discussed my future with the pack. Everyone agreed that taking the job at the elementary school was the best idea. I needed to fly under the radar as much as possible. Blending in and hiding in plain sight was the best thing to do. So today was my first day as the music teacher at Hardin Elementary.

Principal Karen Day's gaze cut to the mate mark on my neck like a blade, a look of disapproval hardening her features. "Sawyer Galloway," she repeated, her voice laced with disbelief. I felt the weight of her stare as she skimmed my resume, the air between us tense and charged. Her smile was a dagger wrapped in sugar as she leaned back. "Bridger," she said, the name edged with an intimacy that set my nerves on fire. "Always good to see you." Her eyes raked up and down his body before returning to me. "Glad to see he provided me with your credentials this time. Even though he already saw fit to go ahead and offer you the job before consulting with me." Her passive-aggressive conversation was awkward to say the least.

Her office was sparse and clinical. A stack of papers marked "Requisition Forms" sat on her desk. After the hell I'd survived, I was determined not to be intimidated by this woman. I met her eyes, knowing she considered me prey in this cat-and-mouse game. "When I visited here, you indicated the position was vacant. I assumed you were ready for it to be filled."

She glanced up at Bridger again, then cleared her throat. "I'm sure..." She glanced back at my resume as though she'd forgotten my name, "Sawyer Galloway." She drew out the name like it was a bitter taste. "You'll be a perfect fit." Her lips curled around her sarcasm like a lover. "Bridger, you seem to have your hands full," she continued, her gaze boring into me. "What with your dealership, dealing with hiring staff at the school, and..." she looked again at the mate mark on my neck, "extra-curricular activities as they may be."

Menace stepped from behind me as anger poured through our bond. He laughed, a sound as sharp as a razor. "Seeing as my money funds this institution and I occupy the seat of Director as well, I can make whatever personnel decision I goddamn well please. You'd do well to remember that Ms. Day." A look of fear crossed her face, then quickly vanished.

"I'll be fine," I assured him as I squeezed his hand, my voice stronger than I felt. The woman's expression made it clear she would keep an eagle eye on me. He turned to me, and I nodded to him, letting him know I didn't want him to fight this battle for me.

Leaning down, he gave me a chaste kiss and whispered, "Give 'em hell, Red," with a wicked smile on his lips. I watched him leave, my own smile of satisfaction crossing my face. He waved as the door clicked shut. The room felt too large, too empty without him.

"So," she said, leaning forward. Her curiosity was a trap. "How does one get a man like Bridger Hardin to mark her?"

I took a breath, steadying myself. "You'd have to ask the Goddess about that," I replied. My pulse raced at the admission. "Seeing as how we're fated mates."

"Is that so?" She sat back, feigning surprise. Her smile vanished. "I'd think a man like him would be more selective."

"I'd be a fool not to have seen Bridger Hardin as the gift he is. But again, we didn't choose each other," I said, the words with boldness. I held her gaze, refusing to flinch under her scrutiny. "I'd never question the wisdom of the Goddess."

Karen's eyes flicked to the mark on my neck, a sneer in her voice. "You're very lucky."

"I'm more than lucky. I hit the mate jackpot." My voice carried my own sneer.

She thought her dismissal could hurt me. I was a princess. She had no idea the pain I'd endured. The office felt cold as she looked down at my file, avoiding my eyes.

"It's so interesting. Our Luna, Juliet wasn't born to the pack either," she said, her tone turning casual, like she was making small talk. "It's harder for some people to accept those who aren't one of us into the pack." Her meaning hung thick between us.

I bristled at the implication. "If the Goddess chose Bronc's mate, that should be good enough for everyone," I replied. My loyalty to Juliet burned fierce and bright.

"Must be nice to feel so confident." Her voice was sweet poison. "But it's different here."

The statement felt like a threat, one I couldn't ignore.

"Bronc is the Alpha of this pack of which I am now a member. As such, I'd never disrespect my Alpha or my Luna." I met her stare, my anger boiling under the surface. "There's no doubt everyone is at least respectful to them around here, regardless of how they may feel." I needed this job. But Karen's certainty that I wouldn't fit in left me raw. "I promise you, I'll do my best for these children even if I wasn't born into this pack," I said, and I meant every word.

Her eye roll was almost enough for me to walk out. But again, I needed this job. "Yes," she sighed. "Feelings have to be set aside I guess."

She smiled, a satisfied smirk that told me she'd always have the last word around here. "Then let's look at your schedule, shall we?" Her tone was clipped, all business.

The paper she pushed toward me was filled with a map that had boxes and times and room numbers that blurred before my eyes. "Five classes a day," she said, as though I should be grateful. "Plus a conference period." Her eyes gleamed with triumph. "And lunch duty."

The breath caught in my throat. "Lunch duty?"

"For the first week," she said, dismissing my surprise with a wave of her hand. "To get to know the students."

I swallowed my anger, my pride, and nodded. "I understand."

"Good." Her smile was as icy as her gaze. "I knew you would."

I left the office with the schedule clutched in my hand, my heart a storm of resentment and determination. The hallways were bustling with children rushing to their classrooms. The fluorescent lights buzzed overhead as I made my way to my room. My first class started in ten minutes.

The music room vibrated with noise and movement as the first class barreled in, small bodies jostling for the best spots. My heart pounded with the tempo of their footsteps. I called roll, names slipping through my mind like water, faces blurring in the chaos. Their voices ricocheted off the walls, a discordant chorus of excitement and shrill laughter. Ms. Galloway, I introduced myself, the alias a fragile mask. We played clapping games, their energy frantic and wild. I let them loose on small instruments, the sound spilling into the hallways like madness set free.

The children swarmed around me, bright eyes and eager hands reaching for attention. Their questions tumbled over each other. "How long have you been a teacher?" "Are we gonna sing?" "Why does your hair look like that?" I laughed, the sound surprising even myself. The intensity of their curiosity was daunting and thrilling.

"Let's start with the basics," I said, trying to herd their energy into something manageable. My own heartbeat matched the frenzy of the room. "Who knows what this is?" I held up a music staff, the symbols as familiar as they were distant.

"Lines!" one child shouted.

"Boring!" another chimed in.

We clapped rhythms, their hands slapping against each other and against desks, the sound sharp and erratic. It felt like I was back in college, lost in a sea of noise and expectations. I showed them treble and bass clefs, and their enthusiasm swelled to a crescendo that shook the walls.

I passed out tambourines, maracas, anything small enough for them to manage. Their chaos became music of its own kind, a symphony of childhood rebellion that echoed in my bones.

The older kids were next, their skepticism a thick cloud in the air. They slouched into the room, eyes rolling, and whispers more cynical than curious. My confidence wavered under their indifference.

"Who are you?" one girl asked, suspicion clear in her voice.

"Ms. Galloway," I said, forcing the name to sound real.

"Where's Mr. Davis?" another demanded.

"Gone." A chorus of disappointment. My grip on the lesson plan tightened. "He's not coming back." I kept the tremor from my voice, kept my shoulders squared.

"What do you know about music?" A boy with an attitude that matched my own fears.

"Enough to keep up with you." I stared him down, feeling the first hint of confidence.

My pulse quickened as I showed them the scales, explained beats and measures. Their interest was grudged, a gift they could take back at any moment.

The two rowdiest boys pushed limits, testing how far they could go. "What's that mark on your neck?" one asked, his tone as defiant as his posture.

"A bite," I said, surprising myself with the directness. "From my mate."

"You're married?" His shock was almost comical.

"Not quite." I hid my amusement as his demeanor shifted.

"Who's your mate?"

"Menace."

The name changed everything. A ripple of recognition passed through the class, the boys suddenly respectful, eager even. I barely knew what to make of it.

My nerves hummed like a taut string, vibrating with the tension of pretending to be someone I wasn't. But my training kicked in, a steadying force. The familiar routine settled over me, comforting and real.

By the time the bell rang, my head spun with names and faces and the intensity of it all. It was almost too much; the pressure of proving myself, of living a life I didn't know I could have.

Lunchroom duty was as isolating as I had feared. The cafeteria buzzed with noise and movement, kids shouting and laughing, their voices clashing with the clatter of trays and chairs. I stood by the door, awkward and out of place, unsure where to begin.

The other teachers were nowhere to be seen, leaving me to monitor a sea of unfamiliar faces. The sense of being alone pressed down on me, heavy and suffocating.

I watched the children as they ate, their energy unchecked, without any proper authority. The assignment felt like a punishment, a reminder that I didn't belong. Karen's handiwork was all over it.

A group of boys crowded around me, their questions fast and relentless. "You Menace's girl?" "Are you gonna teach here forever?" "Where'd you come from?" I answered as best I could, the noise swallowing my replies.

Their curiosity was exhausting, a constant reminder of the fragile lie I was living.

The lunch period dragged, the minutes stretching into an eternity. My determination burned bright, a defiance against the doubt that threatened to swallow me whole. I would prove myself. I would survive this.

But as I watched the chaos around me, I knew I had to be careful.

The stares cut like glass as I entered the teacher's lounge, conversations halting mid-sentence to twist into hostile silence. I felt their eyes like daggers, my back tense under the scrutiny. The air was heavy with distrust, suspicion dripping from every corner of the room. I fumbled with my lunch, trying to ignore the weight of their disdain. Sitting alone at a small table, I felt the edges of their coldness creeping in. Then, a pretty dark-haired teacher with curly hair came over to my table. I couldn't believe she dared to break ranks. She had a wary smile on her face. "Sawyer, right?" She asked, her voice a tentative offering. "I'm Gabby."

I exhaled, the relief in my voice impossible to hide. "Hi." My smile was cautious, a fragile attempt at connection.

She sat down across from me, her expression open and genuine. She was a few years older than me, with a warmth that seemed out of place in the icy room. "You're new, huh?"

I nodded, unsure how much to reveal. "First day." The words were heavy with more meaning than I wanted them to have.

She looked over her shoulder, her gaze lingering on the cluster of women watching us from the far side of the room. "Don't mind them," she said, her voice dropping to a conspiratorial whisper. "They're Karen's favorites. Kind of territorial. I literally call them 'the Karens,'" she said with a quiet laugh. She put her finger to her mouth like she was telling me not to tell.

Her observation cut to the core of my own fears, the ones that said I would never belong, never be one of them. "I noticed," I replied, forcing a lightness I didn't feel.

Gabby's presence was a comfort, a flicker of warmth in the sea of hostility. "Where'd you come from?" She asked innocently but pointed.

"Around," I said, trying to sound casual. "I'm with Menace." His name slipped out, a barrier against the invasive curiosity of the others.

Her eyes widened, then softened into understanding. "Oh hell! Are you the girl? The other one that was rescued when the Luna was rescued?" The look of surprise was genuine.

I shrugged. "That's me."

"Well, you landed in the right spot, girlfriend. Most women around here would have loved for Menace to have rescued them." Her smile was friendly.

I watched the other teachers as they whispered their glances like knives. A part of me hated to lie to these people. I didn't like being dishonest. It wasn't in my nature. Being an outsider was also hard. My mind raced with doubts. Gabby's company eased the pressure, but the fear of exposure still clawed at my insides.

The hostility followed me throughout the day, a shadow I couldn't shake. The teachers cornered me in the halls, their smiles as sharp as their questions.

"Where'd you say you were from again?" one asked, her tone syrupy sweet.

"Dairyville's a long way from anywhere." Another's words dripped with insinuation.

"How'd a girl like you catch Bridger?" The implication stung; the suggestion that I'd somehow tricked him.

My answers were short and defensive. "Guess I got lucky," I said, echoing Gabby's earlier comment. It felt like a lie in my mouth.

They huddled together, exchanging knowing looks. "Lunch duty, huh? Tough break." Their laughter followed me down the hallway, a reminder that I was on the outside looking in. "You were a prisoner in that place? Bet that was a nightmare, huh?" They threw out that question like it was a joke, then whispered to each other and threw more sideways glances. I know wolves tend to be rougher around the edges. But we also feel things deeply.

Gabby caught up with me between classes, her expression sympathetic. "Don't let them get to you," she said. "You'll be fine."

I wanted to believe her, wanted it with a desperation that surprised me. "Does anyone else have lunch duty?" I asked, the question betraying my insecurity.

She hesitated, a slight frown marring her features. "Well, not teachers. It's usually cafeteria staff."

Her confirmation fueled my suspicion, Karen's handiwork becoming more obvious with each passing moment. "Thought so."

"Give it time," Gabby encouraged, her sincerity a lifeline. "You'll fit right in."

I squeezed her arm. "I truly appreciate your being so kind to me." It was important to me that she knew how much it meant.

But the doubt lingered, as relentless as the eyes that followed me through the day.

Karen's office felt colder, more impersonal when she summoned me at the end of the day. The look she gave me was as unfriendly as the one she'd greeted me with that morning.

"Everything okay?" she asked, her tone sharp and condescending.

"I think so," I replied, my voice steady despite my frustration.

"I heard some noise from your room." Her accusation was thinly veiled. "More than I expected."

"Kids were excited." I kept my tone neutral, refusing to rise to her bait.

"Excitement is good," she said, but her expression said otherwise. "As long as it's controlled."

I nodded, my anger simmering just beneath the surface. "Yes, ma'am."

Her gaze was piercing, a challenge and a dismissal all at once. "We have high standards here. It's not like anywhere you've been before."

Her words struck deep, an echo of my own fears. I didn't trust myself to speak, so I nodded again. "I understand."

"You have a lot to prove, Ms. Galloway." The name sounded like a curse in her mouth.

What I wanted to say was- "At least I'm going home to Menace, you bitch, Something you'll never do," But, I just smiled and said, "Ok." I really didn't feel that I had anything to prove. I knew I could be a fantastic teacher. I'd do the best damn job I could do. Unrealistic expectations would not break me.

She watched me leave, satisfaction gleaming in her eyes. The halls were empty, my footsteps the only sound as I made my way outside.

Seeing Menace waiting in the truck, his protective stance a stark contrast to the day's hostility, brought a rush of relief I didn't know I was holding back. I slid in beside him; the tension melted away with the comfort of his presence.

"How was it?" His voice was low, careful.

I hesitated, unsure how much to reveal. "Tough," I admitted, the word too small for the weight of it all.

His hand found mine; the connection grounded me. "Tell me."

As we drove to Pearl's for dinner, the stories spilled out, each one a piece of the larger struggle. The teachers' hostility, Karen's scrutiny, my fear of failing him and myself.

His jaw tightened with every word, his anger a fierce contrast to the calm he usually wore. "You want me to talk to her?" he asked, his voice edged with protective fury.

"No," I said quickly. "I need to do this. I need to prove I can."

He nodded, but his tension didn't ease. "You can," he said, the conviction in his words more reassuring than anything else.

"I hope so," I whispered, the doubt gnawing at my insides.

He looked at me, his eyes meeting mine with a promise I wasn't sure he could keep. "I know so."

We walked into the restaurant together, the scent of grease and determination heavy in the air. I held on to his hand like it was the only thing tethering me to the world I so desperately wanted to be part of. I could feel his love surging through our bond, and already I felt so much better.

Chapter 10

Menace

Bronc eyed me from a corner booth, stress dark in his gaze. I joined him, the diner alive with too many voices and too little space. "This is gonna be a fun breakfast," he said, tossing a paper between us. "Hope you like your coffee with a shot of bad news." The email subject screamed at me. Missing Shifters. Then the body of the email clearly indicated that Rafe was pissed because Iron Valor had knowledge, and neglected to share it. Before I finished reading, I felt Savannah's stress through our bond. My jaw clenched.

"I see how this is playing," I said, bitterness in my voice. "It's not enough that our Luna was our main concern and we had to tread lightly or risk losing her. The other packs are gonna want blood cuz we couldn't save them all."

Bronc signaled to the waitress for two coffees. "We made it worse by not notifying them."

"They failed us before," I shot back. "My sister was abducted, and the council did fuck-all to find her. She's dead because of *them*!" I felt my anger like a living thing inside me, the memory still raw.

Bronc's face softened. I know he loved my sister like she was his own. "Hey, you're preaching to the choir, man. We just have to figure out how we're gonna handle Rafe. He wasn't the reason we lost her," he added quietly.

"I know," I replied, my voice tight. "But he had a representative on the Council. You know how it went down." I didn't have to remind him how her disappearance ended. How the responsible pack only got a temporary sanction for it. My fists were clenched under the table, wishing I'd destroyed Greenbriar completely.

"Should've known they'd be out for blood," Bronc said. "Rafe's pissed." He rubbed his eyes, weariness showing in the lines on his face. "We should've told him what was going on."

"And give him the chance to take over the investigation?" I asked, knowing what Bronc would say.

"If we let the council handle it, Juliet might well be dead. We did the right thing. Rafe will understand that too when we can explain it in person. As far as Savannah? Who the fuck knows?"

"We've got nothing but time and force on our side." I set the paper down, my gaze holding Bronc's. "What's our move?"

The waitress brought the coffee, and Bronc waited until she was out of earshot. "Rafe wants us in Birmingham within the week. Says the missing shifters are our mess now. But Declan's another story. I think we'll wait until we get to Birmingham before we spring that bit of information on him."

"Holy fuck is he gonna shit a brick when he learns that the princess is my mate!"

"Oh, it's hitting the fan. There will be hell to pay. I honestly cannot see how this whole thing is gonna play out, brother. Everyone is gonna get a say in this I'm afraid."

"Listen to me loud and clear, Bronc. I'll kill before anyone takes Savannah from me. I'll die before anyone takes her."

"That's what I'm afraid of," Bronc muttered. "They think we're renegades," he said, his voice low. "They might use this against us."

"They will." I said. My anger ran deep. I remembered the fear in Savannah's eyes when she told me about her father's plans. My mind drifted to how different things would've been if I'd destroyed the Greenbriar pack. I never would've met her.

Bronc poured sugar into his cup. "You want to tell me what else is on your mind?"

I shook my head. "Nothing that matters now. So, what's the timeline, and who's going?"

He sighed. "It'll look stronger if we go as a unit." His gaze met mine, steady and sure. "And we're gonna make this work, Menace. Just like always."

I grunted. "Just like always." The words tasted hollow. The way they dealt with Declan could be the end of us all.

"Leave Savannah and Juliet here," Bronc said. "I want to know they're safe."

"With Arsenal?" I knew his answer but didn't like it.

"Yes," he said firmly. "It's the only way I'll leave."

"They won't be happy."

"No," he agreed. "But they'll be alive."

I sat back, tension easing but not gone. "Yeah," I said, thinking of Savannah and the fire in her eyes. She wouldn't take it well, but I'd convince her. "We leave Skeeter to stew?"

"That's the plan," Bronc said. "Rafe wants answers, not a mess. We've gotta back-burner that shit. At least he's in a place where he can't steal another dime from me."

I nodded. The world seemed a little darker, but at least it was a world we knew. At least we were in it together.

"How's Savannah?" Bronc asked, changing the subject.

"Hanging in," I said, the thought of her lifting some of the weight in my chest. "First day didn't go as planned."

Bronc laughed, a real one this time. "How'd she take it?"

"She's tougher than she looks," I said, proud of her for the way she'd stood up. "But the principal's got it in for her."

"Karen Day," Bronc muttered. "That woman's a piece of work. How'd you date that bitch for six months?"

"Shit? Blue balls maybe? Oh, and she calls Juliet the 'Goddess'," I told him, my own laugh escaping. "And not in a good way. Like, what the fuck? She's the best thing to happen to you and this pack." I meant that too.

He shook his head, disbelief on his face. "We'll keep an eye on her."

"Make sure she's not a problem," I agreed. "Sounds like more than petty jealousy."

"Think Savannah will stick it out?" he asked, curious.

"After what she's been through?" I said, my confidence in her unshakable. "She'll handle it. That woman has a will of iron." I really could see it myself.

"Must be nice having that much faith," Bronc said.

"Nice having something to have faith in," I replied. Savannah had given me more than I thought possible.

We sat in silence for a moment, the weight of everything settling between us.

"Nothing will happen while we're gone," Bronc said, trying to reassure me.

"You sound like you believe that," I said, dry as sand.

"I do." He looked at me, his eyes full of conviction.

"I want to," I said, knowing I couldn't. Not until we had Declan's head. But I trusted Bronc more than any other man alive. If he thought we could pull this off, maybe we could. Maybe it wouldn't be like last time. He also thought Juliet would be safe.

I heard the strength in his voice, the confidence that had led us through wars and blood and loss. If he said we'd survive, I'd let myself believe it.

Maybe.

"We got through worse," Bronc said. "We'll get through this."

"Sure hope so," I muttered.

I felt Savannah's anxiety spike through our bond, pulling my attention. She was stressed, and I had to get back to her.

"You're lucky, Menace," Bronc said, standing to go.

"Not luck," I said, my thoughts already on Savannah. "Pure fucking stubbornness."

The two of us went way back. But she was my future.

The thorns of Savannah's stress cut deep as I drove to the school. I found her outside, tension in her stance and eyes. She was silent during the ride home, an air of resignation heavy around her like dust on old furniture. I pulled into the drive, the colonial house's black shutters stark against the white exterior. She lingered in the truck, unwilling to move. "Made dinner," I said, waiting for her to follow me. The steaks had gone cold by the time she sat at the table, her mind a million miles away. I felt the distance like a wound.

"Did you hear me?" I asked, searching for her gaze.

"What?" Her eyes were vacant.

"I asked how today went," I said.

"Oh," she replied. "Fine."

Her mouth said it, but everything else told me it was a lie.

"Looks like it," I said, my sarcasm not lost on her.

She poked at the steak. "Sorry, Bridger. I'm trying."

"I know you are."

Her silence stretched between us, a void I didn't know how to fill.

"Not much of an appetite?"

She shook her head, the barest movement.

"School's tough?"

She paused, considering how to answer. "Tough," she said finally, the word too small for the weight it carried. Her thoughts were elsewhere, and I had a damn good idea where.

I reached for her hand, feeling the reluctance in her touch.

"Nothing you can't handle, Red."

She gave me a weak smile. "I want to believe that." Her voice was a ghost of its usual self.

"C'mon," I said, pulling her up. "Need to show you something." I led her outside to the woods, the crisp air biting through our clothes.

Her reluctance followed us like a shadow. "Where are we going?"

"Run," I said, watching her surprise flicker to life. "Need it more than you know."

I stripped down, feeling her eyes on me. "Your turn."

"Here?" she asked, glancing around.

"No one but us." I tossed my shirt aside, watching her carefully. "Trust me?"

She hesitated, then pulled her clothes off, standing bare in the December chill.

Her skin glowed in the fading light, but it was her spirit I was trying to revive.

"Ready?" I asked, already feeling the shift in me.

"More than," she said, a spark returning to her voice.

She transformed; her russet and white wolf was magnificent in the evening light. We were off, bounding through the trees, wild and free.

My own white wolf moved with hers, a perfect rhythm that set us both loose. Her stress fell away with each stride, each leap over tangled roots and fallen branches. We ran through the thickening shadows, the cold air filling our lungs and driving us faster. Faster than our fears, faster than the chaos nipping at our heels.

We made it to the ridge, the horizon endless in the distance. The two of us howled into the open air, a declaration of defiance. Of life.

Savannah nipped at my heels, her playful growls a challenge. I lunged at her, and we tumbled through the brittle grass, a tumble of limbs and fur and fire. Her spirit was wild again, free of the restraints that had been closing in on her. My wolf chased hers through the darkening sky until neither of us could breathe.

We made our way back to the house, reluctant to let go of the release we'd found. I shifted first, the crisp night air a stark contrast to my warm skin. She followed, auburn hair tumbling loose around her bare shoulders.

I was on her before she could catch her breath, scooping her up and carrying her inside. "Feel better?" I asked, a growl in my voice. Her laughter was the answer I wanted.

Her eyes sparkled with challenge as she playfully struggled in my arms. I squeezed her tighter, felt her surrender, felt her own desire rising to meet mine. I took the stairs two at a time, my need for her almost as fierce as it had been last night. The run had done its work, had broken through the tension that threatened to pull her under.

"Bath," I said, knowing it wasn't all we'd have before this was over.

She grinned, wild and beautiful. "Spoiling me," she teased.

"You deserve it." I set her down, slipping her robe over her shoulders as I filled the tub.

The water steamed, a hot promise against the cold night air. I poured oil and salts into the tub, the scent of lavender thick and heady. She watched me, her gaze steady and bright.

"Coming in?" She asked, already slipping into the heat.

"Think you can handle it?" I joined her, the water biting at first, then soothing.

Her laughter floated through the room. "That's my line," she said, splashing me.

Her smile was more than I'd hoped for. Her happiness more than I deserved.

I pulled her close, felt her tension finally unwind as the water worked its magic.

My hands found her shoulders, tracing patterns across her skin. I kneaded gently, her soft sighs spurring me on. She closed her eyes, her head falling back, her body relaxed and willing.

"Like this?" I asked, already knowing the answer.

She nodded, her breathing slower, easier.

I gathered her hair in my hands, grabbing a hair tie from the vanity next to the tub and pulled it into a messy bun so I could kiss the nape of her neck.

"So much better," she said, the words soft and sure.

"Good," I replied, kissing her again, letting my lips linger where her pulse beat strong and fast.

The sponge found its way to my hand, and I soaked it, letting the suds drip down her body, watching them trail between her breasts. I washed her arms, her chest, her stomach, each touch teasing, tempting. The water was losing its heat, but we were not.

Her hands found my thighs, and I nearly lost myself right then.

"Savannah," I warned, her name a groan on my lips.

Her fingers dug in, and I knew this bath wouldn't end the way I'd planned.

She turned, water spilling over the edges of the tub, straddling me, before her mouth found mine in a searing kiss.

Savannah's lips were on mine, hungry and demanding, her tongue sliding against my own with a ferocity that made my cock throb against my stomach. She was trying to take control, her hands gripping my shoulders, her hips grinding down on me in the water, the heat of her pussy pressing against my abs. I let her think she was in charge, let her believe she could dominate this moment, but I was done playing nice. My hands slid down her back, gripping her ass with a possessive growl, and she gasped into my mouth, her body arching against mine.

"Menace," she breathed, her voice trembling with need, but I didn't let her finish. My fingers dug into the soft flesh of her ass, spreading her cheeks, and I slipped a finger into her tight pucker, the tight ring of muscle clenching around me. She froze, her body going rigid, and then she moaned, a low, guttural sound that sent a jolt of heat straight to my cock.

"Fuck," she whispered, her voice shaking, and I could feel her body trembling against mine. "What are you—oh, God—"

I didn't answer, just pressed my finger deeper, feeling her body open for me, her pucker clenching and releasing around my finger as she adjusted to the sensation. Her hips rocked back against me, her pussy grinding against my stomach, and I could feel the wetness of her arousal mixing with the water. I leaned down, capturing one of her nipples in my mouth, sucking hard, and she cried out, her hands tangling in my hair.

"Menace, feels amazing," she moaned, her voice breaking, and I could feel her body tightening around my finger. I rubbed her clit with my other hand as she held on to the edges of the tub. I twisted my finger inside her, feeling her pucker stretch around me, and she came with a surprised groan, her body shuddering against mine, as I pressed her clit harder.

But I wasn't done with her yet. I lifted her up, turning her in the tub so she was on her knees and hands gripped the side of the tub, the water sloshing around us as I positioned myself behind her. My cock was rock hard, throbbing with need, and I pressed the head against her dripping pussy, feeling her wetness coat me. I slid into her slowly, inch by inch, feeling her tight walls stretch around me, and she moaned, her head dropping forward as she pushed back against me.

"Fuck, you're so tight," I growled, my hands gripping her hips as I buried myself all the way inside her. She was so wet, so hot, and I could feel her pussy clenching around me as I started to move, as I popped the drain of the tub, thrusting into her with slow, deep strokes. My thumb found her asshole again, pressing against the tight ring of muscle, and she gasped, her body arching as I pushed my thumb inside her.

"Oh God," she moaned, her voice trembling with pleasure, and I could feel her pussy tightening around me as she got closer to the edge again. I fucked her harder, my cock slamming into her with every thrust, my thumb pressing deeper into her tight hole, and she came with a scream, her body shaking as she clenched around me.

"That's it, baby," I growled, my voice rough with need. "Take it. Take all of me." My knot was starting to swell, pressing against her entrance, and she whimpered, her body trembling as I pushed it inside her. She was so tight, so fucking tight, and I could feel her pussy stretching around my knot as it locked us together.

"Menace," she gasped, her voice breaking as I started to come, my cock pulsing inside her as I filled her with my cum. She came again, her pussy clenching around me as she pulled every drop from me, and I groaned, my hands gripping her hips as I fucked her through our orgasms.

When my knot finally loosened enough that I could turn her, she wrapped her legs around my waist, her arms around my neck. I lifted her out of the tub and wrapped a towel around us both. She was trembling in my arms, her body still pulsing with the aftershocks of her orgasm, and I carried her to our bed, laying her down gently before climbing in beside her.

"You're mine," I growled, pulling her close, and she nodded, her body curling against mine.

"Yours," she whispered, her voice soft but sure, and I knew she meant it. She was mine, body and soul, and I would do whatever it took to keep her safe.

"I love you, Red, my little ember," I whispered against her hair.

"I love you, Bridger, forever."

Chapter 11

King Declan Calloway

The shadows of my office clung thick as burial shrouds, stale air crackling with the static of suppressed violence. My pen stilled mid-scrawl when the door creaked open. Another interruption. My assistant's throat bobbed as she spoke. "A Principal Karen Day from Texas on the phone for you. It's about Savannah."

Texas. The word detonated in my skull like shrapnel.

Her voice slithered through the receiver, crisp and clinical, each syllable gasoline on the embers in my veins. Teaching music under an alias. "Sawyer Galloway." Mated to Bridger Hardin. Iron Valor Pack. The leather armrests of my chair split beneath my grip, stuffing bleeding out like entrails.

"Proof," I snarled, already tasting copper on my tongue. "Send me the proof *now*."

The screen flickered—there she was. My daughter's face, a picture taken from a phone, clearly without her knowledge. Her eyes, *my* eyes, alight with freedom's obscene glow. A feral growl tore through clenched teeth; monitors shattered across in a blast of cracked screens.

"You've outrun me," I whispered to her frozen image, thumb tracing the screen hard enough to fracture pixels. "But not outsmarted."

Ms. Day's tinny voice returned with details. Mated to fucking Bridger Hardin, piece of shit Iron Valor pack? Oh, but he and his trouble making Alpha are now absent, gone for days? I stared at Savannah's stolen life unfolding on the screen. Elementary school music teacher in Dairyville? Picnics? My heir reduced to teaching musical quarter notes for peasant pups while her power rotted in this backwater filth?

"Forty-eight hours," I barked into the phone, molten wrath hardening into diamond-edged purpose. Let her savor these final days of rebellion—let her think she'd won. When my wolves descended upon that reeking den of mongrels, she'd learn the cost of humiliating a king. Of betraying blood. I'd have this Ms. Day secure her in a location where she could be extracted without incident. My men would be in and out like smoke.

The phone exploded against the wall in a shower of plastic shards as I rose, a storm given flesh, already barking orders for Callum to get his ass here now. Made commands for jet fuel and silver chains. Her little game ended now.

"Sawyer Galloway," I muttered the name, the alias turning sour on my tongue. A bastardized version of our name. Her music degree, once a source of tension between us, was now the key to finding her. Her audacity infuriated me. Running from me was one thing, but mating with that trash?

I looked at her picture again. Her wild auburn hair and green eyes unmistakable, surrounded by children, the mark on her neck declared her defiance. It taunted me, that brand. She was mated and mated by choice, it seemed. A calculated move on her part, but one that would cost her. I would see to it personally. The more I thought of it, the more certain I was that this mating was a temporary convenience for her. An excuse to hide from my influence and the arranged marriage to King Dominic Madison, the new Midwestern King. Foolish girl. She thought she could rewrite her destiny by scribbling her name over my carefully laid plans. She was wrong.

Savannah was far more valuable to me than she could ever imagine. I watched her from birth, growing into a striking, determined young woman. I molded her, groomed her for the role I required. Now, she'd come back to me as nothing more than damaged goods. I sneered at the thought, my teeth grinding in my jaw. No matter. Once she was within my grasp, Dominic could do with her as he pleased. A less virtuous wife would be his price for more power and influence. He'd take what I offered. My pulse quickened as I imagined her locked in the icy grasp of a life she never wanted. The thought of that cage around her was sweet. Very sweet.

The office felt colder as my plans solidified. Ms. Day's information was valuable, but I wouldn't underestimate Savannah's resourcefulness again. I'd thought her broken, but she had the gall of a thousand wild wolves. She ran when I thought her too weak to walk. I turned my thoughts back to Karen Day. The woman wanted Savannah gone for some reason. I could use that to my advantage. It's obvious she would secure Savannah for me until my men could get to her. Even if she sensed something wasn't quite right, Savannah wouldn't see us coming. I would move fast, exploiting the gap in their defenses. With Bronc and Bridger on the road, she'd have nowhere to turn. Her capture would be a mere formality. I grinned at the thought, my eyes dark with anticipation.

I imagined how Savannah would react when she realized how hopeless her situation was. How futile any attempts at escape were. I allowed myself a moment of satisfaction, letting the certainty of her capture wash over me like an incoming tide. Then, my mind churned with logistics. My team of mercenaries and a few of Callum's most brutal men were more than capable of seeing this through. There'd be no negotiation, no second chances. In fewer than forty-eight hours, she'd not be returning to her nice comfortable family home, but she'd be in the home of her future husband.

The phone felt like lead in my hand as I dialed Karen Day. Her voice was brisk, tinged with expectation. "Ms. Day," I said, my words sharp as blades. "We'll do this my way." I heard her breath catch, her compliance immediate. She would secure Savannah at the school, unaware of what awaited. "If she's not there..." my voice trailed off, letting the implied threat hang like a noose. She assured me that she wouldn't fail. The desperation in her tone was music to my ears. We agreed on a time, a place, the details etched in the cold steel of my intentions. Two days. That was all the time Savannah had left. As I ended the call, I allowed myself a dark, triumphant smile. "Two days," I repeated to the empty room. "In two days, she's mine."

I summoned Callum to my office immediately after ending the call with Karen Day. He entered with military precision, standing at attention before my massive oak desk like a blade unsheathed, posture rigid beneath his tailored suit. When I told him Savannah had been found, his face twisted into something feral. Good. Let him burn with rage; it would sharpen him for what came next. As he paced like a caged wolf, spewing fantasies of tearing Iron Valor apart limb by limb, I leaned back in my chair and let myself taste the sweetness of inevitability.

We discussed logistics, talked about assembling that team of mercenaries, arranging our private jet to Amarillo, and infiltrating Iron Valor territory. I noted Callum's particular eagerness for violence against his sister, even more extreme than my own tendencies. The room grew darker as evening approached, but neither of us moved to turn on more lights; our planning continued in growing shadows. By sunset, we'd finalized our extraction plan. "In hours, Savannah will be in the hands of her future husband, and there's not a goddamn thing she nor anyone else can do to stop it."

Callum's eyes blazed with hatred. He wanted nothing more than to crush the Iron Valor Pack under his boot heel. His rage was a living thing, snarling and hungry, eager to sink its teeth into any threat to our power. "We go in hot," he insisted, his voice cutting through the darkening room like a blade. "Hit them hard, fast, and leave nothing standing."

I considered his proposal, knowing the kind of brute force he loved. But I had always preferred precision over chaos, even if the result was the same. "The goal is her extraction, remember?" I reminded him, my tone icy and detached. "Do not let your eagerness destroy our prize. Your sister's suffering belongs to Dominic first." His jaw twitched at that—not out of mercy for Savannah, but frustration at delaying his sport with her.

His jaw clenched, muscles tight with barely suppressed fury, but he nodded. He understood that our family's legacy, our future, depended on Savannah's return and her marriage to Dominic. He would not fail me, though I had no doubt he'd want to leave a trail of destruction in his wake. I didn't think this was in our best interest, either. "Callum, we need to be forward-thinking here. We'll have our day against Iron Valor. But an unprovoked attack against their men will cause us grief with the Council. They will come for us. We'll exact our revenge in good time, son. Taking Savannah out from under their noses will be sweet enough for now."

He nodded in agreement. Despite his penchant for violence, Callum was a strategist and understood the game. "Yes, father. You're right. I just want to punish them for taking what is ours."

"In good time, son."

We refined our strategy until it gleamed like a scalpel: swift infiltration during Iron Valor's leadership void, minimal engagement...but maximum humiliation for those who'd dared harbor her. Callum grinned when I emphasized stealth over slaughter—not because he cared for subtlety, but because he knew what awaited Savannah once she was shackled in our jet's cargo hold en route to Dominic's estate. His fingers drummed against my desk as we spoke, already itching to leave bruises on her arms when he hauled her away from whatever pathetic rebellion she'd built there among those fools who called themselves wolves.

We moved through each step of the plan; the timing of arrival, the moment of their strike. My office felt like a war room, every detail calculated and deliberate. The shadows deepened as the sun sank lower, and I could see the violent gleam in Callum's eyes as he imagined the delicious victory of finally capturing his sister. "She'll regret running," he said, a savage promise in his voice. "We'll make sure of it." He spat the words out like they burned his tongue, the contempt in his voice almost palpable.

"Once you have her, we move quickly." My voice was as dark as the room around us, each word precise and exacting. "A quick departure will leave Iron Valor reeling. The Alpha and her mate being away will make it so much easier. But the other members of his pack will be there. His enforcers. So stealth is still paramount."

The strategy appealed to Callum's ruthless nature, the efficiency of it satisfying him as much as the violence would. "We'll be ghosts," he said, a grin stretching across his face. "In and out before they know what hit them." He was eager, ready to unleash the kind of brutality that I'd seen him hone over years of training and expectation. It was his gift, cruel and unyielding.

The room grew colder as evening stretched on, but I hardly noticed. My focus was singular; the certainty of success a warm glow in the back of my mind. Savannah's defiance would be her undoing, and Callum and I would see it through. The Iron Valor Pack was formidable, but they would never expect this.

Callum left to gather the men and prepare the jet. His exit was swift, full of the promise of blood and victory. I sat alone in the darkened office, the pieces of the plan clicking into place like the final stages of a long, complex game. I had a call to make. Dominic would be happy to know that his bride was only hours from being secured. I considered inviting him to ride along. I relished the idea of seeing her face when she realized all the months of running still resulted in her falling into the hands of the man I had chosen for her. Dominic and I would be waiting on the plane when tomorrow, she'd see the futility of her choices, the inevitability of her fate. And tomorrow, she'd learn what happens when a Calloway tries to run.

The cold bite of night meant nothing compared to the warmth blooming behind my ribs as I sat alone afterward—a king already tasting victory on his tongue while plotting which pieces of Iron Valor to burn next...once their precious stolen princess was gone.

CHAPTER 12

SAVANNAH

The morning Menace left for Birmingham with Bronc, the air clung to me like static, all prickling unease beneath forced calm. I didn't know if my father was still looking for me, but Menace's reassurances hummed in my head like a mantra: You're safe. He'd unloaded my suitcase and gotten me settled into one of the guest rooms at Bronc and Juliet's in the early hours of the morning. Then, he kissed me hard just inside the doorway to the room, his grip possessive yet trembling, as if letting go might unravel him. "Juliet's got you," he'd said, voice rough. "Arsenal is gonna be staying with you." I nodded as I eased my death grip on the lapels of his suit coat. He and Bronc were dressed for business—if I had to guess, I'd say he was in a Tom Ford suit—navy blue, crisp white shirt, matching vest and tie. This man was more handsome than any man I'd ever laid my eyes on. They'd look right at home in the presence of their king.

Juliet and I walked our men out to Bronc's truck outside their cabin and gave them one last kiss goodbye. Bronc briefly gave Arsenal some last-minute instructions as Juliet and I walked back to the large front porch. We turned and gave a final wave as the truck pulled out and down the dusty road toward the pack's private airstrip about five miles deeper in pack territory.

"Everything is going to work out Savanah." Juliet's voice was warm and reassuring. Her hand on my shoulder a comfort.

"You don't know my father. He's not a man who considers losing an option." I told her. I swear I hated to sound like a pessimist. In my soul, I wanted to be that person who looked at the possibilities and not the obstacles. One day, hopefully that could be me.

Juliet looked me in the eye. "I may not know your father, but I know Menace. That man loves you. With that love comes utter devotion and fierce protection. And I also know Bronc. You are Iron Valor Pack now. He is your Alpha. And he is *not* an Alpha that lets any member of his pack come to harm if it is within his power to prevent it. Trust that they will do all that is in their power to keep you safe and out of the hands of your father and King Dominic Madison." I wanted to trust in them. I really did. There was no point in worrying about something beyond my control. We'd worry about my father when and if the time came.

It had been two days since Menace and Bronc had left for Birmingham. This morning after Arsenal dropped me off for work, walking into the school felt like walking into a hornet's nest—fluorescent lights buzzing, hallways thick with the sour tang of burnt coffee. Something just felt *off* from the moment I stepped inside. Karen smiled at me. *Smiled.* Her lips stretched too wide, like a predator playing with its prey. "Morning, Sawyer," she chirped, handing me a latte I didn't trust. The other teachers—usually icy as January—nodded warmly too. My skin crawled, but I buried suspicion under hope: maybe Menace threatened them.

My classroom was my sanctuary. New violins gleamed in the corner—Menace's doing, subtle as sunrise. He'd been sneaking in instruments for weeks: a cajón drum one day, a few flutes the next.

I ran my fingers over the polished wood, smiling despite myself. This man memorized my Amazon wishlist. The kids' laughter during lessons soothed me, their off-key renditions of "Hot Cross Buns" weirdly grounding. For a few hours, I almost forgot the lie I was living—Sawyer the music teacher, not Savannah the runaway heir.

Lunch with Gabby was my lifeline. She slid into the seat across from me, tossing a bag of Takis between us like contraband. "Spill," she said around a mouthful of chips.

"Who died to make Karen human?" I snorted but didn't answer. Gabby didn't know who I really was, and I hated that. But it was too dangerous for her to know. She'd learn when everyone else did I supposed. "She has been nice to me all day. It's weird. And 'the Karens' have been all smiles, too. I'm afraid Menace has maybe told her to back off or something. Which I hate."

Gabby laughed, mouth full of snack treats. "Oh yeah, how awful. Your big gorgeous mate running interference with the big bad wolf. How terrible." She winked.

"I know, I know. And I'm so thankful for him. But I don't wanna seem like I'm not capable of taking care of myself," I sighed.

She reached over and patted my hand, and I felt for the first time that besides Juliet; I had another real friend here. "I get it, girl. And hey, I think you're amazing. It's tough coming into a place that has its tribes already established. I think you're doing great. And the kids love you. That's the most important thing."

I gave her a smile. She was right, and I shouldn't let any of what they thought get to me.

After my fourth period class, I was about to start my conference hour when Karen popped her head in my classroom door. "Sawyer? Could you help me grab some boxes out of my car?" Her eyelashes fluttered like broken moth wings.

I thought that sounded like an odd request, but I was the only teacher on conference this period, so I gave her the benefit of the doubt. Just chalked it up to more grunt work for me. "Sure," I put on my most cooperative face, following her down the main hall to the back door.

She made small talk as we walked. "How are you settling in?"

"Oh, um, great." I was honestly surprised she'd said anything at all. "Love the kids."

"Really? Well, that's nice." We got to the door, and she opened it, allowing me to go out first. "Maybe you won't miss them too much." She laughed as she quickly shut the door behind me.

I tried the handle frantically, knowing the door would not open, refusing to believe it. Trees surrounded the few parking spaces of the back lot, a promise of abandonment and despair. My thoughts unraveled faster than I could hold on. The world shifted beneath me, my breath loud in the silence. Then it happened.

Callum's arm snaked around my throat before I could scream. "Did you truly think you could hide from me?" His breath slithered hot against my ear, a brother who should protect his little sister, twisted and turned grotesque. Silver chains hissed against my wrists before I could shift, searing through flesh until smoke curled from blistered skin. "Father sends his regards."

I thrashed like trapped prey, teeth sinking into his forearm until copper flooded my tongue. His laughter curdled the air as he wrenched my head back by my hair—roots screaming, vertebrae cracking like dry kindling. I kicked, struggled, desperate to free myself from Callum's grip. It only fueled his rage, making his fists connect harder. A sickening crack as he struck my face, then the metallic taste of blood filled my mouth.

"Still fighting?" He purred as my vision blurred crimson at the edges. "Good. Dominic prefers his whores spirited."

The first punch shattered something delicate behind my eyes—a kaleidoscope of pain blooming bright as his signet ring tore through skin. My knees buckled as darkness swallowed me whole.

Waking was worse.

Pain brought me back to the world. Everything else was darkness. The metal walls pressed in, crushing, suffocating. Each heartbeat crashed against my skull, a thunderous and private hell. My senses screamed with panic. Bound, drugged, trapped. Hopeless. My father had planned this well. Despair tasted like blood on my lips, a bitter promise of what was to come. The vibration and roar of engines filled the space around me. An airplane. I was in the air, miles from the life I wanted. Miles from Menace. Callum's shadow fell over me, but his gloating began before he spoke.

"Rise and shine, my whore of a sister." His voice cut through the dark, as cruel and mocking as the look on his face. "Wouldn't want you to miss the fun."

I couldn't move. Couldn't breathe past the terror that gripped me. His hands were as tight as the chains that bound me, the chains that made my skin blister, burn.

"We're flying to the Midwest territory," Callum taunted, crouching close enough for me to feel the chill of his hatred. "To your new home with King Dominic." The words twisted inside me, sharp and cutting.

"You'll never get away with this." My voice was ragged, a choked whisper. "I'm mated to another."

Callum laughed, the sound dark and hollow. "Not for long," he said. "You'll fulfill your role, Savannah. Your defiance means nothing. Once your mate is dead, you'll no longer be mated to anyone except to the king to whom you were promised. You did this to yourself, you selfish bitch. You've brought shame to your family name."

"Fate decided who my mate was," I said through gritted teeth. I tried to hide my fear, knowing he got off on it. I could see it in his eyes, in the cruel twist of his mouth. He wouldn't kill me, but he could do worse.

"For now, maybe," he said, the words deliberate, slow. "And soon, you'll be Dominic's."

The thought of it shattered me, left me reeling, raw. I had to fight, had to resist. But there was no way out. Callum leaned in, his smile a jagged wound across his face.

"You've got nothing left, sis. No one to save you." His voice dripped with malice, with triumph.

I spat blood at him, defiant. "Menace will find me," I said, clinging to the hope as if it were my last breath.

"Not before I break you." His backhand split my lip again, and pain exploded white and blinding. I slumped against the chains, their silver grip pulling me deeper into despair, weakening my ability to heal.

Time lost meaning in the dark. Every second stretched to eternity. Every vibration of the plane a cruel reminder of how far I was from the life I wanted. From the man I needed. The blood tasted bitter, but it was the chemicals, the drugs, that threatened to pull me under. I fought against it, against the numbness, the helplessness as I tried to reach Menace through our bond. It was weak, but I felt his pull, his love.

But I was as good as gone.

Callum's taunts echoed through the darkness, each word another twist of the knife. Another fracture of my resolve.

"He'll be happy to have you. Damaged goods and all. You're just a means to an end."

I was drowning, every desperate gasp filling my lungs with dread.

"Dominic won't care how many men you've let between your legs. Would you be surprised to know that your future husband and father are on this jet? They think you're still knocked out. Guess I'll go tell them you're awake."

I was nothing to them. Just a bargaining chip, a piece of flesh to trade and own. The metal walls closed in, the vibration drowning out my thoughts. Desperation flared brightly, consuming a fire in my blood that defied my brother, my father, my fate. I clung to the bond I had with Menace, sending out wave after wave of fear and agony and need. He would feel it. He had to.

My hope strained against the darkness, fragile and uncertain. But it was all I had.

I felt the life I wanted slip further from my grasp with every heartbeat, every thunderous, relentless roar of the engines. The plane climbed higher, faster. Blood trickled down my chin, and I let out a silent scream, its echo filling the hollow spaces inside me.

Chapter 13

Menace

The hired driver wore a charcoal suit so stiff it could have stood up on its own, and his jaw never unclenched once during the hour he ferried us from Birmingham's jet center to the estate on the far side of the city. Security at the first gate checked our IDs, then checked them again, as if we might have morphed during the two minutes it took to cross the outer perimeter. "Standard protocol," the driver explained, lips barely moving. "King Rafe's got a few more eyes on him these days."

I caught Bronc's smirk in the rearview, a crooked edge that said he expected nothing less from an old friend with more enemies than friends. The grounds themselves sprawled in a low, rolling way—tennis courts, horse paddocks, the water hazards of a golf course flashing blue between stands of moss-draped trees. The house: colonial, three stories, portico lined with white columns big enough to hold up the damn sky. Workers in overalls and polo shirts zipped past in utility carts, not one of them looking up. I felt the weight of the place before we even stepped inside.

A woman with a platinum helmet of hair and a drawl so sweet you'd get diabetes from it ushered us into the entry hall and through two sitting rooms, both styled like the furniture catalog had a sale on "Confederate-Chic." We passed a man polishing silver trophies, who looked up and gave us a polite, lethal once-over before returning to his rag. "The king's not quite ready," the woman said. "Y'all will be in the Magnolia wing tonight."

We followed her up a split staircase, down a hall painted the color of wet clay, and she unlocked a double suite with a card key that beeped like a miniature alarm. Ten doors lined the corridor. No other guests, no signs of life. Just us. She pointed out the minibar ("compliments of the king, of course"), asked if we required a wake-up call or "special accommodations," then left us to it.

I shut the door behind her and dead-bolted it before Bronc could say a word. "I got it from here."

He nodded, crossing to the wet bar and pulling out a beer. I went straight for my duffel and unzipped the first layer—Wrecker's travel kit. First, the bug scanner. I thumbed it on and swept the ceiling in methodical arcs. The scanner whined low in my palm as I paced the perimeter. Light fixtures, vent grates, even the crown molding. Nothing on the readout. I kept moving.

Bronc drank his beer in three gulps, his gaze following me like I was a lab rat and he was waiting for the data.

"Pretty sure if Rafe wanted to off us, he'd have invited us to a barbecue first," he said finally, voice softer than usual. I ignored him and moved to the bathroom, scanning the mirrors and the showerhead. Again, nothing. Either this place was cleaner than the goddamn CDC or the bugs here ran on tech I'd never seen.

I pulled out the fiber-optic scope next and started on the air vents. "Just because a man's smiling doesn't mean he wants you alive," I muttered, not even bothering to soften it. "You taught me that, Bronc."

He grunted, took the two adjoining steps to the bathroom door, and leaned in. "Yeah, but I also taught you to recognize when a king's just got more to lose than you. Rafe's not like your maybe, soon-to-be father-in-law."

I finished the vents and set the scope on the marble sink. "With all due respect, you only served with him for a couple years. You grew up with my family, went through the loss of my sister because someone decided the rules didn't apply." The words came out flatter than I wanted. It's not like I planned to air my shit in the first five minutes, but sometimes the bottle bursts when you shake it too hard.

Bronc loosened his tie and unbuttoned the top two buttons of his dress shirt. The edge of his mate mark was visible, still faintly pink even after all these months. "You think he's responsible for what happened to her?"

"I think he was in charge of the territory when Greenbriar took her, and I think he's the only king who managed to look the other way for a solid year before the Council called a trial. So yeah, I don't fucking trust him."

Bronc was silent. That silence stretched out, filled the cracks between the marble tiles and seeped into the grout. I could hear the echo of my own bitterness ricocheting off the walls, but I didn't care. I cleared the two bedrooms then set the bug kit back in the duffel, zipped it, and looked at myself in the mirror. The man in the glass looked tired, skin pulled too tight across his cheekbones, a five o'clock shadow that made my scars look like fresh wounds.

Back in the suite, Bronc was on the couch with his boots up on the coffee table, a full glass of whiskey balanced on his knee. "So what's your plan, Bridger?"

I shrugged off my jacket, hung it neatly on the closet rail, and checked the windows for visual contact points. "Plan is simple: keep my mouth shut, watch what Rafe does, and don't take a drink from anyone unless I see it poured myself. If he's playing us, we'll know in the first five minutes."

Bronc took a slow sip, his eyes never leaving mine. "You're not the only one with skin in this game, you know. If Juliet gets so much as a hangnail because of this, I'll end him." His voice was graveled, flat as Texas earth.

I met his stare, and for a second, it was like we were on some goddamn roof in the desert again, waiting for the next mortar. "Copy that," I said, and it was as close as I could come to thank you.

We didn't say much for the next hour. Bronc scrolled through his phone, typing out messages to someone—probably Arsenal or Wrecker, maybe even Juliet. I watched the dusk bleed through the plantation shutters, the blue outside fading to a dirty gray. My hands itched for the comfort of a weapon, but I settled for the cool bite of the whiskey Bronc eventually poured for me.

I drank half, then stared into the glass like it had answers.

Memories came slow, the way they do when you're in enemy territory and trying not to let your guard down. My sister was seventeen when she vanished. All-American, dark hair, sharper tongue than mine but sweeter with kids and horses than anyone alive. She was on my mind all the time, but more so in places like this—places where power grew in thick, humid air and no one ever really left a door unlocked.

The day we found her, she was more dead than alive. The bastard Greenbriar Alpha wouldn't take no for an answer. We knew they were the ones who had her. We went through channels. After Bronc told him his marriage proposal had been declined, he was furious. Two weeks later, Emma disappeared. We immediately went to the council with our suspicions. There was an "investigation." Came up with nothing. Then *we* investigated. Took two hours before we found her in a camouflaged cell outside their compound. Wasn't even well-concealed. She was so badly beaten, malnourished, and wrapped in silver, she couldn't heal. I killed that motherfucking Alpha myself when we raided. Could have taken that pack. Should have. But Bronc said to let the Council handle it. Haven't fully gotten over taking his advice on that one.

Emma never really recovered. Wrapped her car around a tree two months later. Closed casket. My mother's hands, fists balled in her lap so hard her knuckles split. The way that Big Papa's mouth didn't quite close between words, like he'd run out of things to say. I remember vowing never to let my guard down again, and hating the world for daring to expect anything else.

I finished my drink and set the glass down, the clink loud in the dead quiet.

When the phone buzzed on the table, Bronc read the message and nodded. "We see the king in thirty minutes."

"Copy that," I said again, the words as hollow as a spent shell. I straightened my shirt, ran fingers through my hair, and checked the mirror one more time for tells. The man who looked back was good at hiding things, but his jaw was clenched so tight the tendons stood out like cables. I forced a breath through my nose and let it out slow, practiced, the way Doc taught us. Then I followed Bronc down the hall, each step echoing like a countdown in my skull.

If the king wanted a war, he was about to see what it looked like up close.

The king's office was a gunmetal cage at the top of the third floor, all slab glass and uncarpeted concrete, fluorescent lights burning white holes into the dusk outside. Gone were the antebellum ghosts and the sweet rot of magnolia—this was a war room, with floor-to-ceiling monitors, scrolling news feeds, security camera grids, and biometric logs I could read from fifteen feet. Even the air tasted sterile, like something you'd use to clean a crime scene.

Rafe Mayfield was taller in person than any photograph could convey—an inch or two on Bronc, shoulders wide enough to block the morning sun, and a beard as black as the suit he wore. He didn't rise when we entered, just angled his chair and motioned to the two seats across from the desk. Next to him stood his beta, Stetson, who looked more like a wolf than a man: square jaw, stare that could strip paint, hands folded so tight the knuckles were bone white. His gaze raked us up and down, twice.

"Evenin' boys," Rafe said, his voice a bourbon slow pour. "Glad to see y'all made it in one piece." He flicked his eyes to the clock. "Let's not waste time. You got something for me?"

I laid the file folders on the glass—one for Harrison, one for the missing shifters, and one marked "Private." Bronc opened the top folder and spread the photos across the desk: Juliet's hospital records, the before-and-after shots of her mother, the chemical analysis of the serum. Rafe's face didn't change, but Stetson's jaw clenched, sharp and fast.

"We know the Council's been briefed," Bronc began, "but this is what you haven't seen. Juliet's mother was taken when he couldn't find Juliet. He wanted a hybrid. All the others were the known missing from packs generally in the Midwest. Juliet went in to rescue her mother and got taken herself. That's when Harrison realized what he had—omega blood from a fated mate."

Rafe picked up one of the photos and held it to the light. "She's your mate?"

Bronc nodded. "Hastings used her mother to make the first stable batch."

"Council says there's only one dose left." Stetson's voice was flat, dead. "You got it?"

Bronc shot me a look. I answered for us both. "Destroyed it. There was no way to guarantee it wouldn't be used again. We also scuttled the entire underground lab, burned it beyond recognition with everyone in it. Removed all hard drives. And Hastings is dead. Juliet killed him herself."

Rafe looked duly impressed with our Luna. Then gestured to the next folder. "And this is...?"

"Cross-reference of every missing shifter on the east side of the Rockies." I watched Rafe's eyes as he paged through—he didn't flinch at the autopsy photos, but the list of names seemed to slow him.

Stetson finally broke his poker face. "That's a lotta bodies."

"We hope that's all there was." I leaned forward. "The Council doesn't want this getting out, but I think it's important for anyone with missing loved ones. They need closure. But most of all, I care about my pack. And right now, they are in the crosshairs. We didn't cause this. My mate didn't cause this. She didn't have the slightest idea about her shifter heritage when she came to Iron Valor. That was fate, plain and simple. It might be old-fashioned thinking, but I don't give two fucks. The Goddess brought Juliet to me. Can't make me believe otherwise. There is no other explanation for how a wealthy New York socialite, with no ties or knowledge of her shifter heritage, made her way to fucking Dairyville, Texas, to work for the Alpha of a shifter pack. Not her fault those shifters lost their lives. Not Iron Valor's fault."

Rafe set the folder down and laced his fingers together. "I'm inclined to agree, Bronc. So why come to me? You want me to be the shield between the Council and your pack when it comes to any of them pointing fingers your way over the missing shifters?"

"I think it'd go a long way in terms of Iron Valor's credibility as far as our word goes. Some already see us as some kind of vigilantes after Greenbriar." Bronc stood his ground.

Rafe raised a dark eyebrow and looked my way. "What happened with Greenbriar was one hundred percent justified. I dare anyone to say otherwise. Anyone who has anything bad to say about Iron Valor or you or Bridger Hardin over that can discuss it with me."

That took me completely off guard as I made eye contact with him. "Thank you, sir," I told him.

The king stilled for a moment, then continued. "Now, that brings us to our next order of business. The reason I think you are actually here. I understand there is an issue with the power-hungry King of the East, Declan Calloway?"

Bronc answered, voice low and deliberate. "When we took down the Hastings lab rescuing my mate, Juliet, there was another woman there. Bridger is the one who freed her from her chains.

In doing so, he also discovered, amazingly enough, she is also his fated mate."

Rafe's beard twitched, maybe the ghost of a smile. "Oh, come on. This is something out of Disney."

I didn't blink. "It's pretty unfucking believable, but no less true. Speaking of Disney. My fated mate happens to be Princess Savannah Calloway."

Rafe shook his head. "You are shitting me."

Stetson whistled a low note. "She's with you now?"

"She *is* my mate." My voice was as cold as the office.

Rafe stared for a long second. "You're sure about that."

"We're bonded." The words came out in a growl as Bronc put his hand on my arm and Stetson took a step toward me.

Rafe put a hand up as if to push his man back and shook his head no.

"No offense, Bridger. I needed to know. I believe you."

Bronc spoke next. "Declan wants Savannah back. He set her up for an arranged mating/marriage with King Dominic Madison. But she ran, and the son of a bitch is losing face by the day. He'll do anything to get her back—he's already sent several bounty hunters after her. They've all failed. Part of that reason is that she was taken by Hastings. She spent weeks being tortured in his lab."

I waited for Stetson to weigh in, but he just watched me, gaze sharp as broken glass. I stared right back.

Rafe finally broke the silence. "You said Savannah was being hunted."

"She's safe in Dairyville, but we're not stupid enough to think that'll last. Declan's got eyes everywhere, and if he figures out where she is, he'll come himself. She's being guarded, but it's a matter of time."

Stetson snorted. "And you want us to run interference?"

"No." I met his eyes, let him see the steel. "I want you to tell us what Declan's next move is, and how many hitters he's got on payroll. After that, we'll handle it."

Rafe uncapped a pen and tapped it against the desk. "You trust your mate?"

"With my life," I said.

He scribbled a note, then leaned forward, voice dropping. "If Savannah is what you say, the Calloways and the Madisons won't stop at killing. They'll try to break you. Maybe use the Council to void your bond. You need to be ready."

"Already am," I said. I could feel Bronc's silent approval at my back. "If the Council could void a bond, could they uphold a bond? If it can be proven that our bond is fated, would that carry any extra weight? I know it's rare these days. For fuck's sake, it's Goddess-blessed. There are still people who hold that sacred, right?" I knew I could be grasping at straws. But I was willing to grab at anything.

The king of the South watched us for a long moment, then smiled—a flash of teeth, nothing soft about it. "I know many people still hold the tradition sacred, myself included." He snapped the folder shut and slid it to the edge of the desk. "It might be the very thing that at least will give you time. But there's a price. If you're wrong about the bond, the Council will strip you both. Mate marks, rank, everything. So don't fuck this up."

I smiled, tight as piano wire. "Wasn't planning on it."

As we left, Stetson followed us to the elevator, silent and wolf-eyed. I glanced back at the king, who was already dialed into another call. Business as usual.

In the end, it was just like Bronc said. The king had more to lose than we did. He needed his strongest packs intact and at the ready at all times. He couldn't afford for Iron Valor to be decimated.

Morning came with a thick mist hugging the fields outside the window, blurring the edge of the world. I'd slept three hours, maybe less, and spent most of the night cycling through every potential betrayal, every angle that could fuck us before we saw it coming. Bronc's light snoring in the next room was steady, untroubled; I envied him, but not enough to wish for ignorance. I spoke briefly with Savannah. She sounded tired. I tried to encourage her and told her I was doing everything I could to get her out of her engagement to Dominic. We weren't out of the woods yet.

I was dressed before sunrise, black shirt tucked in and cufflinks with our Iron Valor crest secured at the wrists, ready to meet the day like it might punch first. At exactly 0700, the intercom buzzed. "King Mayfield requests your presence, gentlemen."

We took the back stairs this time, led by a silent butler in a navy suit. The war room was brighter now, windows open to a washed-out sky, and the cold light made everything look even more surgical. Rafe stood at the far end of the room, sleeves rolled, tie gone. Stetson waited behind him, and another man—older, white-haired, with the kind of stillness that meant he'd been in worse rooms than this—stood off to the side. Probably security chief, or Council liaison.

Rafe motioned us to the same seats. His eyes were bloodshot, but there was nothing soft about them. "Gentlemen," he said, voice all business. "Last night, I put out feelers on the Madison situation. My people came back with a new wrinkle: I was told that Declan could appeal to the Council to void your mate bond, Bridger. He could say it's not to be recognized because it wasn't approved by her family."

Bronc's lips tightened, but he stayed silent. I let the words settle, then asked, "So what could he do?"

"He could demand Savannah be stripped of her mate mark and returned to Martha's Vinyard. Preferably in pieces, I'm sure." Rafe didn't sugarcoat it. "Then he could try to sanction you for breaking protocol."

I felt the old anger light up behind my ribs. "And the Council would buy this shit?"

Rafe held up a hand, forestalling me. "No. But they have to be seen as neutral. Which means they'd require an outside party to confirm the fated bond. They'd send someone—witch, angel, maybe even a vampire—to do it. If you passed, you're good. If not..." He let the thought hang.

Stetson spoke, voice even. "It's rare, but it happens. You just need to prove the bond is real."

"Savannah's not a pawn," I growled. "She chose me. The Goddess chose us."

Rafe nodded. "Doesn't matter. The Council doesn't give a damn about the Goddess. They care about precedent. And if you can't play by their rules, they'll burn you both."

Bronc jumped in. "If we were to get ahead of this, what would be the Council's timeline?"

"Three days. Maybe four." Rafe's eyes were flat as slate. "You can stay here until then, or go back and prep your case. But you'll need evidence. The Council likes documentation—bloodwork, testimony, physical proof."

I laughed, bitter. "Want me to fuck her on the witness stand?"

Rafe didn't flinch. "Wouldn't be the first time."

The white-haired man stepped forward, hands clasped behind his back. "You have our full cooperation. King Mayfield has secured the best witch in the South. She can do a preliminary test, so you know what you're up against." His accent was Midwestern, probably ex-Council.

I leaned back in my chair, feeling the weight of it all press against my spine. "What if we fail?"

Rafe's mouth twisted somewhere between regret and warning. "Then you run. And you never stop running."

I looked at Bronc, who met my gaze with a quiet, unshakable resolve. "We'll pass," he said. "We don't lose our own."

The meeting ended as abruptly as it began. Rafe shook our hands—his grip a warning as much as a courtesy—and told us to report to the east parlor at 10:00 for the witch's arrival.

Stetson caught my arm as we turned. "Don't let them see you sweat," he murmured, voice pitched so only I could hear. "Council loves blood, but they respect balls."

On the way to the door, Bronc's phone rang. It was Arsenal. He stopped dead in his tracks. He put his phone on speaker. "I've got Menace here with me, and I've put my phone on speaker. Start again." Arsenal's voice came across clearly.

"Savannah's gone. They took her. I think Karen Day set her up."

It was at that moment I felt nothing but agony and pain through our bond as I doubled over and a roar tore through my chest.

The king turned abruptly to us. "Shit. This is a setback. But her father cannot withhold her from the tests, since I've already made the inquiry. She must be presented to the Council for testing, and the mate mark must be left unmarred. But in the meantime, he *can* withhold her from you, Bridger. I'm sorry."

CHAPTER 14

SAVANNAH

Cold was the first thing I felt. Not the sharp, metallic chill of an exam table, but something darker—a gnawing, marrow-deep absence of warmth that radiated through me in waves. My brain trailed slowly behind my senses. I was there but not there, bobbing in a thick sludge of memory and chemical blackout, my thoughts flickering with the last images before oblivion: Karen's face, flat and triumphant, the door slamming home behind me, Callum's arm snaking around my throat, the click of silver cuffs.

Now I was nothing but cold and a noise. An endless, low-frequency vibration that rose and fell with the lurch of my body. I wasn't alone in the dark. Other sounds bled through the engine's whine—a clatter of something heavy against the metal, a hissed expletive, the slow, deliberate drag of someone's boot heel across a grating floor.

I tried to move, and fire shot up my arms and legs. The agony woke me more than any drug or slap could have. I was bound. Silver. It ate at my wrists and ankles with a heat that felt like betrayal, a wrongness that pushed at my body's natural urge to change, to heal, to rage. I whimpered despite myself. My body refused to answer me beyond a sick shudder.

I cataloged what little I could: face pressed against an oil-stained mat, arms wrenched behind my back, knees drawn up, the tang of my own blood in my mouth and the scald of silver at every point of contact. I was wearing my school clothes—black pants and a button-down blouse, the fabric stiff with dried sweat. I could not move my hands, or even flex my fingers; the metal cuffs were locked so tight they had burrowed deep, chafing raw. My feet were shackled together. A chain ran from my wrists to my ankles. The only blessing was they were bound in front of me, not behind. The chains must have been new; there was no give in the links, no evidence of rust. It was a setup engineered for my species.

I tasted old vomit and blood at the back of my throat. When I swallowed, my jaw ached with a thousand miniature detonations. I remembered Callum's first punch—the sharp, wet crunch as his signet ring split my cheek open. Then the world went fuzzy for a long, blank space.

When the pain started to lessen, other details crawled in. The room—no, not a room, a cargo hold. Not on the ground. We were in the air; the floor juddering every time we hit a pocket of turbulence. It reeked of jet fuel and old sweat and the cold, chemical stink of fear. There was a slap of metal every few seconds, a reminder that the walls were not walls but something thinner, weaker. I tried to roll to my side, but only managed to shift my face against the mat. It scraped a scab from my chin, fresh blood stinging on contact.

A voice cut through the dark. "She's stirring." Callum. Even half-conscious, I'd know his tone anywhere. It was the same one he used as a child to gloat over every cruelty, every time he broke my things or hurt our dog.

My heart hammered in my chest, the panic threatening to throttle me, but I forced my breathing to slow. I let my eyes slit open—just enough to see. The hold was lit by a single overhead bulb, its light choked by layers of cigarette smoke and grime. Shadows pooled at the corners.

I was not alone. In front of me, leaning against a reinforced bulkhead, my father watched with the posture of a man who believed he was born to stand over people. He was in a suit, black on black, tie knotted with military precision. His hair, more silver now than red, was combed into an arrogant, perfect wave. His eyes were flat and cold and full of calculation.

A third man hunched on a bench bolted to the wall, arms folded tight across his chest, legs spread in a way that screamed entitled violence. He was younger than my father, his features harsh and beautiful and ruined all at once. His eyes, pale blue and rimmed in red, never left me. My stomach dropped through the floor. Dominic.

My father said nothing. Just watched as Callum crouched down beside me, his grin sharp and awful.

"I told you she'd wake up," he said to no one in particular. "Always did have a weak constitution, didn't you, Savannah?"

I wanted to spit at him, but my mouth wouldn't work. I could only glare, blood oozing from a split at the corner of my lip.

Callum grabbed my hair and twisted my face up toward the others. I didn't make a sound, though my vision flashed white at the pain. "Got your attention, princess?"

"Let her up," Dominic said, the first words from his mouth.

"Why? She's not going anywhere." Callum's grip tightened, yanking my scalp. "Not after what the little bitch pulled. Thinks she's clever."

My father's voice was razor calm. "Enough, Callum. She's conscious now. Let her sit. We have much to discuss before landing."

Callum didn't let go, but he yanked me upright, forcing me to my knees. The silver dug deeper, and I bit back a scream. The world spun for a moment; I retched dryly, nothing left to vomit.

"Welcome back, Savannah." My father's words were perfectly measured, as though I were a misbehaving student in his office. "Your surprise at being here is disappointing. You must have known it would come to this."

I didn't respond. I stared at the floor, willing the nausea to subside.

Dominic kicked a box over to me. It landed with a hollow thunk. "Drink," he said. His accent was unmistakable—Midwestern, polished, predatory. He didn't look at me as he spoke. "Or die of dehydration. Makes no difference to me, but it's not the outcome your father wants."

I ignored the box, ignored the burn of thirst in my throat. I'd been in worse situations. I could outlast them, if not in strength, then in spite.

My father cleared his throat, the sound slicing through the gloom. "We're two hours out from Chicago. Dominic is being gracious enough to host us until the council hearing."

I looked up, letting hatred burn through the fog. "Council?"

He smiled. "There are protocols for these things, darling. Your... mating, for example."

He said it like a slur.

I shook my head, just enough to make the world tilt. "You're wasting your time. As you said, I'm already mated. The bond is real."

Dominic's face flickered with something ugly—jealousy or rage or both. He knelt down to my level, close enough I could see the sheen of sweat on his upper lip. "You think he'll come for you?" he whispered. "You think that mongrel will survive two hours with my men waiting at O'Hare?" His hand shot out and caught my jaw, squeezing until my teeth ground together. "You belong to me. Your father made a deal. That's how these things work."

"You're going to hell," I said, though the words slurred out more like a moan.

He grinned, then let go, letting my head snap forward.

Callum circled behind me, his boots scraping the deck. "Don't bother. She's got nothing left to fight for." He bent low to my ear, his breath hot and venomous. "They're going to rip that mate mark off your neck, you know. Maybe even skin it. Wouldn't that be something? Maybe Dominic will let me keep it as a souvenir."

I turned my face away, trying not to breathe.

My father watched this with an expression of faint boredom. He drummed his fingers on his knee. "You are here to listen, Savannah. That's all that's required. If you can manage not to embarrass yourself for two days, I might even consider some leniency."

He paused, then added, "Otherwise, your life will be very, very short."

Dominic stood and dusted off his hands. "She'll cooperate, Declan. She doesn't have a choice."

I kept my mouth shut. I'd learned in the labs that silence is sometimes all you can weaponize.

Callum was less patient. He grabbed my chin, twisting it so my eyes met his. "Did you hear what father said?"

I stared at him with all the hate I could summon. "Loud and clear."

He slapped me, a backhand across the cheek that made my ears ring. "Show some respect."

I spat blood onto his boots. "Fuck you."

Dominic laughed. "She's spirited. I like that." He squatted again, getting in my face, his voice low and smooth. "You'll learn to like it, too. Eventually."

The three of them conferred as if I were nothing but cargo, a feral animal they had to restrain until its new owner arrived. They spoke in code about "the subject," "the council session," "the protocol for removal." It was obvious none of them considered me a person any longer. Just a liability, a body to be exchanged for power and face-saving.

When they thought I wasn't listening, my father let his true feelings bleed through.

"She's a disgrace," he said. "But if the bond is real, it will be dealt with. If not, we'll take care of her. Either way, Dominic gets what he wants."

Dominic's voice was cold as the hold. "I don't want damaged goods. She'll behave, or I'll have Callum teach her how."

Callum snickered. "Gladly."

The plane rocked through another pocket of turbulence, and my chains pulled tighter. I squeezed my eyes shut, praying for the impact that might end it all.

It never came.

Instead, my father's boots crossed the deck. He knelt, a parody of paternal concern, and stroked a strand of hair from my face. The gesture made my skin crawl.

"Don't be foolish, Savannah," he said softly. "You know how this ends. I don't want to see you hurt. But I will do what must be done."

I let my head sag; the drugs pulling me under. I dreamed of Menace—his hands, his voice, the way he said my name—and woke up crying, the tears cutting clean tracks down my blood-streaked cheeks.

Callum saw and sneered. "Still pining for your hero? Cute. Bet he's already dead."

I ignored him, but the fear burrowed deep. I tried to reach Menace through our bond, tried to send a signal—pain, hope, anything—but the silver burned too hot, snuffing out any magic before it reached my heart.

The hours blurred into one another. At some point, the three men moved to a small compartment at the far end of the hold, their voices muffled by distance and doors. I let my body go slack, conserving what little strength I had.

When the door clanged open again, it was Callum's boots, then his hands, hauling me upright.

"Showtime, princess," he hissed. "Time to meet your future."

He dragged me to my feet and marched me down the narrow aisle, every step a study in humiliation. At the threshold, Dominic and my father waited, their faces masks of contempt and expectation.

The cold air outside bit into my skin as they led me down the steps onto the tarmac. I squinted against the light, blinking through the pain. There were black SUVs waiting, men in suits and guns bracketing the convoy.

No sign of Menace. No cavalry. Only the three men who would decide what happened to me next.

I stumbled forward, determined not to give them the satisfaction of seeing me fall. Even as the world shrank to a pinpoint, even as the silver gnawed at my bones, I held onto one thought:

I would not break.

Not here. Not for them. Not for anyone.

The first thing I registered was the scent—lilacs, maybe gardenia, something sharp and expensive that didn't belong. Then the softness under my cheek: not scratchy wool, not linoleum or caked rubber, but a comforter so thick I could bury my entire arm in it and never touch the mattress. My head throbbed from every direction. My face pulsed in time with my heartbeat, each thrum reminding me of Callum's handiwork. Even my teeth ached. I tried to move and found that, while the silver was gone, my wrists and ankles still burned with the memory of it. The room was sweltering; the lights above me glared like a stage set.

A shadow fell across the bed, and a meaty hand dug into my upper arm. I tried to jerk away, but my body wasn't cooperating, and the hand had no intention of letting me. I was yanked upright so fast that black crept into the corners of my vision. My father's face swam into focus, only inches from mine. He looked rested, satisfied—like a man who'd just collected a particularly rare coin for his collection and couldn't wait to show it off.

He said nothing, just appraised me. His eyes flicked to the cut on my cheek, the swollen lip, the red weals around my wrists where the silver had scorched me. Then, he shook his head in disappointment and released me so I collapsed onto the comforter again.

I became aware of the other men only when they spoke.

"Not much to look at, is she?" The voice came from behind me—Dominic. His words were cold, but what stuck was the hunger underneath. He circled to the foot of the bed, arms folded, mouth drawn into a thin line. His suit was an even darker black than my father's, if such a thing was possible. "I thought you said she was—"

"She was," my father replied, his gaze still pinned on me. "She just needs a reminder of who she belongs to. You know how it is with women."

I tried to stand, but my legs gave out. The comforter caught me, or maybe I just folded into it, my head barely above my knees. My arms hung limp at my sides. My shirt was torn at one shoulder, exposing the bite mark at the crook of my neck.

Dominic's eyes narrowed. "That needs to go."

"Soon enough," my father grumbled. "But not until the Council's finished with it. Their protocols are archaic. You'll see."

Dominic looked at me like I was a puzzle he didn't want to solve. "How long will it take?"

"A week at most," my father told him. "Provided she behaves."

I tried to speak, but my mouth filled with the taste of old blood. I spat it onto the comforter—an insignificant rebellion, but the only one available. My father's hand closed around my jaw, hard enough to make me see stars.

"None of that," he hissed. "You're going to make us proud, Savannah. You will not embarrass this family again."

He punctuated the "again" with a slap—hard, not theatrical, and perfectly aimed to reopen the scab on my cheek. The shock blanked out my thoughts for a few seconds. When my mind cleared, I found I was still upright, his hand fisted in my hair, keeping my head from slumping forward.

A handkerchief appeared in my field of vision. Dominic. He held it at arm's length, as though expecting I might try to bite him. "Wipe your face," he said, the tone one of condescension and bored disgust.

I took the handkerchief, but instead of using it, I dropped it on the floor and glared at him. Dominic's lip curled into the ghost of a smile.

"She's spirited, I'll give you that," he said. "But you'll have to teach her to behave."

My father smoothed a wrinkle from his suit. "I trust you'll be able to manage."

"Obviously."

There was something transactional about their exchange—two men negotiating the price of livestock. It stung more than I could admit, even to myself.

My vision blurred for a moment, and I stared at my lap, the black pants and white blouse a ruined echo of the teacher I'd tried to be. The cuffs at my wrists were ringed with angry red. I pressed my hands together to stop them from shaking. The sight of my own clothes triggered a memory: the school, Karen's smile, the way she'd lured me outside with the promise of help. I saw her face again, lips painted just so, the little upturn at the edge of her mouth when she'd smirked, "Maybe you won't miss them too much." Then the cold slap of metal on my wrists and Callum's voice as the world spun out.

I blinked hard, shoving the memory aside.

"Get up," my father hissed. He didn't wait for me to comply. He hauled me upright again, setting me on my feet. My knees wobbled, but he kept his grip tight enough to keep me vertical.

"We have a schedule to keep," he said. "You will walk, or I will make you."

I could barely stand, but I forced my legs to move, one after the other, keeping my eyes fixed on the floor. The hall beyond the bedroom was a gauntlet of expensive wallpaper and old portraits, every face in the oil paintings scowling down at me like I'd interrupted a dinner party. The carpet was so thick I could feel my feet sink in with every step.

Dominic led the way, his stride unhurried. Behind me, Callum stalked in silence, every so often tapping the back of my knee with his boot when I slowed.

We arrived at a set of double doors at the end of the hall. Dominic opened them with a flourish, revealing an office bigger than most apartments. The ceiling soared overhead. Walls were lined with leather-bound books and the heads of animals I'd never seen in the wild. There was a desk the size of a casket in the center, and behind it, a pair of high-backed chairs.

My father shoved me toward the desk. "Sit," he said. I did, because the alternative was falling face-first onto the marble floor.

The room closed around me. The walls pressed in; heat rising off my skin as if I were about to ignite.

Dominic and my father spoke in low voices, the words impossible to catch. Callum leaned against a window, arms folded, a wolfish smirk on his face. The three of them looked at me like a problem, not a person.

I let my hands rest on the desk, fingers spread wide, every muscle trembling with exhaustion and rage. I tried not to think about the fact that there was no escape; not from this room, not from this house, not from this life.

But I kept my head high, eyes level, daring any of them to look away first.

When Dominic finally turned to me, his gaze was hungry and cold. "You'll want to hear what happens next," he said.

I didn't answer. I just stared, silent and unbroken, waiting for the next act of cruelty to begin.

Dominic didn't bother with a preamble. He perched himself on the edge of his desk, legs crossed at the ankle, his hands folded with an affectation of patience. The gold cufflinks at his wrists caught the office's dim, deliberate lighting and threw it back in sharp daggers, little glints of power in a room built to remind you who ruled here. Even the chairs had more gilt than a cathedral.

He fixed me with a look somewhere between pity and contempt. "Here is the situation, Savannah. The Council does not acknowledge your mating to that—" he paused, smirked, "creature from Iron Valor. They say your father failed to approve the pairing, and that your so-called mate did not follow proper protocol. Even if it were valid, you know what they say about bonds formed in captivity or under stress—they're rarely legitimate."

He let this hang for a moment, like a prosecutor watching a witness crumble. "Tomorrow, you will be taken to Chicago. At Council headquarters, your supposed 'fated bond' will be tested. If it fails, the mate mark is to be burned off. You will then be transferred to me, where you belong. The marriage will take place immediately. If you resist, or cause a scene, the Council will not be as gentle as your father has been."

He glanced at Declan, whose face was impassive but satisfied, then at Callum, who radiated malice from his station at the far wall.

The words felt like they'd been drilled into my skull; every syllable etched in by the cold certainty of men who'd done this before, who'd broken women and called it tradition.

"What if the bond is real?" I said. My voice was so raw I barely recognized it. "What if I pass their test?"

Dominic's mouth twitched. "They have never found one of these 'fated' bonds outside of Council-blessed marriages. But suppose you pass—then you return to your mate, and your family's name is forever stained." He spat the words with venom. "But you won't pass. You'll be proven a liar, just like others before you."

I wanted to scream. Instead, I sat rigid, shoulders back, eyes burning holes through the rug beneath my feet. My wrists tingled where the silver had been, and my neck pulsed with a phantom ache at the thought of what they would do to my mate mark.

Declan spoke up, his voice a precise instrument. "You will not shame us, Savannah. I've tolerated your defiance because I believed you would come to your senses. This is your final chance to prove you are not a mistake."

Callum snorted. "She's nothing but a mistake. We should've taken care of her the moment she started with her little rebellion."

Dominic ignored him, eyes only for me. "Drink some water. Get yourself cleaned up. Tomorrow is a big day."

He gestured to a pitcher and a glass, already sweating on a silver tray. I glared at it as if it might bite me.

"I don't need anything from you," I said. The effort cost me; my voice trembled at the edges, but I held his gaze. "And I will never belong to you."

He stood up, brushed invisible lint from his lapel, and leaned over until I could smell the expensive aftershave he wore. "You will belong to whoever wins. You have no other options." His words buzzed through my skin, setting my nerves on fire.

He straightened and nodded to my father. "See that she's kept under close watch tonight. I want her delivered in presentable condition to the Council."

Declan gripped my upper arm, steering me to my feet. The hallway outside the office was even colder than before. The lights turned down for the night, but no less oppressive. The walk to the guest suite was a blur. My body floated behind Declan's grip, and every step echoed down the corridor like a countdown.

Inside the room, he shoved me onto the bed and stood over me, looming. "You will make us proud tomorrow. That is your duty. Do you understand?"

I didn't answer.

He slapped me again, not as hard as before but just as sharp, a reminder that my body belonged to him until someone took it away. "Do. You. Understand?"

I tasted blood and stared up at him, refusing to give him the satisfaction of a nod.

He left without another word. I heard the key turn in the lock, then his footsteps fading down the hall.

I lay there a long time, staring at the ceiling, tracing the pattern of the chandelier's arms with my eyes. It was hard to believe that, just days ago, I'd been teaching music to a classroom full of children. Harder still to believe that there was any world beyond this suite, this prison of velvet and bone.

But the bond was still there, a thin thread burning through the fog, pulsing in my veins like a beacon. I reached for it, even though the silver had dulled it to an ache. I closed my eyes and sent out a single, desperate plea:

Bridger. Please.

It echoed in the empty cavern of my skull, but the thread flickered in response. Distant, faint, but not gone.

I let the tears come then, silent and hot, burning tracks down my face as I gripped the bedspread with fingers that still shook. I'd always known the odds were against me. But there was comfort in defiance. In knowing that, even now, I could choose whether or not to break.

I pressed my face into the pillow, and through the haze of exhaustion and pain, I made myself a promise.

They would never see me bow.

Not to them.

Not ever.

CHAPTER 15

MENACE

I'd seen men go to pieces before, and it always took me by surprise which ones did. Bronc wasn't a man built for coming apart; he was the kind you expected to survive nuclear fire and walk out with his hair only slightly out of place. But the phone call from Arsenal had pushed him to the brink. After what had happened when he'd lost Juliet just weeks ago, he'd been a man on the edge. He hung up, then spent a minute circling the perimeter of our suite, shoulders so tight it looked like he'd tear through his suit jacket. When he dialed back, I thought the phone itself might dissolve under the strain of his grip.

I sat on the edge of the sofa, hands resting on my knees, body so still it might have belonged to a corpse. I watched Bronc pace, watched the cords in his neck stand out, his mouth opening and closing like he was chewing through iron wire. There was a subtle tremor in his hands—a new thing, and one I catalogued with silent dread.

"Please explain to me how you fucking lost her," he spat into the phone, barely waiting for Arsenal to say hello. The voice coming out of the speaker was measured and slow, but Bronc cut him off at every turn. "You had one job, Jess. One. Fucking. Job. Did you forget how to watch a goddamn door?" A pause, then: "I don't care about the cameras. What happened with Karen Day?"

He stalked to the window, jaw flexing. Arsenal's voice had the calm of a man who knew it wasn't his fault and wasn't about to get rattled by someone else's panic. "She set her up?" Bronc bellowed, slamming the heel of his hand against the glass. "And you just let it happen? How the fuck did she even know who Savannah *was*?"

It sounded like Arsenal was pacing as well. "Apparently she has a cousin who's a member of an East pack. It seems word had gotten around that Savannah had been on the run, and the gossipy bitch and Karen put two and two together. She saw an opportunity to rid herself of her roadblock to Menace, and she fucking took it. She had all the admin keys, alarm codes, and so she could set it up before we had a chance to know what happened. Savannah was gone before I could even get to the rear lot. There was a van waiting."

"Did you get a plate?"

"Covered with mud. But it's in the security surveillance log."

Bronc's eyes slid to me. I met them and shook my head: not worth killing the messenger. He looked back at the phone. "Do we have eyes on the airport? Has the jet left?"

"Gone thirty minutes ago. Decoy SUV stayed parked, but I checked the tarmac myself. She's in the air."

Bronc closed his eyes, pinched the bridge of his nose, and exhaled like a bull before the charge. "Goddamn it. Lock it all down. Nobody in or out, not even for groceries. I want the entire compound on alert. Understood?"

"Understood," Arsenal replied. "What about Juliet?"

A muscle in Bronc's face twitched. He let the silence linger a beat too long. "She's your Luna. She's safe, right?"

"Sir, we're protecting our Luna. There are no threats. Wrecker's with her, and they're in the bunker."

Bronc's nod was slow, deliberate. "Tell Juliet I'll be in touch in a while. And keep a gun on Karen Day."

"She's on lockdown. District's already given her the boot for the breach."

"Not enough. She's *our* problem, and we'll make damn sure she's not anyone's solution, either. Got it?"

"Copy. I'll call you if anything else moves."

The line clicked off. Bronc let the phone drop to his thigh, and for a long second, he just stood there, outlined by the suite's blue-white exterior lights, back rigid as rebar. Then, with a deliberation I hadn't seen since the desert, he turned and walked to the mini-fridge. Pulled a bottle of water, twisted off the cap, and emptied half of it in a single, shaking swallow.

I didn't say a word. It wasn't my place as far as the security of pack territory goes. And besides, I could feel the same rage bubbling in me, just aimed at a different target. I wanted to blame Arsenal, but the reality was this: if you put your trust in anyone, you risk them failing you. It wasn't the first time and wouldn't be the last. Still, Arsenal was a Force Recon man, hard as coffin nails and twice as reliable. If he got taken out of play by a school administrator, it was because she'd set the trap with help.

Bronc pressed his knuckles to the countertop until they blanched white. "Look, I know you want to light it all on fire," he murmured, voice low.

"I do," I said.

"Your restraint is admirable." He looked over, found my face, and the set of his jaw softened. "Didn't think I'd be the one losing my cool."

"You're not losing your cool," I said. "You're pissed because you care. If you ever stop, that's when I worry. And I'm hangin' on by a thread here."

He snorted, the closest he'd come to a laugh since the call. "Well, let's keep each other in check. We lose it, this whole thing goes straight to hell." He straightened and rolled his shoulders, the energy in him shifting from fury to calculation in a heartbeat. He dialed Juliet.

She picked up after one ring. I couldn't hear her side of the conversation, but I didn't need to. Her voice always managed to cut through even the worst storm. Bronc's whole posture changed. He paced again, but his footfalls were slower, less violent. He kept his words clipped, businesslike, but every now and then, a softness crept in. "No, it's not your fault," he said. "She'll be okay. We're going to get her back."

Pause.

"Juliet, I said we will get her back. The Council won't know what hit them. Yeah. I love you, too." His hand trembled for a second on the phone, then he forced it still. "Just promise me you'll stay put. Wrecker's got the house locked up tight." Another pause, then, with a low growl: "Juliet, please."

The call ended, and for a moment, Bronc stood looking at the dark reflection in the TV screen. His voice was softer, but I heard the edge in it. "She's flying to Chicago tonight. She'll be there for the Council hearing."

I raised an eyebrow. "Thought you told her to stay in Dairyville."

"Have you ever known her to listen?" he asked. "At least I'm aware of it this time."

"Must be why you love her." It came out more gentle than I expected. "She's the only person on earth who can tell you to eat shit and make you want to buy her flowers after."

He smiled when he looked at me. "Well, it looks to me like you're well on your way, brother. You're basically about to face a firing squad for your mate."

I just nodded.

The silence stretched, comfortable for the first time since the news hit. I reached for the bottle of scotch in the minibar, poured two fingers into a glass, and slid it over. "Take it," I said. "You need it as much as me."

Bronc stared at the amber for a second, then downed it in one gulp. "You think our pack's falling apart?"

I shook my head. "Fuck no. We have more wolves than we know what to do with, and most of them would rather die than betray their Alpha. If anything, we're overdue for someone to challenge the balance of power. It's what happens when you're at the top. Your father faced it from time to time. Just your turn."

He grunted. "Maybe. Or maybe I'm just getting old."

"You're forty-three, an infant by our standards. I mean, you look like shit, but you've always looked like shit." My attempt at humor landed; he laughed, just a flash, but it made the air feel less like a funeral.

His eyes found mine. "You ready for Chicago?"

"I will fucking burn Chicago down to get my mate back. I'm ready to murder her father, her brother, that fucking king of the Midwest..."

He took a call from Rafe and then shook his head. The energy in him was different—focused, lethal. The exhaustion was still there, the lines around his eyes deeper than they had any right to be, but I could see the wolf in him back at the surface.

He grabbed his bag and unzipped it, and started laying out the hardware: two handguns, backup magazines, a switchblade he kept for close encounters. I did the same, checking my own Glock and the silver-tipped rounds I'd loaded that morning. If the Council wanted a show, we'd give them a goddamn fireworks display.

"Rest up," he said, voice all business again. "Rafe says we fly out in an hour. We'll leave our jet here. Work out the details for how we'll get it and ourselves back to Texas. So goddamn ready. Logistical fucking nightmare."

I nodded, more than ready to get the hell out of here. I wanted to trust that the Council might somehow surprise us and do the right thing. But I sure as shit sat on "go" and waited for them to give us a reason to kill.

The sky turned a deeper blue as we climbed north, and the private jet's window seemed too small for what I wanted: a way out, a way in, any way to get my hands on Savannah. Bronc sat across the aisle, pretending to read a report from Rafe's security team but mostly watching me watch the horizon. We'd each taken up the classic seating—backs never to the aisle, sight lines clear, nothing left to chance.

King Rafe's people didn't skimp on the amenities. The cabin had white leather seats, deep-pile carpet, and smoked glass dividers between each pair of seats. Most would call it comfort. To me it was a slow-burn reminder of just how little money mattered when your mate was somewhere between two states and one step from being sold off.

I'd been locked in the same physical position for forty minutes: left hand knuckles to the window, thumb tracing slow, shallow circles into the padding beneath. The mate mark on my shoulder itched. Then, without warning, it ignited. I choked back a gasp and pinched the muscle, breathing through my teeth.

Bronc snapped to attention instantly. "What is it?"

I flexed my fingers, eyes squeezed shut, waiting for the spike of pain to fade. "I can feel her again," I said, voice gone raw. "The silver's off. For now."

Relief washed over me, hot and dizzy. But it was tainted, because I'd seen what happened to shifters who spent too long in silver. My sister had died that way—thrown into a bunker by the Greenbriar pack, left to stew for weeks in chains. When we pulled her out, there was more scar than skin. I remembered the smell of her as we broke her body from those links, remembered the way she trembled, not from fear but from the craving for release. She'd killed herself months later, unable to shift, unable not to shift. I'd never forgiven the Council for the leniency they showed her captors. Of course, I'd killed their fucking Alpha myself. The Council was still salty about it. Fuck 'em.

Bronc must have seen the direction of my thoughts. "She's not like your sister," he said, quiet.

"I know." I forced the words out. "She's stronger. And she's alive. I can feel that."

He nodded and set his report on the tray table. "Do you want to tell me what you're getting from her? If it's worth hearing?"

I was surprised by the question, and more surprised by the answer that came: "Nothing concrete. Our bond's new—barely enough for sensations, not thoughts. I just know when she hurts, and when she's scared."

"Can you reach her?" Bronc asked.

"No." That stung. "But I can track her, in a way. If I had to, I could find the city."

Bronc's mouth set in a hard line. "Good. She'll be near to where we are."

We sat there, two wolves in a luxury pen, waiting for the next fight. My mind spun with all the ways I could kill those who hurt her, and whether I'd be able to kill my own father-in-law before the Council stripped me of rank or life. What if I killed two kings? I wanted to. But that would take me away from Savannah, and nothing was worth that.

The curtain at the front of the jet snapped open, and King Rafe Mayfield filled the aisle like he was made for it. Six foot four, barrel-chested, with a beard that looked like it had been trimmed for him to appear for the paparazzi. He wore no tie, just a black dress shirt and dark slacks, but he radiated authority like sunlight through glass. He made a show of ignoring the bottle of bourbon in the galley, then plopped into a seat across from us and stretched his legs out.

"You two look like hell," he said, but there was no smile behind it.

Bronc didn't answer, so I did. "We're not here for a vacation, sir."

"Never are," Rafe replied. "But I like to think we can make a little progress before the world tries to bite our balls off."

He leaned in. "Here's how the Council's going to go down. First, you'll meet with an arbitrator from one of the witch clans—she'll be there to test the mate bond and verify it's not a false mark. You'll both submit to bloodwork, magical review, and physical exam."

"Sounds tedious," Bronc said, not quite rolling his eyes.

Rafe ignored him. "After that, the Council will convene in closed session. There are twelve representatives—one for each kingdom, but some serve double roles. They'll hear testimony, then take the findings back to their rulers, who will vote by region. It's not a true democracy, but it's the best we've got."

I interrupted. "Who's likely to side with us?"

Rafe counted on his fingers, as if he'd done this a thousand times. "Not Midwest. Dominic wants to claim Savannah, so clearly he's not for you. Not Eastern Wolves—Declan started this whole shitshow. But you've got the Southern and Western Wolves in your corner, at least for now."

Bronc chimed in. "Vampires?"

Rafe gave a dry laugh. "Western vamps hate the Council, so they'll vote to cause chaos. Eastern are more conservative, if you could consider Kazimir conservative, but they despise arranged marriages. We can count on a split there."

Bronc gave a little sly look at Rafe. "Well, the Eastern Vamps Princess Lucia is my mate's best friend and was a childhood friend of Savannah's. We can at least hope for some sway from her."

Rafe looked incredulous. "Fuck me, Bronc. Iron Valor Wolves never cease to amaze."

I shrugged. "Never count us all the way out." Then I asked, "Witches?" remembering the shrewd, glassy-eyed witch who'd tested me after my sister's death.

"Harder to say," Rafe admitted. "Four covens, each with its own agenda. But two of the four have been on the losing side of mate mark politics for a decade. I think we can get them. The demon and angel factions are a toss-up. The angels are likely a lock for fate, so hopefully they'll be on your side, but they only hold one seat."

I chewed on that for a moment. "So it comes down to three or four swing votes, and who can buy them first?"

He nodded. "Politics isn't much different from organized crime. You want someone on your side, you either pay them or make it impossible for them to cross you."

Bronc's hands balled on the armrests. "Council wasn't worth a damn when it came to finding Emma. Can't help but feel like this is the same song, second verse."

I looked at him with the same sinking feeling. "We're not losing this time," I said, staring him down. "I'll do whatever it takes to bring her home."

"Good," Rafe said. "Because the other side is playing for keeps. Dominic wants to humiliate you. Declan wants to break her. And the rest of the Council just wants the whole thing to go away. Some of 'em might want to make an example of Iron Valor after what happened with Greenbriar. It could go any number of ways."

I let the silence settle. The hum of the engines was a low, persistent threat, a reminder of the speed with which things could unravel. My mate bite still burned, but I welcomed it. It was the only thing that proved Savannah was out there, fighting.

Rafe pulled a notepad from his pocket, scribbled a few lines, and slid it across to me. "These are the names you'll need to watch. I've already sent runners to meet us at O'Hare. You'll have support, but you'll also be tailed from the second we land."

I scanned the list. Four names jumped out: two witches, one vampire, and the demon rep—an ex-marine named Jones, of all things.

Bronc grunted. "We'll handle the pressure."

Rafe's eyes glinted. "You always do. But this time, make sure you leave something standing for the next generation. I'm tired of patching up the messes left behind."

He stood, stretched, and stalked back to the galley. Bronc watched him go, then let his head drop back against the seat.

"Think we've got a shot?" I asked quietly.

Bronc didn't hesitate. "We always have a shot. That's why they don't like the odds."

I grinned, wiped a hand over my mouth, and let my body finally relax.

Outside, the sun was starting to set, the world invisible. Inside, we were wolves among sheep, ready to tear out the heart of anyone who got between us and the people we loved.

I closed my eyes and sent a single, silent message to Savannah: Hold on.

We were coming.

CHAPTER 16

SAVANNAH

The meal sat on the lacquered table for hours before I forced myself to eat it. Cold roast and a slab of cheese, barely unwrapped by the servant who delivered it—he did not look at me, and I did not ask his name. Every movement of my jaw was a small betrayal; I ached to starve, to wither, to resist every shred of this charade, but hunger won out. I needed to heal. The burns on my wrists and ankles demanded protein, demanded salt and fluid. The body is a mercenary, and it always collects its debts.

I ate with my fingers, tearing the meat into stringy bites, chewing until my gums stung. I drank the mineral water straight from the bottle, tilting my head to swallow, ignoring the way the cut on my cheek opened a little with each movement. Blood tasted like metal and memory.

I had counted twelve hours since they stripped the silver from me. Ten of those had been spent here, in the room they called the Rose Suite, and if it weren't for the welts scoring my skin, I would have believed the name a joke. Even the air was sweet, perfumed by a hothouse arrangement at the foot of the bed, its pink blossoms lolling like tongues from cut-glass vases. The carpet was plum velvet, soft enough to bruise underfoot, and I left faint tracks each time I crossed the room. The walls were heavy with gilt moldings and painted angels, their downcast eyes fixed on my every movement. Even the drapes conspired against me, lined with blackout cloth so thick it turned the daytime sun to a pallid, false dusk.

I finished the meal in slow increments, counting each swallow as a victory. When the food was gone, I licked my fingers clean. I would leave nothing behind for them to measure. Every act, however small, would be on my terms.

Time limped by. At regular intervals, footsteps would pass my door—a soft tread, then a deliberate pause, a key rattling in the lock. I wasn't sure if the guards were meant to intimidate or to comfort, but they succeeded at neither. They were like insects, single-minded and relentless, and every time the sound faded I felt more alone. My only company was the memory of Menace's voice, sharp and certain, urging me to hold on.

I would have given anything to hear it for real, even if only in anger. My only solace was the brief moments I felt his love through our bond. It was so new we couldn't really send communication back and forth, only feelings. But anything was better than nothing. Traces of his presence touched me off and on as the traces of the silver they had bound me with left my body.

I had scoured every inch of the room. The windows were fixed, with no visible latches. The only means of egress was the door, a slab of polished walnut with a modern deadbolt and, I suspected, a reinforced steel core beneath the wood. There were no vents, no crawlspaces, no romantic fireplace for me to crawl through. Even the art on the walls had been nailed flush and tight. I traced the outlines of the hidden cameras: one in the corner, disguised as a smoke detector, another in the sconce above the writing desk.

They wanted to watch me. They wanted to see if I would break.

I stretched out on the bedspread, still dressed in the ruined blouse and black slacks from before. It took all my strength not to retch at the smell of myself: sweat, blood, the stink of fear. I pressed my face into the pillow and inhaled. It was clean, so clean it burned my nose with chlorine. I could not sleep. Every time I drifted, I snapped back awake to the vision of tomorrow—the Council chambers, the icy hands that would strip me bare, the ritual that would decide if I kept my mate or lost everything. I tried to picture Menace waiting for me at the threshold, but all I saw was Dominic's smile, wide and white and hungry.

I lost an hour, maybe two. The sky outside the blackout curtains slid from blue to yellow, and I stared at the line of light crawling up the far wall, a soft, jaundiced pulse. I watched it grow, watched the angle change, felt the minutes tick down to zero.

There was a bathroom attached to the suite, and I made use of it. The tiles were marble, cold and veined in blue. A tub sat on lion feet, wide enough to drown in. The mirror was ringed with small bulbs, every one lit, an interrogation in glass. I stripped off my blouse and stared at my torso, cataloguing the marks—four on each wrist, two on each ankle, a pattern of bruising like handprints around my upper arms, a swelling at the cheekbone where Callum's fist had landed. My neck was the worst. The mate mark had gone a sickly color, a bull's-eye of purple and red, angry and raised.

I felt nothing. Not shame, not fear. Just an inventory.

I turned on the water and let it run until it steamed. I poured the perfumed salts into the bath, not for pleasure, but for the antiseptic properties. I slid into the water and let the heat sear my nerves. I scrubbed every inch of myself with the harsh bar soap, dragging the rough side of the washcloth over each burn, each raw place. The pain was pure, and it brought me back from the edge of nothing.

I washed my hair three times, then ran a comb through the tangles, yanking out strands and letting them float in the bath. The water was pink when I finished. I drained it and watched the color spiral away. I brushed my teeth until the bleeding stopped, then rinsed my mouth with the miniature bottle of whiskey I found in the medicine cabinet. The burn was exquisite.

There were expensive lotions on the counter, so I used them to polish my dry skin until it shone. I clipped my nails, buffed them with the emery board, then ran polish over the ragged edges. I took advantage of every product they'd made available to me. After adding leave-in conditioner to my hair, I took the hairdryer and worked a round brush through my long, thick strands until it was dry and laid in soft, pretty waves. I wanted to see myself as someone they could not touch.

When I was finished, I stared at myself in the mirror. I looked like a corpse, but a beautiful one.

Back in the bedroom, I pulled on a fluffy bathrobe from the closet—a white, soft, impossibly plush thing. I tied it tight and lay on the bed, my hair spread out around me. I pulled the covers just over my legs and stared at the ceiling, waiting. For what, I wasn't entirely certain.

I was not afraid of dying. But I was scared to death of them removing Menace's mark from me. Of feeling the bond snap and leaving me hollow. I was afraid of becoming a thing for Dominic to parade, a trophy. But most of all, I was afraid that my father would see the power of the Council break me with bureaucratic precision, that he would win.

I repeated my promise from the night before. I would not let them see me bow.

I rehearsed my answers. Thought of every possible way the hearing might unfold. If they asked, I would tell them everything: the pain, the blood, the way Menace's hands felt on my hips, the sound he made when he came inside me. I would say it all, loud and clear, and let them choke on their rules. I would tell them I'd never known love until Bridger Hardin showed it to me. They would understand that I knew the moment he rescued me from that underground lab, the Goddess told me, not with words, but with an undeniable feeling, that this man, this *good* man, was my mate that she had chosen specifically for me.

I would not let them win. Even if I lost everything, I would go down unbroken.

I closed my eyes just to rest for a few minutes. I kept thinking of how I had to be strong, how I would not break. I would not bend.

I waited for sleep, not expecting it, but welcoming it as a reprieve. In the quiet, the bond flickered—distant, faint, but still there. I sent a message down the line, not in words but in pure feeling.

Hold on. I am holding.

Let them come. I would be ready.

Sleep came in intervals, like drowning under ice. First, the numbing weight, then a gasp, then the world receding behind a pane of frost. I drifted, then I plunged.

Then there were hands. Menace's hands, rough and sure, calloused from years of living and killing. They closed over my wrists, gentler than I remembered, and lifted me from the sheets. His voice followed—a low vibration, not words, but the echo of my own longing. I felt him behind me as he stood me up, his hands on my waist, solid and alive, radiating the scent I could never mistake. Cedarwood, night air, wolf, and the iron taste of blood that lingered from our first kiss.

"Red," he said, mouth against my neck, tongue tracing the edge of my mate mark. "You miss me?"

I shuddered, the dream-logic making every nerve raw. "Always."

He spun me around and pressed me to the wall, his body pinning me in place. My robe parted, the sash untied and fell away, the white pile sliding off my shoulders like a surrender flag. I was bare except for the bruises, which he kissed one by one, lips slow and reverent.

He moved lower. His mouth on my chest, his tongue painting lines of heat over every place I'd ever been broken. "They can't have you," he said, fangs bared, biting down just enough to send a shock through my spine. "You're mine."

I nodded, not trusting my voice. He read it anyway.

Two fingers inside me, sudden and deep, and I gasped. He was merciless in the way I needed him to be. The rest of the world—Dominic, my father, the Council—faded to fog. Only Menace was real, the outline of his body against mine, the rhythm he set with his hands and his hips.

He twisted his fingers, thumb grinding circles against my clit, and I bucked hard against him. "Easy," he murmured. "Fuck, always so wet for me. Always so ready for me. But you're gonna be a good girl and take what I give you."

He drew it out, teasing, then he pulled his hand away and shoved me to the bed. I landed on my stomach; the impact muffled by the sheets. In the dream, I was strong, unbroken; my body obeyed. I spread my knees, arching my back, and he took his place behind me, hands bruising my hips as he pulled me up higher.

He entered me with one long thrust, no warning. The feeling was everything I'd missed—full, stretching, every inch a promise. He gripped my hair, yanking my head up. "Say it," he growled. "Say who you belong to."

"You," I said. I wanted to scream it. "Always you."

His hands reached under my arms and pulled me up until my back was pressed against his hot chest. His mouth was right next to my ear as he panted. "You're goddamn right it's me. They will not take you from me. Not now. *Not ever.*" His hand reached down and rubbed my clit as he pistoned into me from below. His body was incredible as my release was getting closer. "Come for me, Red."

I broke apart, moaning his name as he let go and pressed my head back down to the pillow.

He bent over me, the heat of his chest burning my back, his mouth covering my mate mark, teeth dragging over skin and scar. "You're not a prize, you're not a token. You're mine."

He fucked me harder, hips snapping against my ass, his cock filling me so deep I saw white. I clawed at the sheets, felt them tear under my fingers. He kept the pressure at my neck, never breaking contact, as if afraid I would vanish the moment he let go.

"Red," he rasped, and the sound was almost a plea. "Don't give up on me."

"I won't," I said, breathless. "Never."

His hand reached around, long fingers finding my clit again, and he timed every thrust to the pulse of his fingers. I was nothing but sensation, raw and desperate, the edges of my mind flickering black with each roll of his hips. His knot started to form, the thickening at the base of his cock swelled inside me, a feral pleasure that left me shaking.

He bit down on my mark, hard, and I came so violently it felt like dying. The orgasm snapped through me, a pulse of light and noise, and I sobbed his name into the bedding.

He rode me through it, hips steady, never relenting, never slowing. The knot locked us together, and I felt every twitch, every shudder. His cum filled me, hot and endless, and it was the only thing in the world that felt right.

When the tremors faded, he curled over me, arms bracing my body to his. "Don't let them win," he whispered. "Whatever happens, don't let them erase this."

Another voice invaded our moment. It wasn't right. Menace faded from my arms. I reached for him, clawed at his shoulders, desperate to hold on.

A new hand crashed down on my upper arm, fingers digging in hard enough to bruise. I jerked awake with a gasp, breath caught in my throat, heart pounding so loud it hurt.

The room was ice cold; the bedding twisted around my naked legs. I couldn't remember when I'd shed the robe, but it lay on the floor, the tie stretched out like a noose. Above me loomed Dominic, his face ashen with fury, mouth twisted in a smile that was all teeth.

"Quite the show," he sneered, gaze dropping to the mess between my thighs. "Even in your sleep, you're a whore for him."

The words hit like slaps, but they didn't cut as deep as I expected. I was still in the dream, still locked inside the feeling of Menace's arms. I rolled to my side, covering myself with the sheet, refusing to let Dominic see the tears that burned my eyes.

He grabbed my ankle, yanking me to the edge of the bed. "You're going to be presentable for the Council," he spat. "Get up."

I twisted free, digging my heel into his thigh. He grunted but held on, refusing to let me slip away.

I sat up, chin high, every muscle screaming in protest. "He. Is. My. True. Mate." I said, voice flat.

He laughed, a sound without warmth. "Not after this week. I'll have you branded, then I'll have you fucked. Properly. The way your father wanted."

I met his eyes. "You'll have a corpse before you have me."

He shrugged. "Not my problem." He let go of my leg, stepping back to appraise the damage. "Clean yourself up," he said, voice like acid. "The Council wants a good look at their little scandal."

He turned and left; the door slamming behind him. The lock clicked home.

I lay back on the mattress, body trembling, but I was not alone. I pressed my palm to the bite on my neck, feeling the echo of Menace's teeth in the wound. The mate mark was alive, hotter than the bruises, brighter than the rage.

I let myself feel it for a few seconds; the memory of the dream, the weight of his promise. Then I stood, wrapped the robe around my shoulders, and began to prepare. They would see me. They would see all of me.

But they would never erase what was real.

CHAPTER 17

MENACE

Morning in Chicago. I came awake with a mouthful of her name and a splitting, animal hunger that curled my body around itself like a shell. The room's cold air was a relief and a torment—sheets sodden, skin tacky, the sick-sweet ache of arousal already making an enemy of me before I'd even opened my eyes. The dream was fresh, as sharp as the night she first took my cock inside her, as merciless as the memory of her mouth on my throat. The kind of dream you couldn't shake, not with a century of cold showers. Not with a bullet to the skull.

I lay there a minute, chest heaving, the mate mark on my shoulder burning against the pillow like a live ember. Her scent was nowhere, but my brain made it up: honey and rosewater and blood, an intoxicant more potent than anything the King of the South could offer from his best-stocked bar. The wolf inside me howled and battered at the doors of my ribs, already hungry for the next kill. I rolled onto my back and stared at the ceiling, willing the urge to leave me, to give me half a breath before I had to be human again.

I could still taste her on my tongue, the ghost of salt and sweat, the sharp tang of her fear turning sweet under my hands. I licked my lips and let the memory play out. No sense in fighting the inevitability of it.

In the dream, I'd found her alone in a suite like this, wrapped in a white terrycloth robe that might as well have been nothing at all. The door was unlocked, and she was waiting—hair wild, skin flushed, eyes black with the same need that was currently eating holes through my self-control. I didn't speak, just took her face in my hands and kissed her so hard her lips split. She shuddered, arching into me, and the robe fell open to bare the bruised constellation of my fingerprints on her hips.

"Missed you," she'd said, barely a whisper, but the sound set my nerves vibrating like harp strings plucked to snapping.

I'd pressed her to the wall, hands everywhere at once—palming her breasts, her ass, the soft backs of her knees. She went liquid, clinging to my shoulders, her nails carving furrows down my spine. My cock was out and throbbing before I'd even gotten the sash untied; she reached for it, bold, greedy, as if she could anchor herself to reality by taking every inch of me into her body. I bit her neck—hard enough to bruise—and she moaned so loud it should've brought security. In the dream, nothing stopped us.

The wolf in me loved her best when she was reckless and willing, and in the dream, she always was. I spun her around and shoved her face-first to the bed, yanked her hips up and split her open with a single, brutal thrust. She took it, every inch, pushing back against me with a snarl of her own. My hands fisted in her hair, holding her steady as I pounded her into the mattress. I felt the way her body quaked around me, the electric snap of her coming hard, the wet heat of her cunt squeezing my cock. I came so fiercely it blacked out my vision, knot swelling inside her until there was no way to separate our bodies. Then I bent over her, teeth clamped on the mate mark I'd given her weeks before, and bit down until she screamed.

When I woke, I was hard and aching, the sheet damp from sweat and semen. I lay there for a minute, hating the world and everything in it, including myself, for not being able to bring her into this bed for real.

I didn't have time to wallow. Today was Council day, and if I wasn't careful, it would be my last.

I took a frigid shower, letting the icy scald and burn of the water beat some of the rage out of me. I dressed in a black suit—custom, one of many I owned—and cinched the tie until my neck throbbed with a different kind of need. The Glock sat heavy under my left arm, its weight more comforting than anything else this city had to offer. I checked the chamber and clicked the safety to "on" before sliding on the jacket.

My shoes were polished, my hair combed, but none of it felt like armor. Nothing did, not now. My wolf paced inside me, fur bristling, lips peeled back from its fangs. He wanted blood. He wanted her.

The ride in the elevator was slow torture. Each floor was an eternity. The smell of fresh-cut flowers filled my nostrils. I wanted to rip through my suit, shift on the marble and paint the city red with the blood of every bastard who'd ever tried to take Savannah from me.

But I didn't. I waited, just like I'd been trained. Just like Bronc would want.

Juliet was in the foyer, dressed for war. She wore a dark blue suit, tailored to fit her curves, hair pulled back in a severe twist that made her eyes look even more lethal. She had a pistol holstered at her hip under her blazer, and I knew from experience she'd learned to draw and fire before most men could blink. Bronc stood beside her, hands in his pockets, gaze on the front double doors. His presence reflected a gravity that made people avoid looking at him, stepping wide, even if they didn't know why. The mate mark on his neck had faded to a silvery scar, but I could see the energy it radiated, the way he drew strength from Juliet simply by standing close.

King Rafe joined us, all six feet four inches of him, looming in a suit that cost more than my first car. His beard was trimmed, his eyes bloodshot but steady. He took one look at me and grinned.

"Didn't sleep, huh?" he said.

"Didn't need to," I replied, voice flat.

He laughed, genuine. "Well, let's go see how much of a show the Council wants."

We piled into a black SUV waiting at the curb. The driver—some dead-eyed wolf in a cheap suit—never looked at any of us, just pulled into traffic and followed the GPS like it was a suicide note. The streets were gray and wet, last night's rain leaving everything shiny and raw. The city was awake but not alive, pedestrians marching to work like soldiers to the front. Every so often, we'd pass a patrol car or a private security van, and Bronc's eyes would track them in the rearview until they vanished.

The Council headquarters was a monolith where the city met the countryside: twelve stories of black stone, windowless except for slits near the top, fronted by a line of marble pillars carved with runes and glyphs so old they might as well have been bones. It wasn't built to welcome anyone. It was built to remind you of all the things you weren't.

At the top of the steps, a pair of guards waited—one a vampire, skin so pale it looked like tissue paper stretched over steel, the other a demon, eyes ringed with molten orange. Both wore identical suits, identical earpieces. As we climbed the stairs, the demon's nostrils flared, catching my scent. His face twitched, the hint of a grin, and I fought the urge to show my teeth.

Inside, the air was colder than outside. The lobby ceiling soared three stories above our heads, a ribcage of exposed beams and more carved stone. Every surface was polished to a mirror, but nothing reflected true. The scents here were chaos: old blood, ozone, witch magic, sweat, and under it all, the faintest trace of roses and honey. My wolf lunged for the source, snapping at the leash, and I had to lock my knees to keep from running.

We approached the security checkpoint, a long row of glass barriers manned by yet more guards. They took our weapons—reluctantly, on my part—and scanned us with handheld wands.

Juliet set off the alarm, and the guard ran the scanner up and down her leg before letting her through.

"Nice ink," he said, nodding at her mate mark.

She smiled, predatory. "You'd look better with one yourself."

Bronc smothered a laugh as we stepped into the next corridor. The hallways narrowed, growing darker, the air thick with anticipation and something else—fear, maybe. I could hear voices behind closed doors, the murmur of arguments and deals being struck in every tongue known to man or wolf.

At last, we entered the antechamber. The walls here were plain white; the floors black marble veined with gold. A long table stood at the far end, flanked by two chairs. Another guard—this one a wolf, brown-haired and musclebound—motioned for us to wait. Rafe dropped into one chair, Bronc into the other. Juliet leaned against the wall, arms crossed, watching the room like she expected it to come alive and eat us.

I paced. Back and forth, across the length of the chamber, nails digging into my palms with every step. I could smell Savannah now, her scent leaking through the walls, so close I could almost taste her on the air. My mate mark throbbed in time with my pulse.

"You're gonna wear a groove in the floor, Menace," Bronc said, voice gentle as he could manage.

"Fuck the floor," I replied, not stopping.

Juliet came up beside me. "We'll see her soon. Just hang on."

"I am hanging on," I said. "But if they make me wait another fucking hour—"

"They won't," she interrupted, and I could see the fear in her eyes even as she tried to cover it. She squeezed my arm, strong enough to hurt. "She's stronger than you think."

"Not worried about her," I lied. "I'm worried about me."

She grinned, just a flash of teeth. "You always are."

The waiting was the worst. Every second was a war between what I wanted and what I was allowed. The wolf in me was winning, but for now, I could keep him chained.

The clock on the wall ticked down the minutes. When the guard finally returned and called our names, I was already moving, unable to keep the hunger out of my eyes.

"Ready?" Bronc asked, standing tall, a hand on my shoulder.

"More than," I said. "Let's get this done."

We walked the corridor together, a small army of wolves and their allies, ready to face whatever monsters the Council put in our path.

But nothing they had was scarier than what I'd do if they kept me from my mate.

We followed the guard down a corridor so long and narrow it felt like being funneled into the barrel of a rifle. The walls were bare, no windows, no distractions—just the silence and the echo of our boots. At the end, a steel door slid open with a pneumatic hiss, and a witch waited on the other side.

She was ancient, but only in the way that mattered: not in the sags of flesh, but in the patient, predatory calm of her eyes. Her hair was black streaked with silver, slicked back in a wave that accentuated her sharp cheekbones. She wore a tailored coat, dark purple, with black gloves and boots to match. Her gaze pinned us to the threshold like specimens, and when she spoke, her accent was clipped and transnational—European, but diluted by centuries of careful affect.

"I am Madame Verna," she said, eyes lingering on me a second too long. "You are the wolf known as Menace."

It wasn't a question. "Bridger Hardin," I replied. My voice came out rawer than I meant.

She nodded, lips twitching into something that might have been a smile. "Come in."

The room was an interrogation suite, dressed up as a conference chamber. Table in the center, two chairs on either side, mirror glass on the wall behind her. Another guard—witch, this one, with runes inked along her collarbone—stood in the corner, eyes down but ears open. Bronc and Juliet took seats, but I couldn't sit. I paced the perimeter, trying to look at everything at once, trying to sniff out a trap.

Verna didn't bother with pleasantries. "The Council wishes to confirm the legitimacy of your fated bond," she said. "For the record, please state how long you have known Savannah Calloway."

I snorted. "Six weeks, give or take."

She wrote this down with a fountain pen. "And when did you first suspect she was your mate?"

"First moment I saw her," I said. "She was chained up in a cell, starved, bleeding. My wolf recognized hers before she even looked at me."

Verna looked at me over the rim of her glasses. "And you, as a soldier, believe you can trust the instincts of a beast?"

"It's not instinct," I said. "It's chemical. It's fucking gravity. I walked into the room, and my bones started rearranging themselves just to get closer to her. You think I wanted this?"

She smiled, not unkind. "You would be surprised how many do." She set her pen down and folded her hands. "Describe what happened next."

I shrugged. "I broke the locks, got her out. Carried her through the tunnels. She was hallucinating, almost feral, scared shitless. I had to talk her down, let her smell me. I think she hated me at first, or at least the idea of me. But my wolf wouldn't let go. She had so much she was dealing with. PTSD. She'd already been on the run, but that's her story to tell. I took care of her after I saved her. She was so lost. Scared. I went slow as I could. Had to see if she realized. She did."

Juliet made a small, involuntary noise—a sound of recognition or empathy. Verna ignored it.

"And you marked her?" Verna prompted.

I nodded. "After I made sure she was sure. She said yes. She wanted it. Told me she wanted it more than anything in her life."

Verna raised an eyebrow. "And you believe this is a genuine bond, not the result of trauma or coercion?"

I stopped pacing and leaned over the table. "You ever see a wolf try to mark an unwilling mate? You'd have a corpse, not a couple."

She accepted this without a blink. "I must ask these things. Council requires it."

I sat finally, but only because the urge to throttle someone was fading into exhaustion. "Ask what you need," I said. "But I'm not leaving here without her."

Verna considered me for a long moment, then looked to Bronc and Rafe. "Will you support the claim as witnesses?"

Bronc's voice was calm, but I could see the line of tension at his jaw. "He's telling the truth. I saw it with my own eyes. If you want, you can interview my Luna. She was there for most of it."

Verna glanced at Juliet, who nodded once, sharp as a blade.

"Very well." She reached into a drawer and withdrew a velvet-lined tray. On it sat two glass vials, one empty, one filled with a viscous blue liquid that shimmered in the overhead lights. "The process is simple. Blood from both parties is mixed with a reagent. If the bond is true, it turns gold. If not, it goes black." She said it with a small shrug, as if centuries of heartbreak were none of her business.

I held out my arm before she even asked. She swabbed the crook of my elbow, drew a syringe of blood with clinical speed, and sealed it in a vial. "Thank you," she murmured.

"Now, Savannah," I said, voice gone hoarse.

"Not yet. There are two more tests," she said. "First, the resonance artifact." She set a crystal sphere the size of a billiard ball on the table. "Your mate will hold a matching sphere. If your bond is genuine, they will react."

"What if she's too weak?" I asked. "She was in silver for days. You know what that does."

Verna smiled, but it was sad. "If the bond is real, she could be dead and it would still work."

I believed her. I gripped the sphere. It was cool and rough, but nothing happened.

"We must wait until Savannah is holding the other," Verna said, and wrote something else on her pad.

I barely heard her. My focus was down the corridor, through the walls, hunting for any hint of my mate. Nothing yet.

"What's the third test?" Bronc asked.

Verna looked at him, then at me. "You are both shifters. When together, your auras should synchronize—your heart-beats, your pheromones, even your biochemistry. We have tools to measure this. If the readings do not match, the Council will know."

I bristled, feeling the wolf surge. "I'm ready. Just get her in here."

She made a small note, then stood. "It will take thirty minutes to process your blood. I will fetch your mate then. Please wait."

I couldn't stand it. "Wait? I've waited days. I want to see her now."

She shrugged. "You are welcome to try the door, but the guards are not as polite as I am."

For a second, I weighed the odds. But Bronc's hand closed around my shoulder, an anchor that kept me from doing something stupid.

"It'll be all right," he murmured, low and meant only for me. "You'll see her soon."

I nodded, but it was all I could do not to rip the table in half.

Verna left. The guard with the runes never moved, but I could feel her watching, her power crawling along the baseboards like frost.

Juliet leaned in, her tone urgent. "You have to keep it together, Menace. They want to see if you'll lose control. Don't give them the satisfaction."

"Why do they care?" I snarled. "It's not like I'm going to turn this into a bloodbath."

"They need to know you can control yourself around her," she said. "Otherwise, they'll say the bond is a liability."

I shook my head, furious. "Every bond is a liability. That's the whole point."

Bronc gave a dry laugh. "Council logic, Menace. Just play along for now."

I did, but it nearly broke me.

When Verna returned, she was carrying a new tray—this one with two spheres. She set them on the table, then nodded to the guard in the corner.

"Bring her," she said.

My heart stuttered in my chest. My wolf reared up, ears forward, hackles high.

Juliet reached for my hand. I didn't let her touch me, but she understood.

It took ten more minutes. Each one was a year. When the door finally opened, the scent hit me before anything else—roses and honey, but also fear and sweat and the metallic note of dried blood. I stood unable to help myself, fists clenched so tight the knuckles went bone white.

They brought Savannah in.

But she was still a room away.

I could see her through the glass, hear her voice through the intercom, but the wall might as well have been a thousand miles thick.

Verna gestured to the spheres. "Now," she said, and Savannah reached for hers.

The world went white.

The sphere in my hand lit up, a blinding gold that swallowed the entire room. I heard Bronc swear, heard Juliet gasp, but all I saw was Savannah—her eyes wide and wet, a bruise blooming on her jaw, a smile trying to push through the pain. The spheres pulsed together, faster and faster, until it hurt to look.

Verna nodded, satisfied. "You may put it down."

I did, and in that instant the light vanished. I was cold and empty without it.

Savannah's voice came through the intercom. "Menace?"

I tried to answer, but my throat locked up.

Verna spoke into the mic. "He is here. The bond is strong."

Savannah smiled, small but real. "I know."

The glass wall stayed up. No one moved.

"Can I see her?" I asked, my voice shattering on the last word.

"Not yet," Verna said, soft. "There is still the final test."

And then she left, and I was alone again, pacing the edges of the room while my mate's shadow waited just out of reach.

Chapter 18

Menace

I wore a path in the marble. The room felt smaller every minute, air thickening, gravity pushing down harder than any cell I'd ever known. My wolf pressed at the seams of my skin. My hands shook. My teeth ached.

Verna returned with a tray that contained two vials of blood and a stack of paperwork an inch thick. She set them down without a word, then motioned to the guard in the corner. The witch approached, face blank. I felt the way Savannah's blood, in its own glass tube, waited next to mine, like a reunion in miniature. I kept my eyes on it, hypnotized by the swirl of her cells against the glass.

Verna poured a few drops from each vial into a porcelain dish, then added a single drop of the blue potion. Nothing happened for a heartbeat.

Then everything did.

The mixture flashed gold, so bright it threw shadows on the far wall. The witches stepped back, shielding their faces from the glare. The light built, pulsing, until I thought it might explode.

Then, just as quickly, it faded, leaving only the residue of gold at the bottom of the dish. Verna smiled for real this time.

"That's confirmation one," she said. "You may relax."

"I'm not sure that's possible," I said, forcing a laugh.

She gestured to the next chair. "Please sit. This is the resonance test. It can be...unpleasant."

I obeyed, planting my feet wide, gripping the armrests like they might sprout fangs. The rune witch painted sigils onto my forearms and neck with a brush dipped in what smelled like paint thinner and cloves. The marks sizzled against my skin, cold at first, then so hot I thought they'd peel me alive.

"Ready," I said, though I wasn't.

Verna nodded to the mirror. I saw a reflection flicker, then Savannah's face on the other side of the glass. She was strapped down too, painted with the same runes, her eyes huge and shining in the fluorescent light. My wolf went ballistic, jaws snapping, body straining against the skin that held him in.

Verna placed a crystal disk in my right hand, another in Savannah's. "On my count," she said, "squeeze."

I squeezed. At the same instant, so did Savannah.

The disks vibrated. My entire arm went numb. The room melted away, replaced by a tunnel of sound and sensation—her pulse, her breath, the sound of her voice in my ear. I saw flashes: her face in the moonlight, her hands tangled in my hair, the blood on her lips when she bit me back. Every memory we'd ever made together, flooding me at once.

I saw her chained up the first day. I saw myself carrying her through the rain. I felt the echo of every time I'd fucked her, every orgasm, every whimper, every moan. My cock went hard in my pants, obscene and out of place, but I couldn't stop it. I felt her own arousal, the way she craved my touch, my mouth, my teeth. I felt her fear, too: the silver, the pain, the terror of losing me.

All of it. All at once.

When the vision broke, I was gasping for air, head swimming. The disk in my hand was shattered, splinters of glass driven deep into my palm. I didn't care.

On the other side of the glass, Savannah was crying, but she looked better than she had when she came in. Alive. Alert.

Verna made a note on her pad. "Perfect resonance," she said. "Textbook."

I stared at her, teeth bared. "Let me see her."

She shook her head, almost gentle. "One more test."

I almost killed her. But I sat, and I waited.

The final test was a scan. Verna and the rune witch wrapped an elastic cap around my scalp, each node stitched with what looked like gold thread. I felt nothing, but when they activated the machine, the world started to spin.

"Close your eyes," Verna said. "Picture her."

I did. I pictured Savannah in my arms, her scent in my nose, the feel of her cunt tightening around my cock, the way she called me "Menace" with a tremor of love and awe. I pictured her laughing, I pictured her crying, I pictured her shifting into her wolf and running through the grass at my side.

The machine beeped and then shrieked. On the monitor, a series of jagged lines rose and fell, every one in sync with my heartbeat.

A second monitor displayed a 3D model of my body, luminous threads extending from my heart, my spine, my brain—all of them arcing through the glass, straight to Savannah. The threads pulsed gold, thicker and brighter with every second.

Verna shut off the machine. The room went silent.

"There is no doubt," she said, voice almost reverent. "The bond is genuine. Fated."

The wolf in me howled. "Then let me see her."

She hesitated. "The Council has not yet—"

I don't remember what happened next.

One moment I was sitting; the next I was standing, the chair splintered to kindling beneath me. I flipped the table, sending paperwork and trays flying. The rune witch tried to back away, but I caught her by the arm and slammed her into the wall so hard the mirror fractured. Bronc was on me in an instant, arms around my chest, dragging me backwards. Juliet tried to grab my wrist, but I shook her off, teeth snapping, vision tunneling to red.

"You don't get it," I screamed, voice raw and bestial. "You don't fucking get it! She's mine! You're keeping her from me! You're doing this on purpose!"

Verna stood her ground, calm as a corpse. "I do understand. That is why we test. If you cannot control yourself, the bond is a danger."

"Better a danger than a fucking corpse," I spat, but Bronc tightened his grip, his own Alpha voice crackling with power.

"Stand. Down," he ordered, and for a second I hated him, but the command drilled straight through my skull.

I dropped the witch, hands shaking so bad I thought my bones would snap. I hit the floor, panting, every muscle on fire.

Juliet knelt beside me, whispering something I couldn't hear. My mind was gone, taken over by the need to get to Savannah, to touch her, to make sure she was alive.

Verna nodded, scribbling another note. "We are finished. The Council will review. If they are satisfied, you may have her back by sundown."

I glared at her through the blur. "If you don't, I will burn this building down."

She nodded, as if that was only right.

When they dragged me out, Bronc and Juliet on either side, I kept my eyes on the broken glass of the mirror. I could see Savannah there, still strapped to her chair, watching me with the same feral hunger in her eyes.

I knew we'd make it. Or we'd die trying.

They stuck us in a waiting room with no windows, no clock, and no idea how much time had passed. Juliet prowled the perimeter like a caged panther, high heels echoing with every step. Bronc sat rigid in a plastic chair, fists balled, his entire body one knotted muscle of restraint. King Rafe worked the phone, murmuring into it in a low, measured cadence that radiated threat.

Me, I just stared at the carpet and tried not to explode.

Every ten minutes, a new guard checked in. Sometimes a wolf, sometimes a witch. None of them met my eyes. None of them stayed more than a minute.

Juliet finally stopped pacing, spun on her heel, and fixed the nearest guard with a glare that would have vaporized a lesser man. "Get me a Council rep. Now. I have rights, and I intend to exercise them."

He looked confused, then left.

Bronc exhaled, slow and ragged. "You sure you want to do this here, Jules?"

She looked at him like he was a particularly dim lab rat. "If they think they can keep one of my pack from me, they're wrong."

Rafe covered the receiver, eyebrows raised. "They're stonewalling, but if you push, it'll make them nervous. Might even get us leverage."

"Leverage isn't what I want," Juliet said, voice ice-edged. "I want Savannah. I want her now."

The guard returned, trailed by a Council official: tall, brittle woman in a slate-gray suit, carrying a clipboard and an air of terminal impatience.

"Juliet Baucaum, Luna of Iron Valor?" she said, reading the name without looking up.

"That's me," Juliet said, arms crossed.

"You are aware that under Council code 7.11.3, you are subordinate to this office in all matters relating to—"

"Bullshit," Juliet snapped. "Iron Valor is a free pack, recognized by the Southern King. My mate and I have jurisdiction over all members, wherever they are. That includes Savannah."

The woman's eyes flicked up, surprised. "This is a Council hearing, not a pack run."

"Doesn't matter," Juliet snapped. "Pack law comes first. I am her Luna. You can't keep her from me."

Bronc backed her, voice a growl. "You want a war, you'll get one."

The councilwoman retreated. Juliet looked at Bronc, lips pressed so tight they went white. "They're stalling."

I could feel Savannah's fear through the bond, a spike of cold adrenaline that left me breathless. I squeezed my eyes shut, fighting the urge to shift right there in the chair. My claws punched through the fabric of the armrest. I gripped harder, tearing it to shreds.

"She's scared," I said. "Terrified."

Bronc tried to calm me, but it was no use. My body was changing—bones flexing, muscles bunching, fur prickling at my wrists and neck. Juliet knelt in front of me, hands on my face.

"Stay with me," she whispered. "Just a little longer."

I tried. I really did.

The door opened again, and this time, four guards entered, all armed. Two had silver batons. The air went metallic and hot.

"Don't," Bronc warned, but I was past hearing. The wolf in me wanted out.

Then the temperature in the room dropped by twenty degrees. The fluorescent lights flickered, then went dead. For a second, all was dark—until a new scent cut through the fear.

Vampire.

The doors slammed open, and in swept the Kozlovs.

King Kazimir was an iceberg in a suit, pale as moonlight, his black hair slicked back and his eyes cold, flat disks. He brought with him a wall of air so frigid it hurt to breathe. Beside him, Lucia floated—long black curls, lips painted red, skin like alabaster. Her heels made no sound. The four guards who'd come to subdue us froze in their tracks, like mice in the path of a snake.

Kazimir spoke first, in English, hint of a Russian accent, but so precise it sounded like it had been filed to a razor. "What is the meaning of this? Why is my presence required, and yet my friends are locked away like criminals?"

No one answered.

He let the silence stretch. "Princess Savannah Calloway is under my protection, as is the Luna of Iron Valor. Any who threatens *them* threatens *me*."

The Council official stammered. "Sir, there are procedures—"

He cut her off with a glance. "I know your procedures. I have written half of them."

He looked at me, then at Juliet. "You wish to see the girl?"

Juliet's voice trembled, but she did not look away. "Yes. Now."

Lucia stepped forward, her smile all teeth. "If you do not, I will start killing from the bottom up. Council will not like the headlines. You understand?"

The woman in the gray suit swallowed, hard. "Give me five minutes."

She fled. The guards melted away with her.

Rafe put away his phone and smiled. "Never gets old watching you work, Kazimir."

The vampire shrugged. "Council is made of old men. They fear only what is older."

He looked at me, and something passed between us—a moment of respect, or warning. "Your mate is strong," he said. "But she will not survive this if you do not hold yourself together. Do you understand?"

I nodded, unable to speak.

Lucia hovered near Juliet, hands gentle as she checked for wounds. "You are safe," she said, voice syrup-thick. "But you must be calm for Savannah. She needs you."

I tried. For her, I'd try anything.

The councilwoman returned, eyes wide. "They'll see you now. All of you."

The room moved at once, a single organism. We followed her down another corridor, this one lined with gold-framed portraits of monsters in human dress. At the end, another steel door.

Beyond it: the royal chamber.

And Savannah, closer than ever. I could feel her, her heartbeat tangled with mine.

We were almost there.

The royal chamber was all theater and threat: marble floors, gilded chairs, twelve thrones fanned out in a half-moon like the jaws of some ancient beast. The ceiling soared up into blackness, lost in shadow, as if the Council wanted every guest to feel the weight of oblivion above them. Seated or standing behind each throne were the representatives of every territory and supernatural house—wolves, witches, vamps, even a demon or two, and majestic angels, their eyes like diamonds in the dimness.

Savannah's father, Declan Calloway, sat at the center, king's medallion at his throat, his eyes cold and glittering with malice. Next to him lounged King Dominic, the intended, arrogant as ever, one foot propped on a low table, his fingers drumming on the armrest as if the entire world was just waiting for him to order a round of drinks.

They both smiled when we entered, two apex predators who thought themselves unchallenged.

We walked down the aisle together, Rafe up front, Kozlovs at his flank, Bronc and Juliet on either side of me. My wolf howled, desperate to break free, but I held the leash until my nails dug deep into my palms, drawing blood.

The Council Chairwoman, a witch with paper-white skin and a smile like a paper cut, called the meeting to order. "Let the record show the parties are present. King Rafe Mayfield, King Kazimir Kozlov, Alpha Baucaum and Luna. And..." Her gaze flicked to me, then to the thrones. "Bridger Hardin, mate to the disputed subject. Where is she?"

Dominic's smile widened. "She's being prepared for the test, per protocol."

Lucia cut in, voice cold as ice. "She's being kept from her mate, you mean."

Kazimir spoke next, his accent slicing the air. "Council is in violation. You allow King Dominic access, but not her true mate. This is not tradition. This is torture."

The room rippled with unease. Witches exchanged glances, the vamps bared their teeth in amusement, and Declan's lips tightened, a small tick betraying his anger.

Lucia stepped forward, her presence filling the chamber. "Savannah has been beaten. Starved. Forced into silver. There are witnesses. There are photographs." She flicked a stack of printed images onto the table. They scattered across the marble, each one a still life of pain: Savannah's wrists flayed by silver cuffs, her face swollen, bite marks ringed in purple.

For a moment, there was silence.

Then Rafe spoke, his voice slow and certain. "We demand emergency arbitration. If the Council cannot guarantee her safety, we'll take it to the Assembly of Kings."

The Chairwoman hesitated, then nodded. "Very well. Bring her in."

I felt her coming before the doors even opened—a wave of panic, then hope, then a pain so sharp it nearly split me in half. My bones stretched, fur itched at my scalp, and my jaw ached to crack open and howl. Bronc set a hand on my shoulder, grounding me, but I barely felt it.

The doors swung wide. Savannah stood there, flanked by two guards. She wore a plain white shift, her hair loose, her face pale but defiant. When she saw me, she broke. Just for a second. Then she squared her shoulders and walked down the aisle, never looking away.

She stopped ten feet away. The Chairwoman gestured for her to take a seat. Savannah took it, eyes locked on mine.

"State your name for the record," the witch said.

"Savannah Calloway," she replied, voice so steady it made me want to cry.

"Is it true you are mated to Bridger Hardin?"

"Yes," she said.

"Is it true you were promised to King Dominic?"

Savannah's voice trembled, just a fraction. "Not by choice."

The Chairwoman nodded. "Have you been coerced?"

Savannah's eyes slid to her father, then to Dominic. She hesitated. "Yes," she said, barely audible. "I was forced. They threatened my family. They threatened to kill him."

Dominic laughed, low and ugly. "She's a liar. She ran away from her birthright. This is all an act."

"Enough," Rafe said, and the chamber went still.

The Chairwoman looked at Declan. "Do you dispute the mate bond?"

Declan's voice was ice. "It's impossible. She did not seek my approval. There was no contract. No Council witness."

Lucia laughed, a sound like glass breaking. "You care for contracts, but not your daughter's life?"

Kazimir said, "The bond is proven. Let them be together. End this farce."

The Chairwoman shuffled papers. "It will take a vote."

But the room had already decided. The other royals murmured, not in English, but the intent was clear: this had gone too far. Even the witches looked ashamed.

Bronc leaned in and whispered, "Go to her, Menace. Now."

I didn't walk. I ran.

The guards moved to block me, but the Chairwoman snapped, "Let him pass."

I dropped to my knees in front of Savannah, hands shaking as I reached for her. She gripped me back, knuckles white, her scent flooding every sense. My wolf settled, finally. The world went quiet.

Behind me, the chamber erupted in shouts and arguments and the mad scramble of a hundred old wounds opening at once. But for a few heartbeats, nothing mattered but the woman in my arms.

She pressed her forehead to mine. "Don't let them take me."

I kissed her, gentle as I could, but my hands were bruising her arms, refusing to let go. "They won't," I said, and meant it.

For the first time since this nightmare started, I believed it.

The Chairwoman spoke again. "The Council members will be given the test results. Study them well. Take them to your respective leaders for consultation and we will reconvene in 48 hours for a vote on the matter. Mr. Hardin, Miss Calloway, you will be provided with an apartment here in the Council tower. I strongly advise you not to leave the confines of the building. Alpha Baucaum, you and your Luna will also be provided an apartment. You will all be on the same level as your king." King Rafe looked at me and nodded.

I helped Savannah out of the chair, and we both bowed our heads in reverence to the Chairwoman.

Chapter 19

King Declan Calloway

Night in the Council Tower had its own peculiar geometry. The world above and below fell away, replaced by stone, shadow, and the reek of ancient ambition. My boots found no purchase on the ice-polished marble, only left a fleeting print in the candlelight before the air ate it whole. I stalked the hallways without urgency, a wolf with no need to hurry, because in the end they would all come to me.

The echo of my gait was the only company. No guards, not tonight; the Council had learned better than to tail me after sundown. Even the servants scurried with averted eyes. I let the cold seep in, let it congeal around the bones, because warmth was a weakness in a den of predators. The doors here were heavy, forged from a black wood found nowhere on earth, lacquered so thick it repelled even magic. Each had a sigil, a scent: sulfur for the demons, rosewater for the vamps, burnt honey for the southern wolves. Mine had no marker but the blank, silent threat of absence.

I paused only once, to brush a speck of dust from the brass nameplate that bore my own crest: Calloway, King of the Eastern Territories. It gleamed like a blood clot in the flicker of gaslight. I let my fingers linger, as if by contact I could assure the old bastard inside that nothing had changed. That the world still belonged to those strong enough to seize it.

Inside, the room was a study in discipline. Not a book out of place, not a single chair left unpushed. The carpets were crimson, but only because red did not show the stains. I moved to the window and poured myself a finger of whiskey from the decanter—a habit from a grandfather I'd despised but had become, in some twisted sense, the closest thing I had to God. The liquor caught the moonlight, turned it to amber, and I watched it shudder in the crystal before bringing it to my lips.

The roster was on my desk, bound in rawhide and sealed with three separate chains. The first was symbolic, the second practical, the third a formality. I snapped them all with one hand and let the parchment fan out. Each name was inked in a different hand, a parade of egos and titles so bloated it was a miracle any decision ever passed. But I knew the secret: with the right leverage, the rest followed like sheep to slaughter.

Five votes. That was the game.

Five would tip the balance, enough to override the goddamn charade they called a "fated mate bond." Even after the spectacle that had just played out in the main chamber—my own daughter, blood of my blood, testifying like a common whore that she wanted the wolf who had marked her—I still had options. The evidence was damning, but evidence was only as strong as the hands that wielded it.

I let my gaze fall to the first name on the list:

Shasta Tierney, High Flame Caller of the Emberthorn Witches. Her obsession with tradition was so severe she'd once had her own sister executed for a breach of ritual. She wore purity like a badge, but I knew the rot in her line. She was already on my side; she just needed to be reminded what she risked if her coven ever fell out of favor with the East; a sure thing for the final push.

Next: The Mistress of Shadows, whose real name was buried deeper than the bones of her enemies. A creature of appetites and secrets, she held power over the Gloamreach covens. I knew her weakness—her "daughter," a changeling she'd raised in secret, kept off the Council's census, a crime so flagrant it was a wonder she'd lasted this long. I had the documentation. I had the leverage. I would enjoy watching her squirm.

Then, Wyrdmother Elaina of the Verdant Hollow. A tree-witch, old enough that she remembered when men still believed in gods. She owed me, though she would never admit it. Years ago, when the Southern packs tried to root her coven out, I'd arranged a stay of execution—a single phone call, a single bullet. She would repay me, or she would find herself with a new generation of enemies.

Maltraz, King of the Demons. An utter brute, but practical to a fault. He cared nothing for the politics of mating, only for the balance of power and the contracts that kept his kind from being exterminated. I had promised him a corridor through my territory, a lifeline for his lesser imps. All he had to do was show up for the vote, grunt "no," and enjoy the next century of safe passage. Easy.

Finally, Varic Otero, the vampire king of the Western Territories. This one was trickier. He'd only recently taken the throne after the previous king's "suicide," which I'd arranged with a little help from my friends in Low Town. Otero wanted legitimacy, wanted to be the ruler history remembered. I could offer it, but I would make him crawl for it. He'd oppose the bond, just to cement his own position. He'd hate me for it, but I'd outlive his hate.

My hands shook as I ticked the names, not from fear but from the violence of what was coming. I poured another whiskey. The glass hit the desk with a clink, and I watched a droplet slide down to the surface, stain the roster, then vanish into the grain. I thought of Savannah, her face pale but resolute, the flash of her mother in her jawline. How had I missed it? How had I allowed her to become a liability, a fracture in the line?

I'd seen it coming, of course. The way she'd clung to her music, that insipid fixation on being "happy" when she should have been preparing for her role. The late-night phone calls, the refusal to do as she was told. The fucking piano recitals. Her mother enabled it, pretended not to notice the scent of rebellion that hung over every word. And when she ran and hid. Of course, she wound up in a prison being treated to torture and who knows what else in that lab in the jungle. The thought of it makes me smile. If ever there was an irony, that was it. Except that fucking mutt had to be the one to find her and secret her away. And she'd taken joy in rubbing my face in her rebellion.

Tomorrow, I would begin. Shasta first, then Mistress of Shadows. One by one, I would tighten the noose. I would not sleep until every name on the list owed me a vote, a debt, or a life.

Five votes. Five names. That was all it would take.

I turned back to the window and watched the city tremble under the moon; the towers jutting up like the ribs of some ancient beast. I could hear the howls from the lower wards, the laughter of the damned, and in it, a single thread of music: the sound of my daughter's will, trembling but unbroken.

Let her play her final note. Tomorrow, I'd bring the house down.

Emberthorn lay east of the Council tower, beyond the railroad yards and the salt flats where nothing grew but thornbrush and the bones of animals too dumb to escape the border wards. Even at a distance, you could see its spires: a crown of fused stone and living flame, jagged against the dusk like the teeth of a dead god. The witches had built it as both fortress and cathedral, a place where every wall doubled as a ward, every parapet a pulpit.

I arrived on foot, as custom demanded. Wolves were forbidden to approach in car, bike, or beast form—anyone who tried ended up a pile of smoking ash, and the witches kept the skulls nailed to the outer gates as a warning. I wore my best suit, black silk tailored to hide the bulk, with a single red thread at the collar as a sign of mourning. Even if Shasta didn't notice, the junior priestesses who manned the doors would; it was always the little things that got you killed or crowned in the end.

The walk to the main altar took me through the passage of cinders, a corridor lined with flame that burned but never consumed. It was an old trick, a glamour to remind the uninitiated what it felt like to walk through hell. I passed beneath a dozen archways, each lower than the last, so that by the time I reached the ritual chamber I was hunched, neck aching, eager to stand tall again. It was a clever bit of theater, and I respected it even as I despised the need for it.

High Flame Caller Shasta Tierney was waiting for me, back-lit by the halo of her namesake: a ring of fire that circled the raised dais at the center of the chamber. She wore the ceremonial reds, her hair plaited tight against her skull, her face painted with vertical lines of soot and gold. She didn't rise as I entered, but her eyes tracked me, bright and blue as a gas leak.

I bowed, deep enough to be seen but not enough to lose sight of her hands. "My lady Tierney," I said, my voice carrying in the vast stone space. "Thank you for seeing me on short notice."

She smiled with half her mouth. "You bring the wind of scandal with you, King Calloway. How could I refuse?"

I circled the fire, careful to stay just outside the line of salt that ringed the dais. Tradition said a wolf who crossed it without permission would never shift again; I had no intention of testing the myth tonight. Shasta's hands rested on her knees, fingers working the fabric of her robe in a tiny, perpetual nervous twitch.

I gave her the opening she wanted. "The Council moves fast when it wishes to remind us of its reach. I'd rather not see my family's troubles aired in public, but the Goddess's will is not mine to interpret."

Shasta exhaled, a plume of steam in the cold. "It is the will of the Goddess that brings you here. But it is the will of men that brings shame." She inclined her head. "Your daughter's mate bond is the talk of every coven from here to the Eastern Sea."

"Savannah's actions were... unanticipated." The understatement tasted bitter. "But we both know it's not the bond that concerns the Council. It's the precedent. If wolves can break centuries of tradition at the whim of a girl, what next? Vampires refusing blood oaths? Witches abandoning their covens?" I leaned in, let the heat of the fire paint my face orange. "What happens when a High Flame Caller chooses her own path? Does the world survive that, Shasta?"

She flinched, barely. But it was enough. I watched the gears turn in her mind: the stories of her own line, the cousin who'd defected to the Midwestern vamps, the mutiny that cost her mother her position. Shasta prided herself on being unbreakable, but she understood how quickly tradition became memory, and memory became rot.

"The world survives," she said, "but it is changed. Not always for the better."

"Then we agree," I said, soft as a confessional. "The old ways are not perfect, but they keep us from the abyss. If the Council breaks faith, it breaks everything."

She shifted, robes whispering against the stone. "You came for my vote."

I nodded. "You already know I need five. The rest can be bought or bullied. But yours is worth more than gold. Your word on this will turn the room."

She studied me for a long moment, blue eyes unreadable in the glow. "You are not like your daughter. You know how to ask for things."

"She used to be like me," I said, and let the lie stand.

Shasta pressed her lips together. "You were always a better liar than a wolf."

"I'm whatever you need me to be." I smiled, showing teeth. "That's the whole point."

A long silence, broken only by the sizzle of sap in the flames. Shasta watched the fire as if waiting for a sign, but I knew the real work was already done. Fear of disorder was the mortar that held the whole edifice together.

"If I cast my vote," she said, "I'll expect something in return."

I let the question hang. She wanted me to ask, so I didn't. She filled the silence herself. "There are elements in the Western Territories who want to see the covens split. Otero is making promises he cannot keep. If the Eastern Wolves remain united, so do we."

I nodded. "You'll have your alliance."

She smiled, small and sharp. "You'll have your vote."

We stood at the same time. Shasta stepped down from the dais, the hem of her robe hissing through the salt. She offered me her hand—bare, ungloved, the sign of trust. I took it, squeezed once, and felt the delicate bones beneath her skin.

The deal was done.

Back in the corridor, I let the cold burn off the scent of fire. The first vote was always the hardest; the rest would fall like dominos. I walked the archways with my head high, let the blue flames lick at my shadow, and didn't look back.

The world could go to hell, as long as I got there first.

The sun never rose in Gloamreach. It hovered behind a perpetual veil of clouds, turning the twisted black trees into silhouettes and the ground into a grave of moss and rot. Even the air here was a conspiracy—wet, dense, so thick with spores and secrets you could taste them on your tongue. The witches who ruled these woods liked it that way. They believed in darkness the way some people believed in currency or God.

The entrance was marked by a pair of dead wolves, strung up in the branches and draped with ribbons of sinew. A warning, or maybe a welcome. I passed beneath them, head high, and followed the path of broken stone into the heart of the enclave. No one challenged me, but I could feel eyes behind every tree, every knot of fungus. The Gloamreach witches weren't known for hospitality, especially not for men, especially not for wolves. But the Mistress of Shadows had invited me, and that meant she wanted something.

Her chamber was a nest of woven branches, the walls thick enough to blot out even the suggestion of day. It reeked of mushrooms and burnt cloves, the kind of scent that clings to your clothes long after you've left. The Mistress herself sat in a high-backed chair, a quilt of black feathers draped over her shoulders. Her hair was a riot of curls, half hiding her face, which was pale and sharp as a knife. One eye was painted with kohl, the other bare, and the asymmetry made her look always on the verge of laughter or violence.

"King Calloway," she said, voice so smooth I nearly missed the threat in it. "How rare to see you outside your concrete kingdom."

I bowed just enough to be polite. "Mistress. I trust the moon finds you well."

She snorted, then flicked her gaze to the leather satchel I carried. "You're not here for pleasantries."

"Nor are you." I took a seat across from her, ignoring the way the chair seemed to crawl under my weight. "We can skip the dance if you like."

"Not yet." She poured a drink from a glass decanter—something black and viscous. She didn't offer me any. "Word is your daughter's made quite a mess of things."

"Word is correct." I let the satchel fall to the table between us with a thud. "But that's not why I'm here."

She eyed the bag, then me. "What do you want?"

"A moment of candor." I reached into the satchel and drew out the diary. Small, battered, bound in leather so old it was almost gray. I set it on the table, fingers never leaving the cover. "This was hard to come by. Imagine my surprise when it turned up in the hands of a southern informant, of all places."

Her body went still, except for a tremor at the corner of her mouth. "You've read it?"

"Cover to cover." I flipped it open, careful to keep the ink facing her. The pages were crammed with months of entries regarding a secret. A daughter—no, a changeling; she'd kept hidden all these years.

She was silent, but her fingers dug into the feathers at her collar. "You don't understand what that means."

"I understand enough. I understand that if these notes ever reached the Supreme Council, the resulting inquisition would burn Gloamreach to the ground." I closed the journal, let the silence hang. "But I'm not interested in arson."

She wet her lips, the kohl-lined eye never blinking. "You want something."

"A single favor. A vote." I leaned forward, voice low. "To-morrow, when the Council meets, you will oppose the mate bond between Savannah Calloway and the Iron Valor dog. You will say it's against natural law, or tradition, or whatever fiction you need. I don't care what words you use."

She barked a laugh, harsh and ugly. "You'd blackmail your own daughter out of happiness?"

"She made her choices." My voice was granite. "Now I'm making mine."

She looked away, toward a glass sphere on a shelf that pulsed with a dim blue light. I watched her reflection in it, the way her jaw clenched, the faint panic behind her mask. "If I refuse?"

I slid the journal back into the satchel. "You won't."

A long moment. Then she slumped in her chair, every inch of defiance gone. "This is the last time, Declan. The last time you get to pull my strings."

"We'll see." I stood, brushing the moss from my trousers. "Thank you for your time, Mistress."

She didn't rise. She didn't even watch me go. I left her there, shadowed and small in her own kingdom, the taste of victory sweet and fungal on my tongue.

Outside, the path had changed. The dead wolves were gone, replaced by a tangle of black flowers blooming in the night. A sign, maybe, or just another reminder that in this world, nothing stayed buried for long.

Two votes in hand. Three to go.

I set my course for the next, already thinking ahead to the flavor of blood and fire.

Chapter 20

Savannah

The Council chamber spat us out like bones from a feast, leaving the four of us to gather our dignity in the long, echoing corridor beyond. I felt the blood hammering in my ears, the tremor in my own hands, the unslakable need crawling under my skin—none of it dulled by the judgment of a dozen monsters on their thrones. Beside me, Menace towered, jaw set so hard the muscles corded beneath his skin, the mate mark on his neck livid and pulsing.

Bronc and Juliet walked just ahead, their hands brushing as if they'd never known a world where touching was forbidden. Bronc's suit was rumpled, a wet sheen still clinging to his hairline. Juliet's heels were a metronome on the marble; each click a countdown to something neither of us could name. I felt their glances flick back over us, measuring the distance, calculating the violence it would take to pry us apart.

"Elevators this way," Bronc said, voice flat and barely reined in. I followed, my body electric, Menace's fingers ghosting over the small of my back as if he needed the reassurance that I was real and not another hallucination conjured by need and deprivation.

We moved as a unit, guards flanking us but offering no resistance. It was theater, and everyone knew it. The real threat was inside me, inside Menace, inside every wolf forced to behave in polite company.

The elevator was a coffin lined in gold. Bronc and Juliet slid in first, then Menace and me. The doors snicked shut, and with them the last illusion of safety.

Menace stood directly behind me, his hands braced on either side of my shoulders. I could feel his breath on the back of my neck, could taste the salt of his skin in the air. The energy between us was so thick it might have been visible; I felt his thigh pressed against mine, the minute tremor in his arms as he held himself rigid. My own hands balled at my sides, desperate to reach back and anchor myself in the reality of his touch.

We rode in silence for three floors. The numbers glowed above the door, ticking upward with glacial slowness.

Juliet glanced over, her lips twitching. She nudged Bronc with her hip. "Bet you five bucks they don't make it to the apartment," she whispered.

Bronc didn't turn around. "That's a sucker's bet."

The tension in the elevator was less air, more storm. Each floor intensified the charge, each lurch of the machinery a challenge to the fraying leash of control. Menace's fingers tapped a nervous rhythm against my shoulders, then stopped. His left hand slid to the curve of my waist, fingertips barely grazing the fabric, and I nearly gasped at the heat of it.

"Easy," he muttered, not for me but for himself.

My wolf wanted to snarl, to roll over and bare my throat. I swallowed the urge and instead leaned into him, just enough to feel the pulse at his wrist. He stifled a groan. Bronc, sensing the escalation, took a deliberate step forward and mashed the button for our floor twice.

The elevator shuddered, then creaked to a stop. The doors opened to a carpeted hallway, lit with muted wall sconces. Menace moved first, gripping my hand and tugging me after him. I followed, heartbeat in my throat, vision tunneling to the door at the end of the corridor. Bronc and Juliet trailed behind, exchanging a look that was part playful, part their own lust for each other.

"Don't break anything valuable," Juliet called, her voice sing-song. "We're on the Council's dime, so aim for the drywall."

Menace didn't answer. He moved in long, predatory strides, never letting go of my hand. I had to half-jog to keep up.

We reached the door. Menace fumbled the key card once, then slammed it into the slot. The light turned green. He shoved the door open with enough force that it ricocheted off the wall.

We stumbled inside. The door snapped shut behind us, cutting off the laughter of Bronc and Juliet, the hum of the hallway, the last fragile membrane separating us from the thing we had become.

Menace pressed me back against the closed door, both hands flat to either side of my head, his chest crushing mine in a cage of bone and heat. He didn't kiss me, not right away. He just stared, eyes wolf-yellow and wild, his lips parted as if he was weighing the exact moment to lose control.

"You're sure?" he whispered, the word ragged.

"Always," I breathed.

The dam broke. His mouth crashed into mine, all tongue and teeth and bruising want. His hands found my wrists, pinning them above my head. I felt the scrape of his stubble, the cut of his breath, the way he shivered, as if barely holding himself together. My own body answered in kind—hips grinding, mouth biting back, a raw noise in my throat that could have been a sob or a battle cry.

He pulled away just long enough to look at me, his pupils blown wide, his wolf so close to the surface it hurt to look at him.

There was no ceremony to it. No pause for candles or a practiced hand at my waist, no gentle removal of a shirt or a playful tug at a zipper. Just hands everywhere, tearing, shoving, pressing me so hard to the door the knob left a bruise above my hipbone. He peeled my shirt off in a single rip, the sound obscene in the quiet, and I gasped as the cold air bit my skin. His mouth crushed mine—iron and blood, a tang of something wild—and I bit him back, tasting the salt of his neck as he moved down, down, down. My bra was gone before I felt his hands on my back. He didn't unclasp it, just hooked his thumbs under the cups and yanked it off, leaving red lines on my shoulders.

Menace kissed the line of my collarbone, open-mouthed, his tongue painting heat wherever it landed. His hands were everywhere, greedy, never still; one bruised my breast while the other locked my wrist to the wood above my head. He pressed a thigh between my legs, forcing me to ride it, and I felt him, hard and insistent, through the wool of his slacks.

I clawed at his shirt, desperate for skin, and found the buttons gave way under the force of my hands. I pushed it off his shoulders, running nails over the old scars and the new—each one a litany of pain and memory, each one mapped and memorized. I bit the tendon at his neck, left a mark, felt the growl in his chest echo into mine.

"Fuck," he breathed, voice gutted and shaking. "Missed you so goddamn much."

His fingers were rough, impatient, as he dragged my panties down my thighs. He knelt, nose pressed to the inside of my leg, inhaled deep as if the scent of me was the only air that mattered.

"Could eat you all night and all day."

He licked a line from my knee to my cunt and bit down on the inside of my thigh, hard enough to make me yelp.

"Want you screaming," he said. "Want them all to know what a good girl you are for me when I eat you out. Only me. Only my tongue fucks you like this. Only I eat your pussy like this."

"Don't stop," I told him, and he didn't.

He tongued me, savage and wild, like he was starving and only my pussy could feed him. Nothing delicate or gentle about it. His stubble scraped me raw. He worked two fingers inside, curling them just so, and I lost my footing, knees buckling. He caught me, slung me over his shoulder, and carried me to the bed. The world spun; I laughed, dizzy and high on the violence of it.

He tossed me down, then removed his pants and followed, pinning me to the mattress with his weight. I wrapped my legs around his waist, hooked my ankles at the small of his back, and dug my heels into his ass until I felt his cock throb against me. He was inside me in a single thrust—no warning, no hesitation. The breath punched out of my lungs, replaced by a noise I didn't know I could make. He set a rhythm, brutal and perfect, hips slamming into me over and over. The headboard crashed against the wall, a war drum to the neighbors.

He grabbed both my wrists and pinned them above my head, fingers locked tight around mine. He pressed our hands into the mattress so hard it burned, so hard I thought I'd bruise. His mouth never left my skin—biting, sucking, marking me as his. The mate mark on my neck was a live wire, heat radiating from it, every thrust pushing me closer to a cliff I'd never known existed.

"Say it," he growled, voice ragged.

"Yours," I gasped. "Always yours. Only yours."

He bit the mark, hard, and I broke. My body arched, legs shaking, the orgasm so sharp it bordered on pain. He followed, knotting inside me, the thick swell of him filling every inch. He let go of my wrists, hands cupping my face, kissing me softer now, slower, as if piecing the world back together.

We stayed like that, tangled and panting, for a long time. His sweat cooled on my skin. The sheets were soaked. He pressed his forehead to mine, both of us fighting to breathe.

"You okay?" he whispered.

"Better than okay. I'm alive," I said.

He smiled. "So beautiful."

He pulled out, rolling onto his side, and for a minute we just lay there, listening to the silence. The mate mark still burned, not with pain, with us.

But the hunger didn't fade. It returned slowly, a pulse in the blood, a throb at the base of my spine.

I rolled over and found him watching me, eyes half-lidded but far from satisfied. I ran a finger down the length of his arm, tracing the veins, the old wounds, the story of who he'd been before me.

He grabbed my wrist, not gently, and pulled me on top of him. I laughed and pressed my palms to his chest, feeling the hard beat of his heart. His hazel eyes held mine and I began to rock back and forth, feeling the length of him fill me completely. I threw my head back, loving the feel of him. His hands came around and held me steady on my hips. His thumb rubbing my clit as I rocked. The sensation caused me to lose my rhythm. He sat up and wrapped his arms around me and turned us so I was on my back.

He fucked me slower this time, savoring every inch, every sound. He bit my shoulder, my breast, the inside of my elbow. He licked the sweat from my neck and whispered beautiful things to me.

"Love you, Red," he said, barely audible. "Not gonna lose you. I waited my whole life to find you. Damned if some fucker is gonna take you from me now."

I didn't answer. I just pulled him closer, let the words bury themselves in my skin.

We came together, slower this time, the pleasure an ache instead of a blaze.

Afterward, he held me, arms circled around my waist, breath hot in my hair.

The afternoon crawled by in a haze of exhaustion and pleasure. We moved to the shower, washing each other with hands more tender than I'd thought possible. He soaped my back, traced the ridges of my ribs, cupped my ass in both palms and lifted me so I could wrap my legs around his waist.

He fucked me in the shower, water slicking our bodies, his cock sliding in and out with obscene ease. I bit his ear, left crescent moons in his shoulder with my nails, and when I came this time, I bit over my mate mark on his neck, drawing blood.

He shuddered, let go, and I felt his knot swell again, locking us together. We stood like that, breathless, forehead to forehead, the water turning cold around us.

We dried off in silence. He wrapped me in a towel, then carried me back to the bed, collapsing in a heap of limbs and wet hair.

We lay together, staring at the ceiling, listening to the city's pulse below. His fingers traced patterns on my thigh. Never still.

"Do you think we'll make it?" I asked, voice a whisper.

He didn't answer right away. He just tightened his grip, held me closer.

"Doesn't matter what they say," he said at last. "We're makin' it."

I wanted to believe him. I chose to believe him.

We had room service deliver food and nibbled on meat and cheese throughout the day. But mostly we stayed tangled in the sheets long until the room had gone dim around us as the city bled to dusk. The only light came from the edge of the curtains, a knife-blade that painted everything a shade between bruise and bone. I lay with my head against his chest, listening to the stutter in his pulse as if the next arrhythmia might be the last. His hands moved in slow, drifting circles down my back, fingers tracing patterns like he was trying to remember every inch in case the remembering was all he had left.

Neither of us spoke for a long time. The clock ticked somewhere—cheap, electronic, the kind of noise made for hospitals and council chambers. The mate mark on my shoulder was a fevered spot, burning hot against the cool of his skin.

He broke the silence first, voice a low scrape. "If the vote goes against us, we have three options." He said it like he was reading the results of my biopsy, like it was a fact he'd practiced for years.

I propped myself up, pulling the sheet with me. "Okay," I said, waiting for the punchline.

He didn't look at me. Just stared up at the ceiling, the muscle in his jaw flexing as if he were chewing through the words. "Option one, we run. Council will hunt us, but I have the contacts. We could make it months. Maybe a year if we stay mobile."

"And never sleep in the same bed twice? Always looking over our shoulders?" I tried to keep the bitterness out, but failed.

He nodded. "It's something I'm good at."

"Option two?" I asked, voice smaller than I meant it.

His eyes flickered to mine. "We fight. Bronc and Rafe would back us, maybe the Kozlovs. We could make a stand. But it would be ugly. Casualties on both sides. And they'd never stop coming."

I pictured the Council chamber; the thrones lined up like mausoleums. Pictured Lucia and her fangs, Juliet's laughter gone brittle, Bronc holding a pistol to his own head before letting them break his pack. "You'd die for me?" I whispered.

He barked a laugh, humorless. "I'd kill for you. That's the difference."

I rolled onto my back, staring up at the darkening sky. "Option three?"

He exhaled, slow. "We let them have you. They strip the mate mark, give you to Dominic, and send me to rot in whatever hole they use for shifters like me. Life goes on for everyone except us."

I touched the mark on his neck, fingers gentle. It pulsed under my touch, a living thing.

"They can't just erase this," I said.

He shrugged. "If they want to, they will. Council's done it before." His hand found mine, squeezed. "But I think it kills you. Maybe not right away, maybe not a conventional death, but…yeah. Of course, Dominic would try to replace my mark. The Goddess wouldn't stand for it."

He pulled me close, lips at my ear. "They will not win, Red. Even if I have to burn the world down. It may be a last-minute decision, but I'll come up with something. I'm counting on the Goddess to inspire me, hopefully."

I wanted to believe it. I wanted to be as certain as he sounded, and maybe I did feel a tiny seed of faith. But it sure seemed like a long shot.

Chapter 21

King Declan Calloway

Verdant Hollow had a way of lulling you into peace, then reminding you just how little you deserved it. The air was sweet; the wind perfumed with wildflowers and damp earth, every step cushioned by a carpet of moss so thick it felt obscene. But the beauty was a trap: the deeper you wandered, the more the trees closed in, the more the sky became a memory. It was said that Verdant Hollow could kill you with kindness, and if you looked at the number of vanished envoys on record, you'd believe it.

I followed the winding path to a grove of ancient oaks, their branches locked in a silent argument that had gone on for centuries. The roots bulged above ground, tangled and black, making the whole place feel like a set for a funeral. In the center, seated on a low stone, was Elaina Rowan—Wyrdmother of the Hollow, the oldest living witch on the Council, and the only one I feared in my bones.

She was waiting for me, as I knew she would be. Her skin was the color of old bark, her hair a mass of silver-white curls that framed a face more wrinkled than alive. But her eyes were clear, cold green, and they saw through every lie before you'd even spoken it. As I stepped into the grove, she didn't move, didn't even blink.

"You have nerve, Calloway," she said, her voice a dry rustle. "Not much else, but plenty of that."

I bowed, slow and shallow. "Wyrdmother Rowan."

She cocked her head. "You never come unless you want something."

"That's true of everyone."

She made a noise—a click of the tongue, or maybe a curse in her native tongue. "Sit then. Let's get this over with."

I did, perching on a mossy root across from her, the damp seeping through my trousers in an instant. "I'll be quick," I said. "You remember the Purge."

Her lips thinned. "I remember a lot of things."

"In the third year, the hunters had you cornered. You lost a dozen priestesses, more in the fire. But I intervened. I brokered a truce. I gave you a path to escape."

"You gave me a week," she said, voice sharper now. "It cost me thirty years of penance to the Hollow. My people still bear the scars."

"It was better than extinction."

She was silent. The wind whistled through the branches, carrying the scent of sap and wood smoke.

"You owe me a favor," I said. "That was the deal."

She looked at me, and for a moment I saw the animal in her—something old, dangerous, desperate to be free. "You waited all this time for this?"

"It's important."

She closed her eyes, as if savoring a foul taste. "You want my vote."

"Yes."

She shook her head, curls bouncing. "You're asking me to go against natural law. The mate bond is not some contract. It's the bedrock of the world."

"My daughter violated pack law first. She set this in motion." I let my voice soften just a little. "You know as well as I do, the world doesn't run on love. It runs on balance. If the Council bends for one, it'll snap for all."

She studied me, the icy green of her gaze rooting me to the spot. "Do you believe that? Or are you just playing the part?"

"I believe in what works," I said.

"Always did." She glanced away, fingers tracing the fissures in the stone. "If I do this, the favor is spent. No more debts between us. I don't care if your house is burning and the only water is in my well."

"One favor," I agreed. "And then we are done."

The wind gusted, lifting strands of her hair and making them dance like white fire. For a second, I thought she'd refuse, call my bluff, unleash the Hollow on me and let the forest swallow my bones.

But she nodded once, the movement so slight I could have missed it.

"I'll vote your way," she said. "But don't mistake this for loyalty. I'd sooner see you rot."

I grinned, showing teeth. "I'd expect nothing less."

I stood bowing deeper this time, and turned to leave. The trees parted for me; the roots shifting just enough to let me through.

Three down. Two to go.

But as I walked away, I felt the weight of the bargain. Some debts, once paid, never really vanish.

The portal to the Demon Kingdom opened behind the Council Tower, tucked in a ruin that was once a power substation, now just a tangle of wire and rust. No one came here on purpose unless they had a death wish or a standing invitation. I had one of those, so I stepped through the ring of smoldering sulfur and let the air dissolve around me.

Hell wasn't what the books promised. It was worse. The sky was a furnace, all reds and oranges with no relief, and the ground was a crust of black glass that sliced your shoes with every step. The wind was constant, hot as a blast furnace and thick with the taste of blood. I wiped sweat from my brow and kept moving. You didn't linger here, not even if you were a king.

The obsidian throne room was built into the side of a volcano the world was oblivious to. The walls pulsed with veins of magma, casting the whole chamber in a living, hungry light. Maltraz sat at the far end in his monster form, half-man, half-monster, his body covered in black scales, his horns twisted like a ram's, his fingers ending in knives. He lounged on a throne made of fused skulls, each one still faintly aware.

He watched me cross the room, eyes burning gold.

"The Wolf King comes begging," he rumbled, smoke curling from his mouth.

I ignored the heat and the smell. "Not begging, Maltraz. Collecting."

He grinned, sharp teeth flashing. "It is rare for your kind to collect here and leave whole."

I approached, stopping just outside the reach of his arms. "You remember the Angel Wars. You remember who kept your lines open when the celestials tried to purge you from the east?"

He nodded, a slow, ponderous gesture. "You slaughtered a choir for me. That was a good day."

"You owe me a favor."

His tail flicked behind him, gouging a furrow in the glass floor. "Always with the favors, Declan. What is it this time?"

I glanced at the fire pits lining the room, the small demons chained there for warmth, or maybe just for show. "Tomorrow's vote. I need your voice."

He leaned forward, scales clicking. "The Council's old game?"

"Yes. My daughter's bond. I want it broken. I want the Council to stand by the old laws."

Maltraz snorted a cloud of cinders. "Family troubles? How... mortal."

"I know what happens if the wolves fracture," I said. "So do you. The Council falls, and then the celestials come again. No more songs, just silence."

He let out a laugh, the sound like a tree snapping in a fire. "You are still the only one who understands consequence, Wolf King." He rose from his throne, looming over me, the heat radiating from his skin like an open furnace. "If I vote your way, you will owe me nothing. Our ledger will be clear."

"Agreed."

He grinned again, and this time the flame in his eyes softened, almost friendly. "It will be a pleasure to watch the world burn with you, Calloway."

He offered his hand. It was three times the size of mine, tipped with obsidian claws. I shook it anyway, feeling the skin blister where our palms met.

"Done," I said.

"Done," he echoed.

He let me go, and I staggered back, the air filling my lungs with smoke and power. I bowed, just enough to acknowledge the beast, and turned to leave. As I walked out, his laughter followed, echoing off the walls long after I'd crossed back to the ruins and the taste of sulfur faded from my mouth. When I saw him for the Council vote, he will be in his more palatable, less monstrous form. I can't say I'm not happy about it.

Four down. One to go.

And the last was the most dangerous of all.

The vampires didn't do subtlety. Otero's local compound was almost as grand as his one on the west coast. It was a cathedral of marble and crystal, every wall a mirror, every corridor designed to make you feel small and hungry. The air was icy and thick with the scent of rare flowers, cut with the tang of old copper and expensive cologne. Even the servants here glided—no footsteps, just a sense of passing breeze and a flash of dark eyes.

I was ushered through three sets of doors, each guarded by twins with perfect skin and teeth so white they hurt to look at. No one spoke. No one needed to. I was expected, and the expectation pressed down with every step.

Varic Otero waited on a terrace overlooking the city, his body framed by the moon and the pulsing grid of traffic below. He wore a suit three shades darker than blood, a high-collared shirt, and a ring on every finger. In one hand, a goblet; in the other, nothing but patience.

"Declan," he said, nodding once. "The wolf who would be king of all things."

"Otero." I matched his stillness with my own, refusing to let him pace me.

He gestured to the seat beside him, a spindly thing of polished bone and velvet. "Care for a drink?"

I took the chair but not the offer. "I don't mix."

He smirked, a flash of fang. "Your loss." He sipped, and I saw the red line left on the crystal. "I assume you're here about your daughter."

"I'm here about tomorrow's vote."

He made a soft sound, almost a purr. "You're losing, you know."

I let that pass. "It isn't over until the last hand is shown."

He glanced down at the traffic, fingers tracing the rim of his glass. "Your daughter's happiness means so little to you?"

"This isn't about happiness. It's about order. If you want chaos, let the southern packs off their leash and see how long you keep your empire."

He looked at me then, eyes so dark they swallowed the light. "You threaten me?"

"I warn you." I leaned in, letting my own hunger bleed through. "Without structure, everything falls. Even your house, Otero."

He nodded, a slow, measured beat. "And what do you offer in return for my... compliance?"

"Exclusive hunting rights in the East Territories, for one. And next time the Council selects a leader, I'll cast for you."

He laughed, a cold, brittle sound. "You'd make yourself my puppet?"

"I'd make us both kings," I said, and smiled. "With greater reach."

He studied me for a long moment, the silence between us cold enough to raise frost. "You'd sell your daughter for a piece of territory?"

"I'd sell myself for a larger kingdom. My daughter is a casualty, not a currency."

He raised his glass. "You're more honest than your predecessors."

"I outlived them for a reason."

He sipped again, the wine or whatever it was staining his lips. "You'll have your vote, Declan. But know this: the day you fail me, I will drink you dry."

I stood, brushing imaginary dust from my sleeves. "The day you can, you may."

He didn't answer. He just watched me leave, the glint of his eyes following until I was out of sight.

Five votes. The ledger was set.

I walked out into the night, the city below a tangle of light and noise, and wondered for the first time if I'd traded too much for a win. But that was the curse of kings: you never knew until the blood was on the floor.

Tomorrow, Savannah would learn what I already knew.

There was no such thing as a happy ending.

CHAPTER 22

MENACE

The knock came at 12:03 a.m., just as the digital clock on the nightstand blinked its second colon and erased the hour before. The sound wasn't loud, but it was final. The kind of knock that changed fates, ended families, started wars. I felt it in my sternum before I heard it. Savannah slept with her back to me, red hair riot over the pillow, her breathing shallow and even. She didn't stir, not even when I slid out of bed and padded naked to the door. My body was already on edge, mate mark burning, heart running double time.

I cracked the door an inch, but Bronc forced it the rest of the way, face braced for what he'd have to say. King Rafe was behind him, beard shadowed and jaw locked so tight the lines cut deeper than I remembered. They wore the same expression—grim, tired, like men about to dig a grave in wet dirt.

"What is it?" I asked, already knowing.

Bronc didn't answer, just jerked his head for me to follow. I pulled on a pair of jeans, and we moved down the dim corridor, past the soulless council art and the dustless carpets, until the door to the stairwell clicked shut behind us. I could smell the stress on Rafe, the cold sweat behind his ears, the sour tang of coffee on his breath.

Bronc stood with arms folded, making himself the wall between me and the news.

"Declan's got the votes," he said. The words were flat, but I could see the anger curdling under each one. "Midwest, East, three of the four witch clans, plus the swing demon and the west Vamp. Dominic has the Supernatural Council wrapped tight."

Rafe's eyes narrowed. "If they call it as expected, they'll strip the mate bond by dusk. Maybe sooner. Then they ship Savannah to the lake house until the wedding ceremony."

I wanted to ask if it was a joke, if this was just some game of chicken and we were still in control of the car. But the way Rafe kept glancing at the exit, the way Bronc's hands fisted and unfisted, told me there was no bluff here. They had counted the bodies, lined the coffins, prepared for a defeat they'd always suspected might come.

I felt the old self wanting to howl, to split the walls with a rage that would bring the council running. I wanted to take Bronc's head in both hands and break it open until his doubt ran out. Instead, the anger passed through me like a hot wind, and left behind a vacuum. My hands went cold; my vision tunneled.

It was Rafe who spoke first. "There's always a chance, but—" He stopped, searching my face. "You good, Menace? Because you look like a man about to shoot up a police station."

"I'm good," I said, and heard the death in it. "Better than good. I'm ready."

Bronc shot a look at Rafe, then back to me. "We'll file the injunction, but there's not much precedent. If they strip the mark, the bond won't kill you. But it'll—"

"I know what it does," I said. I thought of Bronc when Harrison destroyed Juliet's mark, how he'd almost lost his mind. The way he couldn't think straight. But Savannah would have a replacement mark. I wondered if the witchcraft would leave her hating me. It was bad. There was no question.

Rafe stepped in, voice low. "I need you to stay put tonight. No heroics. No phone calls. Tomorrow, if there's a move to make, I'll make it. We're not losing this fight in the dark."

I nodded. "Copy."

Bronc hesitated, then touched my shoulder. "If you need to talk to Juliet—"

"No," I said. "Let her sleep. If I need her, she'll know."

The three of us stood in silence for a long, empty minute. Then Rafe broke it, with a hand on my forearm, firm and grounding. "We'll get you through this," he said.

"I know," I said, and it felt like a lie even as I meant it.

They left, the door hissing closed behind them. I waited, breathing, counting the heartbeats until I was sure I could walk back without breaking.

Savannah lay on her side, knees drawn up, fists curled under her chin. In the pale blue light of the room, she looked more like a child than a queen. She spoke. "Bad news I assume?"

"The only thing you need to concern yourself with is how very much I love you." I told her and then I kissed her with every bit of myself I had to give.

I took her into my arms and made love to her like there was no tomorrow because there might not be. After, I lay down beside her and wrapped my body around hers, not for comfort, but for the knowledge that I could. That she was still here. The room was quiet except for her breathing. The white noise of the city filtered through triple-paned glass.

I did not sleep. I traced every possible contingency, every path to violence, every last-ditch ploy and gamble. I counted the minutes to sunrise, and when she turned in her sleep and pressed her face to my chest, I held her there until my arms went numb.

I let her have the illusion of safety. For now.

But I would never let them have her. Not while there was a drop of blood in my body. Not while I could still tear the world open and drag her through it, screaming or not.

Let Declan have his votes. Let the Council make its plans. I had mine.

Morning arrived with the taste of metal in my mouth, like a knife left to soak in tap water. The hour was gray and soured by anticipation. I lay on my back and watched the first cracks of light crawl across the hotel ceiling, tracing the faint lines where the drywall had been joined and sanded, painted over again and again but never made seamless.

Savannah woke with a sharp intake of breath, her hands clutching at the bedsheet as if she expected it to be a shroud. I said nothing, and neither did she. We got out of bed like convicts summoned for a last walk.

She drifted to the window and stared out, naked, unself-conscious, her body marked by the bruises and bites I'd left on her, my claim written in purple and gold across her skin. She didn't ask me to cover her, didn't shrink from the light. If anything, she seemed to take strength from it.

I showered first, turning the water so hot it skinned the residue of sleep from my muscles. I dressed in the suit Rafe's people had hung in the closet—black, sharp enough to cut, the tie a matte burgundy that looked almost brown unless you knew what to look for. I fumbled with the knot, fingers too thick and angry for the fine work, and had to re-tie it three times before it looked like something a living man might wear to his own trial.

She chose a black dress from the suitcase; something simple and sleeveless, no jewelry except for the crescent-moon pendant Juliet had given her. It was a mourner's dress, a dress for any woman who expected to be seen and remembered. She topped it with a black leather blazer. Simple. Elegant. Her hair was a deep red warning sign against her pale skin, big waves resting at her waist.

We stood in front of the mirror, side by side. I hardly recognized the two of us.

"You ready?" I asked. My voice came out hoarse.

She didn't answer, but slipped her hand into mine. Her fingers trembled, but only a little.

The walk to the Council was an exercise in denial. The lobby was empty except for two vampires and the few other staff who were milling about. The streets outside were washed clean by last night's rain, but the city's grime lay just beneath, waiting for the sun to fail.

The Council's building was a crypt from another age: stone older than the Republic, steel and glass added like afterthoughts to impress a line of visiting dignitaries. A line of flags hung limp on their poles, the wind dead or too frightened to move.

Inside, the guards wore earpieces and bored expressions, but their eyes tracked every movement, every hitch in Savannah's stride. She walked with her chin up, but I saw the way her shoulder blades tensed under the fabric, ready for a blow.

We passed the checkpoint, took the elevator up, and emerged into the corridor outside the main chamber. It smelled of old incense, burnt coffee, and the recycled air of a dozen power struggles. I saw the Kozlovs at the far end, Lucia and King Kazimir flanked by a pair of identical, silent ghouls. Lucia caught Savannah's eye and gave her a tiny nod, less encouragement than recognition—two survivors passing in the hallway of a ruined girls' school.

Bronc and Juliet were already waiting. Bronc's tie was off-center, his hands in his pockets, but his eyes had the look of a man running out of time. Juliet wore blue again, her hair tight, her lips the color of dried blood.

They spoke in low voices until the doors to the chamber yawned open and a guard beckoned us in. We filed inside, two by two, like animals onto an ark with only one level and a leaky hull.

The Council chamber was a cathedral of authority, every stone soaked in the sweat and excrement of centuries of wrangling. Twelve thrones in a semicircle, each occupied by a representative of some supernatural territory or species. The rest of the seats were filled with spectators—witches in severe dresses, vampires with faces like surgical instruments, the odd warlock or hellhound in borrowed human skin.

At the far end of the aisle, behind a stone dais, Declan waited. He wore a suit the color of dried liver, his tie knotted perfectly, every hair in place. Beside him was Dominic, the rival king, who looked bored already and was scrolling through a phone as if awaiting a lunch reservation. I felt my wolf rise and bristle at the sight, but I kept it chained in the back of my mind.

The crowd noise dropped to nothing when we entered. We took our seats near the front, Rafe on my right, Savannah on my left, Juliet and Bronc behind us. The air was cold, the kind of institutional cold that no radiator or body heat could ever soften.

The Councilwoman—same paper-white witch from the day before—banged a gavel. "This session will address the disposition of the disputed mate bond between Bridger Hardin and Savannah Calloway, with respect to Council law and existing treaties."

She flicked her gaze to Savannah. "The defendant may speak."

Savannah stood, the black dress falling straight as a blade from her collarbones. She looked smaller than the day before, but her voice was clearer, more measured.

"My name is Savannah Calloway. I was born the property of Declan Calloway, and for twenty-four years, he has treated me as such. My only crime was existing. My only hope, for most of my life, was to avoid being noticed. My brother Callum's fists taught me obedience. My father's indifference carved me into something cold, sharp-edged, but independent. I learned to swallow my screams, to let bruises bloom purple under my skin like funeral flowers. Love? A fairy tale for fools. Survival was the only hymn I knew."

Her words echoed, cold as snowmelt. She wasn't speaking for the Council; I realized. She was speaking for herself, and for the ghosts of every girl like her.

She went on. "I never dreamed of a mate. Not once. The concept felt like an unimaginable nightmare, something brittle, bitter, destined to crumble. My father's voice always at the forefront of my mind, venomous and certain: 'You'll kneel for whomever I choose, girl. Your purpose is to bleed power into this family.' I'd seen what that looked like. My mother, hollow-eyed and silent at his side, her true mate found only after being mated and married to my father, now beyond her grasp. Too late for her. I saw what it was to be chained to a monster. My only hope was to survive. So I ran." She took a deep breath.

"Then Bridger came." Her eyes found mine.

"He found me in that lab, silver burning my wrists and ankles raw. I didn't recognize hope until I saw it on his face—all fury and fire, eyes like a storm hunting vengeance. His hands didn't shake when he snapped my chains. His voice didn't waver when he gently told me to rest easy. He had me. And in that moment, I knew it was true. Someone had me."

A tear ran down her beautiful face.

"Bridger's love was not gentle. It was a blade, yes—but one that carved away the rot, leaving me raw and trembling and new. When he looked at me, he didn't see a pawn. He saw a queen. A partner. A soul the Goddess herself had forged to walk beside him. The day I met Bridger Hardin, I knew it was fate. Not because he claimed me, but because he *saw* me—not as a pawn, not as a prize, but as a person. The only person in my life who ever did."

I could feel the tension building behind me, the eyes narrowing, the ears tuning in.

"My father tried to have me killed. My brother beat me. Dominic Madison wants to brand me, take what my mate gave me, and then pretend I never existed. I would rather die than let that happen." She turned, faced the Council. "If you take this bond from me, you will kill more than a shifter woman. You will kill the idea that any of us can be more than the tools of men like Declan Calloway."

She stopped, breath shaking. "The Goddess chose us. Deny us at your peril, for Her wrath is terrible to behold."

There was a silence then, not the dead air of fear, but a living, breathing quiet as every eye in the room reevaluated what they'd been told. The Councilwoman made a note, the pen scratching like a nail over bone.

"Thank you, Miss Calloway. The plaintiff may respond."

Declan stood, face unreadable, the mask of a man who's already convinced himself of his own lie.

"I have always loved my daughter," he began, but the words sounded so wrong I thought he might choke on them. "But she has been ill. Unbalanced. She was taken from her home, brainwashed, made to believe that this man—" he gestured at me, "—is her mate. There is no evidence the bond is legitimate. No evidence she can survive the ritual of stripping. But if the Council decrees it, I will support the law."

He sat, hands folded, and did not look at her.

Dominic didn't even bother to stand. He smiled, slow and reptilian, and said, "She will adapt."

A ripple of disgust, not laughter, rolled through the audience.

The Councilwoman tapped her gavel. "Mr. Hardin, you have the right to speak."

I stood. The bond burned like holy fire in my veins.

"The Goddess carved Savannah's name into my bones long before I knew to beg for mercy. I'd laughed at fated mates once, spat at the notion like the arrogant fool I was. But Savannah... She wasn't a choice. She was a revelation. A reckoning. Every cell in my body howled *mine* the moment I scented her fear in that lab, bloodied but unbroken. I'd have torn the world apart then. Now? Now I'd salt the earth."

I stared at Declan across the council chamber, my wolf's snarl vibrating behind my teeth. "You think your bribes and threats matter?" My voice dripped venom, low enough to slit throats. "I know you've been busy calling in favors. Five votes bought like cheap whores." The chamber hissed, but I didn't blink. "Your council's a rotting theater, Declan. A pantomime of power."

I leaned forward, the wood groaning under my grip. "You want to play games with fate? Fine. But know this—" My gaze swept the room, lingering on every compromised face. "I didn't survive hell to kneel to cowards. You vote to strip our bond?" A feral smile split my lips. "I'll raze every fucking kingdom here to ash before I let your greed touch her."

The truth of it sang in my blood. The Goddess didn't make mistakes. Savannah's laugh in the dark, the way her wolf curved against mine like two halves of a blade—that was divine work. And me? I was the weapon she'd forged.

Declan's jaw twitched. Fear, sour and sweet, bled through his cologne. Good. Let him choke on it.

"Burn your protocols," I said softly. "Your votes. Your lies." Savannah's breath hitched beside me, pride and fury tangling in our bond. "The Goddess will have the last word."

I wasn't quite finished. "And just for good measure. Further proof that Declan Calloway is a liar, there was a battery of tests that proved beyond a shadow of a doubt that we are, in fact, fated mates. Every test we willingly submitted to. Every test we passed. Someone here may have diminished mental capacity, but it is *not* Savannah Calloway."

I sat. Savannah reached for my hand under the table. Her fingers were still trembling, but only a little.

The chamber fell into a clamor.

The Councilwoman again scratched her pen across paper. The plaintiff again may respond.

Declan stood. "I say those tests were not accurate." Then he sat.

A hush fell over the chamber. The type of hush that dragged out, stretching to a thin wire that vibrated with every heartbeat in the room. Even the Kozlovs had gone quiet, eyes glittering like predatory insects in the gallery. Beside me, Savannah's hand curled into a fist, the knuckles gone white against the black of her dress.

The Councilwoman finally lifted her head, lips already pursed in a verdict.

"Council will now render its judgment," she said, and the timbre of her voice was all the warning I needed.

"For the separation and nullification of the disputed mate bond, as proposed by the Eastern and Midwestern Kingdoms are as follows. The witches' votes are split; three aye, one nay. Vampires are split; the West aye, the East nay. Wolves are split; two aye, two nay. Demons are, aye. Angels are a nay."

Her gaze was cold as a morgue's drawer. "The ayes have it. As per Council law, Savannah Calloway's mate mark will be stripped, and she will be remanded to the custody of King Dominic Madison pending further review."

A sound like a punctured lung went up in the gallery—shocked indrawn breath, then the hiss of a hundred minor predators relishing the kill.

Guards moved at once. Two advanced on Savannah, hands out, their eyes fixed not on her but on me. I felt the wolf in my blood rise, claws prickling at the beds of my nails, every bone in my body shouting for release. But the next moment, everything went cold, then brilliantly, terribly clear. I heard a voice—not my own, not even the beast's, but older than either. It said: *She is yours. The Council does not matter. Remember who you are.*

I stood up before the guards could reach her. The entire chamber tilted on its axis.

"I invoke ancient law," I said, my voice ringing through the stones.

Every head turned. The guards froze.

"I challenge Dominic Madison for the right to my mate," I said. "By ritual combat. Witnessed. Final. No substitutions. You know the words."

The Council Chairwoman's face drained of blood, and for a moment I thought she might faint. Instead, she turned to the scroll at her elbow and scanned it with trembling hands.

"There has not been a challenge in a hundred and fifty years," she said.

I ignored her. "But there is precedent."

Bronc was on his feet now, every muscle wound tight. Rafe looked at me, not with shock, but with a kind of raw pride. Juliet grinned—she was the only one.

Dominic rose to the bait at last. He stood, face darkening, fists balled at his sides.

"I accept the challenge," he said.

Declan tried to interrupt, looking at Dominic. "You *do* realize what that means, don't you? The winner takes all. Kingdom. Power. Life. Are you prepared to lose?"

"Too late. He already accepted. I came here prepared to die," I told Dominic. "Did *you?*"

All the color washed from his face.

The Chairwoman tried to reassert control. "This is most irregular. There are—"

Rafe interrupted her with a wave of his hand. "You *know* the law. It supersedes even the Council. The challenge is binding."

Kazimir Kozlov spoke up, voice as soft as falling ash. "You should allow it, Madam. Else we will. And your precious Council will look quite foolish."

She nodded once, defeated. "So be it. The challenge will be held in three days' time. This will allow everyone time to travel to King Dominic's estate where the challenge will occur on the battlefield there. No weapons allowed, but those the Goddess gave you. The result is final, as it is a fight to the death. Savannah will remain with her current pack until the challenge is decided."

The guards retreated, not quite sure where to stand. Savannah sagged into her chair, stunned, eyes wide. When she looked at me, there was fear, but also something like awe.

Dominic smirked, but the confidence was gone from his eyes. He was a wolf, but I saw the man in him, saw the cracks.

Declan slumped back in his seat, jaw working, but he said nothing. For the first time, he looked mortal.

I took Savannah's hand again. The tremor was gone.

"We have a few more days," I said. "Eat. Rest. Whatever comes next, I want you strong."

She nodded. "I trust you," she whispered, so quiet I barely heard it.

I didn't trust myself. But I trusted the voice that had spoken to me. The voice of every ancestor who'd ever fought to keep what the world tried to steal.

I would win, or I would die. There was no third path.

I looked at Dominic and smiled a toothy grin. I saw him sweat.

Chapter 23

King Declan Calloway

Menace's snarl echoed in my skull for hours after the Council adjourned. Even now, alone in the second-floor study of Dominic's estate, I felt the vibrations of that inbred mongrel's arrogance rattling the marrow of my bones. The moon hung low and bulbous over the lake, casting its leprous light through the room's stained glass and painting the shelves with black and crimson bars. I stalked the perimeter of the office. A wolf denied a kill, trailing the scent of rage with every step.

Dominic Madison—King of the Midwest Wolves, but less a ruler than a parasite in a bespoke suit—sat hunched behind his desk, shoulders bunched, fingers spidering over the edge of a leather-bound folio. He hadn't spoken since the Council's gavel struck. Not a word, not a cough, just the rhythmic twitch of his cheek muscle, a tell that grew more pronounced with each minute of silence.

I slammed my fist against the corner of the bookcase, sending a rain of dust from the top shelf and nearly toppling the bronze bust of Dominic's own face. It caught on the edge, rocked back and forth on its chin, then settled, staring at me with dead, perfect eyes. "There must be a loophole," I growled, barely aware of the words tumbling from my mouth. "No shifter of common blood can challenge a king without consequence. It's anarchy. We are not animals."

Dominic flinched. His hand went to his throat, fingers resting on the pale flesh where his mate mark should have been. The absence of it radiated through the room like the stink of a rotting carcass. "You heard the Council. The invocation was ancient law. The Council can't override a direct challenge before so many witnesses. Especially not after Lucia and Kozlov backed it. The vampires live for this sort of spectacle." He said it like a prayer, but I could see the despair in his eyes.

I reached for the next shelf and ripped a thick volume free. The gold-embossed title, The Law of Challenge and Ascension, glinted in the lamplight. I flipped it open, the pages brittle as old snow, and skimmed the index for any precedent to undo this farce. "You do realize," I said, "that if you lose, not only will you die, but your line, your Council seat, your territory—all of it passes to that mutt. I will not watch the Midwest fiefdom bequeathed to a Texan nobody with nothing but a birthmark and a service medal."

Dominic winced. The words 'service medal' always stung; he'd never served a day in his life, though he'd worn more than a few uniforms for ceremonial photographs. "Declan, I... there is still time. He's just a brute. We'll have days to prepare. You could bring in the twins, or Callum, or... gods, anyone else with teeth. I know how to fight. I've won my fair share of tournaments."

I laughed, a joyless, cracked sound that bounced off the oak paneling and died in the velvet drapes. "It is a ritual challenge, you simpering little twit. If I sent in an assassin, even a half-wit like Rafe would see through it. Besides, you're the one who wanted this done 'by the book'. Well, now the book is writing your obituary." I flung the legal tome onto the desk, scattering the neat stacks of Dominic's correspondence.

He snatched at the papers, trying to restore some semblance of order, but his hands shook so badly that he only succeeded in shuffling the mess around. "Maybe... maybe there's something in the Codex of Challenges. The addenda. The devil is in the footnotes. You always said that."

I prowled to the window and stared down at the lake. On the far shore, I could see the shimmer of black SUVs parked at the curb, the glitter of security glass. "You know what the real devil is, Dominic?" I said, letting my breath fog the windowpane. "It's that you spent your entire reign buying votes and selling favors, and now you're surprised when the rest of the world moves your pieces for you. This was supposed to be an arranged marriage. A transaction. Instead, you let a nobody with a Southern accent and a hard-on for my daughter throw your kingdom into open challenge." I turned, letting him see my teeth. "You make me sick."

He tried to meet my gaze, but his eyes kept drifting to the pile of lawbooks on the table, or to the empty glass of whiskey at his elbow. "She's not worth it," he said at last. "Savannah. She's a liability, always has been. I could align myself with another house."

"Savannah is my blood," I said. "She may be a miserable disappointment, but she's a Calloway, and we will have this merger of our houses. And I will not let the Calloway name be sullied by that white-haired trash. Not after everything I have built. It's too late for anything else anyway. You accepted his challenge." I circled behind the desk, looming over Dominic. He sat defiantly, knowing I was right.

I reached for another book and slammed it onto the blotter. The Codex of Royal Succession. I thumbed through it, ignoring Dominic's protests, until I found the passage I wanted: "Any King, when challenged by a lesser, may invoke trial by proxy, should his own fitness be in doubt." I jabbed the page. "Here. We can name a proxy. Callum will do it. He's young, but he has the training. And the strength."

Dominic shook his head. "That's only if the King is physically incapacitated. If I even suggest it, the Council will demand a medical review. They just saw me today. Clearly, I'm in perfect health. They'll know."

I spat onto the floor, hating his lack of fighting skill more than I hated Menace's impudence. "Then we find another way. We prepare you. We get you stronger. We make sure that when the day comes, you are more wolf than man. For fuck's sake, you are a king! You come from generations of the strongest alphas known to wolfdom! Just because you've allowed yourself to become soft doesn't mean your DNA isn't up to snuff."

He looked up at me, hope and terror warring in his eyes. "Could it be done? In three days?"

I considered the question. Dominic had allowed himself to become soft, yes, but he still had the bearing of an alpha. He was still powerful. With the right training, the right enhancements, the right threats—anything was possible. I nodded, letting him see the steel in my conviction. "You will win, Dominic. You will not embarrass the royal houses. But we won't stop looking for another solution we might find as well."

I stood surveying the room. The library was a fortress of paper, every wall lined with treatises and manifestos and thick, leather-bound histories. But it felt as brittle as a mausoleum. All this knowledge, and none of it had saved us.

I crossed to the sideboard, poured myself a glass of whiskey, and downed it in one long swallow. The burn was nothing compared to the bile that rose in my throat every time I thought of Menace's sneer.

I walked to the far wall and pulled a slim volume from between two dictionaries. The binding was black; the title embossed in silver: Rituals of Augmentation and Debasement. I traced the runes on the cover, felt their chill seep into my fingertips.

If there were no loophole, I would make one.

This was my world. I would not lose it to a mutt and a daughter too proud to kneel. Not after all the blood I'd already spilled to build it.

After hours of looking at the books in this room, I realized it was futile.

"This is wasted effort. The answer isn't in here." I slid my gaze to Dominic, letting him see the calculation on my face. "It's not in the open."

He stared at me, then the lightbulb moment happened. He straightened in his chair. He finally seemed to realize he was king, and managed, "You mean the archives."

"That's where the deepest truths are hidden," I said.

He walked to the far trick wall built by his father, a man who was at least half as clever as he was cruel. You wouldn't see it unless you were looking for the minuscule seam above the third shelf. He pressed a finger to the spot, then pried the board loose. Behind it, a metal panel with a thumbprint lock. He pressed his finger to the glass, waited for the cold needle to bite, and then the panel slid away with a hiss of exhaled air.

He looked at the contents of the shelf, then looked at me. "Any idea what we're looking for?"

Inside was a row of books—short, thick, some wrapped in tanned hide, others in black scales, one bound in what I had always suspected was tattooed human skin. I pulled the largest one free, ran my palm over its slick, diseased surface, and let the lamplight catch on the etched runes across the spine.

"I believe these are forbidden," Dominic commented, but his eyes never left the book. "Council says—"

"Council says a lot of things," I answered. "None of them matter when the wolves come for you." I set the tome on the desk, opened it with care, and watched the dust spiral up in thin, gray tendrils. The pages were heavy and stuck together at the edges; it took force to peel them apart.

The language was Old Tongue, but I'd been schooled my entire life in languages. I scanned the index, then flipped to a dog-eared chapter: Rituals of Enhancement, Under the Old Moon.

Dominic read over my shoulder, voice barely above the breath of a dying man. "You think this... this could help me?"

I smiled, but only with my mouth. "You have the natural strength of an alpha, but you haven't bothered to keep yourself as strong as you should Dominic. But with this? You could be as strong as Menace. Maybe stronger."

He didn't even protest the insult. "Is it safe?"

"Probably not," I said. "But neither is facing a superior fighter."

He closed his eyes. "What does it require?"

I skimmed the first page, then traced a finger down the column of glyphs. "Blood," I said. "Yours, mostly. Some... other elements. A wolf to channel it. But mostly, just blood."

He looked at his hands again. "Fuck. How bad is this going to hurt?"

I shrugged. "All power hurts. That's why it's power."

He laughed, a small, brittle sound. "What's the worst that could happen?"

I didn't answer. The worst had already happened: he'd let himself get cornered by an inferior, and now he was mine to shape or break.

I flipped to the instructions, scanned the supplies. Most were trivial—herbs, silver, salt. The rest would require some creativity, but I'd procured worse for less noble causes.

Dominic stood, straightening his tie even though it had wilted to a wrinkled cord. "How soon can we do it?"

I glanced at the clock. "We need to do it close to the time of the fight so it will be a peak potency." I closed the book, ran a thumb along the edge, felt the prick of the binding needle. "Tonight, you rest. I'll arrange the rest."

He almost smiled, the pathetic bastard. "Thank you, Declan."

I didn't answer. Instead, I lifted the book and slid it back into the wall. As I closed the panel, I turned to Dominic. "Remember this, King. When you win, it's because you did what was necessary."

He nodded, and left the room with the bearing of a man who finally understood his role: the weapon, not the wielder.

When I was alone again, I poured myself another glass of whiskey. I drank, then stared out at the lake until the glass was empty and the sun began to stain the far shore with the color of old bruises.

It was done. My daughter would kneel, or she would die. Either way, I would prove who was the strongest.

The study's atmosphere had just begun to curdle into a sort of stagnant peace when the door burst open, scattering the heavy silence into tatters. Callum stalked in, hair wet with rain and eyes bright with mischief, a little too satisfied with himself. He moved with the insolent grace of a favored son, but his gaze was all wolf—calculating, hungry, always searching for the spot of softest flesh.

Trailing him was a woman swaddled in a dark, ragged cloak. The hood shadowed her face, but even from across the room I felt the cold spill off her in waves, a temperature drop sharp enough to crack the wax puddles on the desk. Dominic straightened in his chair, went pale as cream cheese, and tucked his chin in as if to avoid the sight.

Callum stopped a foot from the desk. "Father," he said, with an exaggerated bow, then jerked his chin at the cloaked woman. "Moira Blackthorn. You said to fetch her if things went sideways."

"Things have not gone sideways," I said, but even I could hear the lie in my voice. "They have gone terminal. Thank you, son."

The woman peeled back her hood. Her face was a contradiction: smooth, ageless skin stretched over the fine bones of a child, but the eyes... the eyes were bottomless, tar-black, no white, no iris, only the infinite night. I felt them rake my soul, weigh and measure every secret, every debt owed.

"King Declan," she said, and the syllables dry-brushed the air like leaves scudding across tombstones. "Your son tells me you require a remedy for an... impasse."

I stepped forward, carefully, as if approaching a loaded trap. "We require certainty. The ritual challenge must be won. No room for error, no room for mercy. My daughter's future—and my own—is on the table."

Moira's lips curled, not quite a smile, but something far more obscene. "Blood magic is always happy to oblige the proud and the desperate." She glided to the bookshelf, her long fingers trailing across the spines with the delicacy of a blind pianist. "Which flavor of certainty do you desire, King? Invulnerability? Madness? Death in the shape of your enemy's face?"

Moira's fingers stilled on the shelf. The cold radiating from her deepened, frosting the air in my lungs. "You've already begun," she said, less a question than an accusation. Her black eyes flicked to Dominic's as he sat at his desk, then back to me. "With an ancient book."

I didn't flinch. "You know it?"

She laughed—a sound like ice snapping underfoot—and withdrew her hand as if the spines had burned her. "Know it? It's a corpse's breath given form. The Black Codex should've been ash five centuries ago." For the first time, her ageless face twitched, a spiderweb of tension fracturing her composure. "Where did you—?"

"Irrelevant." I crossed to the panel, pried the Codex free again. Its binding needle bit my palm, drawing a bead of blood that sizzled against the leather. "Can you work it or not?"

Moira didn't touch the tome. She leaned in, nostrils flaring as if scenting rot, then recoiled. "This isn't blood magic. This is... communion. With things that gnaw at the roots of the world." Her voice wavered, just a tremor, but I stored it away like a blade. Fear. Genuine fear.

Dominic stirred, knuckles white on the chair arms. "Declan, maybe we should—"

"Quiet." I didn't look at him. Kept my gaze locked on Moira's endless eyes. "Name your price, witch. Triple your usual."

Her tongue darted out, wetting lips gone gray. "Triple won't save you when the debt comes due."

"But it'll buy you prettier headstones," I said. "Do we have an accord?"

A beat. Two. The cold sharpened until my teeth ached. Then—

"Dawnbloom petals. Still dripping sap," she snapped, suddenly all business, though her shoulders remained rigid. "The heart of a storm-struck oak. And a living vessel—something with teeth enough to bite back when the void starts chewing."

"The wolf," I said, nodding toward Callum, who grinned like a feral dog scenting blood.

Moira's gaze swept over him. "He'll do. Barely." She turned to Dominic, and I watched him try to sit up tall under her attention, sweat glistening on his upper lip. "You. Strip to the skin. Scour yourself with salt and vervain. No metal on your flesh when the moon crowns."

"Why?" he croaked.

"Because when the Codex opens you," she said, smiling now with all the warmth of a grave's shadow, "you'll want every barrier gone. Pain is the kindest part of this."

Dominic's throat bobbed, but he nodded.

Moira swept toward the door, her cloak billowing like a storm cloud. "One hour," she threw over her shoulder. "Pray your wolf doesn't piss himself before then."

The door slammed.

Callum chuckled, cracking his knuckles. "Feisty."

"Out," I ordered. When the room emptied, I pressed my bleeding palm to the Codex. The leather drank greedily, runes flaring copper-bright.

Let her fear, I thought. Fear made servants of wolves and witches alike.

Dominic lingered, trembling in the lamplight.

"Go prepare, King," I said softly. "Your mate awaits."

He fled.

Alone, I poured another whiskey. The lake outside mirrored the sky's gathering colors—purple, violent, beautiful.

Soon, Menace would learn the cost of defiance.

Soon, the Codex would feast.

I stared into the bottom of my glass, waiting for the last drop of courage to dissolve. Then I set it down, wiped my mouth.

Whatever it took. Whatever it cost.

CHAPTER 24

SAVANNAH

Council headquarters had the smell of old books and even older violence, the kind that soaked into the stone and never washed out. I sat at the end of the meeting table, wrists resting atop the polished oak, the trembling in my hands a secret only the wood would remember. Above me, the arched ceiling dwarfed us all. Centuries of plotting had stained it with candle soot and a whisper. At that hour, we were the only ones in the room—Juliet, Lucia, and me—alone with the aftermath and the fear that tomorrow would bring the end of everything I'd started to want.

Juliet was the definition of unshakable, with crossed arms and ankles, nails painted a shade of navy so dark it was nearly black. She watched me with the patience of a mother wolf, but every so often she would twitch, as if she wanted to bite the air itself. Lucia Kozlov, in contrast, was perched on the arm of a high-backed leather chair, her black curls a wild cloud that haloed her porcelain skin. She kept flashing her teeth, as if daring the world to bite first.

The longer we waited, the more the room pressed in. I watched the red pulse of my own finger where it tapped a steady rhythm on the table's edge. Even now, my body wanted to move, to run, to never stop.

"You're going to wear hole through that table, love," Lucia said, accent thick as old blood. "This room survives assassination attempt, vampire wars, but not nervous shifter girl, da?"

I tried to laugh, but it snagged in my throat. "You can go if you want. I'm not very good company."

Juliet put a hand over mine, her touch as cool and unyielding as marble. "I think you're exactly the company we need." She glanced at the door. "They said it would only be a few minutes."

"Bronc and Rafe are probably fighting over who is the talking one," Lucia said. "You know how males are. They want to appear decisive." She slid off the chair and stood in front of me, blocking out the chandelier. "But that's not what you think about? You think about Bridger."

I didn't answer.

Juliet's voice softened, losing its edge. "Is it that bad?"

I wanted to shake my head. I wanted to say it wasn't, that I was just tired, just hungry, just a little cold. But the words would have been a lie, and I was tired of lies.

"It's worse," I said. "I keep seeing him dead."

The table was long enough for ten, but in that moment it felt like an altar, and I was the only thing on it worth offering.

Lucia stepped closer, her heels making no sound on the stone. "He is strong. Stronger than any here. Maybe stronger than even you think."

"That's not what I'm worried about," I said. My voice came out hollow, barely a whisper. "It's my father. And Callum. They'll cheat. They always cheat."

Juliet nodded, as if this was the most logical thing in the world. "They might try. But the challenge is public. Judges will surround the arena."

"Dominic is still king," I said. "He could have anything hidden. Poisons. Traps. Witchcraft. The last time my father had an enemy, he buried her in concrete and used her bones as a garden ornament."

"Sounds like my kind of party," Lucia said, but there was a hardness behind the joke. "I will be there. My father too. If anyone tries things, they answer to us."

I looked up into her eyes, surprised by the ferocity there. "Why are you so invested?"

"Because you are friend," Lucia said. "And because your mate saved my life once, long ago. Debt is debt." She glanced at Juliet. "Besides, your father is dick."

Juliet smiled, just a fraction, and squeezed my hand. "It's not just the men who stand with you, Savannah. It's all of us. Iron Valor is family."

I nodded. "I just... I can't lose him. Not now. Not after everything."

Juliet leaned in, lowering her voice so only I could hear. "You need to trust in the Goddess. She wouldn't have given you Bridger just to rip him away. That's why you're going to survive this," she said. "You're the only one who's not afraid to say what scares you. The rest of them, even Bronc, they bury it. You let it out." She tapped my shoulder, right over the mate mark, which still throbbed with feelings of love and concern. "That's what makes you dangerous."

"Dangerous?" I shook my head. "Some days I can barely think."

"Exactly," she said. "And yet, here you are."

Lucia straightened, rolled her neck, and popped her knuckles one by one. "Let them cheat. Let them try. Menace is not so easy to kill."

The door opened then, letting in the scent of cigar smoke and the rustle of expensive wool. Bronc led the way, his expression thunderous, followed by King Rafe, who looked more priest than king in his charcoal suit and white shirt. Both men took seats at the far end, but Bronc's gaze pinned me with all the weight of a freight train.

"Sorry to keep you waiting," he said, and the lie was so obvious I almost laughed. "We've got confirmation. The Council is sticking to the ritual. No exceptions. No substitutions. Dominic has to face Menace in the flesh. No seconds, no magic, no weapons, but their own teeth and claws."

"They'll still try something," I said. "They always do."

Rafe held up a hand, calm and deliberate. "There'll be an army of witnesses. Vampires, witches, even a few demons and angels. They want this clean. They want it legendary."

Juliet arched an eyebrow. "Demons?"

Rafe smiled, but it didn't reach his eyes. "Even the underworld likes a good underdog story."

Bronc leaned forward, elbows on the table. "I know you're scared. I know you think this is a death sentence. But I need you to hold it together, Savannah. Bridger's counting on you. If he thinks you've given up, he will."

I tried to match his intensity, but my hands shook harder. "I believe in Menace one hundred percent. If it's a clean fight, nobody can beat him. It's hard to think they'll keep it honest. I don't know what to do about it."

Juliet's grip tightened. "You sit here, and you wait. And when the time comes, you stand in the front row and you let him see you're not afraid."

Lucia bared her fangs in a grin. "And if anyone tries to break rules, we break them first."

The table went quiet for a minute; the tension settling over us like a blanket of lead.

It was strange, the way council headquarters could shift shape depending on who occupied it. By the time Bronc, Rafe, and Menace herded the rest of us into the strategy room on the seventh floor, the air already felt different—charged, tense, almost military. The table was covered with maps and dossiers and a tray of untouched sandwiches, as if the entire fate of our lives could be solved with a working lunch. The room was windowless, but the walls, thick as the hull of a submarine, muted the world outside into a faint, reassuring hum.

Menace stood behind my chair, one palm flat on my shoulder, the heat of him radiating through the fine mesh of my dress. He didn't say anything at first, just squeezed once, a signal that stated I'm here, don't drift. Juliet sat on my left, scrolling on a tablet and muttering to herself. On my right, Lucia traced the rim of a wineglass with her finger, looking bored out of her mind until her eyes landed on my mate.

King Rafe held court at the head of the table, a roll of butcher paper unfurled before him and a red marker already uncapped. He drew a rough circle, then a line connecting it to a smaller X. "This is where the challenge will happen," he said, voice calm and deep. "Dominic's estate, Naperville, Illinois. Private grounds, but the Council's secured the perimeter and brought in their own security. They've also agreed to a fifteen-foot neutral zone—no one in, no one out, not even medical, until the fight ends."

Juliet scrolled, then stopped. "What about Council interference? Or third-party actors?" She didn't look up from her screen.

Bronc, looming behind Rafe, shrugged. "There'll be enough witches and demons to keep even Declan from stacking the deck. And Kozlov's people will be there too."

That's when I noticed him: Kazimir Kozlov, standing in the corner like a negative of a man, skin pale as rice paper, eyes black as a vacuum. He smiled at me, just a little, and inclined his head. Next to me, Lucia rolled her eyes. "Father is here for moral support, not to start war. But if war happens, we are ready."

Menace's grip on my shoulder tightened. "What's the plan for travel?" His voice was even, but I could hear the coil of energy underneath it.

Rafe pointed to the map. "Tonight, we leave Chicago. It's only 33 miles from Council headquarters to Dominic's estate in Naperville. I've ordered my Sikororsky S-92 helicopter to take us to the property I've rented for us. The copter seats 12. I believe

Bronc has his team flying to Birmingham to pick up the Iron Valor Jet to bring it to O'Hare?"

"Arsenal, Doc, Wrecker, and Big Papa are already en route," Bronc said, looking at me, not Menace. "We also have a group of other Iron Valor pack members en route to O'Hare. Menace is not going into this battle alone." He then turned to Rafe. "Sir, I believe you'll have SUVs arranged to pick them up when they arrive?"

"Absolutely. They know their assignments." Rafe's reply was exacting and sure. These men were like a well-oiled machine.

I felt Menace exhale, the knot in his shoulders loosening by a millimeter. "And after the fight?"

Rafe hesitated. "If you win, you're king of the Midwest territory even before a coronation, since challenge won the crown. And that's a whole new ball of wax. Declan will be incensed at having lost. I don't know how the Midwest packs will take it."

Kazimir spoke next. "You must obtain fealty from all pack Alphas immediately. None would dare challenge you."

"If you lose, Savannah gets safe passage to wherever she wants. That's my guarantee."

Lucia's eyes snapped to mine. "He won't lose," she said, her tone not entirely reassuring.

"Declan *will* try to cheat," I said. My voice didn't shake. "He doesn't know any other way."

Kazimir spoke again, this time directly to me, voice low and elegant. "My daughter tells me your mate is worth a thousand King Dominics. We will provide additional security. Discreet but effective." He eyed Menace. "You have my word as vampire sovereign of the East."

Menace nodded, solemn. "Thank you."

Rafe drew another circle on the map, this one farther out. "Once we're on the property, everyone sticks together. Council's put us all in the same wing—no splitting up, no wandering. Challenge is at dusk on Wednesday. Basically gives us two days."

Juliet flicked her eyes up from the tablet. "And you're *sure* Dominic will play it straight?"

Bronc answered. "No. But if he doesn't, the repercussions will be biblical. This is a trial by blood, not by lawyers."

For a moment, no one spoke. The only sound was the tap of Lucia's nail against her glass and the almost imagined thrum of jet engines in the distance.

Menace's fingers slid from my shoulder to the back of my neck, a motion so subtle only I would notice. He leaned in, lips brushing the shell of my ear. "You okay?" The question wasn't for now, but for what came next.

I nodded. The bond between us was a live wire, bright and thrumming, but beneath it was the certainty that I would rather die than let him walk into this alone.

Kazimir said, "And if anything happens, my people are authorized to kill on sight. No questions. No witnesses."

The meeting wound down after that; the plans distilled into a single sheet of paper, signed by Bronc, Rafe, and Kazimir. They left us alone in the room for a few minutes, the silence as thick as sleep.

Menace pulled out the chair next to me and sat, body turned to face mine. "I'm ready."

"I know," I said. "I just wish I could do it for you."

He gave a soft laugh. "If it were up to me, neither of us would be doing this."

Lucia stretched and then rose from her chair. "I need to find coffee. Or something stronger." She looked at Menace. "Try not to get blood on my shoes, okay?"

He grinned, teeth flashing. "No promises."

Juliet closed her tablet and snapped the case shut. "Come on, Savannah. Let's go pack."

As we left the room, I looked back once, saw Menace alone at the table, tracing the red lines Rafe had drawn with the tip of his finger. He looked like a man studying the pattern of his own veins, trying to find the artery that would let the pain out.

Outside, the halls were already emptier than before. The world had shifted again, and we were moving with it, hurtling toward a collision none of us could escape.

But for the first time since this nightmare started, I felt something other than dread. It was hope, raw and sharp, and it left a taste in my mouth that lingered long after we'd left the building behind.

The estate looked like something out of a rich man's fever dream: three stories, limestone front, lights blazing in every window even though dusk was still thickening the sky outside. Our driver pulled through a set of iron gates, up a drive so long I wondered if the house would ever materialize. As we rounded the last bend, the headlights swept over a line of cars—some black SUVs, others that looked like they belonged in a war zone. Beyond them, the mansion loomed, squat and watchful. Even from the curb, it radiated a kind of patient peril.

Menace led the way inside. The front doors were heavy oak, ancient and iron-banded, and they swallowed us one by one into a foyer bigger than most people's entire living spaces. The floor was black tile, polished to a mirror, and every step echoed forever. In the middle of the foyer, Arsenal and Doc waited—both in jeans and t-shirts, both looking like they'd never been further than five feet from a loaded firearm.

"Menace, you old bastard," Arsenal said, clapping him on the back so hard the sound rattled the chandeliers. "Can't leave you alone for ten damn minutes."

Menace grinned, the first genuine smile I'd seen on him in days. "I move fast for an old guy."

Doc shook his head. "We got bets running through the pack. Half the guys think you're gonna snap Dominic in half. The other half think you're gonna literally tear him limb from limb."

Arsenal elbowed Doc. "The money's on you, man. Nobody wants to see the pussy king win."

Menace's hand found mine, gave it a squeeze. "That makes all of us." He nodded toward Bronc and Rafe, who trailed in behind us. "You bring the whole circus?"

"Couldn't leave the pretty people at home," Bronc said. "Besides, they wanted front row seats."

The reunion was fast, loud, and obscene in its familiarity. For a while I stood off to the side, watching the choreography of brotherhood: the shoulder slaps, the hugs that were closer to wrestling holds, the way even their insults were stitched through with something like love. Juliet joined me, arms folded, eyes scanning the crowd with practiced indifference. She caught me staring at Menace, then at Arsenal, then back at Menace.

"They're a different breed," she said, not unkindly. "Like a litter of dogs that never grew up. But nobody better to have by your side in times of trouble."

Lucia drifted over, glass of vodka in hand, and shrugged. "At least they're loyal. Most men are not."

The house was too warm, the air dry and scented with lemon oil and the faint metallic note of spent adrenaline. I felt the sweat bead under my collar, but it was nothing compared to the chill that crawled my spine every time I caught a glimpse of the long hallway that led off the foyer. The shadows there moved wrong—too fast, or not at all. I wondered if anyone else felt it, but the men were too busy with their rituals, and Juliet was busy pretending not to care.

Wrecker appeared next, arms crossed and smile wide enough to unhinge his face. He punched Menace on the shoulder, then glanced at me. "Hey Savannah." I nodded. He looked at Menace, then back at me. "I know we don't know each other well, but he's talked more about you than he's ever talked about anyone. Never said you were this pretty, though."

I managed a weak smile. "He lies a lot."

"Not about this," Wrecker said, and there was something so genuine in his eyes that it hurt to look at him for too long.

The dining room was set like a funeral feast: enormous table, candelabra at the center, enough food to feed a pack of wolves. Doc ushered us in, then poured wine into heavy crystal goblets. The men took their places—Bronc at the head, Juliet to his right, then Arsenal, Big Papa beside him. Menace was to Bronc's left, then me, Lucia, Wrecker, and Doc. Lucia was a nice block against all the testosterone that was flowing. Rafe took his place at the other head.

At first, the talk was all business. Arsenal mapped out the plan for tomorrow—wake at 0500, gym, then breakfast, more strategizing with Rafe and his team, then transport to the arena. Menace would fight Dominic at dusk, alone in the ring except for the Council witnesses and the cameras. There were big screens that flanked the arena, so everyone who watched got a bird's-eye view of the carnage. If, Goddess forbid, he died, the rest of us were to run, not look back, and never speak of this day again.

"Don't die," Arsenal said, voice flat. "I don't want to have to lie to your old lady."

Menace grunted. "I'll do my best."

I didn't say it aloud, but I told myself, *if he dies, I die too*. There was no life without my fated.

The men ate, piling their plates high with steak and bread and potatoes. The food was good, but none of them seemed to care. I picked at my meal, appetite gone, and watched the way the room seemed to close in around us, the dark outside pressing against the windows like a second skin.

After a few minutes, the tone shifted. The stories started; some funny, some ugly, all true. Wrecker told about the time Menace talked a suicide bomber out of detonating, only to knock him cold and handcuff him to a light pole. Doc recounted the time Menace took a bullet to the thigh and kept running, dragging three men to safety while cursing the whole way. Even Big Papa chimed in, voice deep and sonorous, telling how Menace once held a dying teammate's hand for five hours, not leaving until the body was cold.

The men laughed, sometimes too loud, sometimes not loud enough. They talked about pain like it was a badge, about fear like it was a joke they'd all heard, but no one quite remembered the punchline.

I watched Menace, saw how the stories softened him, how the lines in his face smoothed, how the anger faded to something almost gentle. For a while, I let myself believe this was a normal night, that tomorrow would be another day, that men like him got to live forever.

When the meal ended, the men drifted into the living room, voices dropping to low, urgent murmurs. Juliet disappeared with Bronc. Lucia vanished, probably to hunt something in the woods. I lingered, not wanting to leave, not wanting the night to end.

Menace caught my eye from across the room. He moved to me, silent as a ghost, and took my hand.

"Come with me," he said, and I did.

He led me to a side hallway, away from the others, down a corridor lined with portraits of people who looked like they'd never known happiness. At the end was a sunroom, the glass dark and streaked with rain. He closed the door behind us, then turned and put his arms around me.

"I'm not afraid," he said. "Not anymore."

I buried my face in his shoulder, breathed in the scent of him—cedar wood, smoke, and home. "Then neither am I."

He kissed the top of my head.

I looked up at him and saw the way his eyes glowed gold in the dim light. "I wish I were half as strong as you."

He laughed. "You're stronger. You've survived worse."

We stood there for a while, not moving, just feeling the world tilt and shift around us. For the first time, I thought maybe we could win. Maybe the universe wasn't always rigged in favor of the monsters.

When we went back to the others, the men were already heading up to their rooms. When they saw us, Big Papa stopped and grabbed our hands. I was moved beyond measure when he quietly prayed for Menace.

Outside, the wind picked up, rattling the old glass in its frame.

If tonight was our last night together, we were going to go out with all the passion we could muster. When we got to our room, I grabbed his face in my hands and kissed him like there was no tomorrow.

Chapter 25

Menace

Savannah hit me like a bullet at the threshold, mouth already on mine, legs tangled around my waist. The door was barely shut, and she was clawing at my shirt, tearing open buttons with a desperation that almost hurt to see. Her hands went up into my hair, fists clamped tight. She bit my lip hard enough to draw blood, and when I flinched, she growled—low, raw, nothing human in it.

The air between us went brittle. My own hands found her hips, the slip of her ass beneath the thin fabric of her dress, and I hoisted her higher, pinning her against the wall with my body. She made a sound—half sob, half snarl—and locked her ankles at the small of my back, grinding against the hard line of my cock through my jeans. I tasted salt and iron, sweat and her. The world outside the door was gone, burned to nothing.

I carried her into the bathroom, flipping on the light with an elbow. The place was all glass and cold tile, designed for men who drank their whiskey neat and never shed a tear. I sat her on the counter, knocking aside a glass and a little bottle of mouthwash. The shiver that went through her was pure animal lust and hunger. She yanked at my belt, fingers clumsy, cursing under her breath.

"God, I need you," she said. Not a plea. A fact.

I tore the dress from her in a single motion, fabric splitting at the seam and falling away. She was naked underneath, except for a sliver of lace I ripped off with my teeth. She giggled, just a flash, then went still when I ran my palms up her thighs. Her skin was so pale it reflected the light, every goosebump and scar lit up for me. I kissed her knee, her inner thigh, her hipbone, and she closed her eyes, chin tilted up like she was praying for mercy.

"Shower," I said, and she nodded, sliding off the counter with a grace that was almost obscene.

I stripped, and we stepped in together. The water was already running—scalding, perfect. Steam billowed up around us, turning the bathroom into a pressure cooker. The first blast hit her shoulder, and she gasped, arching her back as the heat ran over her. I watched the way the water beaded and ran in little rivers between her breasts, down her belly, over the scar on her thigh.

She turned to face me, green eyes shining, mouth parted. "You going to stand there, or you going to do something about it?"

I pressed her against the glass. My hands shook as I lathered the soap, dragging lavender and slickness across every inch of her body. I washed her like she were made of crystal, careful and methodical, except when I wasn't. I spent minutes on her tits, running the pad of my thumb over her nipples until they peaked, red and furious. She shivered at every touch, hair plastered to her face, breathing in little hitched gasps. I kneaded them in my hands, loving the feel of them. Soft and firm, the contradiction a mystery I didn't care to solve. When the soap washed away, my mouth was on her, sucking each peak, my tongue twirling until my teeth pulled at them. Her hands were in my hair, pulling me to her.

"Don't stop," she whispered, but I could barely hear her over the hiss of the water.

I dropped to my knees. The tile felt cool against my skin. I pulled her hips toward me and pushed one thigh over my shoulder, spreading her open. She braced against the wall, hands splayed, head thrown back. The scent of her was sweet and sharp under the lavender—pure Savannah, pure mate, mine.

I started slow, dragging my tongue through her slit, tasting every drop, every shiver. She moaned, low and shamed, trying to muffle the noise with her hand.

"Don't you hold back on me, Savannah. Give me everything I demand. I want your sounds. All of them."

I bit the inside of her thigh, and she whimpered, so I did it again, harder. The water pounded her back, and I devoured her, tongue working circles over her clit until her legs shook.

"Please," she choked. "Please—fuck—don't stop, don't stop!"

I sucked her clit between my teeth and she screamed, not caring who heard, not caring if the whole damn house listened in. Her body locked up and she came, flooding my mouth, her fingers digging so hard into my hair I thought she'd rip it out by the roots. I kept going, kept licking her through the aftershocks, until she was sobbing my name and begging me to let her breathe.

I stood, mouth and chin glistening. She slid down to her knees, and before I could say a word; she reached for my cock with both hands and shoved it into her mouth so deep her nose pressed my pelvis. She gagged once, then relaxed her throat and took all of me, eyes shining up at mine as she swallowed. The look in her eyes was pure challenge. Can you handle this?

"Baby, fuck. That feels so good."

I braced both hands on the slick tile, vision going white around the edges. She worked her tongue along the underside, twisting her wrist at the base, the other hand clutching my ass, pulling me closer. Every time she pulled off, she licked the tip, never breaking eye contact, before plunging down again. The shower was a sauna now—steam thick, air electric, every surface dripping. The sound of her mouth on me was the only thing I could hear, wet and filthy and alive. She took me to the back of her throat over and over. I couldn't tell if it was the shower or tears running down her cheeks. Either way, it was beautiful.

"I'm gonna come, Savannah, and you are gonna swallow every drop. You understand?"

Green eyes found mine, her eager nod telling me she want-ed it. It didn't take long. My balls tightened, a lightning flash at the base of my spine, and I warned her—once, twice—but she just sucked harder, refusing to let go. My hands were in her hair as my hips pushed my dick further to the back of her throat. When I came, I shouted, slamming a fist into the glass so hard it rattled. She swallowed every drop, then licked me clean, spit running down her chin.

I lifted her up to me and kissed her deep. Our tastes mingled together.

She looked up at me with a savage little smile, eyes glassy and wild.

"That was the hottest fucking thing I've ever done," she said, her voice shredded.

"We're just getting started, Red."

I pulled her onto my lap and held her; the water sluic-ing us both clean. She buried her face in my neck and sobbed once—just a single, sharp cry—before she laughed and wrapped her arms tighter.

We stayed like that until the water started to run cold, until her skin was puckered. I carried her to the pantry and grabbed one of the thick towels and wrapped her up, rubbing her dry with hands that trembled and shook. She looked at me with a contentment I'd never seen, not in her or anyone.

I carried her to the bedroom, her skin glowing under the dim light of the room. Her hair was pulled up in a loose bun, wet strands escaping to frame her face, and I couldn't help but think how fucking perfect she looked. Like she was made for me, for this moment. I let her legs down gently, standing her with her back to my chest, my hands tracing every inch of her perfect body. I wanted to memorize every scar, every curve. Should I die tomorrow, I wanted every detail of my mate to be the last thing my mind saw. My fingers felt the contour of her waist and hips, soft under my calloused fingertips—felt gooseflesh rise with every stroke. Her head fell back against my shoulder.

She fit so perfectly against me. I pressed my hand fully over the mound of her pussy, loving the feel of her bare flesh under my touch. "I'm going to have this body several times tonight. My entire being will be tattooed upon your soul before I'm through." I pressed two fingers inside her channel that was dripping wet with her need. "Fuck, you make me happy, Red." I told her, my lips against her ear as she moaned and I circled her clit, bringing her closer to release.

I walked her two steps closer to the bed and gave her back a gentle push. "I need you bent over the bed for me, beautiful." My foot kicked her legs wider for me. I groaned at the sight of her—her pussy glistening with her arousal, her ass just begging for my cock. I ran my hand down her back, over the curve of her ass, and then down to her pussy, slipping my fingers inside her so they were good and wet. When I slipped one inside her tight pucker, she moaned, pushing back against my hand, stretching her as I pulled her back slightly then hit my knees to lick her clit.

"Menace," she whimpered, her voice breaking as I pushed a second finger into her tight little hole. She was so wet, so ready, and I couldn't wait any longer.

"I fucking swear, Red. If I survive tomorrow. My dick will have this hole someday." I pulled my fingers out and positioned myself at her entrance, pushing into her beautiful pussy slowly, savoring the way she clenched around me.

"Fuck," I groaned, burying myself balls deep in one smooth thrust. She cried out, her back arching as she pushed back against me, taking every inch of my cock. I grabbed her hips, pulling her back onto me as I thrust hard and fast, the sound of our skin slapping together filling the room.

"Yes," she moaned, her voice trembling with pleasure. "Fuck me, Menace. Harder." There was desperation in her words. She needed to feel everything I could give her. It needed to be as real as we could make it.

I didn't hold back, slamming into her with everything I had, my cock hitting that spot inside her that made her scream. I reached around to rub her clit, feeling her pussy clench around me as she came again, her body shaking with the force of it.

"That's it," I growled, fucking her through her orgasm. "Come for me, baby. Let me feel you."

She did, crying out as her release continued, her pussy squeezing me so tight I thought I might lose it. But I wasn't done with her yet. While I continued to fuck her, I could feel my knot start to grow. I wet my thumb and pressed it against her asshole, rubbing it against the tight little ring of muscle.

"Menace," she gasped. "It's too much, feels too good."

"You'll take what I give you, mate. I want you to feel everything tonight."

My knot was making my thrusts more difficult, but I knew it was close to the spot inside her that took her beyond reasoning. I felt her ass tightening around my thumb, her pussy choking my cock as her release came on like a freight train. I leaned over her and sank my teeth into my claiming mark one last time. Her blood filled my mouth, and the bond surged stronger than ever. I felt every emotion of love, longing, fear, and anguish flood my soul. We were so connected I didn't know where she began and I ended.

I collapsed on top of her, both of us breathing hard as we came down from the high. My knot had begun to release, and I was able to turn her to where her legs could wrap around me. Her arms came around my neck as she cuddled her head to my chest. Sitting on the bed, I gently took her hair down and stroked her back.

"I love you," I whispered, my voice rough with emotion. "No matter what happens tomorrow, you're mine. Always."

We lay on the bed for several minutes in silence. I rolled her over, kissed her mouth, then licked the sweat off her neck and breasts. She was crying, but she was smiling, too.

"You're all I ever wanted even though I didn't know it at the time."

She nodded, still catching her breath.

"And tomorrow, I'm going to kill Dominic. I'm going to tear his head off and throw it at your father's feet. Then I'm going to come back here and fuck you until you can't walk."

She giggled, wiped her eyes, and buried her face in my chest. "You promise?"

"Scout's honor."

She started tracing circles on my chest, her fingers soft and warm. We lay together, listening to the tick of the mantel clock and the distant sound of nature outside. The bed was soaked, ruined, but neither of us cared. It smelled like us.

"I feel like our bond is stronger," she whispered.

I kissed her hair, breathed her in. "I feel like that too. That will help me tomorrow. You make me stronger."

She fell asleep before I did, hand still curled over my heart.

I listened to the rhythm of her breathing, let the exhaustion seep into my bones, let the blackness at the edge of my vision spread and take me.

Tomorrow, there would be war.

But tonight, we were alive.

Chapter 26

Savannah

When I woke, the world outside the window was a wash of nothing, a dry December sky faintly colored by the threat of sunrise. The bed beside me was cold—Menace's absence a divot in the mattress, a mate-shaped outline pressed into the sheets. He was already gone, and I didn't need to reach through the bond to feel the afterimage of him: a hot filament of energy echoing with pain, focus, anticipation. The clock read six a.m., but it felt like the final hour.

For a long time, I lay there and measured my own heart. It ran a jittery, broken rhythm, never quite settling into a pace that matched the dead silence of the house. I closed my eyes, hoping for more sleep, but the dark behind my lids was alive with dreams of fur and fangs and the blood on Menace's hands. When I couldn't take the crawl of my own mind anymore, I threw off the covers and swung my feet to the floor. The hardwood was glacial, and the air felt hollowed out, as if the house itself was holding its breath for what was to come.

I washed, brushed my teeth with hands that trembled too much, and then stood naked before the closet. My body was mottled with bruises, evidence of the night before—his teeth, my need, the fact that when we made love, it was more violence than tenderness. My mate mark looked inflamed in the mirror, a red glyph just below the hinge of my jaw. The flesh around it was mottled, like the petals of a dying peony. I traced it with one finger, felt the heat of it, and pretended that some of Menace's courage could be drawn through the skin and bone, right into my blood.

I had never dressed for badassery before, but by God I did now. I chose black. A high-necked turtleneck tucked into velvet-soft leggings, boots that crested above my knees and zipped up the inside seam. Over the top, I wore a black leather vest, the kind the Iron Valor women wore when they wanted to look intimidating and untouchable. I raked my hair back into a high, tight ponytail. I was going for a look that said, *'my man is a killer, I can't wait to see it.'*

Just before I left, I noticed the long coat draped over the edge of the chair. It was black leather, heavier than any jacket I'd worn before, with an Iron Valor patch sewn over the heart. The red lining was shot through with satin, but gave me a feeling of armor. I shrugged it on, and for the first time since childhood, I almost didn't recognize myself in the mirror. I looked like the villain of someone else's story—pale, lips bitten red, eyes the green of pond algae and panic. There was nothing of the Calloway princess left. Just a wolf's woman, ready for the last battle.

I hesitated at the threshold, hand on the knob, and sent all the encouragement I could muster through the bond. *Menace*, I thought, *you're not alone. You never will be.* I pushed it hard, hoping he'd feel it, that the heat and light would hit him mid-stride and knock the doubt from his chest.

I didn't see anyone in the hall, but I could hear the scrape of chairs and the hiss of a percolator from somewhere down the stairs. The dining room was already alive with the wreckage of men preparing for war. Arsenal and Doc sat closest to the door, hunched over mugs of black coffee like priests at a pre-dawn mass. Wrecker and Big Papa were at the buffet, loading their plates with enough food to choke a horse. At the far end of the table, Lucia Kozlov perched like a wraith, elegant in a long sleeve red velvet dress, her black curls drawn up in a messy knot that only highlighted the porcelain of her face.

But it was Menace who nearly made me catch my breath. He was sitting with his back to the window, light cutting a white stripe across his bare shoulder and the thick silver scar at his jaw. He wore sweatpants and nothing else, his chest slick with post-workout sweat and the vapor that steamed off him in the chill of the house. He was laughing, a low growl of sound, and for a split second he looked younger—beautiful, the way some wolves are when the blood is up and the teeth are hidden.

Then he saw me. He stood up so fast the chair shrieked against the floor, and the room went silent.

"Holy shit," Arsenal said, half under his breath.

Even Lucia, who'd seen more death than any man at the table, was momentarily stunned. "You look..." She searched for the word, then gave up.

"Fucking hell, Red. You look like pale rider come to collect."

Menace crossed to me in three steps. He ran his eyes over every inch—slow, hot, unashamed—and when he reached the Iron Valor patch above my heart, he stopped. He put his hand over it, fingers splayed, palm warm through the layers.

"You look like a queen," he said, voice rough. "Not the kind that sits on a throne. The kind that burns the fucking castle down."

He kissed me right there in front of everyone, hands flat against my back, mouth open and hungry. The room erupted in catcalls and applause, but I shut the sound out. The bond roared between us, a current that pulsed with so much love and trepidation I thought it might crack me open.

When he pulled away, there was blood on his lower lip—mine, from where my teeth had split in the force of the kiss. He licked it off and grinned, feral and sweet.

"I could eat you right here," he whispered, low enough that only I could hear it. "But we'd never get to the fight."

I smacked his arm, just hard enough to sting. "I'm ready," I said, and it was true.

Lucia poured me a mug of coffee, then slid it across the table with a smile. "You will not need this. But it helps, yes?"

I nodded thanks.

The men talked, voices tight with adrenaline and old grievances, and for a moment I felt like I'd always been here, like I belonged in this den of broken wolves and dying hope. Juliet entered the room last, dressed much like me, only her top was red and her hair was down, her eyes alive with the kind of wild, steady rage that only a Luna can wield. She gave me a once-over, then nodded, as if to say, *now you get it*.

We ate in silence for a while. Menace never let his hand leave my thigh.

There was a clock on the far wall. The numbers ticked closer to the hour when everything would change, but in that second, with him beside me and the pack all around, it almost didn't seem like his life was on the line.

Almost.

After breakfast, the house shifted from a lair to a command post. Menace and Bronc started clearing plates before the last of the eggs were gone, shoving them into the sink with a violence that didn't match the eggs themselves. Arsenal, Doc, and Wrecker migrated toward the living room, but were called back in with a barked order from Bronc, who was already unrolling maps and scattering them across the scarred dining table. The room filled, one by one, with the rest of our war council: Juliet, serious and intense, with her hair loose, golden, wild waves around her face; Lucia, still barefoot, padding across the tile with a mug of vodka in hand; and King Rafe, who wore a shirt like it was a uniform and stood behind his chair as if he meant to interrogate it.

"Let's do this," Menace said. His voice wasn't loud, but it cut through the low buzz of caffeine and nerves. The men took their seats. I pulled up a chair beside Juliet, who winked at me as she produced a legal pad from a briefcase somewhere beside her.

The table was covered with printed diagrams, aerial photographs, and what looked like a hand-drawn layout of the fighting pit. At the center was a glossy full-color map of the arena, marked up with red and blue Sharpie lines.

"First thing," Bronc started, "we go over the arena. No surprises. This is where they'll try to fuck us."

Menace leaned forward and traced a line along the map. "There's three main exits—here, here, and here. Security will be tightest at the entry, but the Council's running all external checkpoints. That means no one gets in or out without at least three signatures. They'll have private guards in all the corridors." He jabbed a finger at the edge of the pit. "The fighting area itself is open, with no barriers, no cover except for the arena cover itself. Other than that, just dirt and blood. The Council Chairwoman will announce the challenge, then they will lock the doors until it's over. No interference, no medical, no second chances. You win or you die."

"Sounds like home," Arsenal muttered, but no one laughed.

"Judges will be posted along the perimeter," Doc said, pointing to the small red circles along the outer ring. "One from each species—wolf, vampire, witch, demon, and angel. They have kill-switches for anything magical or tech-based. The moment it starts, the rules are absolute."

I looked at the map, trying to picture the fight. "So it's just... you and Dominic. No weapons, nothing?"

Bronc shook his head. "Just teeth, claws, and what the Goddess gave you. Anything else is grounds for immediate execution. And they will do it, Savannah. They'd rather kill you both than risk a scandal."

"Dominic's wolf is bigger, but slower," Menace said, voice hard. "He's used to bullying smaller prey. I'll have to run him out, make him tired, and then take him when he's desperate. His left hind leg is weak from an old injury. If I can bait him into lunging, I can take it out and end this fast."

Arsenal grinned. "And if you can't?"

"Then I'll die trying," Menace said, and there was no bravado in it.

I cleared my throat. "What about the Council? The ones who voted for us—they should all sit together. In our box. Show strength."

There was a pause, then Lucia nodded. "Is good idea. Looks like unity. Makes them less likely to betray."

Juliet scribbled a note, then spoke without looking up. "Iron Valor officers will be first row. The rest of the pack fills the general stands. We'll have eyes everywhere. And Rafe's people are running external logistics—communications, transport, everything."

Bronc added, "I'll serve as first. That means if Menace gets hit with something dirty—poison, spell, whatever—I'm allowed to intervene if the Council agrees it's not fair play."

"And if they don't agree?" I asked.

He shrugged. "Then we burn the place down and run."

A ripple of nervous laughter went around the table, but it died quick. The mood was a wire pulled tight, waiting to snap.

"Juliet and I have practiced a new thing," Bronc said. "We can communicate through the mate bond. Actual words now—not just feelings. If anything is off, I'll get it to her, and she'll relay it to you." He looked at me, eyes clear and direct. "Nothing will get past us, Savannah. Not this time."

Menace's hand slid over mine, calloused fingers curling tight. "If I go down, you run. No heroics."

I didn't answer. He knew the truth—if he died, I'd never leave.

King Rafe stood, flattening his palms on the table. "The challenge is at six. Once it starts, no one can help. You can scream, you can cry, but no one will listen. The only rule is: last man standing."

Menace nodded. "That's all I need."

Lucia stood, drained her glass, and set it down with a click. "Time to get ready, da? No one wants to see my father cry if you lose."

Juliet closed her notebook. "We'll meet at the cars in two hours. Don't be late."

As everyone filtered out, Menace caught my elbow and pulled me close. "You scared?"

"Of course I'm scared," I said. "I just look better in black."

He kissed the top of my head, lips lingering. "Stay alive, Red. That's all you have to do."

I watched the others go. The house was suddenly too big, too quiet, like an abandoned church after the congregation had given up hope. The maps and plans were already obsolete—by this time tomorrow, we'd be either dead or kings.

I pressed my hand to the Iron Valor patch on my chest, felt my heart kick beneath it.

One more hour. One more shot.

I'd never been more ready for anything in my life.

They said to meet in the foyer at 2:45, and when I stepped into the hall at 2:43, everyone was already there, down to the second. The Iron Valor men in black suits with pressed collars and hands fidgeting at their sides. Juliet and Lucia flanked me, both in their best approximation of "funeral-wear"—Juliet in severe navy, Lucia in a velvet black maxi with a high neck and a Russian cross at her throat. Menace had traded his sweats for slacks and a thin cashmere shirt, the kind that clung to every ridge of muscle and made him look like he'd just stepped out of a torture scene. He had that shine in his eye: the one that came right before a gunfight, or maybe a wedding.

Rafe and Bronc conferred with the drivers in the driveway, surrounded by five black SUVs. The cars were already running, little clouds of exhaust ghosting in the December air. The cold was biting, but the adrenaline running through my system made it feel like the surface of the sun.

When Bronc saw me, he stopped mid-sentence, mouth twitching. "You ready, Savannah?"

"Ready or not, we're doing this, so I'd say I'm ready," I said, and he grinned, proud and sad.

We piled into the cars, men up front, women in the back. Menace tucked me under his arm, thigh pressed hard against mine. The car smelled of cologne and upholstery and the faint, coppery tang of impending violence. We didn't talk; we just held each other, and I matched my breathing to his heartbeat.

The ride lasted exactly fourteen minutes, but it felt like a parade into the unknown. We rode in silence, staring out at the frosted fields, the leafless trees, the clouds gathering at the horizon in long, pastel-colored lines. Every few miles we passed a checkpoint: more black SUVs, bored-looking Council police with sunglasses and earpieces, dogs bristling at the ends of their leashes. The closer we got to the estate, the more it felt like a siege.

The arena was visible from a mile away, a white scar on the earth shining under the winter sky. It looked like a mausoleum or a stadium built for gladiators—massive, square, the windows all mirrored. There were already cars lined up along the access road, a procession of royalty and hangers-on here to watch someone die. I thought of how they must have this place glamoured so the human world didn't notice it.

The SUV slid up the ramp and into a gated lot beneath the building. We stopped at a security booth, where a vampire in a three-piece suit checked our badges and then bowed his head, just enough to show respect but not enough to admit fear.

"Good luck," he said, and Menace's eyes flashed gold.

Inside the structure, it was colder. The air smelled of bleach and concrete, and our footsteps echoed in the long hallway that led from the garage to the inner sanctum. The Council had gone all-out: everything was sterilized, security guards stood at every intersection, and there were cameras every ten feet, tiny red lights blinking in the corners of the ceiling. The corridors twisted, a labyrinth designed to make escape impossible.

A Council escort—a witch with blue hair and a voice like crushed ice—led us down a staircase and through two sets of reinforced doors. On the far side was a locker room, cinderblock walls, a row of battered wooden benches, and a single full-length mirror. The door out to the arena was already propped open, and I could hear the low roar of the crowd, like the pulse of a dying god.

Menace sat and pulled off his boots, moving with the efficiency of a soldier. He stripped to the waist, baring his scars and the tattoo that ran down his back: the Iron Valor wolf, jaws open, eyes red, fur inked with the names of every man he'd lost in battle. He caught my eye in the mirror, and for the first time, he looked afraid.

I went to him, rested my hands on his shoulders, felt the tension in the knots of his neck. "Don't let them break you," I whispered, and he smiled, but it was all teeth.

Juliet and Bronc stayed near the door, whispering in a language I didn't know—something secret and ancient, the way wolves used to talk before men forced them into suits and jobs. Lucia sat alone, feet tucked under her, reading a battered paperback. But her eyes were sharp, flicking up every time someone moved.

At five o'clock, the crowd upstairs went insane. The sound was less a cheer than a wail, a million voices layered over each other. The stands were full—Council dignitaries, supernatural media, even the royalty from other houses. The big screens at each end of the arena showed looping video of Menace and Dominic, their faces staring out like wanted posters.

A Councilwoman in a gray suit appeared at the door, her clipboard tucked to her chest like a shield. "You have fifteen minutes," she said. "Then the challenge is called. Please make your way to the staging area."

She left without waiting for a reply.

Menace pulled on a pair of black drawstring pants. He didn't bother with shoes or a shirt. "You look good," I said, and he laughed—a single bark.

He pulled me close and pressed his forehead to mine. "I want you to promise me something," he said. "If I lose—"

"You're not going to lose."

"If I lose," he repeated, "don't wait. Don't grieve. Just burn it down and walk away."

I didn't reply. There was nothing I could say that wouldn't be a lie.

He kissed me, slow and hard, and when he let go, he touched the mate mark at my neck with the pad of his thumb. "I love you," he said.

I gripped his wrist, squeezed. "I love you more."

Bronc called, "Menace, it's time."

The staging area was another concrete bunker, this one lined with ancient runes that glowed faintly blue. There was a viewing slit, like in a prison, and through it I saw the pit—just dirt, packed hard, ringed by ten-foot walls. The air was thick with anticipation and fear. Juliet took my hand and didn't let go.

Chapter 27

King Declan Calloway

The chamber beneath the arena was colder than the grave, wet stone bleeding chill through the soles of my shoes. It was almost dusk, so the moon was barely visible in the winter sky. Down here, light filtered in only as sickness, a thread of mercury seeping in through the grates and falling in trembling streaks over the table, the altar, the floor where Dominic would either die or become unkillable. The place reeked of centuries-old sweat and the yellow of fresh fear. I breathed it deep. The copper in the air would be worse soon enough. I made sure no one could make entry.

Dominic was already in the circle, stripped to his skin as Moira commanded. His flesh was marbled with pale, bloodless streaks, his veins webbing blue beneath the surface like worms pressed between glass slides. He shivered. Not from the cold—no, I recognized the shudder of a man preparing himself for a pain he could not conceptualize. His tongue darted across his lips, flicked at the dust of words he couldn't say.

Moira circled him, barefoot and silent as a shadow, drawing lines in the salt with a sprig of something brown and leafless. Her eyes were voids; even when the candlelight splashed across her face, it was as if the light gave up and drowned there. Her hands moved with predatory grace. The sigils she drew on the stones seemed to shimmer, then fix, as if the world itself was reluctant to let them stick.

"Do not move," she whispered to Dominic, not looking at him. "If you move, you'll tear the boundary and invite everything in at once."

He looked at me, desperate for assurance. I gave him nothing.

Moira muttered in her death-dry tongue. I heard only fragments—words about teeth, and debt, and the part of the moon that does not turn to face us. Then she leaned in, pressing her palm to Dominic's chest. Her fingers left behind a smear of gray powder that began to sink into his skin, as if his body was thirsty for it.

Dominic gasped. Not a scream. Not yet. But close.

Moira's hands blurred. She produced a knife from her belt—its blade old, blackened, the hilt a tangle of wire and bone. She made the first cut below his right collarbone, and the sound it made was not the sound of a knife going into flesh, but the wet rasp of something burrowing out. Dominic's back arched, muscles clawing up from beneath his ribs. Moira slashed again, down the length of his sternum, then along the curve of his hip. She was drawing runes—not simple lines, but entire alphabets—onto his body, inking them with his own blood.

He screamed now. The sound wasn't human. It was the scream of a wolf gutted and hung upside-down, of a kingdom's last heir dying for nothing. I felt the hair rise on my neck.

Moira chanted. The wounds did not clot. Instead, they blossomed, the edges writhing, knitting and unknitting as if the flesh was thinking about what it wanted to be. Dominic bucked, heels pounding the stone, but the salt ring held. Moira's eyes rolled back, the white showing and then going gray as ash.

She bent low and whispered into his ear. Dominic's jaw clamped so tight the bone creaked. Blood streamed down his chest, pooling in the hollow above his belly. Moira dipped her fingers in it, then painted the last sigil on his forehead. She stepped back, out of the circle.

The power hit like a car crash. Dominic's spine bent backward, and for a second I saw every rib through the skin, straining to break free. The runes on his body caught fire, blue and orange, burning without heat, and the air filled with the stink of ozone and black pepper. His eyes rolled, turned black, then gold, then something else.

Moira watched, arms crossed. "It will end soon," she said, but she looked at me when she said it, not at him.

Dominic thrashed, then stilled. His body jerked, every muscle spasming at once. I thought he would snap in half. But then, with a final convulsion, he collapsed into a heap, panting, half-conscious. The runes on his chest had stopped bleeding. Instead, they seemed to have sunk under the skin, glowing faintly, like the filaments of a light bulb behind thick glass.

Moira knelt, finger to his throat. She nodded, satisfied. "It's done."

I stepped forward, careful to avoid the lines of salt and the crust of drying blood. I gripped the king by the back of his neck and hauled him upright. His head lolled. Then his gaze snapped into focus, hard as a diamond. He looked up at me with pupils so wide there was almost no blue left.

He flexed his hand. It cracked like dry wood. Then he grinned, feral, and reached for the metal goblet on the table. With a flick of his wrist, he crushed it to a wad of tin and let it clatter to the stones.

"I can feel it, Declan," he hissed, his voice a grate dragged over wet stone. "I could tear Menace limb from limb with my bare hands now."

"You may have to," I said. I let him stand on his own, watching his balance. He trembled, but with the excitement of a dog straining at a leash, not from weakness. "Do not overplay your hand. The first minutes are critical. They'll expect you to fight like a wounded animal. Give them what they expect, then break it off in the wolf's throat."

Dominic nodded, still flexing his fingers. "You want his head, or should I rip out his heart?"

"Both. And you will make it memorable. The Council needs to see the old law reasserted. But above all, you must finish him. Leave nothing for the scavengers."

Moira lingered behind us, cleaning her blade with a scrap of salt-stiff linen. "It is not permanent," she said, her voice hollow. "He will be strong for a little over an hour tonight. Then the body slowly starts to weaken. If you want it to last, you will need to repeat the ritual. Or accept the consequences."

Dominic didn't even look at her. "I only need an hour."

I dismissed Moira with a flick of my hand. She gathered her things and faded into the dark. I'd already resolved to have her killed once this was over. Menace was a problem, but witches with debts to my family were a liability that grew teeth in the dark.

Dominic rolled his shoulders. The wounds on his chest had already stopped bleeding. His skin was hot to the touch, his pulse rapid as a hummingbird's. I handed him a cloak, the old kind, thick and black, the lining stiff with velvet. He shrugged it on, wincing as it settled over his raw flesh.

We walked together up the corridor, away from the salt and blood and wet stone. At the foot of the stairway, I stopped him. "When you go out there, you'll be watched by every king and traitor who did not stand with us. Do not let them see your fear. Remember, you are more than a king tonight. You are a weapon."

He smiled, teeth sharp as razors. "I am."

"And what of Savannah after?" he asked, not as an afterthought, but as a man considering the problem of leftovers from a particularly rich meal.

"You will keep her sedated until the bond is cleanly gone. We cannot have her running, or killing herself in a fit of romance. If you win—and you will—you will hold her, and you will let her see what her choices have cost."

Dominic licked the blood off his lips. "And the witch?"

I didn't hesitate. "She must be eliminated. No one can ever know what we've done here today." I made a note to call Callum later. He was always best at cleanup.

Dominic laughed, the sound gone ragged with the echoes of agony. "Let the Council try to prove it. The witch will be dead before dawn."

He started up the stairs, climbing two at a time, the black cloak flaring behind him. I let myself smile. Relief that I'd have my miserable daughter under my control in a matter of hours and secure not only the Eastern territories but the Midwest as well.

I lingered a moment in the quiet, then followed. By the time I reached the top, the sounds of the arena were already pulsing through the walls: the drums, the howl of thousands, the promise of violence waiting for us above.

Whatever it took, whatever it cost. My kingdom would remain and expand.

The corridor from the chamber to the arena was a throat lined in bone. The stone overhead sagged with the weight of two centuries' worth of challenge, every inch scarred and pitted from the passage of kings and killers. The guards who met us at the foot of the stairs did not speak. They wore the livery of the Council—silver on blue, hoods up, faces shadowed—but their heads dropped as we passed, the deference automatic, the kind of obedience you only get when everyone believes you capable of anything.

Dominic walked ahead of me, the black cloak trailing in a wake of velvet, the edges already sticky with old blood and the sweat of the condemned. The silver chains that bound the front were thick, heavy, but they did not slow him. If anything, they seemed to amplify his stride, each step a slow-motion violence.

He flexed his fingers as he went, the new runes beneath his skin itching for release.

"Remember, they'll be watching for the change," I said, low enough that only he could hear. "Don't let it take you too soon. If you lose control, you'll go feral before you ever reach Menace."

Dominic rolled his neck until it cracked, then shot me a grin. "I can hold it, Declan. I've never felt more alive." He meant it, too; the usual tremor in his hands was gone, replaced by a tremor in the air itself.

We reached the final landing, the iron gates that divided the underground from the stage above. Two more guards waited here, armed with pikes that glittered with a fine dusting of silver. They stood aside when I nodded, their eyes fixed firmly to the floor. The rules were the rules: at this point, the king's word was as good as law.

Above, the crowd was already a living animal, its voice a thousand-headed thing that vibrated the mortar loose. I could smell them—sweat, wolf, vampire musk, the ozone of demon magic. Every great house had sent an envoy. The cameras would be streaming to every territory. I watched as one of the guards checked Dominic's wrists for forbidden weapons, then drew back, confused to find nothing but bare skin, the runes all but invisible under the darkening flesh.

I stepped close, straightening his collar, readying it to fall away with his shift. Dominic bore it like a child suffering a final fuss from an overbearing mother. But when I touched his jaw, I felt it: the furnace heat under the skin; the heart drumming triple-time. He was ready.

"This is not just a fight," I whispered. "It's a reckoning. If you lose, your line ends. If you win, no one will dare question the old laws again. Do you understand?"

He nodded. "Of course I do. Remember, I am also a king, Declan."

I let the words hang between us. I wanted to say something else, but the moment for royal sentiment had passed centuries before either of us was born.

One of the guards signaled, and the gates began to rise. The scrape of iron on stone was nearly lost in the roar from above. Dominic braced himself, flexed his hands one final time. I took my place at the side, in the shadow where the firsts wait for their fighters to prove themselves or die.

At the top, the Council's stage was set: a circle of packed dirt, surrounded by tiers of stone benches, every seat filled with something dangerous or beautiful or both. The arena was rimmed with torches, their flames blue and white, burning without smoke. At the far end, the dais for the Council, the Chairwoman in her robes of authority, flanked by the other adjudicators.

I could see the box where Menace's people sat. Savannah sat with Bronc's whore of a Luna, and all the traitors who voted against us also joined them. They'd somehow even had the Kozlovs—Kazimir and Lucia—with the patient hunger of old money in their box. They'd all feel my wrath when their man fell.

Across the pit, Menace and his first Bronc appeared. Menace stood in a cloak of battered leather and arrogance. Soon he'd be nothing but blood and memory.

Dominic took a breath and stepped into the light. The runes on his chest were hidden from the eyes of everyone. No one would know he had a significant advantage over the mutt. There was a ripple in the crowd, a collective intake of air.

The Chairwoman's voice rang out over the arena: "Let all witnesses record the rite of challenge. By ancient law, by the will of the Council, by the blessing of the Goddess, two men enter, and one will leave. No weapons save those born of flesh. All debts paid in blood. Once the battle begins, it shall not end until only one stands."

A hush fell. The only sound was the torch flame; the animal whisper of wolves on the wind.

Dominic let his cloak fall. He wore nothing underneath. The crowd's roar rose again.

I locked eyes with Menace across the pit. He gave me a small, mocking nod. He knew somehow, that we had cheated, that the deck was loaded. But he was still here. Still ready to die for a girl he'd only known months.

Dominic stepped forward, and so did Menace.

The next moment would decide everything.

I stood at the edge, hands clasped behind my back, every muscle locked. There was no prayer for what was about to happen. There was only law, and blood, and the hope that when it was over, my daughter would know the pain that she had caused me.

The horn sounded, and both Dominic and Menace instantly shifted, their wolves both magnificent.

The battle had begun.

Chapter 28

Savannah

There's a word for a sound that makes you want to crawl out of your own skin. A word for the howl that's half birth-cry, half execution order. There's not a word for how it felt to hear Menace's wolf split the world open in front of me, but if there was, it would be something guttural, something wet and bladed.

I stood at the edge of the pit and let my nails gouge the railing. Blood welled under each thumb, a prayer for luck offered to a goddess who'd already weighed us and found us insufficient. The air stank of blood, old and new, the audience's anticipation sharpening it into something bright enough to slice cartilage. The blue fire in the torches painted everything in morgue-colors, even Menace's white wolf, who gleamed like a cauterized nerve.

Dominic's wolf was larger than I remembered. It wasn't just the mass, though he was easily seventy pounds heavier than Menace, his shoulders corded with obscene new muscle. It was the way he moved, a sinuousness that looked borrowed, as if the body wasn't entirely his to command. When he lunged at the opening horn, the movement was wrong, too fast for the bones underneath. I smelled magic instantly—a tang of rot, sickly and high-pitched—and the crowd did too. They shrank back from the rail, supernaturals who'd seen enough sorcery to recognize a ticking bomb when it flexed its claws.

Menace met the charge head-on, no hesitation, no calculation. His body was a coiled spring, every muscle cabled to snap at the first feint. But Dominic's leap was pure physics, not strategy, and Menace barely evaded the snapping jaws, his white pelt losing a ghost-patch to the black wolf's teeth. The crowd roared. Menace circled, head low, and his lips peeled back in a grimace of calculated rage.

The first exchange was brutal, but it wasn't the worst thing I'd ever seen. Not yet. They clashed, then separated, then clashed again, both landing blows, but Dominic was cheating—healing, even as Menace opened fresh wounds. Every time Menace scored a bite or a rake, the skin sealed itself with a rippling shiver, closing up the way a mouth does when you clamp your jaw tight against a scream.

Menace switched tactics, going low, aiming for the underbelly. He feinted left, darted right, and went for the femoral. It worked—Dominic's wolf shrieked as Menace's jaws closed around his thigh, twisting, worrying the bone. But Dominic just reared up impossibly, and slammed his full weight down, crushing Menace to the dirt. The thud reverberated through my spine. I thought I felt a rib crack.

I doubled over the rail, bile burning my throat. For a moment, the world narrowed to the two of them: white and black, hope and extinction, a metaphor so on-the-nose I would have laughed if I wasn't swallowing the taste of my own fear.

Dominic's magic-enhanced wolf pressed the advantage, pummeling Menace into the arena floor. I saw white fur turn pink, then red. I saw the way his tail curled protectively over his flank, the way his eyes never left the enemy's. Even as he bled, he calculated. He waited for the moment the black wolf's teeth reached too far, and then—like the world's most beautiful trap—he snapped his head up and caught Dominic by the lower jaw.

Menace held on with everything, legs scrambling for purchase. He twisted, hard, and Dominic yelped. But the sound didn't last. Dominic's claws raked Menace's face, blinding him on one side, leaving a flap of skin dangling over his left eye. I screamed, and so did someone in the crowd.

The fight went on. It had been minutes, but it felt like hours. The arena was a centrifuge of violence, every turn escalating the damage. Menace was on defense now, staying low, dodging the worst of it, but the black wolf's stamina was obscene. Every time I thought Menace would get a breather, Dominic was on him, a storm without end.

At the twenty-minute mark, they were both streaked with gore. Menace's coat was mostly pink now, and there were tufts of fur littering the sand. Dominic's right eye hung half-closed, oozing something blue-black, and one ear was missing entirely. Menace was panting, tongue lolling, every breath a gamble. I could feel the pain through the bond, each new laceration sending aftershocks through my chest. I clenched the rail until my fingers went numb, then dug my teeth into my arm to keep from screaming.

There were times when Menace looked to be out. Twice, he went down and stayed down, just long enough for the crowd to start murmuring in defeat. But each time, he got up. Not because he was stronger— he wasn't—but because something in him refused to give the bastards the satisfaction.

At the thirty-minute mark, Dominic tried to end it. He went for the jugular, literally. Menace sidestepped, let the jaws close over nothing, and then leaped for Dominic's exposed throat. He barely missed. Dominic caught him mid-air and flung him into the pit wall, hard enough to leave a bloody streak. Menace slid to the ground and lay still, sides heaving, one leg at a sick angle.

The arena went silent. I wanted to die. I wanted to charge the pit myself, tear at Dominic with my nails, my teeth, my useless, fragile body. But my knees buckled, and I hung there, draped over the rail, watching the end approach.

Dominic prowled the length of the pit, savoring it. He barked once, a sound of pure triumph. He padded to where Menace lay and nudged him with a paw. Menace didn't move. Not even a flinch.

Dominic circled, jaw open in a wolf's grin, waiting for applause. He turned his back to the body and raised his head to the gallery, inviting them all to see the victor.

That was his mistake.

Menace didn't get up. He lunged straight from the ground, legs splaying out behind him as he rocketed forward and up, catching Dominic's back leg in his jaws and yanking with everything left in his ruined body. The crowd erupted. Dominic went down hard, Menace following, jaws locked on the hock. He twisted. I heard the snap from fifty feet away.

The black wolf howled, and Menace didn't let go. He climbed up the body with his teeth, inch by inch, working through muscle and tendon, until he was at Dominic's throat. This time, he didn't miss.

He bit down. The bite was obscene, an arterial spray that painted both of them red. Dominic thrashed once, then twice, but Menace hung on. I screamed, everyone screamed, and the blue flames in the torches went wild, shooting high into the air.

When it was done, Menace let go and staggered backward. He limped, dragging the dead leg, and the whole left side of his face was an unrecognizable mask. Dominic's wolf twitched, then went limp. Blood puddled beneath him, soaking into the sand.

The crowd was dead silent, except for the sound of Menace's breathing, which was ragged and shallow and desperate.

I screamed again, this time wordless, the sound echoing off the pit walls. Menace swayed, then collapsed, his body stretched out next to Dominic's corpse. He didn't move.

I stood there, not breathing, not moving, waiting for him to get up.

He didn't.

It took eight seconds after the final kill for anyone to move. In that time, I counted every place Menace had bled, every place the sand was stippled with something vital and unrecoverable. I counted my heartbeats too, but they didn't line up right, skipping and doubling in a pattern that felt more like malfunction than rhythm.

Menace's wolf lay stretched out in the dirt, a white pelt ruined to pink, the left eye swollen shut, and the right still faintly open. I watched for the breath, the twitch, the twitch that meant he hadn't died at the finish line. It came eventually—a convulsive jerk, as if the spirit inside him had to be cajoled back by the world's most belligerent paramedic.

He shifted slowly, agonizingly, as if every cell had to be dragged one by one from the animal to the man. There was no drama to it, no shuddering glamour, just a blur of pain and an anti-climax of bone and skin. He came out raw and naked, his body mapped in bruises and bites, a fresh set of claw tracks scored down his chest. He made it to all fours, then one knee, and then finally to his feet. The crowd was still silent, but the white noise of horror was starting to leak in around the edges.

Bronc was the first to break protocol, jumping from the box seat to the edge of the pit. He vaulted the rail and was at Menace's side in seconds, draping a Council-branded robe over his bare shoulders and half-carrying him toward the stairs. Juliet was there too, her arms outstretched, her face a mask of incredulity and bone-deep relief. They flanked him, bracing him, the three of them a battered tangle limping toward the arena's exit.

I found my legs then, and I ran. The moment I hit the stairs. I got to Menace as they reached the top, and for a second I didn't know what to do. Hug him? Collapse at his feet? Just stare? In the end, I did all three. I wrapped my arms around his ribs, felt the wet heat of his blood soak the front of my clothes, and then slid boneless to the ground, clutching him and sobbing into the meat of his thighs as we stood at the edge of the arena.

He grunted, the sound closer to a laugh than a scream, and ran a hand through my hair. "Red," he rasped, "you're getting me all sentimental in front of the fucking Council."

Juliet pulled me up, set me on my feet, and looked into my face like she needed confirmation the world was real. "He did it," she whispered, shaking her head. "He actually fucking did it."

I nodded, not trusting my voice, and pressed my face into Menace's neck. I felt his pulse, erratic but alive, and tasted salt and iron where I bit him by accident.

The crowd was finding its voice now. There were cheers, yes, but also gasps and the low, ugly rumble of the Council's own guard, who lined the perimeter and bristled at the sight of their champion's death. There was a second, deeper layer to the noise, too—a kind of animal yelp, sharp and panicked, as the scent of fresh blood reached the balconies. If you'd never heard a room of supernaturals scent a kill, you don't know what fear is.

We barely made it two steps before a klaxon sounded and the whole arena went pitch dark. Spotlights slammed on, blinding everyone, and the big screens above the pit flickered to life, showing a blurry security feed. For a second, I thought they were going to replay the fight. Instead, the camera zoomed in on my father, Declan, standing in a cold stone room with a witch beside him.

The sound cut in, echoing around the chamber: "You promised he would win," Declan hissed at the witch, voice shaking with more than just rage. "You said the mutt would never survive him."

The witch's face stayed calm. "I promised a temporary advantage, Your Grace. I made it clear to Callum—your son, as he explained so forcefully—that the magic would wear off with time. I cannot control your daughter's betrothed's incompetence."

A gasp ran through the gallery. They were broadcasting the evidence of cheating, and not even the most loyal bastard in the room could deny it.

The video cut to another feed—Callum, my brother, in a hallway with the same witch, handing her a fistful of gold and a vial of what looked like my own blood. "It's hers," he hissed, "straight from the source. Use it."

The video cut again. Declan, pacing, ranting: "If the Council discovers this, you are dead. We all are. Is that clear?"

The screens went dark. The house lights snapped back on.

All hell broke loose. Council members shot to their feet, some shouting, others turning on each other, a few openly laughing. The East's seats emptied in a slow-motion exodus, the faces in those rows tight and ashen. At the head of the dais, the Councilwoman banged her gavel, the sound useless against the chaos.

Amid all this, I was still holding Menace, half-sobbing, half-laughing. We'd won. We'd actually fucking won.

Then I heard the scream. Not from the pit, not from the Council, but from directly behind me.

Declan barreled through the mass of bodies, shoving guards out of the way, his face a color I'd never seen—bloodless, veins showing blue under the skin. He fixed his eyes on me, and I realized with a sick certainty that nothing in the last twenty-four hours mattered. I would always be prey, and he would always be the wolf at the end of my story.

He hit me hard enough to knock the air from my lungs, driving me into the stone wall. I heard Bronc shout, and Juliet curse, and someone in the crowd start to laugh—a thin, brittle giggle that belonged in a hospital ward, not an arena.

Declan's hand closed around my throat. He squeezed. The world went gray at the edges, then white. I clawed at his fingers but got nothing. He leaned in close, his breath sour with whiskey and hatred. "You think you've won?" he spat, voice a splinter. "You will never be free. You'll never—"

Menace broke him off. He wrapped his arm around Declan's neck and yanked him away, the movement so fast and savage I barely saw it. They went down together, rolling across the ground, a tangle of blood and muscle and old, unspeakable fury.

They wrestled, less a fight than a slow-motion homicide. Declan clawed at Menace's face, and Menace just kept squeezing, cutting off the blood to his brain. They rolled across the arena floor, into the legs of Council guards who only watched, too shocked or too delighted to intervene.

Finally, Declan went limp. Menace let go, shoved him aside, and staggered back to me. He knelt, cradling my face in his hands. "Red," he whispered, "you okay?"

I tried to nod, but my neck wouldn't hold me up. "You're bleeding," I said. "Everywhere. Please. You have to—"

He smiled, blood in his teeth. "Don't worry. We're wolves remember? My wounds are already starting to heal."

In the lull, the Councilwoman's voice rang out. "The challenge is decided. The mate bond stands. The Council recognizes the new—" She never finished.

Declan got up. His face was purple now, veins bulging, eyes wild. He didn't run at me, though. This time, he aimed for Menace. There was a knife in his hand, pulled from somewhere in the folds of his ruined suit.

He screamed, "You've destroyed everything!" and drove the blade at Menace's chest.

I moved, but not fast enough. Menace blocked the first blow, but the second caught him just under the ribs. A wet, sickening thunk that made me want to vomit. Declan twisted the blade.

The guards swarmed him then, pinning him to the ground. But it didn't matter. The knife was in Menace's chest, all the way to the hilt.

He fell, catching himself on his hands. The blood pooled around him, dark and spreading. He looked up at me, and his eyes were full of something I'd never seen before—fear, maybe, or the sudden, animal knowledge that everything he'd fought for could be taken away in an instant.

"Savannah," he said, and then collapsed.

I caught him as he went down, blood turning the front of my clothing into a sticky second skin. I pressed my hands to the wound, trying to hold him together. His heart was still beating, but the tempo was wrong again, slowing and skipping and then stopping for whole seconds at a time.

He looked at me, and his mouth shaped my name, but no sound came out.

The world shrank to a tiny dot. Just the two of us, his dying, and my inability to do anything about it.

I screamed for help, but it wasn't enough. It never was.

Menace's blood was hot and too slick for me to grip the wound closed from where the knife had been, but I pressed my palm there anyway, bracing his body on the sandy floor of the arena. He blinked, once, and the eye that wasn't swollen shut rolled up to find me. "Savannah," he said, and the word was wet with red. "My mate." His fingers tightened on my wrist, then twitched away.

I kept calling for help, not knowing who was around me or what they were doing. Maybe it was the Council, maybe Juliet, maybe just the dead wolf inside my head who refused to believe in endings. I heard Bronc cursing, heard boots shuffling in the sand, but the world had collapsed to a hole barely big enough for the two of us. I threw myself across his body as the bond between us shrank and shrank, thinning to a thread, a wire, a ghost of itself. I felt his heartbeat stutter and then skip. Once, twice. The third time, it didn't come back.

"NO! Don't you leave me! Bridger! Come back to me! You can't leave me alone! You won! We won! Please!" I sobbed uncontrollably.

He went slack. The blue of his lips bled into gray. I pressed my mouth to his, desperate, as if I could give him my own air, but the world's best CPR couldn't raise the dead. The thread snapped. It was the sound of a violin string breaking in a dead-silent concert hall. The pain was so sharp and final that for a second I thought I'd been stabbed too. Maybe I had.

I wailed, my face in his throat, the world refusing to end but also refusing to keep going. His body stayed warm, but the soul inside it was gone. I rocked him, muttering his name over and over until the noise dried up in my mouth.

That was when the hush hit the arena. I didn't notice at first. But then the silence was a weight, a tidal shift that crushed every living thing flat. I looked up, expecting the Council to have fled, or the guards to be dragging Declan away for execution.

Instead, the entire crowd had parted in a ripple, everyone staring at the far stairwell.

A figure was descending the steps. He was tall, seven feet, and he wore white, just white, not the blue of the Council or the silver of a king. His hair was long, white-gold, and it trailed behind him like a sheet in a hurricane. His face was beautiful the way icebergs are beautiful: too sharp, too old, too indifferent to care who it killed.

He moved with a slowness that was not hesitation but mercy, as if every step down the stairs was a gift to the crowd, giving them time to reckon with what they were about to see. He never took his eyes off me. Not once.

When he reached the pit, he walked through the guards as if they were smoke. I'd moved off to where I was seated next to Menace's body, and he knelt at my side and set a hand on my shoulder. His skin was cool, but it didn't sting. It just was. He looked down at Menace, then at me.

"May I?" His voice was so low I didn't know if I heard it or just felt it vibrating in my chest.

I nodded. I couldn't have said no even if I'd wanted to.

He placed his palm over the wound. I expected fireworks, or light, or some movie-bullshit about grace and salvation. There was none of that. There was only the slow, steady pressure of his hand, and the way the blood seemed to flow backwards, rising from the sand and knitting into the torn skin.

He whispered something in a language I didn't know. The syllables wrapped around my brain, slippery and untranslatable, but I understood them anyway: hunger is not the same as evil, mercy is not the same as weakness, all debts are paid in flesh.

The wound closed. Menace shuddered, once, then again. The coldness in his body drained away, replaced by the animal heat I had always felt burning under his skin. His chest rose. He coughed, spat blood, then sucked in air like he'd never tasted it before.

The bond flared back to life, and I gasped from the feel of it. Other than that, I didn't move. I just stared.

The white-haired man sat back on his heels, wiped a streak of blood from his wrist, and looked at me with eyes that were the color of winter sunlight on new snow. "This one's important," he said. "Try not to lose him again."

He got up, flicked the blood onto the sand, and left. Just like that. No applause, no explanation. I knew the angels didn't interact with the Council more than necessary and was shocked he'd taken the time for us. Something profound had just occurred.

Menace's eyes opened. They found mine. He smiled, small and weak, but real. "Did you miss me?" he croaked.

I was too spent to cry, too empty to laugh, but I held his face between my hands and said, "Never do that to me again."

He nodded. "Not if I can help it."

I kissed him. I didn't care that it was bloody and awful and the whole world was watching. He was alive. We were alive. Sometimes that was the only miracle that mattered.

The Councilwoman banged her gavel, but I didn't hear the verdict. The only thing I heard was the thrum of the bond between us, alive and electric, the thread rewoven, unbreakable.

After what seemed like forever, Bronc and Juliet helped us to our feet. Menace was stronger than he had a right to be. I guess when an angel breathes on you; you bounce back quicker than not.

He had entered the arena Bridger "Menace" Hardin, VP of Iron Valor MC. He was walking out Bridger "Menace" Hardin, King of the Midwestern Wolf Territories. And I remained his one true fated mate.

CHAPTER 29

MENACE

They'd thought to whisk us away from the arena like a pair of war criminals awaiting execution. After what I'd just been through, though, I was not in whisking shape. The guards in Council blue flanked us, rifles slung but unnecessary. My people followed us here, so no one in this castle was going to start a riot, not with the mutt who'd just killed their king, bleeding a river down the front of his own chest. Every corridor stank of ozone and disinfectant the deeper we went. The stone walls and ancient radiators stuttered to keep up with the late fall chill.

Savannah never let go of my arm. Even as we were funneled through the marble halls of the Midwest King's estate—once Dominic's, now mine by right of blood—she clung with the tenacity of a bulldog with a bone. I wanted to hold her close, to carry her on my back, but the wound in my side made every breath a warning shot, so we walked together, two ghosts leaving a trail for the living to follow.

At the medical ward, Savannah put her foot down. She braced herself in the threshold, green eyes flicking to the nurse on duty—a severe type with black lipstick and a stethoscope like a noose. She moved too slowly as far as Savannah was concerned. With too much ambivalence. "This. Is. Your. New. King. That makes me your queen. He'll be tended to. Now get him a bed and get the healer." The nurse suddenly understood the meaning of respect. Her eyes finally took one look at the mess of me and set to work, barking orders for bandages and saline and to fetch their healer. They stripped my robe and laid me on a clean table.

The healer's hands on me were professional as she went about healing various injuries from the fight with Dominic. But I felt a slight tremor in her fingers as she finally unwrapped the wound left by Declan. She peeled the crusted bandage from my skin. There should have been a hole, a tunnel bored straight through my ribs. I closed my eyes as I remembered Declan's blade singing with each inhale. But when she cleaned away the gore and blood, all she found was smooth skin as pink as a newborn's. No gash. No scar. Nothing but the faintest ring where the angel's hand had snuffed out death.

The healer paled, the color draining from her face. Something that I'd seen only a few times before—usually after a bombing, when the living realized they were the only ones left breathing. "Impossible," she muttered. "You were stabbed. I saw—everyone saw—" Her voice dropped to a whisper, equal parts awe and fear. "The angel's touch. As a healer, I have the ability to knit wounds together, but there is always evidence that the wound was there. This—this looks as though you were never touched by the knife. It's extraordinary."

Savannah had watched it all, arms folded tight around her ribs. I caught her gaze, saw the aftershock of it there. She'd loved me, lost me, and gotten me back in less than five minutes. No wolf should have to survive that much loss especially not in one lifetime.

I reached out and brushed her cheek with the back of my hand. "I'm fine," I said, and for the first time in years, it was true. The healer cleaned the area, more for her own comfort than mine, then shuffled away, muttering prayers to herself.

We were alone in the exam room for a heartbeat.

Savannah blinked hard, then set her jaw. "You died, Bridger." The words vibrated with the sweet music of her voice , something I would never tire of hearing. "I felt it. Your soul left your body. Mine was fighting to go with it."

I shrugged, or tried to. The movement pulled at the phantom wound, and I made a face. "Didn't take."

She let out a noise somewhere between a laugh and a sob. "You idiot," she said, but softer than before. "You absolute idiot."

"I had to be sure you'd remember me if I came back *wrong*." I was only half-joking. I saw the shadow flicker behind her eyes, a memory of every man who'd tried to own her and failed. She was mine now, but only because she chose it. The thought was humbling.

She bent low, pressed her lips to my forehead—gentler than a nurse, rougher than a saint. "Go. Clean up. You're due in the conference room in an hour."

"And you?" She still had my blood caked on her clothes and body.

"I look like *I* battled in the arena. I'm going to get cleaned up too. Meet you in the conference room?"

"Wouldn't miss it." I told her.

She nodded, then slipped away, her scent trailing after her, a thread of honey and roses.

The staff had assigned me a guest suite. I guess it was a bit macabre for me to take Dominic's chamber while his body was barely cold. I didn't care. This room was opulent, with velvet curtains and a huge shower with several showerheads. I stepped in, let the water run as hot as I could stand. For a long time, I just stood there, waiting to see if the blood on my hands would ever come off. It didn't. Not that it could be seen. The stain was in my bones.

When the hot water scalded away the last of the surface pain, I stepped out and looked at myself in the mirror. The face staring back at me was a horror even though the healer did a good job and things were looking and feeling better. My left eye was swollen, but at least I could see out of it now. Jaw was puffy like I had a rotten tooth, my scar looking more silver than usual. The split places on my lips had closed, so at least I'd be able to eat without too much discomfort. My chest and arms were crosshatched with new bruises, the color of twilight on a battlefield.

But there was no wound over my heart, just the perfect oval of fresh skin, paler than the rest of me. I stared at it, wondering if the angel had left anything behind—a message, maybe, or a ticking bomb. I couldn't shake the feeling that I was now a haunted house, and something old and divine had moved in for good.

I dressed in the clothes provided by the staff: dark jeans, black button-down, boots of the most expensive leather. Everything fit better than I expected, but I felt like a child in his father's best suit, pretending at adulthood.

Before I left the room, I pressed my palm over my heart, expecting to feel the echo of the knife. There was nothing. Only a steady, perfect pulse. I let my hand linger a moment longer, then turned and walked out, ready to face whatever came next.

The conference room was dressed for a feast, but it looked more like a wake. Someone had laid out platters of roast meats and cheeses, silver urns of coffee, and trays of rolls that steamed in the ambient heat from the chandeliers. Everyone feasted. This was a hard-won celebration. I was fortunate to be alive, and everyone was damn happy I was. At least *my* people were. And though the wine flowed, serious discussions had to take place, so moderation was the word of the night.

Savannah was already there, hunched at the table next to Bronc and Juliet. Her hair was pulled into a messy bun, and she wore a stylish long dark green long sleeve emerald color dress. Whoever dressed her recognized she was indeed their queen. She gave me a small nod when I entered, but her eyes skipped past mine. I recognized the look. It was the same one I wore after every op that left bodies and headlines in its wake: Don't touch me, I'm radioactive. She'd mount me on the goddamn conference table if she could. I couldn't help but grin. My mate. Fuck. She was every good and fierce thing in my life. I made a beeline straight for her and kissed her hard. I didn't give two fucks who saw. And she kissed me right back.

The Council Chairwoman stood at the head of the table, all sharp angles and silver hair, her eyes like two holes punched in heavy paper. She raised a glass—not to the victor, but as if she needed something physical to keep her upright. She cleared her throat.

"Let the record show the Eastern throne stands empty," she announced; no preamble, no time for anyone to catch up. "Declan Calloway, by Council order, will be put to death by public execution at sunrise for the murder of Bridger Hardin, Vice President of the Iron Valor Pack. His resurrection notwithstanding. His son, Callum Calloway, is now a fugitive, wanted for conspiracy and the murder of witch Moira Blackthorn. All parties should update their records accordingly."

The words rippled down the table like a chemical spill. At the far end, Rafe sat with his arms folded, impassive, the muscle at his jawline ticking every time the Chairwoman uttered a new fact. He was playing the long game, but his scent betrayed him—he reeked of pride and fury, and I couldn't tell which weighed heavier.

Juliet reached for Savannah's hand and led her to the table. I followed her and Bronc. I took my seat to the right of the Council Chairwoman, Bronc to her left. Savannah sat next to me with Juliet next to her. Juliet leaned over Savannah to me. "Is it true?"

She whispered, eyes flicking to me and back. "They're going to execute him?"

I nodded. "He's not getting up this time."

Savannah flinched at that, but she didn't cry. Instead, she stared at the centerpiece—a twisted arrangement of black calla lilies and bone-white roses—and I could see her inventorying every moment of her father's life that led to this. There wasn't enough space in the world for that sort of math.

The Chairwoman cleared her throat again, bringing the room back to order. "Mr. Hardin, you are entitled to claim the spoils of victory—title, territory, and all assets. You may also decline, in which case the Council will appoint a new Alpha for the Midwest Kingdom. Either way, you must decide tonight. Protocol."

I shrugged, then looked at Savannah. "It's your choice, too," I said, voice soft. "If you want out, now's the time."

She finally met my eyes. "I'm not leaving you," she said, and I believed her. "But... my family—my mother and Griffin—they need to know. Can I have a minute?" The last word was a plea, and the Chairwoman waved her off with a flick of her hand.

Savannah took Juliet's phone and left the room. Through the glass panel, I watched her shoulders shake as she dialed. I felt every emotion she was experiencing through our bond. The most remarkable was relief. There wasn't really any grief to be found. Fear was the most troubling. I felt that fear when she told her mother that Callum was missing, then joy when she shared she was safe. Finally, there was so much hope when she told her mother that nothing would ever be the same. I double-checked with the Council Chairwoman that Savannah's mother and brother were under the protection of the Council until Callum was found. She assured me that their estate was under heavy guard.

I turned my attention to Bronc. He poured two fingers of whiskey into his coffee and drank it in one swallow. "Never saw you as the king type," he said, grinning like it hurt. "Thought you'd stick to the MC until your liver gave out."

I shrugged again, then clapped him on the shoulder. "I thought I'd have more time to disappoint you."

He snorted, but his eyes were red. "You'll make a fine king. Just don't forget about us. How you gonna handle living with all these Yankees?"

I bellowed a laugh at that. "Fuck, I don't know, man. What are they gonna do when I have a big ol' Texas barbecue out on that pristine back lawn?"

Juliet leaned in, her voice a conspiratorial hush. "When you're in charge, will you finally outlaw polyester blends? Half the Council dresses like they're headed to a job interview at the DMV."

"Council's got bigger problems," I said. "First order of business: not getting murdered by the next psycho with a knife and an inferiority complex."

The Chairwoman rapped her knuckles on the table, impatience fraying her calm. "We need to address the matter of evidence. The video that aired during the challenge—exposing Declan's treachery—originated from inside the Council's own surveillance system. We want to know who provided it, and why."

Every face turned toward the screen on the far wall, frozen on the last frame of the broadcast: Callum passing a vial of blood to the witch. The air in the room thickened. A predator's pause before the kill.

No one spoke, so I did. "Someone wanted to expose a corrupt king. Any number of people on the Council could have simply wanted the truth out, maybe just a bored tech with a sense of justice. Doesn't matter. It's done. There are lots of families who deal in secrets, and everyone knows it." Of course, the only family that truly deals in secrets is the Kozlovs. They are the only supernatural mafia family represented on the Council.

At the mention of secrets, no one dared to look at Kazimir at the end of the table. But my eyes landed on Lucia. She was resplendent in a crimson sheath dress, black curls wild around her face, lips painted with the same shade as fresh arterial blood.

She caught my gaze, held it, then winked. A slow, deliberate movement that caused me to give her a subtle nod of my head.

Savannah returned then, her face streaked but resolute. She slid back into her seat next to me and set her hand over mine. Her grip was cool and unyielding. I was hers, and she was mine, and every person at this table knew it.

The Chairwoman closed her binder, signaling the end of the session. "You have until midnight to decide. If you decline the throne, the Council will appoint. If you accept, your investiture is at dawn. Until then, this castle is yours. Use it wisely."

The others filed out, murmuring to themselves, the ghosts of old power trailing them like a scent of dead flowers. Bronc and Juliet hung back for a moment, then left together, arms around each other like survivors of a shipwreck. Rafe nodded to me on his way out, a small, private salute.

Lucia lingered at the door, lips parted in a hungry smile. "Congratulations, King," she said, the word twisting in her mouth like something alive. "May you reign with a heavier hand than the last."

When the room was finally empty, I turned to Savannah. She was still holding my hand, tighter now. The emerald dress clung to her in all the right ways, but her face held questions and fathomless forevers.

"We did it," I said, because I didn't know what else to say.

She let out a breath, the weight of the world deflating with it. "*You* did it," she echoed, then pressed her lips to my knuckles, a queen in a ruined palace.

There would be a hundred battles tomorrow. But tonight, the world belonged to us.

Chapter 30

Savannah

Dawn curled around the drapes like a hand, slow and probing, prying at my eyelids. I let it, for once. Last night's exhaustion was a memory drowned in bourbon and adrenaline, and Menace slept on, the rise and fall of his ribcage the only proof the battle hadn't been a fever-dream. In the room's hush, I catalogued the other evidence: bandages now gone, bruises already faded to the color of old violets, blood scrubbed from the floor by unseen hands. The only thing they hadn't erased was the pillowcase, still tacky where I'd wept into the fabric before finally passing out in his arms.

I curled toward him, greedy for the heat, for the fact that he was still breathing. The fine, silvery line of his jaw with just the right amount of blonde stubble. He'd cleaned up his beard in the night, probably just before crawling into bed, and the scent of expensive aftershave still clung to his throat. My mate, the king-killer, looked every bit the hero. He also looked like a man who'd been devoured and then spat back into the world.

It was the mark on his chest that drew me. I'd seen it last night—the circle the angel left when he undid Declan's last cruelty—but in the morning, it had turned a faint, uncanny hue, lighter than the surrounding area. It pulsed in time with his heart, a living sigil just below the skin. I let my fingers hover there, afraid to touch it at first, then caving in, the way one always caves to gravity. The skin was warm, softer than the flesh around it.

He didn't wake, not even when I leaned in and pressed my lips to it, light as a leaf.

I lay there a while, letting my palm map his ribs, the stories they told: the scar from a childhood where he'd been bucked off of a horse, a dip where a bullet had once splintered bone, the pale ridge from his last tour of duty. His hand, always so quick, so restless, now twitched only once—curling into a fist before softening again. I traced the line down, letting it be a prayer of thanks. I didn't know I'd have this body to touch again. I was afraid he'd be taken from me. I was forever grateful he was here.

Below his waist, he was already half-hard, the logic of sleep and survival running on a different clock than the rest of him. I palmed him through the sheets, careful and slow. The first touch made him shift, a small sound in his throat. He didn't wake, but the cock in my hand twitched, thickening with the promise of a whole new violence. I let the sheet fall away, exposing the pale arch of his hips, the dusting of blonde that led straight to where I needed him.

I didn't need to be gentle. But I wanted to be. There was a reverence in it, a slow unraveling. I slipped down the bed, nuzzled against the root of it, breathed him in—the mix of sweat, laundry powder, and the faint copper of blood that lingered no matter how much we scrubbed. I licked a stripe up the shaft, circled my tongue around the head, and tasted him. He was salt and skin. There was a violence to the size of him, an arrogance in the way his body insisted on being worshiped. I did.

He started to stir then, an intake of air, a flex in the thigh that made my head jerk back just enough to watch his face. His eyes weren't open, but his mouth parted, a sigh blooming from his chest. I swallowed him down, let the crown hit the back of my throat, and held it there, breathing through my nose and counting the beats as I sucked. My hand wrapped around the base, thumb stroking the vein just under the skin, the way I knew would break him if he was conscious.

He was, a moment later. I felt it in the shift of his hips, the shudder down his spine. I looked up and saw him watching me, one hazel eye open, a wolf's smile flickering in the ruined geometry of his mouth.

"You're a fucking queen," he rasped, voice not quite awake but already claiming me. His hand tangled in my hair. Not rough, but firm enough to make it clear who was in charge. I let him guide my head, let him set the pace. Up, down, slow, then quick. I could have died this way, and I think he knew it.

He fucked my mouth. Not with the aggression of a brute, but with the solemnity of a king who knew the world was watching. His breath hitched;gasped every muscle locked. He whispered my name, the real one, not Red, and it was so raw I almost lost my rhythm.

I took him deeper, relaxing my throat, my nose pressed to his belly. The skin there was still marked, still strange, and I let my fingers roam over it as I sucked, as if the act could heal both of us. He gasped, louder now, the sound filling the small, cold room. I felt his body tense; the cock swelling harder, thicker, the warning clear.

"Swallow it," he ordered. Not a request. Not a plea.

I did.

The cum was bitter, but I held it on my tongue, savoring the way his body jerked, the way his hands knotted in my hair. He groaned, full-throated, animal. I swallowed, then licked him clean, slow and careful, until he softened against my lips.

He didn't let go of me for a long time.

I crawled back up the bed and curled into his side, head on his shoulder, my hand still tracing idle circles over the healed wound on his chest. He kissed my hair, his breath still ragged, the aftermath of pleasure mingling with the memory of pain.

"Was that a dream?" he asked, voice hoarse.

"No," I said. "But if it was, I don't want to wake up."

He laughed, the sound softer than I'd ever heard. "You're fucking dangerous, you know that?"

"So are you," I shot back, and nipped his shoulder, just hard enough to leave a mark.

He pulled me closer, hand splayed over my lower back. "Don't let anyone on the Council see you do that. They'll think I've gone soft."

I bit back a smile. "You're the king now. You can do whatever you want."

He mulled that, eyes fixed on the ceiling. "You sure you're okay?" he asked. "After yesterday?"

"Are you?" I countered.

He considered. "Wasn't ready to die. But if I had to, that would have been the way."

I propped my chin on his chest, the sheet pooling around my waist. "Can I tell you something?"

"Anything."

I hesitated, then let it out. "On the call with my mom..."

He raised an eyebrow. "Yeah?"

"She's... free," I said, and felt the truth of it. "She never said it, not in front of him, but she hated my father. She said she's been waiting years for him to die. She wanted to thank you."

He blinked, surprised. "For what?"

"For saving me. For giving her a reason to keep going. For letting Griffin take the throne and not making her deal with it anymore. Mostly for just... surviving." I swallowed, the words thick in my throat. "And she's happy. You know why?"

He shook his head, bemused.

"Because she gets to be with her mate now. Her true mate. He's been waiting for her for twenty-five years. She told me that last night. First thing she did after getting the news—she ran to him. She gets to be loved finally."

Menace was silent, letting the words sink in. He wrapped both arms around me and just held on.

I could have wept for my old life, for all the years I'd lost, for the way trauma kept bleeding through the future like dye in water. But instead, I let myself hope for what was to come.

I ran my hand down his body one last time, savoring the shape of him, the miracle of him. I kissed the angel mark on his chest, the place where death had tried and failed.

"Thank you," I whispered, not for the act, not for the rescue, but for just existing, here, now, alive.

He kissed my forehead, then my lips. "Anytime, Red."

The day was just beginning, but for the first time in years, it felt like it might not end in tragedy.

We lay there a while, not speaking. Not needing to.

We could have laid there forever, burrowed under the quilt, but the world was nothing if not insistent. At seven a.m. sharp, a knock split the silence—three hard, staccato raps. Not a question, not a suggestion. The day demanded us.

Menace answered, wearing only a towel and a snarl. The woman on the threshold blinked, caught herself, then handed him a folded parchment. "Council requests your presence at nine. There will be a formal witness to dress you both." Her voice was flat, her eyes never dropping below his collarbone, as though acknowledging any part of him might dissolve her professionalism. She set a lacquered trunk on the carpet, then fled, heels clacking down the corridor like castanets.

Menace whistled, low and mocking, and closed the door. He flicked the parchment open. The wax seal was already broken. "We're to be in the anteroom at eight for prep," he read. "Then the crowning at nine. You up for this?"

"I think I am," I said with a grin.

He smiled back, then peeled away the towel and started digging for fresh clothes. I let myself watch—the lean muscle, the angel mark now faded to the color of a clear sky, the ease with which he wore his own nakedness. He caught me staring and winked.

"Want me to help you get ready?" he asked, the wolf in him still alive and hungry.

"Tempting," I said, "but the attendant might faint. And you're supposed to look respectable for once."

He made a face but didn't argue. By the time I'd slipped into the bathroom, the air was already steaming with the scent of his shower, water still pelting the tile like rain. I washed fast, letting the heat bake the knots from my neck, then wrapped myself in one of the guest robes and padded back into the bedroom.

The trunk was open now, and inside, layers of folded fabric—velvet, brocade, the deep, bruised colors of midnight and dried blood. On top, a note: "For the Queen Consort."

The title made my stomach twist, but there was no time for reflection. Another knock, softer this time, preceded the entry of a different woman, younger and less rigid, her hair pinned in a severe twist and her eyes already tracking every detail. "I'm here to assist with the attire," she said. "If you'd please?" She gestured toward a chair at the window, and I obeyed.

She set to work, fast but not unkind, her hands braiding and twisting my hair, pinning it with jet combs and metal sticks that shimmered in the early light. She lined my eyes, dusted powder over my cheeks, but left my lips bare—"To let your own color come through," she said. The dress was a thing of weight and armor, black and deep green, the bodice boned and laced so tight I felt like I'd been trussed for the slaughter. She finished with a brooch, set high at my throat, the insignia unfamiliar but heavy with history.

Menace appeared at the door in his own finery: black suit, high-collared, with a sash of deep burgundy and the same insignia at his lapel. He looked every bit a king. If he were uncomfortable, you'd never know it. He made it work. He always did.

The attendant handed him a set of matching cufflinks, then stepped back. "You're ready," she said. "The guards will escort you to the antechamber."

Menace offered his arm. I took it. The corridor outside was already lined with Council blue—guards at every third door, eyes forward, hands hovering over their sidearms.

We walked, and the mansion walked with us. The route wound through stone passages and up shallow stairs, every turn offering another view of the history of the territory. New paint had freshened up the corridors. Floors had been polished in honor of the occasion. Every servant and staffer we passed paused, eyes wide, then dipped their heads in deference—sometimes to me, sometimes to Menace, never to both at once.

On the last landing before the Council hall, we paused. Menace squeezed my hand, grounding me. "Ready?" he asked.

"I was born ready." I truly was.

He grinned. "You are a queen."

"Don't you forget it."

The doors to the antechamber were old, probably as old as the country itself, carved with the runes of every house that had ever held power here. The guards on either side swung them open, revealing a room that was massively large and probably had room for a thousand ghosts.

There was a hush when we entered. Not silence—nothing in this world was ever silent—but a hush like the air just before a tornado. Every seat was filled: Council members, envoys, the supernatural elite and their proxies. Vampires in tailored black, witches in blue or bone, and the occasional demon or angel in some fashion that defied all good sense. At the far end, on a dais a full story above the floor, stood the twelve thrones—ten occupied, two empty, the absences more terrifying than the presence of any living monster.

In the front row, Rafe watched us with an expression that was all amusement, no malice. Kazimir sat beside him, the white-haired vampire king, hands folded like he was praying for someone else's soul.

Menace and I took our places before the dais. The Chairwoman of the Council rose, her robe a river of silver and shadow, her hair braided in a crown across her scalp. She banged the gavel.

"Let it be entered in the record: the former Midwest King, Dominic Madison has fallen; his line ended. In accordance with Council law, the victor and his chosen mate present themselves to be crowned."

She gestured to the side, and two attendants approached: one with a velvet cushion bearing the crown—a circlet of black iron set with stones the color of wet hematoma—the other with a scroll of parchment. The script crawled across the page, ancient words in an alphabet I couldn't read.

"Bridger Hardin, do you accept the mantle of King of the Midwest Territories?" the Chairwoman intoned.

Menace nodded, never breaking eye contact with her. "I do."

"Do you bind yourself to the laws of the Council and the Goddess?"

"I do."

She turned to me. "Savannah Calloway, do you accept the role of Queen Consort, and with it, the charge to protect this kingdom and all who dwell in it?"

I swallowed, felt the rawness of it in my throat, then nodded. "I do."

She read the oaths, slow and steady, every word a weight. When she finished, the attendants brought the crowns forward. The Chairwoman lifted the black iron circlet, held it aloft so the room could see, then brought it down carefully onto Menace's head.

He did not flinch. Not even when the metal settled over the wound left by last night's violence. He looked every bit the king now, eyes cold, spine straight, the scars on his face a testimony instead of a flaw.

The Chairwoman picked up the smaller circlet, more delicate, rimmed in silver and green. She was turning to me when a hidden door at the back of the chamber exploded inward.

The noise was thunderous. The guards at the threshold went down in a heap, and through the smoke and splinters came my brother.

CHAPTER 31

SAVANNAH

Callum's hair was wild, his suit torn, one sleeve soaked in blood. He carried a gun—not a ceremonial one, but the ugly matte black of a tactical Glock. He didn't raise it, not right away. He just stalked down the aisle, every eye in the chamber fixed on him.

"Stop him!" the Chairwoman screamed, but no one moved. The rules of the arena didn't apply here, but the law of spectacle did. No one wanted to be the first to die.

Callum saw me, and his face twisted, hatred and loss braided tight together. "You think you can just erase us?" he spat, his voice echoing off the marble. "You think you can murder our father and take what's ours?"

I glanced at Menace. He didn't blink, didn't even move. The wolf in him had learned patience.

Callum aimed the gun, finger white on the trigger.

Bronc reacted before anyone else did. One second he was in his seat; the next he was airborne, all six foot three inches and two hundred thirty pounds of him. He hit Callum at full speed, tackling him into the aisle. The gun went off; the shot ricocheting up to the ceiling, a chunk of old stone raining down onto the benches.

They hit the floor hard. Callum rolled, caught Bronc with the butt of the pistol, but Bronc already had his hands locked around

Callum's wrist. They wrestled for it, a tangle of limbs and spit, until Bronc wrenched the gun free and tossed it across the floor.

Callum went for Bronc's throat. It was animal, desperate, the same rage that had fueled every day of his life. He only managed to bite his forearm, hard, drawing blood. Bronc didn't scream. He just slammed his forehead into Callum's nose twice until the cartilage shattered and blood spattered both of them. Then Bronc locked his hands around Callum's neck and squeezed.

The struggle was brief, brutal, and final.

Callum's eyes bulged. His heels drummed against the floor once, twice, then went still. Bronc didn't let go. Not until the guards came and pried his hands off, leaving Callum's body limp and leaking blood onto the pristine marble.

A silence followed, heavy as a tomb. Bronc staggered to his feet, breathing hard. He straightened his jacket, took a tissue from Juliet and wiped the blood from his face, and casually walked back to his seat. He never looked at me. Never looked at the carnage. He just sat and waited for the world to resume.

The Chairwoman banged the gavel again, louder this time. "Let it be recorded," she said, voice trembling, "that the challenge to the throne has ended. The blood debt is paid."

She picked up the silver circlet and set it on my head. It was heavier than it looked.

The crowd erupted, not in applause, but in the low, dangerous hum of power acknowledging itself. Every face turned to us, some in awe, some in terror, all knowing that the world had shifted, and that from here on out, there was no going back.

Menace leaned close, lips brushing my ear. "There will be no other fucking queen like you," he whispered.

I believed him.

I stood there, bleeding inside, crowned before a chamber of monsters and saints.

It fit better than I ever dreamed.

They gave Callum's body five minutes before the staff swept it from the marble. The blood lingered longer—a thin, glistening rivulet that ran through the cracks, pooling under the table where the Chairwoman sat. She ignored it. By the time the reception started, someone had scattered enough sand and salt to soak up the worst of it.

We didn't leave the dais, not right away. There were formalities, a dozen of them, each one more senseless than the last: the stamping of seals, the witnessing of signatures, the muttered oaths between new lieges and their would-be subjects. My mouth tasted like rust, and my heart had slowed to a tired, exhausted crawl.

But when the doors opened for the reception, everything changed. The world rushed in: kingdom envoys in strange, tailored suits, vampires with blood-wet lips, the rare witch who floated across the floor without ever quite touching it. Goblets of wine—red, of course—passed from hand to hand, and the food was a parade of things I barely recognized, each more decadent than the last.

Menace stayed close, always within a hand's reach, but he let the other monsters come. Rafe was the first, his hug a backslap that would have caved my ribs if I'd been human. He didn't even bother to hide his delight at being alive and watching someone else do the fighting for a change.

Kazimir shook Menace's hand next, then kissed my knuckles, lips cool as ice. "If you ever grow tired of dis one, you may call me," he said, voice soft but knife-sharp.

Menace just snorted. "You wish, bloodsucker."

Then there was Juliet. She wore Iron Valor red now, the shade of love and heat, her mouth stained with pink and her laugh bigger than her body. She hugged me so hard I thought I'd shatter, then whispered, "You did it, Red. You're really fucking free." Her eyes were misty, but not from crying. Just from too much emotion for one body to hold.

The party swirled around us, a hurricane of old money and new wounds. I watched the Council members maneuver—some to congratulate, others to glare, all of them already running the numbers in their heads. Some handshakes were a threat; some smiles, omens.

There were moments of beauty, too: the glass windows throwing shards of morning sun across the floor, the old paintings flickering in the torchlight, the music that thrummed from a string quartet at the edge of the room. Even the food had a strange, animal poetry to it—slabs of rare meat, pomegranate seeds glinting like spilled blood, hunks of cheese so pungent they nearly walked off the table.

Menace and I played our roles, king and queen, but the wolf in both of us stayed wary, never relaxing, believing in the adage: trust but verify.

When the last of the guests had either drunk themselves senseless or been carried out, a guard summoned us to a side chamber. It was smaller, lined with books, the table set for only a handful of people.

Rafe and Kazimir waited there, along with Bronc, Juliet, and the Chairwoman. The air was thick with the smell of coffee and cigar smoke. Kazimir poured himself a glass of clear liquor, took a seat, and gestured for us to do the same.

"Congratulations," he said. "Dat vas one of the better coups I've vitnessed in a century."

Menace grinned. "Didn't exactly go as planned."

Rafe laughed, big and booming. "That's the best kind. The ones you can't script." He leaned in, dropping his voice. "Now comes the real fight. You need to secure the loyalty of every Alpha in your territory. And you'll need a witch to read them all. Anyone gets clever, you'll know."

Kazimir nodded. "My Lucia recommends Eliana Meinhardt. Young, but ruthless. Can read man's heart like tea leaves."

The Chairwoman set down her gavel, eyes weary. "You'll also need a council of your own. The wolves are not used to centralized power. They need the illusion of representation, or they'll revolt before the year is out."

Menace accepted it all, the advice and the threats, as if he'd been born for this. Maybe he had. He shot a look at me, checking for signs of breakdown or revolt. I gave him nothing. I was too tired for either.

Juliet, slouched in her chair, piped up. "Don't forget about us little people. Somebody's gotta make sure you don't fuck this up."

Bronc snorted, then said, "He'll do fine. He's got Red. She's the brains. He's just the teeth."

They all laughed, even the Chairwoman. For a moment, the room felt almost safe.

But Kazimir wasn't done. He raised his glass, eyes glittering. "You are King of Midwest now, Menace. But remember—every throne is just fancy guillotine. Rule well, or you'll end up like the last one."

Menace toasted him, unbothered. "I look better in red, anyway."

Afternoon crawled in, and with it, the realization that the world would not pause for us. There were calls to be made, agreements to be signed, and a thousand details that required attention.

But before any of that, Iron Valor gathered one last time. They met us in the lobby—Bronc, Juliet, Wrecker, Doc, Arsenal, Big Papa, all looking battered but whole. Bronc gripped Menace's shoulder, then pulled me in for a hug that lingered just a beat too long.

"You're sure you'll be alright?" he asked, worry peeking out from under the Alpha mask.

Menace nodded. "It's a kingdom, not a prison."

Bronc didn't buy it, not entirely. "Your dealership—"

"My GM will handle it," Menace cut in. "I'm not selling. I'm just... taking a sabbatical."

Bronc grinned. "Heard that before. Usually means you're coming back twice as crazy."

Juliet grinned too, eyes dancing. "Just promise you'll help with the Skeeter problem once we know who's behind it. You're still our problem solver."

Menace looked at me, then back at them. "Soon as you call, I'll come running."

Wrecker shook his hand. "You need backgrounds on any of those Alphas, call me. I'll dig so deep their mistress's boyfriends won't be safe." The bro hug and laughter told me he appreciated the reassurance.

Arsenal told him to find the biggest, baddest enforcer and keep him close. Doc had visited our healer. He liked her and told us she could be trusted. That was a huge relief. Of course, Big Papa gathered us all in a circle and prayed over everyone. The tears fell then. I silently prayed that Menace would find a group of men he could trust in our new home.

The group dissolved into hugs and backslaps. It was over too fast. Everyone loaded into SUVs, and that left Menace and Bronc. I knew it was killing him to have his mentor and best friend leave. But I also knew Texas was only a couple of hours away by plane. And we had the miracle of FaceTime now.

I stood with Juliet as these two amazing men said their good-byes. I didn't want to let her go, either. "What am I going to do without you?"

"Well, *Sawyer*," she laughed.

"Yeah, *Julia*?" I laughed back.

"Our journeys started out as mirror images didn't they? And look at where we are now." I pulled her into the tightest hug. "I sure am glad I have you in my corner."

"I'll always be there, girl. You call me if you ever need any-thing. I love you." She wiped the tear that had escaped her eye.

I wiped my tears. "I will. I promise. Love you, too."

When they'd gone, the lobby felt hollow. The silence was deafening.

Menace turned to me, all the bravado gone. "You ever think we'd wind up here?" he asked, voice low.

I shrugged, then pressed my head to his chest, over the healed wound. "Not on a bet. I was just hoping they'd let us stay mated."

He kissed the top of my head, then led me up the stairs, through the quiet hallways, back to the room where we'd started.

We stood together at the window, looking out over the king-dom that was now ours: the fountains, the manicured gardens, the sky that would never again be the same.

I thought about my mother, about my brother Griffin, about how their lives were about to change. I thought about the ghosts still rattling around this mansion and wondered if we could ever teach them to rest.

Menace pulled me in, arms around my waist, and I let him.

"I love you," I said, and I meant it down to my toes.

He smiled. "I know. That's why we're going to burn this world down and build something better."

Outside, the last of the day's light hit the horizon.

It was ours now.

And I was not afraid.

Epilogue

Wrecker

I stepped into the church room at the compound, the air thick with sweat and old gun oil, and the burn of the overhead fluorescents strobing each man's face into a mask of ruin. It was built to look like a regular boardroom—shitty paneling, heavy Texas Star table, a print of the Alamo to give outsiders a history lesson—but that was a lie. The ghosts here weren't colonial; they were recent, and they all had my name carved into their teeth.

Bronc sat at the head of the table, forearms spread like a bar bouncer's barricade, eyes fixed on the documents in front of him but not seeing them. He looked older than usual, and for a moment I wondered if the weight of Menace's departure had settled the decades he'd always managed to outrun right into his spine. If it had, I owed Menace a beating for leaving me alone with this crowd.

Arsenal was to Bronc's right, next to an empty chair, his hands locked in a cathedral, face unreadable. Most would call him taciturn; I called him a human polygraph with a hair trigger. On Bronc's left, Big Papa nursed a cup of black coffee, calm radiating off of him, belying the scars he carried. He watched me walk in, his eyes following me like I had the answers to the universe. At the end, Doc leaned back in his chair, black frame glasses, like fucking Superman looking for a phone booth.

Mine was the only empty chair besides Menace's, sitting there reminding us our second was no longer here.

Bronc didn't say anything for a minute. He just waited for me to take my seat, which I did. We all were looking at him. The clock on the wall ticked at quarter speed.

"Let's start," he said, not so much an order as a mercy killing. "First thing—" and here he picked up a single piece of paper, then set it back down, as if the effort of holding the truth was just too much, "Menace is gone."

He let the words hang. No surprises in the room; just the way it needed to be said, to be ritualized.

"You make it sound like he's dead," Arsenal grumbled, so flat you could iron a shirt on it. "He's just King of the Midwest now. But might as well be the same thing."

Bronc cracked a smile, but it was the kind of smile you give a dying dog before you put the bullet in.

"Means we're down a VP," Bronc continued, glancing at the list but not reading it. "Rules are rules. Even if the last six months have proven we're the only pack or MC in America that gives a fuck about rules anymore."

He looked at me, and I braced for the axe.

"Wrecker, I want you as VP," Bronc said.

I didn't move, didn't even blink, because to do so would be to admit I hadn't seen it coming, and nothing is more dangerous than being predictable in this club. But my stomach did a weird somersault, and a thin vein in my temple throbbed so hard I thought it might tap out on its own.

"Vote?" I said, because someone had to say it.

Arsenal's hand went up instantly. "Aye." He looked at me as if daring me to question it.

Big Papa followed, slower, but with more weight. "Aye."

Doc shrugged. "No one else on the payroll could keep up with Bronc's disaster curve. Aye."

That left Bronc. "I don't get a vote," he said. "But if I did—" and here he dropped the mask for just a second—"it'd be a fuck yes."

I could have said something glib, something to bleed the tension out, but my throat was suddenly full of static. I just nodded, letting it settle over me like a bad tattoo.

"Good," Bronc said. "Gavel it." He rapped a fist on the table. "Next, we need a new enforcer. Arsenal, thoughts?"

Arsenal didn't hesitate. "Finn. 'Gunner' Walsh. Cattle foreman. Busted two coyotes last month with his bare hands, then made breakfast for the ranch crew before the sun was up. Never missed a church service. Never missed a Sunday ride. Never snitched, never soft."

Doc looked skeptical. "He's what, twenty-six? Kid's got the emotional IQ of a whitetail."

"He's got the fear response of a tornado siren," Arsenal said, dry. "That's what I want in an enforcer. Loyalty, speed, and the willingness to go through a wall if I tell him to. He learns the rest."

Big Papa nodded. "We've seen worse."

"Wrecker, thoughts?" Bronc asked.

"Never had a problem with Gunner," I said. "If you want him, I'll break him in."

Bronc signed off with a wave. "Done. I'll talk to Gunner tonight." He eyed Arsenal. "Get the initiation planned. Make it memorable. Next."

The rhythm of these meetings was clockwork—officers first, then the club business, then the dark shit. The last category was always the longest.

"Now, Skeeter," Bronc said. "We got him locked up. Someone was pulling his strings, and he ain't sayin' who. Before I beat him to death, got ideas?"

"Yeah," I said. "I gotta lead."

I leaned in, because the walls had ears, even here. "Server breach two weeks ago wasn't just the MC. The Dairyville Bank's database got mirrored. Someone's been filtering withdrawals and deposits for over a month. I built a dummy network off our own router to feed them fake logins, but they keep coming. Whoever's running Skeeter is smarter than we thought."

Arsenal actually looked impressed. "You're feeding them honey-trap data?"

"Every day," I said. "So far, they think they're bleeding us dry. But the money they're stealing doesn't exist. Not in the real world. It's a shell game."

Doc grinned, the first time all morning. "Beautiful."

Bronc drummed his fingers on the table. "You got a trace?"

I nodded. "Last ping was from an IP block outside Plainview. Rural. Could be a relay, could be a trailer park. But I'll find out tonight."

Big Papa frowned. "Going alone?"

"Yeah, I got this. It needs to be quiet." He knew I had it under control.

Bronc eyed me one last time, like he was measuring the difference between what I was and what he hoped I'd become. "Don't die, Wrecker," he said, not unkindly. "I need someone to give Menace shit when he comes back for a visit."

The meeting ended in a slow dissolving of bodies—Arsenal out first, then Doc, then Big Papa. Bronc and I were last, and when it was just us, the air in the room got thinner.

"Anything else?" I asked.

Bronc looked at me, and for a moment, he didn't look like an Alpha, or a boss, or a soldier. He just looked like a man who'd lost too much.

"You sure you want this?" he asked, quiet. "It's never what you think it's going to be."

I thought about the last week—the blood, the betrayal, the way every old story had replayed itself with new actors. I thought about Savannah and Menace, alone up there in the dead heart of the country. I thought about the hollow place inside me that had never gone away, not since I was a kid, and learned what it meant to be prey.

"I never wanted anything more," I said, and for once, I meant it.

Bronc nodded. "Good. Then go break some heads."

He left, the door closing with a soft click.

I sat in the silence for a while, counting the cracks in the ceiling. There could be a war coming, and for the first time in my life, I wasn't just a weapon. I was the man who pointed it.

Outside, the sun was starting to sink. I zipped my jacket, checked my sidearm, and got on the road.

There was a job to do.

Dusk had already gone gray when I ditched the bike behind a patch of scrub brush, a mile out from the mark's location. I walked the rest, boots silent on the powder dirt, the loaded 9mm bouncing against my ribs with each stride. The wind was sharp, dry, and full of the distant stink of livestock and burning mesquite. It felt like every molecule in the world was waiting for the next mistake.

The house sat on an acre of nothing, a white box with a black shingle roof and fake colonial shutters, the kind that always came pre-aged from a manufactured lot. This one had a deck built all the way around. The windows were shut, curtains drawn, but warm light leaked from the living room, a bad yellow that made my eyes ache. There was a single car in the gravel drive—a basic sedan, silver, with a vanity plate bracket for a college no one outside of Texas would recognize. I slid around the perimeter, eyes cataloging the vulnerabilities: one camera on the eave, a motion light over the porch, locks from the seventies. I'd seen harder targets at the Dairy Queen.

First move: kill the video. I dropped prone behind the back fence, rolled out the pocket laptop, and pinged the signal. The camera was live, but routed through a generic Chinese app, so it took two minutes to set a loop, twenty seconds to spoof the timestamp, and less than a breath to render the system blind to everything that mattered. I checked for other cameras on the network. Four pointed inside—living room, bedroom one, bedroom two, and the kitchen. Nobody home. All cameras looped for the same twenty seconds.

I put the laptop away, slid on my leather gloves, and eased up to the kitchen door. It was locked. I picked it in less than a minute, the rattle of tumblers as easy as flipping a light switch. I ghosted inside and closed the door behind me.

The kitchen was immaculate. No dishes, no stains, nothing in the sink but the silver gleam of the garbage disposal mouth. The only clue that anyone lived here was a single mug by the coffeemaker. I palmed it, checked the lipstick, and put it back exactly where it was.

I moved room by room. The living room was a catalog spread: mid-century couch, a rug that probably cost more than my first car, everything arranged with obsessive symmetry. The TV was wall-mounted; the remote nested perfectly parallel to a paperback book on the glass coffee table. I flipped the book open—no annotations, but the title was some kind of stalker romance. I scanned a few pages. Wow. Dark shit.

I ventured into the first of the two bedrooms. Looked like a guestroom, barely slept in, a hospital-cornered twin bed and a bookshelf full of more questionable romance novels. I pulled one and found lots of dog-eared pages. My eyes scanned a few paragraphs that contained some fucked-up shit. I put the book back, stifling a laugh.

The main bedroom was next. The bed was made, the closet open. No men's clothing, no shoes larger than a size seven. I touched the hangers, let my fingers glide across little black dresses and a variety of concert t-shirts. Some brands were everyday wear, some were high end—Marc Jacobs, Calvin Klein, a few pieces with French names I couldn't pronounce. I checked the dresser, finding nothing but folded lingerie, all black or red, and a collection of silk scarves. I looked under the tray of jewelry—no gun, no drugs, just a box of business cards from banks and title companies in Amarillo.

The nightstand was more interesting. Second drawer: two paperback romance novels with the spines broken and a dog-eared page in each. Beneath, a baggie with a spare key and a prepaid Visa. At the bottom, a small zippered pouch with a high-dollar pink cordless dildo. In another velvet pouch, a silver butt plug with a jeweled heart at the top, a bottle of lube, and a small black notebook with an elastic band.

I pocketed the notebook. If it turned out to be a sex journal, it'd be the second-most embarrassing thing I'd read tonight.

Last, the office area. The desk was spotless, but the desk calendar was full of names and numbers, each scribbled in a different colored pen. I used my phone to photograph each page, then searched the desk for a laptop. Not here. She must have it with her.

I went back to the kitchen. I was about to leave when I saw, pinned to the fridge by a smiley-faced magnet, a cheap five-by-seven photo in a plastic frame. The kind you'd get at a fair.

Four people in the photo: a man, grinning like he was about to kill the cameraman; a woman in a pastel dress; and two teenagers—a boy and a girl, almost identical except for the length of the hair. The boy was Axel Reid and the girl, his twin sister, fucking Parker.

The Reids were Iron Valor Pack until Valorie and Roger died in a car accident several years ago. Tragic. We stood by their kids Axel and his fucking twin sister, Parker. Took care of them. Axel handled the books at Bronc's shop for two years while Parker went to college. She graduated, and they both decided to leave the pack. Gotta do research to see where they supposedly went.

Fucking traitors.

A car crunched onto the gravel outside. I blinked the sweat from my eyes, shoved the photo back, and headed to the back door as her feet hit the front porch. I heard the front door lock code beep as I let myself out.

I'd put on the mask I used anytime I needed to conduct any kind of stealthy shit. Black with creepy as fuck white eyes and mouth. Wearing black from head to toe, there was no way she could identify me. I fucking wanted the bitch to see me.

She turned on the back porch lights and pulled back the curtains on the large picture window so she could check the back deck and yard. That's where I waited just off to the side. Then she turned out the lights, and I took a step directly into her line of sight. Mother fucking fuck. She was gorgeous as she stood frozen, with a look of terror on her face when she saw me standing just feet away from her on the other side of that window. My dick was instantly hard.

I blew her a kiss with my gloved hand and walked away. I knew she wouldn't call anyone for help. Matter of fact. My bet was, she went straight to her bedroom nightstand.

THANKS FOR READING

There are nights when I write with my heart wide open, the quiet so thick it hums like a hymn, my fingers steady as they trace the shape of something brighter than fear. This is how I want you to feel here: safe enough to linger, brave enough to believe.

Thank you—first, last, always—for walking this path with me. For seeing past the masks of wolves and vampires and demons to the fragile hearts beneath, the ones that bled and yearned and dared to love, anyway.

You stayed through every storm, and you did it with a tenderness that told me you understood: monsters are just people who forgot how to hope. But Menace and Savannah? They never forgot. Their love outran death itself. Stitched back by grace, by an angel's stubborn hands, they proved that light always finds a way to bleed through the cracks.

Sometimes I think these words will outlive me, that they carry more faith than I ever knew I had. But stories, even the truest ones, fade without hearts to cradle them. So if you loved reading about how good rose from the ashes—if you believed, even for a moment, in a love that defied graves and angels who wore ordinary skin—would you leave a review? It's the fuel that keeps me writing, the warmth that carries me to the next dawn. Without you, these words are just whispers. With you, they're a hymn.

I can't wait for you to read Wrecker and Parker's story. The epilogue is just a taste. Eli "Wrecker" Leonard is full of dark surprises, and if you think Parker will get out unscathed, you haven't learned a damn thing from me.

Thank you for reading. For bleeding. For coming back, even when you know what waits in the dark. I do what I do for you.

Yours, always,

Dex

P.S. Better lock your windows... If you ever need to debrief after this emotional rollercoaster (or demand more details about the wolves), find me on my socials: Facebook (www.facebook .com/dexhavenauthor) Instagram (@authordexhaven) or Tiktok (@authordexhaven), or haunt my website (dexhavenauthor.com) for previews, deals, and confessions I can't make anywhere else. You can even email me dex@dexhavenauthor.com

ALSO BY DEX

If you loved Menace and you somehow missed BRONC Book 1 read it NOW! And of course, Wrecker Book 3 I'm sure is already on your TBR.

And if you're a fan of romantasy, my first series is a fun tale of an orphan from Texas who realizes she's actually not so much from Texas as she is from an entirely different realm. She's tasked with saving the realm from destruction by a power-hungry goddess. Along the way she meets her mate, a dreamy shadow-wielding vampire king, as well as a host of other fabulous creatures, including dragons, of course. Read the completed hot and steamy Kingdoms of Eldoria series **Claiming Starlight, Starlight & Luna Rising, and Starlight & Fire**, where you'll meet Olivia and Cade as well as the Dragonia and group of wonderful friends and family she comes to know and love. You'll find yourself on the edge of your seat with the heart-stopping action and needing a fan to cool yourself off as the steam heats up between several couples.

ACKNOWLEDGEMENTS

Having people I trust read what I write and give me honest feedback and catch mistakes before the book goes to the masses is so damn helpful. I'm lucky to have a couple of ladies willing to do this for me. And they do it simply because they are kind. **Denise Pruitt, Patti Kapusta**, and **Ann Dearnley**, my heartfelt thanks to y'all. **Kathy Connley**, your words of encouragement always mean so much.